YOU HAD ME *at* JAGUAR

TERRY SPEAR

sourcebooks
casablanca

Published by Sourcebooks Casablanca, an imprint of Sourcebooks, Inc.
P.O. Box 4410, Naperville, Illinois 60567-4410
(630) 961-3900
Fax: (630) 961-2168
sourcebooks.com

Printed and bound in the United States of America.
OPM 10 9 8 7 6 5 4 3 2 1

To Carol Smith, who loves my bears, books, and photos! Thanks so much for being a friend, and give all the little bears a hug for me.

Prologue

Outfitted in black cargo pants, shit-kicker boots, and a black T-shirt, Valerie Chambers was ready to take on physical training with the rest of the Enforcers. Their job was taking down the worst rogue shifters, and sometimes the humans who were killing jaguars or shifters in the wild, so they had to be fit.

Valerie always thought of the training as a challenge, but also viewed it with a fair amount of dread, knowing that if she failed an activity, she'd have to repeat it several times. Which meant she was wired as she went through the various stages of the multiday training.

She was going through her paces: rappelling off the seventy-five-foot tower, making her way across a rope to reach the other side of the "ravine," and low-crawling under wire. It was all strenuous work, meant to keep the agents in shape and test their skills, to help them learn their weaknesses and strengths and work on them. A couple of the guys were giving her a hard time, in a joking way, about moving too slowly under the wire. But she moved at her own pace. If she got hung up under there, she'd have to do it again, ten more times. The low-wire crawl was what she hated most of the individual training components. No matter how hard she pushed herself, she could never beat the clock.

She noticed a group of male jaguars fighting each

other in a different area, trying to pin their opponents down without really hurting each other. She'd have to do that in the training tomorrow.

Next, she had to do hand-to-hand combat with different opponents. She was petite, like many of the female Enforcers. But even the taller ladies had the same problem. They didn't have the muscle strength to handle the male jaguars. Instead, they had to use deception, feints, distractions, any tricks they could to incapacitate their opponent. In the field, it would be different. The shifter would often be unprepared for the female Enforcers' combat maneuvers, so the agent could take them down that way. In training, the Enforcer males were prepared to take the women down. No male shifter wanted to be the butt of jokes if he failed to do so.

After having successfully thrown a woman, Val moved on to her next opponent. Howard Armstrong was rough edges and hard angles, and had stern blue eyes and a growly voice. Muscular build, black hair, and a brooding expression defined him. Yet even before they tangled, he gave her a small smile, the corner of his mouth turning up just a hair, his eyes sparkling. She didn't know if he was so cocky because he thought she would be easily defeated, or because he appreciated having a woman to tackle this time.

She'd seen him tackle three men to the mat individually before she was paired with him, so she knew he wasn't going to be a pushover. She was trying to think positively and not let feelings of defeat sabotage her efforts.

At least twenty other agents were paired up all over

this part of the Warehouse, men versus men, men versus women, women versus women, standing on gray gym mats, ready for the signal to begin.

Val really, really tried to relax. She was already sweating from some of the other training she'd done, and so was he. Sweat dribbled off his brow, his biceps gleaming. He was beautiful in a dark, predatory way. The thing she noticed most was that he stood perfectly relaxed, as if he had nothing to worry about.

Despite trying, she couldn't shake off the stress she was feeling. Her muscles were taut with tension.

His smile grew, as if he knew she was afraid of how this was going down.

She lunged for him. She didn't remember hearing the bell ding. Maybe it had. Maybe it hadn't and she'd made it up in her mind because she was so wired. It was too late now to stop her action. And it worked! He wasn't ready for her, and with one quick sweep of her leg, her hands grabbing his strong wrists, she managed to unbalance him enough to slam her body against his and take him down. Pinning him down with her body wasn't part of the program, but they were always taught to improvise when necessary.

He was actually grinning at her! Maybe because she was grinning back at him, delighted she had bested him, feeling the tension leave her all at once. Not bothering to extricate himself from underneath her, he didn't seem to mind where she was resting against him.

Then a chorus of woots and hollers filled the Warehouse. No one else had tackled their opponents in the hand-to-hand combat arena yet. They were all standing where they had been when she'd taken Howard down. Well, except that they had turned and were all watching her and Howard.

"That's how it's done," one of the testers said, smiling.

Val quickly moved off Howard, but before she could get to her feet, he did and offered his hand in friendship. She couldn't believe he wasn't angry with her. She took his hand and pulled herself up.

Then the bell rang. *Now* the bell rang? And the others quickly tried to take their opponents down, with thuds on the mats following.

"You're quick," Howard said. "No one has ever taken me down. Ever."

She smiled and patted his steel-hard abs. "There's always a first time for everything." And then she hurried off to navigate one of the water-hazard trials, though after getting the best of Howard, she was going to have a hard time keeping her mind off just how sexy he was.

—⁓—

Watching Val head to her next training, Howard chuckled, thinking how much he'd like to date the spirited woman. She was trying to tuck her red hair back into its bun, while loose, silky strands curled down her back.

He liked a woman who could throw him off-balance, give him a challenge, and do the unexpected. Val taking him down before the bell rang had shocked him, which was the only way she could get the best of him. Though he had to admit to himself, once she'd made her maneuver, he hadn't tried very hard to take charge of the situation. He had wanted to see just where she would take it.

Her landing on top of him was definitely unexpected. All he could think of were the straggles of red hair framing her face and her beautiful green eyes, mixed with aqua and a hint of amber, staring down at him in disbelief.

He always felt he didn't need the extra training and would rather be taking care of the bad guys. But today, one smart female Enforcer agent had made the whole week of exercises worth it.

The next day, Howard had training mixed with other branches: Enforcer, Guardian, and JAG. It was something they'd never done before, and he really hadn't wanted to do it. They needed it as a way to improve communication and work ethics between the branches though.

He'd started out as an Enforcer. Then before he knew it, he was working with a Guardian and a JAG on a case. Not long after that, he became a member of a team on the United Shifter Force. His only regret had been that he would most likely never see Val again, in Enforcer training or otherwise.

Until he'd been assigned his current mission. He suspected she wouldn't like it one little bit when she learned he was assigned to watch her back.

Chapter 1

Drinking a beer at the San Antonio Clawed and Dangerous Kitty Cat Club, Howard Armstrong looked more relaxed than Val had ever seen him. Although she'd only seen him working vigorously in training exercises. Why was he here? She should have known she'd run into him again—they were working for the same jaguar police force, after all. He made her think of long, hot nights and impossibly sexy dreams.

She had been astonished to learn he had left the Enforcer branch to work with the JAG's new United Shifter Force unit. And a little disappointed. She'd thought she might see him again during training. She had wondered if he'd gotten as much ribbing about her taking him down as she had.

"He let you so he could get close and personal." A couple of the women she worked with had made that comment or something similar. "Good move to take him down as if we were in the field and not in training," one of the guys had told her, impressed with her wiliness. "He must be getting soft," another male Enforcer had joked.

Howard was all hard muscle, nothing soft about him.

The Enforcer branch was a specialized jaguar policing force that eliminated jaguar shifters who were guilty of committing violent, deadly crimes against humans and shifters alike. The agents of the USF worked as a combined force of wolves and jaguars. Howard had made a great Enforcer because he did things on his own, a loner. Many of the Enforcers were like that, which was why Val couldn't understand why he changed jobs to be a team player with a mix of shifter types.

Howard still worked out of the Houston office, as far as she knew. She'd wondered if he was working on a case in San Antonio. When she'd spied his vehicle here for days with no sign of him, she'd asked her boss—and Howard's—if he was on a mission. They'd both denied it. She didn't think the USF agents went solo on missions. Was he really just on vacation?

Sipping a margarita at a table across the club from him, Val watched Howard snack on chips. Then he was joined by a brunette—pretty, petite, and wearing a short red dress and low red heels. Was the woman a jaguar or a wolf? Maybe a date?

When Val had seen Howard's black pickup truck with the distinct jaguar in a jungle painted on both sides and smelled his scent around the vehicle, she'd figured he still owned it. Even so, she had run his license plate to make sure someone else hadn't bought it. She had learned it was still his truck. She suspected Howard was after someone. But this was the first time she'd actually seen him or the woman, which meant he had to be undercover.

The jungle music made Val involuntarily tap her boot on the tile floor, and she had the greatest urge to get up and dance. The smell of sweet mixed drinks, beer, humans, jaguars, and a few wolves drifted to her. Palm trees in pots, vines stretching to the ceiling, and a skylight way above simulated a jungle scene like most jaguars loved. The summer sun was still high enough to spread sunlight through the windows filtering down through the living foliage.

Since she couldn't get away to the jungle very often, she enjoyed going to these places to immerse herself in the jungle feel from time to time, more so when she wasn't on a mission. Here it was air-conditioned, with a light mist spraying the plants and water droplets collecting on the leaves. Jaguar shifters wearing leopard-print fabric danced on elevated stages, and bright lights flashed across the stages and dance floor, making the scene appear otherworldly.

She glanced again at the tables that were cast more in the dark, in case Benny Canton had already arrived and she'd missed seeing him when she had walked through the place earlier searching for him. This was the kind of job she loved. Eliminating rogue jaguars, the murdering kind. She hadn't heard of a case like this in a good long while—a jaguar who'd murdered his wife, just because she threatened to leave him. That was one of the differences between the wolf shifters and jaguars. The wolves mated for life; jaguars could divorce.

She watched the door open when someone new arrived—two single males, neither of them her perp. Benny was known to frequent this club, having left his job as a construction worker after murdering his wife. He had no family, and she hadn't found any other place he could have holed up. So she'd staked out the club for the past three days, watching for him or some of his friends, who'd proven to be just as elusive as he was. She'd had no luck running into him or the others. But this club was the only lead she had.

She'd considered that he might have gone across the

border, because the shifters often did so to play in the jungle as wild jaguars. And for a rogue, he would have extra incentive to leave the country.

———∿∿∿———

Taking another swig of his beer while the jungle beat seemed to raise the roof of the club, with its loud drums pounding and the surround-sound amplifying the effect, Howard tried his darnedest not to look in Valerie Chambers's direction. Not that he ever would have revealed that he'd been attracted to her from the first time he'd actually seen her in advanced training as an Enforcer a year earlier. He still couldn't believe his boss had asked him and gray wolf Jillian Greystoke to watch Val's back surreptitiously. He'd much rather be up-front about what he was doing when helping out other agents.

As soon as he'd seen the striking redhead again, he was reminded of how she'd pinned him down during training. She'd cast him the wickedest smile. With his back on the floor and her on top of him, he couldn't help smiling back at her. Of course, after her unorthodox move, the testers had made a new rule—no one was to move before the bell rang—because they were afraid they'd have chaos otherwise. When they'd mentioned the new rules, Howard had glanced in Val's direction, and she'd given him a cat-that-ate-the-mouse look similar to the one he'd given her when she was lying on top of him at the training. He'd smiled back at her, thinking they might really have had a chance to date.

The three branches—the Enforcers, JAG, and Guardians—all had a common mission: deal with jaguar shifters who posed a threat to humans and shifters alike, though each handled different situations. The Guardians focused more on providing aid to injured jaguars, while the JAG went after the rogues, or humans who were dealing in jaguars. The end result—incarceration or death for the rogues—depended on the situation. The Enforcers were sent to terminate murdering jaguars. Period. They didn't consider jail time for the offender.

Howard and Jillian were now with the USF, a special section of the JAG that took care of jaguars and wolves creating trouble or in trouble. They were currently the only two agents who had a break between cases. Since Howard was a former Enforcer, his boss felt he would be right for the job. The branches worked together when necessary, but usually all the agents involved would be well aware of the situation.

Jillian was mated to Vaughn, a gray wolf SEAL who was busy tracking down a murderous wolf with the two other jaguar team members of the USF. They hadn't needed Jillian and Howard too.

Jillian got another text, the fourth one in a half hour. She texted back.

Howard didn't have to guess who it was from. "Vaughn should have taken you with him."

"This guy that Val is trying to neutralize is supposed to be a lot less violent than the one Vaughn's team is trying to track down. At least as far as the general population is concerned. Benny's wife was a different story."

"I still wish Martin had allowed us to tell Val we are here watching her back."

"The boss said she doesn't like working with anyone else. Since many Enforcers work alone, she'd think her boss felt she couldn't handle the case on her own. How well do you know her?" Jillian asked.

"I've been in training with her. Never worked with her though. She's got some kick-ass moves, and I have to say she's extremely quick-witted."

Jillian smiled at him. "Did she ever get the best of you?"

He gave her a dark smile back. "Not that I'd ever admit to." He ordered another beer. "You know, her mother, Gladys, was the first female Enforcer we had, and she and her mate, Jasper, are still on the force."

"Wow. They don't want to leave all the excitement behind?"

"That's about it. They're both good people, wanting to right the wrong and deal with the bad guys. And Gladys wanted to prove to her dad, who was an Enforcer, that she could do as good a job as any man. She and her mate have one of the highest success rates for eliminating rogue jaguars. They make a great team. But there has to be a time when Enforcers need to retire, when they might not be as quick to react or as strong as they had once been. Their boss just doesn't want to force retirement on them. Not while they've been so successful, despite being in their golden years."

"I think it's great. Better to die doing what you love than live to an old age wishing you were still fighting the good fight."

He smiled at Jillian. "Easy for you to say. Your kind lives much longer than we do. What a deal."

"True. You know, Val's been watching you. And she's been watching the entrance. Do you think she's onto us?"

"I doubt it. What would the odds be that Martin

would send two of his USF agents to protect an Enforcer in a simple takedown operation without her being informed?"

"Not likely. Do you want to dance?" Jillian grabbed Howard's hand before he could object.

"Hell, do you want this to get back to Vaughn? As a SEAL wolf, he'd kill me."

Jillian laughed. "He knows we're undercover, and this is just for fun. You never dated Val?"

"No. I never dated anyone in the Enforcer branch. How do you know she's been watching me?" he asked as they danced to the loud beat, the lights flashing all over the dance floor. "Wait. It was when you went to the ladies' room. That's why you took so long to return. You were observing her."

"And others. And you."

"Me? I wasn't about to blow our cover. What if she had a meltdown because we're here to protect her?"

"You did good. You only looked her way five times and only when she was busy ordering a drink, telling a patron to bug off, and looking around at other people at the time. If you had caught her eye though, then what?"

"I would have waved. She knows me. I know her. It would be foolish to pretend I didn't recognize her."

They continued to dance to the faster beat, which Howard was glad for. He really didn't want Vaughn to get any ideas about him and Jillian.

"You ought to ask her to dance. You're no longer an Enforcer. Then she'll know we're not together in a boyfriend/girlfriend way. It might help our mission if it looks like we're just here to have fun."

"She's on a job."

"Right. But you aren't supposed to know that. You'd be her cover too, though she wouldn't realize it."

"All right. You just don't want it to get back to your mate that I only danced with you."

Jillian laughed.

He led her back to the table, but the next dance was a slow dance, and he wasn't going to ask Val then. Not that he didn't want to, but he hated being here under false pretenses, as far as Val was concerned. What if they got a little too hot and heavy on the dance floor, as he'd like to with her, and then she learned he was only there on an assignment?

He sat down across from Jillian.

She smiled. "Coward."

"Next dance." But it was a slow one too. "Next fast dance," he clarified.

Then again, Val might wonder who Jillian was. A date? Even though that would work for a cover, he didn't want Val to think he was on a date. So much for really getting into this assignment. And here he was, always a professional when it came to his missions.

The next dance was fast-paced, so he rose from his chair and saw some guy trying to take a seat at Val's table. Howard headed for the table, though he told himself he wasn't in rescue mode. Not when he was sure she wouldn't appreciate it. So why was he making a beeline straight through dancers in his path, his gaze hard on the man at her table, and why was he walking so damn fast?

Maybe she wanted to be with the guy, but he suspected not from the way her brows furrowed and how she was motioning for him to get lost. She'd probably do the same with Howard.

The guy suddenly noticed Howard advancing. The guy had had too much to drink, smelled of whiskey, and was unsteady on his feet, finally planting a hand on the chair back next to her as if to keep from falling down.

"Hey, Val," Howard said in greeting. "Is this guy hassling you?"

The human glanced at her, then turned his attention to Howard.

Howard had dealt with enough ugly drunks to know the guy was trouble.

"What's it to you?" the human asked before he tried to shove Howard, but Howard didn't budge and gave him his growliest look. Though he would have preferred to do so as a jaguar. That would have gotten the guy's attention. "Get. Lost. Now," Howard growled.

The drunk glowered at him. Howard made a move for him, his posture threatening, and the drunk quickly backed off, then headed for another table.

Val folded her arms and focused on Howard, raising a brow as if to ask what *his* problem was.

He wasn't surprised. He knew she could have handled the drunk, but it still bothered him enough that he wanted to step in and protect her.

"Did you ditch your date already?" Val asked.

He didn't offer her his hand in greeting or an explanation but just asked, "Do you wanna dance?"

"I've heard you're a high guardian. Or noble watchman." Val toyed with her glass.

"You've totally lost me."

"Your name. Howard. Suits an Enforcer more than a Guardian." She frowned. "Why USF?"

He'd never looked up the meaning of his name.

Probably a good thing, as he normally saw himself as an Enforcer. Though he did serve in more of a guardian role on this assignment. He shrugged. "I guess I just got in with the right people, and I'm still up for terminating the bad guys when I need to." He wondered how she would know what his name meant, unless she'd been interested in him just a little bit. Maybe not so much now that he was no longer an Enforcer though.

She gave him a half smile, then motioned to Jillian. "Your date must be getting lonely." Then she eyed him with speculation. "Unless you're here on a mission." She glanced back at Jillian, considering her for some time. "I've never seen her before. Wolf? Jaguar? Human?"

"Wolf, mated." He still hadn't blown his cover, but he wanted her to know they were looking after her, whether she liked it or not.

Val raised both eyebrows this time.

"Her mate is a SEAL wolf. Jillian and I are on a job."

Val leaned her head back and smiled. "Okay. And you're undercover so you want to dance with me in case her mate gets upset with you for not dancing with anyone else." Then she frowned again. "You don't suspect me of anything, right?" she joked.

He shook his head. The only thing she was guilty of was being stubborn when it came to having a partner on a mission. At least, that's what his former boss, Sylvan, had said about her when he'd briefed them on their mission.

To Howard's surprise, Val rose from her seat and moved toward the dance floor. "What's your case? Jaguar murdered wolf? Wolf murdered jaguar?"

Howard hurried to join her. So she didn't realize he

was here because of her. He could understand what she thought they were looking for, because those were the kinds of cases they normally handled. Still, he really didn't want to have to lie about this. Her attention switched from him to someone to their left. Howard turned to look, and sure enough, it was Benny, the guy she was after. Shaggy blond hair, blue eyes, wearing jeans and a muscle shirt, showing off a lot of bicep. He was into construction work, and he looked like he did some heavy lifting on the job.

"Problem?" Howard asked. She had to know he suspected the guy was *her* case.

"Have to take a rain check on the dance."

When she frowned, Howard looked to see what was going on. Benny was dancing with a blond-haired woman who looked similar to his former wife. The music changed to a slow dance.

"Can I help you with anything?" Howard asked Val.

"Still an Enforcer at heart?" She pulled Howard into her arms and began dancing with him, not rubbing her body against him in a way that said she wanted more of this, but just to add a bit of realism, he thought.

He smiled, glanced over at Benny, and realized why Val was dancing with him. The perp and the blond were close by. "You'd better believe it."

"And Jillian?"

"Absolutely. And the truth is *you* are *our* mission."

Val patted him on the chest. "Good to know you're ready to come clean."

"You already knew?"

"I saw your truck parked near the club three days ago. It made me suspicious that you were here every night that I was, yet…weren't here. Once I called your plate number in to ensure you still owned the vehicle, I did consider you were here on a vacation. Or a case. But I wanted to learn the truth."

Howard figured where this was going. She didn't seem to be upset about it, so that was good.

"I contacted my boss, and he said in no uncertain terms that he hadn't sent anyone to watch my back. Which surprised the hell out of me, because I really didn't think you were here because of me. I thought you were on another case. I told him who you were and that you were USF. And he said he didn't know anything about the USF agents' cases. Except that he would, if he and your boss were in collusion. I called your boss. He gave me the same song and dance. Only it was *way* too similar. When my boss has something to hide, he says, 'Let me make it perfectly clear and in no uncertain terms…' When your boss does, he says—"

"'The truth of the matter is—'"

"Right. So they were in agreement. But I still didn't know what you were doing down here. Were you on some secret mission that had nothing to do with mine, and they didn't want to break your cover? Maybe, but then I thought it would be too much of a coincidence, particularly with the way our bosses responded to my inquiries. I didn't think they'd be so underhanded as to have other agents take down my perp."

"We're not here to take over your case. We're strictly here to provide backup. Your boss was worried about this guy and about you."

She looked relieved, sighed, and pulled Howard closer to her. This time, Benny was dancing farther away from them, and Howard fit her even more snugly against his body. He was taking protecting her to heart, wrapping his arms around her waist.

"You must already know the situation. Benny murdered his wife in cold blood for the insurance money and to stop her from divorcing him. He'd turned her six months earlier, so the consensus is that she wasn't dealing well with the changes. Maybe he felt he couldn't handle her like he thought he could. And living with her was getting out of control. For whatever reason, he murdered her, and he's going down."

Howard couldn't believe it. "Who all knew she was human to begin with?" No one had told them that bit of news.

"It wasn't something we knew until after he'd murdered her. You can't tell when someone's newly turned, unless they have the urge to shift and don't have any control over it. He must have kept her locked up so no one would know about her. Every jaguar who knew him thought he had mated a jaguar. But when I began interviewing her friends and family, learned they were all human and she hadn't been adopted, we put two and two together. It all fit.

"She had frequented this club, then dropped out of her family and friends' lives as soon as she met Benny and they were married. Everyone worried about her, thinking he was keeping her hostage, controlling her. But he couldn't let her out of his sight for fear she'd shift into a jaguar at any time. At their home, claw marks were all over the place, doors mainly. The arm of one of the chairs was crushed, so it looked like she had been one angry cat. Who could blame her, really."

A jaguar's bite could crush a tortoise's shell, so Howard could visualize the whole scenario perfectly. "But it was her saliva on the crushed arm of the chair, not his?"

"Correct. You sure don't know much about the case, do you?"

"We're here strictly to be your protection."

"*Why* are you undercover?"

"According to your boss, you refuse to work with—"

"He's on the move."

The blond Benny had been dancing with was leaving the club with him, but Jillian was nowhere to be seen.

"Where's your partner?" Val asked, sounding annoyed.

Howard was already on his phone, texting Jillian.

Howard: Where are you?

Jillian: I'm in your truck, getting ready to follow the perp if he leaves the… He's leaving the club.

Howard: We're right behind him.

Howard was trying not to crowd Benny and the woman, though he was attempting to smell their scents. Jaguar and…hell, human? Planning to take a new human wife and see if she did better with the change?

Jillian: He's headed north toward the parking lot up the street. At least I assume that's where he's going.

"Where's your vehicle?" Howard asked Val.

"Where he seems to be headed. Up in that parking lot."

Howard: Jillian, I'm sticking with Val. You follow
his vehicle if he gets in one and takes
off. We're heading toward Val's car in
that same parking area.

Jillian: OK

He and Val quickly exited the club, pausing outside to
find their target. Benny and the woman had turned into
the parking lot, but now Howard and the others couldn't
see them for the buildings. Howard and Val sprinted for
the parking lot, but they didn't hear the sound of any
vehicle's engine starting up.

"Do you know what else is back there?" Howard
asked Val.

"An alley leading through the buildings to the next
street."

He got on his phone to Jillian. "No engine starting
up. He might know we're after him and have taken off
through a back alley."

"Do you want me to drive down the other street?"

"No. Stay there in case he suddenly leaves the parking area. I'll keep the phone open in case I need to talk
to you fast."

When they reached the edge of the building, Howard
and Val slowed their run to a fast walk. She grabbed his
hand and pulled him close, wrapping his arm around
her waist as they moved around the side of the building.
She chuckled and pulled him down for a kiss. He knew
it was all for show, like two lovers having a tryst. But
damn, she tasted good: of sweet margarita mix, tequila,
and limes, and hot, sexy jaguar.

Hell, who said Val didn't work well with others? He

wrapped his arms around her and gave her a kiss back, which she allowed, even playing with his tongue with hers for a moment again, wanting to have done that the day she'd taken him to the mat in training.

And then she pulled him into the parking lot. "Ha! Can't remember where I parked the car. Can you?"

"No. I wasn't paying any attention." He was glad she gave them the perfect reason for sniffing around the cars, if the jaguar was nearby watching them.

They looked at each of the cars, trying to see if there was movement in any of them. But they didn't see anyone.

Jillian asked on the phone, "Hey, what do you want me to do?"

"Go to the next street over. I think we might have lost him." Howard hated that they had, if they had, but his mission was to protect Val at all costs.

They began following Benny's and the woman's scent weaving around the cars, down one row, and then the next. Either Benny couldn't find where he'd parked or he'd been attempting to lead them astray.

Howard heard his own truck driving onto the next street, and he and Val headed through the narrow brick alley to the other street. They continued to follow Benny's and the woman's scent. They saw no one walking anywhere. Howard glanced up at the brick buildings, many of them warehouses converted into condos.

"Would he be living in one of those?" he asked.

"He had money, but I wouldn't think he'd be able to buy one of those so soon after his wife's death. Unless he owned one already under another name, or he rented one. The only place he owned was the home he murdered her in. And since it was in both of their names, it's tied up for now."

They kept walking, down another narrow alleyway and onto the next street. They followed Benny's and the woman's scents a few blocks, and then lost them at another parking lot.

Howard said to Jillian on his phone, "We've lost him. They probably took a vehicle from the parking lot we're standing in. We're on Sycamore."

Val got a call, and she said, "Yeah, Mom? No, lost him." She glanced at Howard. "You and dad were behind this? Sheesh, Mom. Yeah, I know about it. They're not really that great at undercover work." She gave Howard a cocky smile.

It depended on the kind of undercover work she was talking about. Howard smiled back at her.

Jillian drove around the block and pulled up in front of them.

"No, we lost him, Mom. So, see? It didn't help to have them watching my back. With so many of us after him, we probably spooked him. I'm returning to head-quarters. Where are you going to be? Belize? Tell me you are going down there for a vacation this time. You and Dad need to retire." She rolled her eyes. "Be…care-ful. All right? Okay, talk to you later."

"You're headed back to Houston?" Howard asked Val. He was surprised.

"I could stake out the club and keep searching this area, but I'm afraid he won't return now. I'm worried about the new woman he's hooked up with. What if he turns her too, and she doesn't like it any more than his wife did? Maybe he won't marry this time though. Just see if it works or not. Though it makes me wonder if he's done this before. Turned human females and killed them when it didn't work out."

"That would be bad news."

"It sure would. I'll just walk through the alleyway and back to the parking lot."

"I'll go with you." Howard wasn't about to let her roam around in the dark by herself. Streetlamps only lighted so much of the street; the shadows darkened in the alleyways. Sure, because of their jaguar genes, their night vision was phenomenal. Their hearing and scenting abilities were vastly superior to those of ordinary humans too. But his job was to watch out for Val.

He was afraid she meant to continue to look for Benny and the woman on her own, believing—as she'd told her mom—there had been too many of them looking for him.

"All right. Fine. You can drop me off." Val climbed into the front passenger's seat, leaving Howard to take the back seat.

Jillian glanced over the seat back. "Did you want to drive?"

He shook his head. He decided right then and there that he didn't trust Val one little bit. She'd agreed too readily to accept their help as backup. She didn't even seem to be bothered that she'd lost Benny. He thought she had some clue as to where Benny might have gone.

"Are you leaving for Houston tonight?" he asked Val.

"It's nearly midnight. I'll stay at my hotel another night and leave in the morning. So what case will you be working on next?"

"Nothing on the agenda, as far as we know," Howard

said. Nothing except continuing to provide Val protection. And that wouldn't end with her leaving for Houston.

"Why don't you go by the name of Thorsen? God of thunder? Or Thor?" Val suddenly asked.

"How in the world do you know my middle name is Thorsen?" Howard was really surprised. He didn't share it with anyone if he could help it.

Jillian chuckled. "I like it. God of thunder. Suits you, Howard."

"One of your friends called to you during one of the training exercises," Val said. "And then another said, 'Yeah, the mighty Thor, who has lost his hammer.' You quickly took the one down to the mat and then the other. They were laughing their heads off but in good fun. I was impressed. Especially when I had the god of thunder under my control shortly thereafter. I asked the boss, and he told me your name was Thorsen but some called you Thor for short."

He'd known that would come back to haunt him, but he hadn't expected her to mention it in front of Jillian, who chuckled. "Next time, I will have you right where I want you," Howard said to Val.

"Oh?" Val's comment was a challenge. *She* was a challenge.

"Next training session."

"You no longer work for the Enforcer branch."

"I'll be there. Just for you."

She smiled.

Jillian pulled into the parking lot near the club, and Val got out. "Thanks for the ride."

Howard left the truck and climbed into the front passenger's seat. "We'll follow you to the hotel."

"Naturally." Val crossed the parking lot and climbed into a red Subaru.

He shut his door, and Jillian and he watched Val as she drove to the entrance to the parking lot.

"Do you think she's still going to search for the perp?" Jillian asked Howard, following Val's car as she pulled onto the street.

"Yeah, I do."

"Are we following her back to Houston tomorrow?" Jillian sounded concerned for Val's welfare.

"Yeah. Until we've been reassigned to another case, we continue to do our mission and watch her back. I don't trust her. I think she believes we caused Benny to run and she wants to do this on her own, just like her boss said she would."

Jillian turned onto the next road. "What if Benny knows she's out to get him now? She puts herself at more risk by not having us to watch out for her."

"I agree. Which is why we're sticking to her." The training exercise reminded him of how unpredictable Val could be. Which might be why she was so success-ful on her own.

"Do you think she knows of some other place he could have gone?"

"Maybe. Which means we need to take turns watch-ing her vehicle tonight." Howard gave Jillian the choice of whether she would stay up first to keep an eye on Val's car. He had no intention of losing track of Ms. Valerie Chambers.

"Maybe you shouldn't have told her we were her backup. I take it that's what happened in the club when you danced with her."

"She had seen my truck parked out here several nights. She hadn't seen us, but she checked my plate and called the boss to see what I was doing down here."

Jillian laughed. "Maybe she just wanted to see you again."

"I doubt it. She guessed we were here because of a job, despite our bosses denying it."

Smiling, Jillian shook her head. "So much for our undercover work, if even our chiefs couldn't convince her otherwise."

Once they arrived at the hotel, Jillian went up to their suite of adjoining rooms while Howard followed Val to her room to ensure they knew which one she was really staying in.

"Don't you trust me?" Val pulled out her key card.

He just smiled and waited for her to use the key on her room.

"See?" The green light flashed, indicating it *was* her room. She pushed open the door. "I'll call you if I get another lead."

He wouldn't hold his breath. "It's not that late. Do you have a swimsuit? Do you want to go for a dip in the pool?"

"Nope—to the swimsuit." Then she gave him an interested smile. "But yeah. What jaguar wouldn't want to try out the pool?"

Her phone rang. She pulled it out of her pocket and glanced at the caller ID. "Yeah, Mom? Are you still up?"

"See you in a few minutes here?" Howard asked.

She smiled at him, nodded, and shut her door.

He left for his room on the next floor up. He would have preferred being right next door to Val, but the hotel hadn't had any rooms available on this floor. Jillian would be watching Val's car from her window after Howard and Val went swimming, just in case Val tried a disappearing act.

Chapter 2

"YES, MANUEL, I HAD TO...TAKE CARE OF SOME BUSI-
ness. Otherwise, I would never have called you my
mother. Did you learn where else Benny might have
gone?" Val asked. He was one of the agents who did
investigations in an office at the Enforcers' headquarters. She didn't want Howard and Jillian to learn she
might have updated information on Benny, follow her,
and spook him again.

She began pulling off her blouse and then her skirt.

"That's why I'm calling. I've been checking the air-
lines and finally found Benny booked on a flight leaving
for Belize at 12:30 tomorrow afternoon. The next flight
out is 5:30 that evening. You can try to fly standby on the
earlier flight. There are still seats available on the later
one. Hey, the other business you mentioned wouldn't
happen to be with regard to Howard Armstrong, would
it? It sure sounded like his voice."

"Yeah, you're right. He and a wolf with the USF were
given the mission of watching my back undercover."

Manuel laughed. "He's too good at his job to get
caught. He must have wanted you to know he was
there watching out for you. You know, rarely do any
of the guys take him down in training. For you to have
managed…"

"Don't tell me you think he planned it that way."

Manuel laughed again. "Since your parents are down

there, you can probably work together. Then Howard and his partner won't have to tail you any longer."

"Thanks! I'll let Howard know. And I'll tell my folks I'm on my way down there." Val had never worked with her parents on a case. Her dad had always taken charge anytime they did anything all the years she was growing up. She could just see that if she signed on with them, she and her mom would be relegated to the role of the Enforcer crew, while he was the captain of the ship. She could captain the ship on her own just fine. But if they needed her once she finished her mission, she would be there for them, since she'd already be in the country.

"Just let me know which flight you end up getting on."

"I will. Thanks for the tip."

They ended the call, and she phoned Howard's number. "Hey, it's me, Val."

"You didn't change your mind about swimming, did you?" Howard sounded as if he was going to be disappointed if she had.

She smiled. "No, you can come down and get me. I'm joining my parents in Belize to help out with their case. You and Jillian can tell your boss, and he can assign you a new case to work on."

"Belize. What happened to catching up to Benny? The guy needs to be taken down at once."

She didn't want to tell Howard the real reason she was going to Belize. What if Howard didn't believe she would have her parents' protection while she worked her case? Especially since they were already on a case. What if he thought he had to follow her down there?

"I'm sure we'll get another lead soon, and then I'll jump on it."

"When are you going?"

"Five thirty tomorrow evening. The earlier flight is booked."

"Okay, see you in a few minutes." He ended the call.

She frowned at the phone, surprised he'd end the call so abruptly. She suspected he was going to call her boss to try to learn if she had a new lead. Or confirm she didn't have an earlier flight. Didn't he trust her? She smiled.

She tied back her hair in a ponytail and glanced at her matching purple bra and panties that had no seams so they looked enough like a bathing suit. She should have thought to bring one on the trip. Though she hadn't believed she'd be swimming with a sexy jaguar in a hotel swimming pool.

Before long, Howard was at her door, but before he could knock, she was opening it, courtesy of her jaguar hearing. He dropped his hand and looked her over, frowning. "I thought you didn't have a swimsuit."

"I don't." She headed for the stairs; she always used them to stay in shape.

"You could have fooled me. Nice…underwear," he said.

She smiled as she headed down the stairs. They often stripped naked in front of other jaguars before they shifted, so she wasn't embarrassed to be wearing underwear that looked like a bathing suit in front of the very interested male jaguar. Glancing back at his trunks, she said, "Like your suit."

"I always take it on trips, just in case I can get in some swim time."

"I thought I was going to be busy doing surveillance

so late every night that the pool would be closed before I was through for the evening."

"I'm glad to be able to do this tonight."

"What about your partner?"

"Jillian is texting her mate and told me to have fun."

"She must really miss him."

"She does, but she's fully dedicated to the job. She just figures only one of us needs to be down here safeguarding you."

Like Val really needed them to watch her back, but she didn't make any comment.

When they reached the floor where the pool and bar were, they went inside. They had an hour before closing, and no one was in the pool area. *Thankfully*. Val really didn't feel like swimming with noisy kids or trying to swim in a pool crowded with adults.

She grabbed a towel from a stand and put her key card and cell phone on a table. Howard did the same. Then she moved to the pool and sat on the edge. Howard dove into the deep end as if he couldn't wait to go swimming. For a moment, she observed him creating small waves in the water, his muscles rippling with his powerful strokes. God, he was magnificent. She slipped into the pool and began swimming laps like he was doing, until she noticed he'd paused to take a break at the deep end of the pool, treading water, watching her.

She should have continued to swim and not looked to see what he was doing, but she couldn't help herself. Howard did intrigue her. Now she was treading water, not drawing closer to him. He suddenly pushed off the wall and dove under the water, heading straight for her. She could see his muscular form growing closer and closer under the water. She wanted to stay, she wanted to flee: both natural instincts for a jaguar being hunted.

She was going to hold her spot, come what may. She wasn't going to swim away. She *wasn't*. But the thrill of the chase was in her blood, and she suddenly dove under and away from him, turning in a wide circle to reach the deeper end. The chase was on. He was a powerful swimmer and quickly touched her foot. She swam faster. But she couldn't keep out of his longer reach, and he soon caught her foot, pulled her close, and they both came up for air. He was testing her to see if she would kick at him to release her or allow the intimacy.

Then he was holding her close in the pool, treading water to stay afloat with her hanging onto his hips in a light embrace as he wrapped his arms around her waist. He wasn't smiling. She was. He was turned on, his eyes lust-filled, his gaze on hers but slowly drifting to her mouth. It couldn't be helped when he was swimming in the water, chasing after a she-cat, and she had allowed herself to be caught.

"Now what?" she asked, wondering just where the hunky cat was going to take this.

"I've wanted to do this ever since you got the better of me in training." And then he lowered his head and she lifted hers and they kissed.

She was so glad no one was here as she wrapped her arms around his neck and gave in to the hotness of the kiss, their tongues caressing, his hands sliding down to her bottom and pulling her snug against him. She instantly felt his full-blown erection. Ohmigod, he was such a jaguar. She almost regretted she had every intention of leaving him behind and going after Benny on her own. Then again, her mission was her mission, and she was certain she could take him down without any problems. Having the male jaguar and female wolf trailing her? That would only hamper her.

For now, she gave in to the kiss, licking Howard's wet mouth, nibbling on his wet neck, loving this unexpected bit of bliss. But then she heard the telltale sounds of kids' noisy chatter and adults telling them not to run. Her time with Howard was abruptly at an end. Or at least she thought so. He was either too wrapped up in his lust-filled thoughts, or he was just ignoring the inevitable.

So she continued to kiss him as if there was no tomorrow, which there wouldn't be. Not like this.

And then three boys flew into the pool room, a woman yelling at them, "Walk, don't run!"

Howard nuzzled Val's cheek, making a disgruntled sound. She imagined he'd need a towel to cover up, if what she was feeling against her lower belly was any indication.

"Guess it's time to head on up to bed." She almost regretted having to say that, but the kids hit the pool and were wild and excited, splashing about—which she would have done as a child—but as far as she was concerned, this was late enough to be adult time only. The kids should have been in bed hours ago.

"Yeah." Howard's voice was husky, raw with passion, his eyes hot with hunger.

She smiled and pulled away from him. "Come on, hot stuff. Time to go."

It was time to end the brief fascination she had with the god of thunder. But man, did he have some moves.

She climbed out of the pool at the deep end, and

Howard followed her. She shouldn't have looked, but she had to. Yep, he was hotly built, muscles and *all* the rest, his swim trunks plastered to his arousal.

They grabbed their towels from the table where they'd left them and started drying off. Wrapped in their towels, they picked up their keys and phones and hurried out of the pool area, racing to her room to avoid the hallway's chill.

As soon as she was at her room, she unlocked the door and turned for a brief good night. As cats, they could have sex at any time and it didn't mean they were mated, but she really didn't want to do that with him and then leave, which was what she was getting ready to do.

"Night, Thor. That was some swim."

He gave her a wicked smile. "Hell, anytime."

She hadn't planned to kiss him again, but slipping into her room like a scared rabbit just wasn't her. She kissed him briefly. "Pleasant dreams." Then she slipped into her room.

"Yeah, you too." His voice was still rough and deep.

She closed her door and leaned against it. Wow. Why did he have to leave the Enforcer branch?

She quickly removed her underwear and took a shower. After drying her hair, she got dressed, throwing her wet underwear into a plastic dry-cleaner bag, and then sat down on the bed, intending to leave the hotel and stay at another as soon as she thought Jillian and Howard might be asleep. Then she got a call from her mother. It was ten o'clock. Why in the world was she calling at this hour? "Mom, is anything wrong?"

"Howard called and said you were coming to help with our case. We're so glad, dear."

Val would kill Howard. "I'll check in with you when I get down there. I have some business to take care of too, so I don't know how much time I'll be able to spend on your case."

"Oh, that's wonderful." There was a significant pause. "I asked if you'd taken Benny down since the last time we talked. He said no."

"No new leads as of yet."

"When will you be getting in?"

"Not sure. I'll let you know when I arrive at the airport in Belize. How's your case going?" Val was certain if she told her mom she was looking for Benny in Belize, her mom would call Howard right back.

"We're staking out a house right now where Eric Erickson usually stays when he's in country, according to one of our sources. The deed is in his name, but he's not often here. He's been selling purple heroin, but we haven't spied him, or anyone else, there. We're sure that when we take him down, others will take his place. But with any luck, they won't be our kind."

"I hope not. You don't have any leads on where he might be?"

"No. The man that informed on him said for certain Eric comes here about this time of year."

"I trust you'll be able to eliminate him soon." She wished they could deal with this on their own without getting hurt. Every time they went on one of these kinds of missions, she worried about them.

"You said you were coming to help." Her mom paused for a moment, and in that pause, Val knew her mother suspected what she was up to. "Benny's headed down this way, isn't he? That's why Howard called, isn't it? To ensure you really were coming down here to help us with our case. You wouldn't be coming down here to help us—or take care of other business, as you put it—if he was still at large. You would be following him to where he was headed next."

"I *will* help you with your case. I'll be in the country. And if I eliminate Benny before then, I'll be free to just work with you."

"All right. Let us know when you get in."

"Will do. Be safe. Night." Val ended the call, knowing her mom would call Howard back and tell him where she was going and to continue to watch her back. Val had called the airport to get on the 5:30 flight but would go to the airport and try to get on standby for the earlier one.

She paced across her hotel room, waiting until she thought Howard and Jillian might be asleep. She also figured the two of them might be taking turns watching her car to see if she tried to slip away in the middle of the night. Which was why she had pretended her car was in the parking lot down the street from the club. She'd looked for a car that was the same size and color as hers and that had only had human scents on it. She hadn't wanted to borrow a car that had any shifter scents on it. Not when shifters could possibly track her down by scent later. While Howard and Jillian had watched her, she'd found one that was unlocked and hot-wired it. Then when they had reached this hotel, she had parked it at the side entrance so she could slip out through the front entrance without Howard or Jillian seeing her if they were observing the car.

She packed her bag and checked out of the hotel, then

called a taxi. When the taxi arrived, she had the driver take her to a parking area near the club where her car really was, paid him, threw her bags into the trunk of her car, and drove to a new hotel near the airport.

She worked alone. Had for two years now. And she wasn't going to lose the perp again.

In her new room, she removed her clothes and tossed them on a chair. Then she pulled out her wet underwear so it could drip-dry in the shower. After pulling the floral bedcover aside on the bed, she climbed under the sheet. She wondered how long it would take Howard and Jillian to discover she was no longer at the hotel and that the car wasn't hers. Would they return home for another mission or search for her?

She let out her breath. She needed to get this done before the creep turned another woman and decided she didn't suit him either. And she hoped Howard and his partner didn't waste her time and theirs searching for her. But she suspected they'd end up at the airport when she did.

She got a call from her boss and answered it, wondering what was wrong now.

"I just wanted to give you a heads-up. Rowdy Sanderson, a Bigfork, Montana, homicide detective, has been questioning our people at the crime scene in San Antonio where Benny's wife was murdered. When our agents asked what he was doing there, he said he'd gotten a call from her, saying she was afraid her husband was going to kill her. But she told him that whatever Sanderson did, he wasn't to call the local police. So he didn't. When asked how he knew her, he said they were friends back in Bigfork.

"Hopefully, he won't learn where Benny's gone and follow him to Belize. If you hadn't heard, Rowdy's the human who knows about wolf shifters. He doesn't know about us jaguars, and I want to keep it that way. No matter what, don't turn him. Try not to kill him." Sylvan sent her a couple of pictures of the detective. Rowdy's hair was military short, dark brown, and he had blue eyes in the head shot, a professional photo. In the other photo, he was wearing a white parka in a wintry snow-filled scene at a frozen lake, giving an interview, the headlights of a car poking out of the ice.

As if her situation wasn't complicated enough.

⁓

Howard had the last shift to watch Val's car that morning and hadn't seen any sign of her, but he suspected she wasn't sleeping in. After her mother called him and let him in on the news—that Val had a tip Benny was taking a flight out to Belize—Howard and Jillian had set plans in motion. He'd known not to trust Val.

Jillian knocked on the connecting door to their rooms.

"Come in."

"No sign of her?" Jillian asked. Her hair was tied neatly back, and she was wearing jeans, a floral shirt, and boots.

"Nope. Want to check on her to see if she wants to have breakfast with us?"

"What if she leaves while we're walking down to her room?"

"Yeah, that's a distinct possibility. You stay here to watch her car, and I'll go to her room," Howard said. "Call me if you see her headed for her car. If she agrees to have breakfast with us, I'll let you know and you can meet us at the restaurant."

"All right. We're still going ahead with the plan, right?"

"Absolutely. We'll both get in line for the first seats available on standby for 12:30. If she gets on and I can't, then you stick to her, and I'll follow you on the 5:30 flight."

"If she doesn't make it on the earlier flight, she'll be stuck flying with you." Jillian smiled. "She's good at playing cat-and-mouse games."

"Tell me about it. Call you in a few." Howard jogged down the stairs, reached Val's floor, and soon knocked at her door. No one answered. He called her phone, but she didn't answer. He didn't have a good feeling about this.

He called Jillian and headed down to the lobby. "She's not answering the door or her phone."

"Her car's still here."

"I'm going to the lobby to make sure she didn't check out." When he reached the lobby, he told the clerk, "I'm looking for my friend, Valerie Chambers. She said she was leaving early, but she left her phone with me by accident. I checked her room, but she isn't answering, and I can't call her because I've got her phone." He waved his phone at the clerk a little to emphasize his point. "Has she checked out already?"

"Let me see. Uh, yes, several hours ago."

Howard couldn't believe it. "Okay, no problem. I'll catch up to her at the airport. No one can live without their phone for long, you know. She's probably already missing it and wonders where she left it."

The clerk laughed.

Calling Jillian, Howard left the lobby and headed outside. "She checked out hours ago."

"You're kidding. But her car's still here."

"Yeah, I'll have the license plate run, just to verify the vehicle is hers. If it is, she must have taken a taxi to some other place. My guess is she went to a hotel near the airport for the rest of the night."

"She wouldn't want to abandon her car here for however long it would take to go there and return. They could have towed it."

"That's what I'd figure. Get back with you in a few minutes." Howard stalked out to the vehicle Val had driven last night and called in the license plate to one of the agency clerks who did investigations for them behind the desk. "I need to know who the vehicle belongs to."

After a lengthy pause, the clerk at headquarters got back with him. "The car belongs to Whitney Bishop."

"Whitney Bishop? Thanks. Can you report to the police that it was left at the Kingston Hotel in San Antonio?" Howard smelled around the car. Except for Val's jaguar scent, all he smelled were human scents.

"Will do."

Howard thanked him, ended the call, and phoned Jillian. He headed back into the hotel. "She stole the car. It belongs to a human."

"She's a bit of a rogue."

"Yeah and smart too. I wouldn't have guessed she'd go to that much trouble to leave without alerting us." He headed inside the lobby and entered the stairwell. He could take the elevator, but he liked to run up the stairs for endurance training whenever he had the opportunity, and it wasn't as though they were in a rush to go anywhere now.

"Do we search for her?"

"Nah. We might as well get breakfast and then leave for the airport. At least we packed summer clothes for the San Antonio heat, which will work well for hot Belize this time of year."

"I've never been there. I was Googling it, and they still have jaguars that roam freely in the rain forest. No wolves though."

"Yeah. In some of the states, you're in your element. The jungle is the big cats' playground." He opened the door to his hotel room. "I'm back."

Jillian tucked her phone away. "Do you ever feel the urge to live there?"

"No. Visits are fun, but we have enough roaming-around land where I live. What about you?" He grabbed his bag and Jillian took hold of hers, and they left the room. "Do you ever feel the urge to live somewhere that wolves live wild so you'd blend in more?"

"No. Though some wolf packs chose their locations for that purpose, to run as wolves where humans wouldn't be shocked to see them. Like you, I don't mind visiting places like that, but it's the local wolves' territory. If we moved to a place like that, they'd smell we were wolves and want to protect their territory. There's only so much food to go around for a pack."

"That's so true. Did you tell Vaughn you're going to Belize without him?" Howard escorted her to the western-themed restaurant and took a booth near a window overlooking the parking lot. The restaurant was nearly empty. He hoped it was because everyone was taking off for other destinations or still sleeping—not that the food was bad.

"Yeah. He wished he could go too and we could go snorkeling and do other fun things while there. He was glad to learn Val's Enforcer parents are down there to help out if this gets complicated."

The server brought them menus and coffee. "I'm Sue, your server. I'll let you have a moment to look over your menus."

"Thanks," Howard said.

Sue headed for a table across the room.

Jillian glanced at the breakfast menu and set it aside.

Howard was still reading his. "I'm afraid Val's parents are busy with their own case. I hope they get it resolved soon, but they're just staking out the drug dealer's house for now." He set his menu on the table. "I didn't think I'd ever be working with a partner, let alone that you and your mate would be wolves."

Jillian smiled. "I never thought I'd be working with big cats either. About last night—"

Hell, he hadn't minded that Val had seen and felt the way she'd aroused him, since she'd seemed intrigued, but he really hadn't wanted his female USF partner to see it. He'd tried to duck into his room and take a cold shower, but Jillian was his partner and she had wanted to know if he'd made any headway with Valerie. Which, knowing she'd left them last night, meant he hadn't.

He raised a brow at Jillian.

She just smiled and looked outside. Jillian had gotten the biggest kick out of how much Val had heated him up last night and had told him he was doing a great job. Not that anything he'd done with Val had been part of the job. That had been a hell of a lot more personal.

A few minutes later, Sue came to take their orders, but then paused. This time, she was close enough that Howard smelled she was a jaguar and she smiled at him, but she looked puzzled about Jillian.

"We're agents with the USF, United Shifter Force," Howard said.

"Oh. I've never heard of that organization. I've never met a wolf shifter before either. Do you need a minute to look at the menu further?" Sue asked them.

"No, thanks. I'll have eggs over easy and sausage links," Jillian said. "And we'll both have a glass of water too."

"I'll have the steak and eggs, medium rare on the steak," Howard said.

"I'll have these right out for you."

Before long, Sue brought out their meals while Jillian was texting her mate. They were so newly mated that Howard had been surprised she wanted to go with him on this mission. But she'd vowed to watch his back. Vaughn and jaguar mates Everett and Demetria were watching one another's backs.

When Sue left, Howard said to Jillian, "Okay, here's what we know. Lucy Harding was married to Benny Canton. She was a jaguar shifter when she was murdered. We assumed she'd been one all along, but Val spoke to her family and friends and they're all human."

"We know for certain Benny murdered her?" Jillian asked.

"Yes. As a jaguar. Saliva proved it. We'll take him down, one way or another." Howard was certain of that.

They finished their meal, and when they left the

hotel, they saw the police and a man standing next to the car Val had stolen, talking to each other.

"I hope Val called it in and not just us," Jillian said.

Howard drove his truck to the airport, hoping they'd beat Val there. "I plan to mention it to her when we catch up to her again. We *are* supposed to be the good guys."

Chapter 3

VAL FINALLY GOT SOME MUCH-NEEDED SLEEP AT THE hotel and then took the complimentary shuttle to the airport, which was one reason she'd stayed at this hotel. She could leave her car here for the duration of her trip without paying for airport parking, compliments of the hotel. She made it through airport security and headed for the gate where the earlier flight would take off, hoping she would be able to get a seat on standby. What she hadn't expected was to see Howard and Jillian at the check-in counter.

Val came to a full stop. She'd truly thought she'd get there way before they did!

Howard turned and saw her, offering her the most devilish smile. She wanted to growl. Especially if she missed getting on this flight because one of them, or both, made it instead.

Still, she smiled back, admitting they were a step ahead of her this time. She added her name to the standby list and glanced at the board, hoping she'd come in ahead of one of them at least. But the board didn't change. She was in third place. Not that she really hoped anyone would miss their connection—because she knew what a pain that was—but she still wished she'd end up with a seat on this flight.

"Cute trick," Howard said to her as the three of them took seats in a little windowed alcove so they had some privacy. "About the car, I mean." But he didn't appear amused.

This time, she gave him a genuine smile. "Thanks. I did report the borrowed car, just for your information. I used the hotel phone. I didn't want the person who owned it to think it was trashed or long gone, or for the police to spend a lot of time looking for it."

"Good. I reported it too," Howard said.

She raised her brows, hoping he hadn't mentioned who had stolen it. She suspected he wouldn't have. Not when they were all shifters and she had an important mission to accomplish. She was glad to hear they'd discovered what she'd done. She would have been disappointed if they hadn't been that good at their jobs.

"When did you figure it out?"

"When I went to your room to escort you to breakfast."

She chuckled. She couldn't help herself. "That late, huh? How did you know I was taking a flight out? Manuel told my boss, who told your boss, right?" Val should have known Manuel would keep her boss in the loop. And her boss would have told Howard's boss, who would have told Howard and Jillian. "Or my mother told you."

"Something like that."

"Okay, look. This is my job. I work alone. You did too when you were an Enforcer. You know how it is. Since I can't seem to convince you that I don't need your help, if you're going to watch out for me, you have to do it from a distance. I don't want Benny being spooked and disappearing again. He's a jaguar, wily and dangerous."

"Which is why we're here to protect you. We'll stay

out of your hair, but you need to keep us informed of where you're going at all times." Howard spoke in a no-nonsense tone.

Val suspected she was going to have trouble with him not letting her do her job her way.

"Do you know any specific reason why he's gone there? Other than it's a jaguar hot spot," Howard said.

"It's possible he knows people there," Val said.

"Or he's just so familiar with the territory that he figures he can keep ahead of us," Howard said.

"Keep ahead of me, you mean," she reminded Howard. "This is *my* assignment."

Howard nodded. "Right."

Val was afraid Howard was too much of an Enforcer at heart to mean that. "Benny is supposed to be on the earlier flight."

"Haven't seen any sign of him. He might be in one of the restaurants or a bar," Howard said.

"Do you have any idea where Benny's going to be staying?" Jillian asked.

"Yeah. I got a text before I reached the airport. He's rented a cabin at the Tropical Rain Forest Resort."

"For just him? Anyone else?" Jillian asked.

Val shook her head. "We don't know. He ordered the plane ticket for himself, one-way ticket. We assume he's going to be alone, unless he meets someone there." She paused. "We have another issue."

"Oh?" Howard asked, sounding wary.

"Okay, my boss called last night and mentioned that a Rowdy Sanderson, homicide detective out of Montana, is looking into Lucy's death too. He's human but knows about wolf shifters."

"Hell. A homicide detective is involved now too? I can't believe this." Howard shook his head.

"Yeah, he could be a total pain in the butt if he intends to take Benny into custody. And that a human even knows wolf shifters exist and hasn't been turned or eliminated is a big no-no. I can't believe a wolf hasn't done something about this."

"Any guidelines from Sylvan?" Howard asked.

"No killing or turning."

Howard snorted. "That leaves telling him what all of us are if we run into the detective in Belize, and I'm sure Sylvan wouldn't go along with that."

The call came for passengers to begin boarding. All the shifters stood, ready to go if they were called on the standby list. Four names were now ahead of Howard and Val. Jillian's name was still at the top.

Jillian's name was called. "Good luck," she said to her partner and Val.

"I'll see you there." Howard frowned, looking a bit uncomfortable that he wasn't going with her.

"I'll take your place," Val offered, "so the two of you can stay together." She smiled, knowing they wouldn't go along with it, but she had to make the offer. Just in case.

Jillian smiled back. "That's all right. See you there in a few hours." She hurried to board the plane with the others while Val and Howard watched and waited to see if they would make it. But they were also looking for any sign of Benny boarding the plane.

Two more passengers were called on standby. That was it before they closed the doors.

Val was trying to relax and not feel so tense about missing this flight. There wasn't anything she could do about it, but all she could think of was losing Benny completely. She took a deep breath and let it out. "Did you see anyone who could have been Benny getting on the flight?"

"Yeah, at least three men were wearing hats. The men were all the right size, build, and age. But I couldn't see their faces to make a positive ID."

"We need to get to the ticket counter and just sniff around for Benny's scent. Do you have a ticket for the later flight?"

"I do," Howard said, sounding glad about it. Or maybe that he would be on the same flight as Val. Though she suspected he was also worried about his partner. "You?"

"Yes." At least Val was glad about that.

Then they moved closer to the check-in counter and both smelled Benny. He was on the same flight as Jillian, and Val hoped she would be all right.

Howard texted Jillian to ask her to be careful: Benny was on the plane.

———⚡———

As soon as Jillian's plane took off, Howard received a text from Vaughn, wanting to know why his mate was going to Belize alone, without her partner to back her up, when the rogue jaguar was on the flight with her.

"Trouble?" Val asked as they took their seats again in the waiting area.

Howard texted Vaughn back, explaining the situation, which he was sure Jillian had already done. He assured Vaughn they'd be back together in a few hours while he watched over their mission priority—keeping track of Val.

Vaughn didn't respond. Howard knew the wolf was worried, but he was also giving him a hard time. Howard loved to reciprocate, and Vaughn had gotten the best of him a few times.

"Why do you prefer working alone?" Howard asked Val after finishing the text to Vaughn, still not answering her question. She didn't need to know that Jillian's mate was on edge about her being alone.

"You have to ask me? You were the same way!" Val said, not answering Howard's question.

Howard let out his breath. "You're right. When we had to deal with really bad cases or take care of a group of shifters, we went in pairs, sometimes more. At one time, I had a partner. We worked well together for two years, but then he went through a divorce. On our last two missions together, he was distracted and foolhardy, not cautious like he normally was. I swore it was like he didn't care if he got hurt, but that meant he couldn't watch my back either.

"I wanted to leave him at the office for the second mission because he'd been reckless the day before on a case, but he insisted on coming with me. He was offended that I would even consider leaving him behind. I reminded him he couldn't pull what he had the day before. He assured me it wouldn't happen again."

Val frowned. "What had happened?"

"He rushed into a house where the perp lived without taking any precautions. He was lucky that time, but I gave him hell for it. The perp was hiding in the attic. If he had been prepared to fight us, my partner could have been killed before I could reach him.

"Anyway, he assured me, again, that he was fine. He

was cool. No problem. And really, up until the point we had trouble, everything was going as well as could be expected—until he got a text from his wife telling him he had to sign some papers. Shortly after that, we were in a second cat fight, and either he wasn't thinking straight or he just didn't care. I could have taken the perp down. I was ready for him. Just as I went to lunge for him, my partner leaped into my path. The perp tore out his throat before I could get around my partner and kill the cat," Howard said.

"I'm so sorry."

"Yeah, well, I was angry with him and his wife for a long time after that. I worked alone and did fine by myself. There's nothing worse than losing a good friend on a mission. I was constantly second-guessing myself. What could I have done differently? What could any of us have done differently? I just couldn't deal with it."

"I agree completely." Val settled against her seat. "I had a similar experience but different circumstances. I was partnered with another female Enforcer, and she fell for the perp."

Howard was surprised to hear it. He would have thought he'd have heard about that through the agent grapevine.

Val continued. "I couldn't believe it. He was like Ted Bundy. Good looking, charismatic, had a way with women. He didn't fool me with his charm. He murdered her and nearly killed me. I vowed I'd never work with another agent while I'm with the Enforcer branch."

"I thought that too, until I began working for the USF. Wonderful group of agents, and the great thing is we all have our special talents. Jillian is a gun expert and can hack into computers. She'll be armed by the time we see her in Belize."

"And you're a big, dangerous, male cat," Val said.

Howard smiled. "You are sneaky, quick-witted, and easily take advantage of a situation."

She smiled at Howard wickedly.

He motioned to the eateries down the hall. "We have quite a lot of time to kill, and it's lunchtime. Do you want to get something to eat?"

They agreed on a steak place, since they had another three hours before they boarded their flight. They found a booth and both ordered rib eyes, baked potatoes, and broccoli. When they received their orders, Val got a text and responded to it.

"Have you got anything more on Benny?" Howard asked, passing her the basket of rolls.

"We're monitoring a credit card he's been using." Val cut into her steak. "He picked up groceries close to the airport."

"Wouldn't he figure out we could be monitoring it?" Howard couldn't believe the guy could be that careless. "Are you sure he hasn't given the card to someone else? Or left it behind so someone else would steal it and use it to throw us off his track?"

Val sipped some of her water. "You'd think so, but he was using it at the club, and then he paid for a trip to Belize."

"He didn't leave it in the club for another jaguar to find, and the thief is going to Belize?" Howard asked.

"Two jaguars identified him at the bar using that same credit card on other occasions. From what we can learn about him, he hasn't murdered anyone else, just his wife. And he hasn't committed any other crimes. Not everyone who commits a crime is a master criminal. From all accounts, he was in a rage when he murdered her. It appears he's going to his old haunts—like the club in San Antonio and Belize—unsure what to do. He doesn't have any family to speak of. He doesn't have his phone with him, or we could track him that way."

Howard thought Val might be right. Not all criminals were very bright. Still, he had his doubts. What if they arrived in Belize to find Benny had never gone to the resort? That someone else was staying at the cabin?

They talked and continued to buy sodas and water to keep their table longer until they had to leave on their flight. It was better than sitting in the waiting area. They finally ordered cheesecake and coffee before they were kicked out of there. Val got another text and answered it.

"News about Benny?" Howard asked. He couldn't help it. Whether she liked it or not, she had two more partners on this job.

She smiled.

Howard let out his breath. "We stick together."

"Sure we will. The tech that's following his credit card usage sent me a description of the car Benny's driving. It's a red 2017 Ford EcoSport."

Howard shook his head. "I still can't believe he's using the same credit card."

"Good news for us."

"True."

After they finished their dessert, they headed to the gate to catch their flight. Howard couldn't wait to get to Belize and make sure that Jillian was fine.

"Worried about your partner?" Val asked as they made their way onto the plane.

"She can handle herself, but yeah. I didn't think we'd be separated like this."

"Have you worked with her long?"

"For several months. The entire force has always been together until now."

"I still can't believe you went to work with them and didn't continue to be an Enforcer." Val reached her seat and smiled at the passenger sitting next to it. "You wouldn't mind letting us sit together, would you? We're newlyweds and couldn't get seats together."

The man got up from the seat. "Sure. Which seat do you have?" he asked Howard.

"The single one across the aisle, two rows further back." Howard was astonished that Val wanted to sit beside him on the flight, though he was trying not to look shocked about it.

"Even better. Thanks."

Val and Howard thanked him, and Val moved into the row to sit next to the window.

Jillian texted Howard to tell him that she had arrived safely in Belize, and he was relieved to hear from her.

I'm in the lobby at the Belize Airport Hotel, grabbing some lunch. I'll wait here until the two of you get in. Got a cabin at the resort!

Howard texted back: We'll be there before you know it and decide where to go from there. Great on the cabin!

"Did you get a cabin?" Howard asked Val.

"Yeah." She settled back in her seat. "You?"

"Yeah. Jillian just texted me that she got one."

"Better be on the other side of the resort."

He didn't know where any of their cabins were located. It didn't matter. He was following Val wherever she went after they arrived at the resort.

"You didn't want me to protect you. I didn't think you'd want me to sit by you on the plane," he remarked.

Val surprised Howard at every turn.

"You're not protecting me. Not right now. Here, I'd rather sit by a fellow former Enforcer and talk. I mean it about you two staying out of sight though." Val fastened her seat belt.

"We will, as long as you keep us informed about where you are." He still didn't trust that she would keep them apprised of her movements.

―⁓―

When they finally landed in Belize in the middle of a rainstorm, Howard called Jillian right away. "I've got this on speaker," he told her. "We just arrived at the airport."

"I'm so glad to hear from you. Vaughn is driving me nuts, checking up on me until you arrive. I'll let him know we're together again once you get here."

"Val's getting a rental car after we get off the plane, and we'll meet you at the hotel soon," Howard said, getting the directions.

"I'll be waiting," Jillian said.

They left the plane, and Val dug out a rain jacket. Howard hadn't brought one with him. Maybe he could pick up something here. They got their bags, and Val paid for a rental car. He knew Jillian would already have a car, so he followed Val out to her car, getting soaked in the process.

"You should have brought a rain jacket with you." She seemed amused.

"It's on my list for next time I have an unscheduled trip to Belize during the rainy season."

As soon as they settled in the car—with her in the driver's seat—she handed him her bag. "Tissues in the front top pocket, if you don't have any of those either."

"Thanks." He pulled out a couple and mopped up his face and arms.

Val drove out of the airport to the hotel.

"So why is Benny staying at the Tropical Rain Forest Resort?" Howard asked. "Do you have any intel on that?"

"He's gone there before. I guess it's familiar ground to him," Val said. "It's the rainy season, and the tourist rush hasn't begun, or we wouldn't have been able to get cabins there."

"What about your parents? Where are they?" Howard asked Val.

"They're in another area of Belize, a couple of hours away."

"Are you going to tell them you're here?"

"I will. After I finish my mission, I'll help them with theirs."

"Who all are they attempting to take out?" Howard asked.

"Jaguar Eric Erickson. He's pushing purple heroin, and five people have already died from his drug sales that we know of."

"Sounds like a good candidate for termination."

"He is the perfect candidate. He doesn't care anything

about ruining people's lives. All he cares about is making money off their misfortune." Val turned onto another street, and they saw the sign for the hotel.

After they parked, they found Jillian sitting in the lobby waiting for them. She hurried to join them. "Got us a great two-bedroom cabin." Jillian smiled at Howard.

He knew that expression meant she had pulled a fast one on Val. He wondered what that was all about.

"Better not be next to my place," Val said. She jerked her thumb at Howard. "Before we get to the resort, Howard needs to buy a rain jacket. There's a store near here where we can pick that up and any groceries you want before we head out to the boonies."

Howard couldn't have been more surprised about Val's suggestion. He'd expected her to take off and keep her distance from them as much as possible while she tried to track down Benny. Then again, she'd need some groceries too.

They rode in her rental car to a shopping area. Val parked. He didn't expect the two women to stay with him when he went into a clothing store, nor did he expect them to try to figure out which jacket he should get.

He realized the only woman who had ever gone clothes shopping with him was his mother. He couldn't help being amused. He tried on a gray rain jacket when Val held up a jungle-green one, shaking her head at the gray one. Jillian had a blue-gray one she liked best. If it had been completely up to Howard, though it still was, he would have gone with the gray one. To appease the ladies, he tried on their choices as well.

"The green one. It has all kinds of hidden pockets for anything you might need to keep…hidden," Val said.

"She's right. And it would blend in better with the rain forest if you aren't wearing your wilder coat." Jillian lowered her chin and gave him a look that said he'd better go along with the suggestion.

He eyed the gray jacket again. Wouldn't he blend in with a gray, rainy day just as well wearing it? He suspected Val would be more agreeable about working with them if he went along with her suggestion. "The green it is. Perfect for jungle rain warfare." Though if he was going to be battling it out with Benny, he intended to be wearing his waterproof jaguar coat.

"Good. Let's head to the grocery store and leave for the resort," Val said while he went to pay for the jacket.

Once they'd picked up what they wanted at the grocery store, they returned to the hotel, and then Howard and Jillian followed Val in their rental car.

"I was about ready to punch you if you didn't pick the green jacket," Jillian said to Howard.

He chuckled. "I figured that from the stern look you gave me."

"She seriously likes you. A woman who didn't wouldn't have suggested shopping for a jacket for you. And that means she could very well be changing her mind about working with us. That only makes our situation easier. She might be coming around. I hadn't mentioned it before because I wasn't sure if there was anything more to it at the time, but she sure was dancing close to you. If it had been your idea only, I doubt she would have allowed it. And then swimming with her? Oh my."

He smiled. "She did ask the guy who was seated next

to her on the plane if he'd take my place so she could sit with me—as newlyweds."

Jillian laughed. "You see? What did I tell you?"

"That's only because Benny wasn't around. She even said so. I asked."

"Still, it sure sounds like a step in the right direction. I was so glad to leave you two alone for a while so you could get to know each other a little better."

"Where is our cabin in relation to hers?"

Jillian chuckled.

Howard glanced at her and smiled. "I figured the look you gave me when you said you reserved a cabin meant you did good."

"Right next door. Each of the cabins is surrounded by rain-forest trees and shrubs, so each has plenty of privacy, but it's still next door to ours."

"Did you happen to learn where Benny's place is?"

"I hacked into their reservation system and learned his cabin is on the other side of us."

Howard laughed. "Val will have a conniption."

"Right. But she's our mission, and if we're between the two of them, we can watch out for her. And if we happen to see Benny and have the opportunity before she does, we can take care of him."

Smiling, he shook his head. "I don't think me agreeing to take the green jacket will be enough to smooth things over once she learns where we're staying."

"She had the first opportunity to take the cabin next to his. The others were way too far away. I didn't want to risk us being on the other side of the resort."

He chuckled. "She won't like it."

"She doesn't have to. This is our job."

So much for them trying to convince Val to agree to working with them. But he totally agreed with Jillian.

———∿∿———

Two hours later, they reached the lodge to pick up their keys for the cabins.

"You have my number, and you can text me if you see Benny before I do," Val said for their ears only before they entered the lodge.

"We'll let you know if we spy him. And if you're after him, let us know," Howard said, his voice stern.

"Sure will."

They went inside, and Val got her key first. "You know what I said about keeping your distance from me."

"Gotcha," Howard said, fighting to keep from smiling about it.

"All right. See you later." Val hesitated before she headed outside.

He swore she really hadn't wanted to leave without them. Maybe she was getting used to them being around. He didn't want to see her go either. But they would be at their cabin soon enough, and he was shifting and checking out the area right after that. Jillian would have cabin watch. If he'd known he would be going to jaguar country, he would have taken one of his jaguar teammates with him instead. He didn't want her running around here as a wolf. Too conspicuous, unless people thought she was a dog. He smiled.

They waited until they thought Val would've had time to settle in, then drove to their cabin. Where they parked was hidden from her view. Unless she roamed around the area, she wouldn't know they were there.

All the cabins were raised on stilts. Water was puddled in places as Howard and Jillian grabbed their bags and headed for the stairs.

Rabbits scampered into the rain forest. Squirrels dashed up trees covered in trailing orchids. The aroma of blackberries, coco palms, and cashews scented the air. Orchids' heavenly perfumed scent added to the wondrous fragrance.

Howard didn't smell any jaguars that had been in the area, but he would check around Benny's cabin next.

They had brought the prerequisite hunter concealing spray to minimize the chance Benny would smell them. Howard hoped Benny wasn't also using the spray to hide his scent. Howard didn't think Jillian needed to wear it because the chances of a wolf searching for a jaguar shifter to take down would be unlikely. Not many people knew about the USF, unless they were agents who worked at one of the branches.

"Wow, this country is so beautiful," Jillian said as she and Howard carried the groceries and bags up to the deck of their cabin.

Howard had forgotten Jillian had never been to Belize, and it was fun seeing her so in awe of the place. All the scents and sounds and sights really did take a newcomer's breath away.

Howler monkeys called to each other as they swung through the trees, and birds chattered all over. Howard and Jillian both looked up at the canopy to see one watching them from a branch.

It was still raining, and Howard was glad to have a rain jacket for the trip, no matter the color or number of hidden pockets it had.

"Now what do we do?" Jillian unlocked the cabin and he followed her inside, stepping into a spacious living room with a pullout sofa and five chairs, all covered in tropical fabric, and a dining table and kitchen right off that and open to the living room.

"I'll check out the area in my fur coat. You stay here and—"

Shrieking at the cabin next to theirs—Val's cabin— penetrated the sounds of the rain forest and the steadily falling rain.

Howard raced out into the rain, Jillian hot on his heels, her gun out and ready.

Chapter 4

VAL HAD JUST UNLOADED HER GROCERIES AND WAS unpacking her bags when she heard rustling and a chittering noise in the kitchen. First thought she had was that Benny knew she was here and had come to eliminate her before she could take him out. But it sounded like…animals, rather than a person.

She peeked around the corner of the hall into the kitchen and saw two black howler monkeys eating four of her oranges on the beige tile counter. They were spitting the peelings onto her floor. As soon as they saw her, they shrieked and she shrieked too. She hadn't meant to, but they'd startled her as much as she'd startled them. Then one threw an orange at her!

Val couldn't believe what she was seeing.

What she hadn't expected next was for Howard to rush into her cabin and strip off his clothes. Standing there naked for a moment, he looked at the monkeys and then around the cabin, ensuring *that* was the only problem.

She had to laugh. The jaguar had some serious muscles. Jillian came in through a back door, gun in hand, but then she saw the monkeys and laughed.

Howard quickly shifted into his jaguar, and the monkeys raced out through Val's front door. Then Howard shifted back to his human form and grabbed his boxer briefs off the floor. He began pulling them on, offering her a little smirk. "We're here for you as your backup for any threat, big or small."

Okay, she deserved that.

He didn't pull on the rest of his clothes. "You're okay, right?" He was suddenly very serious.

"Uh, yeah, I guess you could hear all the shrieking from a mile away."

"We could have, but we're in the cabin next door," Howard said, smiling.

"What? *Not* between Benny's and my cabin." She should have known. She didn't rent that one because she wanted a buffer between her and Benny so she wouldn't spook him.

"Yeah, we're your protection," Howard reminded her.

"That's *not* what I meant by you being here on the other side of the resort." She was surprised he hadn't bothered to dress yet. Was he trying to show off? He *was* impressive. "Why aren't you getting dressed? Not that the sight of you standing there mostly naked doesn't appeal, but…"

"I was going to go for a jaguar run to check out the area. Want to go with me? Jillian is staying behind to watch over our places."

Totally exasperated, Val folded her arms. "Okay, so then if he sees the two of us running around as jaguars, what is he going to think?"

"That you and I are here on a vacation, as so many of our kind are when they visit here."

Jillian tucked away her gun and asked Howard, "Do you want me to stay here or return to our place?"

"You can return to our place and, if you would, let the boss know we are all here and safe."

"Okay. See you in a bit." Jillian headed out the back.

Val began to strip off her clothes, throwing her things on the sofa. "The problem with us being lovers coming here for a visit is that you're staying with Jillian. Now, how will that look?"

"Like I'm having an affair with my next-door neighbor?" Howard smiled. "I'll wait outside for you." Then he stripped off his boxer shorts again, opened the front door, and shifted. He loped outside.

He was just as sexy in his beautiful, golden jaguar form as he was in his human form. Gold and tan, covered in black rosettes.

Val stepped outside, closed the door, and finished pulling off her bra and panties to shift, then sprinted after him. It was late at night now, after all their traveling and shopping. It was still raining, but the canopy of the forest kept the rain from reaching them. Still, it wouldn't matter in their jaguar coats.

They ran until they came to a pond where catfish and bay snook swam, turtles were sleeping on rocks, and in the center of the pond, a small island was situated. Val saw two iguanas perched on top of a stack of rocks on the island.

Howler monkeys screeched a warning that jaguars were on the move down below. They probably wouldn't steal into her place again, now that they'd learned jaguars roamed the cabins. Spider monkeys were warier of people, so she and Howard didn't see them until they were farther away from the resort, deeper in the rain forest. Jaguars and cougars were known to prey on spider monkeys, so as soon as they saw the two jaguars, the spider monkeys let out a ruckus and took off.

Val and Howard ran alongside a river, closer to where a baboon sanctuary was located. The baboons began to make a ton of noise, warning of the predators nearby, as the breeze blew their big-cat scents into the sanctuary. Or at least her scent. She hadn't had time to put on the hunter's spray yet. She couldn't smell Howard, so she knew he was wearing it.

He was in the lead part of the way, but then she ran alongside him. She hadn't gone running with another jaguar in forever. It was usually safer to do it solo, easier to disappear if anyone spotted her. But she enjoyed being with Howard in a nonwork way. Which made her realize she hadn't taken a vacation in years. The last time had been with a male cat she'd had fun with but who hadn't been mate material. She was all about work ethic, and he didn't have any. More a playboy, live-for-the-moment kind of guy. Which made him fun, until he was hitting her up for money so he could continue his freeloader lifestyle.

It felt good stretching her legs. They turned around and raced each other back to the cabin. Howard leaped over a fallen tree, and she leaped over it right alongside him.

She wouldn't run near Benny's cabin, not until she was wearing hunter's spray. Howard licked her cheek, and she nipped at his ear, telling him she wasn't playing, even though she liked the idea that they could. But she was on a job, and that took priority over anything else.

His tongue was hanging out, and he looked like one happy big cat. She felt that way too, just from the freedom to stretch their legs in the rain-forest environment as if they lived there.

Then she thought back to the business with the

monkeys. Eyeing Howard, she hoped he'd never tell anyone he'd rescued her from a pair of cute little orange-stealing howler monkeys on the mission in Belize.

When they returned to her cabin, Howard shifted and began to dress. She did the same.

"Did you want to come over to our place and have a barbecue later? I've been thinking about this. It can look like we're friends, renting two of the cabins. So we can share meals and pretend to be here just on vacation." Howard pulled on his cargo pants.

"You don't think it will look suspicious that two jaguars showed up with a wolf, and the jaguars aren't staying together?"

"Yeah. I think I need to stay with you, and Jillian is on her own."

"Ha! What would her mate think of that? Not that I'm considering it, mind you."

"Vaughn would think we made a new plan to get the job done. He knows that when we go into the field, we have to be flexible and change arrangements when a new one seems to be the best choice."

"You wish."

Howard chuckled. "I do. Jillian's just as highly trained as we are. Her shifter half works against her here. Otherwise, she's a fantastic shot with about any kind of gun. And she knows martial arts too. It actually helps that she's a wolf because that should throw off Benny if he suspects anything. She's also been through cyber-warfare training in the military. So she knows her way around computers and, specifically, how to hack into them."

"That would sure come in handy. I was going to put

on some hunter's spray and check around Benny's place to see if he's there a little later tonight."

"I'll go with you, if you want."

Val hadn't expected him to offer instead of demand. "As my lover?"

"If that works for you."

"Not happening." She pulled on her shirt, then pointed to the mess the monkeys had made. "Don't you dare tell anyone what went on here." She began cleaning up the monkey-chewed oranges. She'd really wanted to have those for breakfast.

"Mum's the word. Are you coming over for dinner?" Howard pulled on one of his boots.

"Sure."

"We'll be ready in an hour." He pulled on his other boot.

"All right. See you then. And…well, thanks for coming to my rescue." She really hadn't thought she'd be having meals with the USF agents. She wasn't sure whether this was a bad plan. She wouldn't be certain until the matter with Benny was resolved or they ran into trouble.

"Anytime." Howard winked, then left her cabin and headed to his.

He was a charmer, just like when she'd taken him to the mat that one time. Not to mention chasing her and catching her in the swimming pool.

Val finished cleaning up the mess in the kitchen and wondered what she was getting herself into with Howard. She hadn't been that fascinated and annoyed with a guy in she didn't know when. When she called her folks to inform them she was in Belize and staying at this resort, they put her on speakerphone.

"Thanks for letting us know. Any sign of the murdering bastard?" her dad asked.

"Not yet. What about Eric, the drug dealer?" she asked. "I know you would have said if you'd taken him out."

"He hasn't returned to the house where he was staying. We're afraid he might have gotten word we're here. We sure hope not. We had a devil of a time finding this location. Our source stated implicitly that he's in the area, so we're staying put for the time being," her mom said.

"Well, let me know if you need my help with him."

"Will do. Same thing goes for us. How's your protection service doing?" her dad asked.

"They rented the cabin between mine and Benny's."

Her dad laughed. "Good."

"You know, this could hurt my chances at taking Benny out, again."

"You'll get him, but we want you to be safe too," her mom said.

Val sighed. She really appreciated her parents' concern, but they'd never asked her boss to provide cover for her before. "I'm about to go over and have dinner with them. I'll keep you posted on how things go here."

"Same here, Val. Talk later."

She just hoped they didn't get into any real trouble and wished that Howard and Jillian would protect her parents instead of hanging out here. Hopefully, Benny would show up so she could eliminate him and get this done with. Then she could aid her parents, though she was reminded of how in charge her dad could be. She figured that for this one job, she could deal with his attitude if her parents still needed her assistance by then.

—₩₩—

When Howard returned to the cabin, Jillian had already started to make spaghetti for dinner. He'd have to barbecue ribs tomorrow for lunch or dinner. "Dinner smells great."

"Thanks. I figured you would be hungry after your run. I'm starving. I didn't see any sign of anyone while you were gone."

"Okay. I invited Val to dinner. That way, if Benny sees us, he'll believe we're all friends. She said she'd love to join us. I mentioned being her lover, but she wasn't buying it."

Jillian laughed. "Subtle you are not. We can talk on the back deck at some point, establishing our cover, and if he's around, he'll hear our conversation." Then she frowned at Howard as she stirred the spaghetti sauce. "You're not going to leave the USF if things start to heat up between you and Val, are you?"

"Why? Because of Val? We're just on a mission."

"I can smell that your pheromones have kicked up a whole bunch since you've been with her. You can't hide how you feel about her. Not with her or with me. Nor can she hide how she feels about you."

"I keep forgetting your wolf senses are as keen as ours are. Nothing is going to happen between Val and me, but if something did, we might continue our respective jobs, or she might even join us."

"Or you might return to the Enforcers to work as her partner, just as her parents work together as a team."

"Maybe. But you have to remember we're not wired like wolves. We can be interested in another cat and then later not."

"I keep forgetting how it is with jaguars. Everett and Demetria are so happy together."

"Yeah, they're perfect for each other." Which was how Howard wanted to be with his jaguar mate, if he found the right woman. He'd known Everett and Demetria from the beginning of their relationship, and they were great partners in the war against jaguar crime. He wanted to be with a woman who understood how it was to work these kinds of jobs, who could work with him.

"How was the run? Besides invigorating and stimulating?"

"Good. We spooked a bunch of baboons. I was worried about you running as a wolf, but we could take a run together. People would probably just think you're a big dog that befriended a jaguar."

She grunted.

Dogs originally came from wolves, but wolves didn't like to be thought of as dogs, which had a lot to do with how dogs mated with any old dog instead of for life as wolves did. Still, it would be a way to explain how a wolf would be running through the rain forest in Belize.

He eyed the spaghetti on the stove. "I told Val I'd barbecue, but I can do that tomorrow."

"I hope she doesn't have her heart set on the ribs. I just figured I'd get this started and it would be ready about the time you returned."

"I guess I should tell her in case she doesn't like spaghetti." Howard called Val and told her about the change in menu.

"Sounds good. I love spaghetti."

"Great. It's done, if you'd like to come over now."

"Sure thing. Um, got a text. Be over in a moment."
She ended the call.

"She'll be over in a few minutes, Jillian." Howard
started to set the table, wondering who was texting Val.
Someone who was keeping her informed about where
Benny was headed? He hoped so, and that she'd keep
them informed about where she was going.

"I hope this isn't a bust and Benny doesn't show up."
Jillian began serving garlic toast.

Howard placed bottles of water on the table, then set
out the silverware and plates. "Hopefully not."

A knock on the door sounded, then Val called out,
"Just me."

"Come in," Jillian yelled. "I'm just getting ready to
serve up the spaghetti. Salad and the toasted garlic bread
are on the table."

Val entered the cabin and shut the door. "Sure smells
great."

"Thanks," Jillian said. "Is everyone up for a glass of
wine? You have to have red wine with spaghetti."

"Yeah, sure, thanks."

"I'll get the bottle." Howard returned to the kitchen
and brought the bottle out of the pantry.

Val found wineglasses. After Howard poured the
wine, Val took two of the glasses to the table, and
Howard brought the other.

They all sat down to eat, Val at the head of the table
and Howard across from Jillian.

"I let my boss know about the two of you and that
having the three of us here could cause complications."

"What did he say?" Howard asked, dishing up some
of the garlic bread and salad.

"You know how Sylvan is. He said to do whatever it took to get the job done without causing civilian casualties. And that whatever I did, I shouldn't turn anyone or get myself killed."

"That goes without saying. Trying to get a newly turned shifter back to the States from south of the border can be a big problem when they can't control their shifting." Howard took a bite of the garlic toast. "Great toast."

"Thanks," Jillian said.

"What I want to know is what is going on with Benny? Is he here already, off barhopping maybe? Running as a jaguar?"

"Let me see what I can learn." Val pulled out a business card and called the owner of the resort, putting the phone on speaker. "Hi, I just checked in at one of your cabins, and friends of mine are staying at the one next door. We have more friends who talked of joining us, if they could get the cabin on the other side of number three. Is that one occupied?"

"Yes, a gentleman is staying there. He picked up his key already."

"How long does he intend to stay?"

"Three weeks."

"Okay, I'll let my friends know."

"We have other cabins available."

"I'll let them know that too. If they decide they want to come down, they'll call you and make arrangements directly with you."

"*Muchas gracias, señorita.*"

When Val finished the call, she breathed a sigh of relief. "I was worried Benny had decided not to show up, but since he picked up the key and has rented the cabin for three weeks, he should be around soon. We can go search around the place, but this time, I'll put on hunter's spray."

"I take it I'm cabin-sitting." Jillian took another piece of garlic bread.

"I think that would be for the best, don't you?" Howard asked her.

"Yeah, I do."

—⁓—

Val liked that Howard had asked Jillian what she wanted to do instead of just ordering her around.

After they finished eating, Howard and Val washed the dishes. Then he went into his bedroom to strip and shift. Val did the same in the living room, spraying hunter's spray before shifting. Once they had shifted, they went to the back door.

"Be careful, you two." Jillian opened the back door for them, and they bounded out of the cabin and down the steps.

Val and Howard moved silently through the trees, staying off the lighted pathways and listening for any sound of movement in Benny's cabin. She noticed a faint light on inside. She smelled Benny's scent and that of the woman he'd been with at the club. Great. Had she bought her own ticket to Belize?

Trying to take care of him without the woman learning about it was going to be a bigger chore. They didn't want her calling the local police to tell them her boyfriend went missing.

Val and Howard moved around the back side of the

cabin and saw light spilling from a bedroom window into the woods. Unless they'd left a light on and departed, Val assumed someone was home. No vehicle was parked near the cabin though. And she didn't hear anyone talking or any lovemaking.

Then she saw the shadow of someone walking around in the room. Val and Howard moved farther into the shadows of the trees and watched as the blond-haired woman looked out the window.

Thankfully, she appeared to be fine. Val indicated to Howard with a nudge of her head that she wanted to look for Benny. She thought he must have taken off in a rental car, unless he and the woman had used some other transportation to get here, but if he was running as a jaguar, she hoped to take him down tonight.

Usually, Val took care of a perp, headed home for a break, and then took on her next assignment. This time, she'd have to ensure the woman got home all right. But the issue of the woman calling the Belizean police could be a real problem. Unless they could convince her Benny had abandoned her because he was on the run from the American police for having murdered his wife.

Val and Howard spread out from each other and began to canvass the area. She smelled where Benny had run before as a jaguar and wondered just how long ago he'd moved through there. Luckily, rain didn't wash away scents. He had circled the huge pond a couple of times and run along the river in the opposite direction they had taken earlier.

They were all creatures of habit, unless something forced them to see a particular path as dangerous, and then they might change their route. She and Howard just had to learn when Benny would take another jaguar run and nail him.

She realized, as she was making up a plan of action in her head, that she was already including Howard in her plans. She swore he'd gotten under her jaguar coat the first time she'd trained with him. He was pure male and hot testosterone, domineering and decisive, but also willing to let her decide what she was going to do about Benny while protecting her back.

They headed back to Howard and Jillian's cabin in a roundabout way. When they finally reached the cabin, Val slapped the door with her paw. It wasn't a loud sound, her claws retracted, but with their sensitive hearing, she knew Jillian would realize it was them.

Jillian opened the door, phone in hand, and smiled. "What did you learn?"

Howard loped down the hall.

Val shifted and began to dress, yanking on her panties and then her bra. "The woman he was dancing with at the jaguar-owned club is here. She was at the cabin. We didn't see a vehicle parked nearby, and we found the paths he's taken as a jaguar through the rain forest." She pulled on her shirt.

"Oh, the woman being here isn't good," Jillian said.

"I agree. Any news from Vaughn?" Val pulled on her pants, socks, and then her boots.

"They're still after the guy. I sent Vaughn pictures of the resort. He wants to come here with me when we are both free sometime."

"It's beautiful. There's lots to see and do. You'll have fun." Val wasn't sure about the wolves running as wolves, but snorkeling, diving, canoeing, and all kinds of fun activities for them to do as humans would make up for it.

Howard came out of the bedroom and joined them. "If we hear a car drive into their area, we'll let you know. If you do, if you can give us a heads-up, that would be great. We'll try to intercept him."

"Will do. Do you want to meet up with me and go out really early in the morning if we don't hear him tonight? Maybe he'll run before there's much activity around the place," Val said.

"Yeah, let's do that. Even earlier if we hear his car come in later tonight. I had an idea though—about the woman. What if you and Jillian try to befriend Benny's girlfriend while he's gone? Not tonight. It's too late, and she might be afraid if you showed up over there. If you're together, you can protect each other if Benny suddenly shows up. You'd be wearing hunter's spray, so he wouldn't know you're shifters. Maybe if you visited with her for a bit, we could learn where he's gone and who she is. Then we can look into her background. I'd go, but she might feel more at ease talking to a couple of women. That way, you can both tell her to call you if she wants some company or needs anything else," Howard said.

"Like he gets weird with her and she needs a place to retreat to. Sounds like a winning idea to me," Val said. "If she tells him we've been there, he won't think anything of it. Just more Americans staying in the resort and being super friendly."

"I like it. So what's the story you and I would share?" Jillian asked. "My boyfriend is in the States and couldn't get free from his job, so I came with the two of you?"

"She might wonder why I'm staying with you and not with Val if she learns about it," Howard said.

"Right. The two of you are dating, and that's why you're staying together. I'm here because my boyfriend couldn't get away to vacation with us. Maybe we'd had this planned for a year, and suddenly he couldn't come with us," Val said.

"That sounds like it would work," Jillian said.

"Do you have a specific reason you're over there bothering her?" Howard asked. "If she's not out and about and you just happen to run into her, it might seem odd that you knock on her door and say hi."

Everyone was thinking, trying to come up with a good reason for starting up a conversation with her.

"I've got it," Val said. "We thought she was a girl we knew from high school." And that would be the way in, if Benny was gone and Val and Jillian could see the woman on her own. "We could talk more about it over breakfast."

"Sounds good," Jillian said, and Howard agreed.

"All right. Night all," Val said.

Jillian and Howard said good night to her.

Val thought things couldn't get any more complicated until she'd left their place and was heading through the forest when she saw a man skulking around in the dark, heading toward Benny's place.

This was *not* good.

Chapter 5

HEART POUNDING, VAL ENTERED HER CABIN QUIETLY
and quickly, intent on going after the prowler heading
for Benny's cabin and leaving her door slightly ajar.
She didn't turn on any lights and hurried to remove her
clothes, then shifted. She wasn't about to waste time
and lose the opportunity to discover who was prowling
around in the dark and stop him, if it meant he'd chase
off her prey. As soon as she'd slipped out the door and
leaped off the steps, she raced after the man. Wearing
camo pants and a shirt, he was partly crouched like a
hunter would be, still moving through the woods in the
direction of Benny's cabin. But he didn't smell like
Benny. And he was human.

She growled a little, afraid whoever it was would tip
Benny off that someone was looking for him. As soon
as the man moved closer to the light that was on in one
of the bedrooms, she could make out his features better.
It was Rowdy, the homicide detective from Montana.
He *wasn't* going to arrest her perp. She couldn't let him.

Without giving her actions another thought, she
pounced on him, knocking him out with a swipe of her
paw, silencing him before he could cry out. She dragged
him back to her cabin. A jaguar was capable of carrying
a deer into a tree, so one human was no trouble at all.
But man, was she pissed. Now she had to deal with *him*!

She dragged him up the steps—had to shift to open

the door, then shift back to move him again—and pulled him into the living room. Then she ran to shut her door, shifted, and locked it. She turned around and thought she saw Rowdy's eyes slam shut. Ohmigod, had he seen her shift? She studied him. She had to know: Did he now realize jaguar shifters existed along with wolves? She knew he did!

Her boss would be furious with her.

At least she had plastic ties so she could bind Rowdy and tape for his mouth to keep him quiet. What if he managed to get up and take off while she was getting the ties? She raced into her bedroom and grabbed a bag that had the essentials she needed. Then she ran back into the living room, watching him before she approached. He smelled of fear, and his heart was pounding. He wasn't unconscious then, and he had to have seen her shift.

What the hell was she going to do with him for however long it took to deal with Benny? Then she realized she had another problem. If Howard or Jillian came to her place, they'd know she'd had a visitor. She needed to move him to the spare bedroom. She'd have to keep them away from here until she could figure out what to do with him.

Still lying on the floor, Rowdy suddenly opened his eyes and looked straight at her, though he appeared to be dazed. As soon as he saw the ties and tape, he tried to sit up. She quickly knocked him out with a well-placed kick with her bare foot to his head. Then she tied his hands behind his back and taped his mouth.

She shifted into her jaguar again and dragged Rowdy into the spare bedroom. His heart rate was racing, so he was okay, thank God, but he had to know he was in trouble, more so than if she was just human. A little harder swipe with her paw and she could have killed him. But if he had alerted Benny that people were after him and Benny had run off… She growled.

Val raced into the living room, shifted, and hurried to dress. Once she had her pants and shirt on, she returned to the spare room.

She hoped she didn't get kicked off the force for this. What else could she have done though? She hadn't killed him. She'd just tell him that Benny was a shifter, and they had to eliminate him. Would the detective go along with that? Maybe not. He was a homicide detective, working to put murderers behind bars. And if she eliminated Benny, Rowdy would probably feel justified in taking *her* in.

She could bite Rowdy. And then, as Howard had said, the real nightmare would begin. Returning Rowdy to the States so someone could watch over him until he got the shifting under control would be a real chore. Which would mean *she* would have to take care of him. No way did she want that.

She was dead tired, needing to sleep. She took a pillow off the guest bed and put it under his head. Then she sat on the bed and waited for him to stir.

She must have dozed off on the bed, because the next thing she heard was the faint sound of a car driving down the road and parking at Benny's place. At the same time, she heard Rowdy struggling to get free of his wrist ties. Then her cell phone buzzed.

Her heartbeat quickened, and she yanked her phone out. *Howard*. Texting her that he'd heard Benny's car arrive. At least he thought it was. Did she want to go with him to check it out? He'd meet her on her porch steps.

No! He'd smell that Rowdy had come up her steps. She quickly texted Howard back.

Heading to your place. Wait for me there.

She flipped on the light in the guest bedroom, and Rowdy stared up at her from the floor, his blue eyes wide.

"Okay, listen, are you after Benny Canton for what he did to Lucy?"

Rowdy just gawked at her.

"Nod your head."

He didn't.

"All right, he's a shifter. Got that? A shifter. And he can't go to jail. We know you know about some of us. And we know you also understand we have to take care of our own. You need to leave this to us and return home. Okay?"

Rowdy nodded, but she didn't trust him to go along with the plan. "Just…go to sleep, and when I return, we'll talk some more."

She hurried out of the bedroom and opened the door to her cabin just enough for her to squeeze through, then moved away from the door, stripped, and shifted. She was hoping Howard wouldn't come to see what was taking her so long to join him.

She tore off to meet up with Howard, figuring she was in so much trouble, but she had no idea how to fix this.

⁓

Howard was afraid Val had taken off to check on Benny herself, but he thought she'd been sincere when she'd said she'd go with him to see if Benny was now home. Howard was watching Benny's cabin in case he went for a jaguar run when he heard movement behind him. Val hurried to join him in her golden jaguar form. She wasn't as stealthy as she usually was, so he figured she was in a rush to meet up with him. When she got close, he was surprised to smell the scent of a male on her. Someone he hadn't smelled before. A human.

He frowned.

She nudged his face in greeting, then headed for Benny's cabin as if nothing was amiss.

Who would she have been seeing at this time of night? Maybe some of the staff at the resort? That didn't make any sense.

As he followed her, his mind was supposed to be on the case, but he couldn't help glancing back at her place. Was that why she was so late to meet up with him? She'd met some man at her place?

Howard couldn't figure it out. As soon as he could, he would check around her cabin to see if the guy had actually been at her place or if she had just run into him on the way back to her place after dinner.

His mind again on business, Howard watched for any signs of a jaguar running around the forest and listened to hear if anyone was speaking inside the cabin. The lights were out, and he heard a couple having sex in the room.

Not that he was surprised, if the woman was Benny's new girlfriend. Would she still want to be with him if she learned he'd murdered his wife? Howard wished they could take Benny down, but Enforcers and USF agents were supposed to be careful about showing anyone what they were, if they could help it. And in a case like this,

barging in as jaguars and killing him in front of his girlfriend wouldn't work. They didn't want to traumatize
her any more than they had to. Nor did they want the
police searching the area afterward for two man-killing
jaguars they had to terminate. Any jaguar could become
a prime suspect then.

Val and Howard sniffed around the car and the area
to ensure the man inside was really Benny. He was.
Then Howard smelled that the man who'd left his scent
on Val had traveled in this direction too, a little farther
from Benny's cabin. Who the hell was he?

He wondered if it was the homicide detective. That
was a complication they didn't need.

Val paced for a few minutes in the woods, and he
speculated on whether she was unsettled about Benny
and not being able to do anything about him, or if it was
more about who she'd seen.

She finally indicated she wanted to return to their
cabins, but she went straight to Howard's place when
he tried to walk her to her own. She paused at his cabin,
then shifted. "In the early morning hours, we can wait
outside his cabin to see if he leaves for a run."

Howard shifted. "Who is the man I smell on you?"
He tried not to be all growly about it, but he wasn't dis-
missing his concern.

Her lips parted, but she didn't answer him.

Howard narrowed his eyes. "Rowdy? Did he show up?"

She shifted into her jaguar and ran off to her cabin.
He shifted and chased after her.

Hell. Now what?

She ran inside while Howard paused at the entrance
and smelled the same man all over her steps. He had a

bad feeling about this. If she had tried to keep Rowdy from finding Benny…

She couldn't have taken the homicide detective hostage. Or worse, killed him. But Howard didn't smell blood.

He walked inside the cabin, smelling the guy's scent. He followed it to one of the bedrooms and recognized Rowdy from the picture he'd seen, sitting on the floor, his hands restrained behind his back, his mouth taped. His eyes were wide as he stared at Howard in his jaguar form. He had to have seen Val run past the guest room door in her jaguar coat too.

Hell, Val.

Howard heard her in another room, and then she joined them, completely dressed and holding a white towel. "What was I supposed to do? He was prowling around Benny's cabin. What if he had caused Benny to run? Or worse, Benny had killed him? We had to let Rowdy know that Benny is a shifter and can hear, see, or smell Rowdy, unlike a human."

Howard shifted, took the towel Val handed him, and wrapped it around his waist. He should have known the homicide detective would learn where Benny was staying sooner or later. Howard couldn't fault Val, except for not telling him what she'd done right away. They were in this together, whether she wanted to admit that or not.

Then again, she probably had wanted to go after Benny, and Rowdy had been her second priority.

"Rowdy Sanderson. What are we going to do with you?" Howard folded his arms across his chest.

"I told him he couldn't take Benny down. That *we* have to," Val said. "If it wouldn't be such a pain to try to move him back to the States, and such a trial to teach him our ways until he could get the shifting under control, I'd say we should just turn him."

As much as Howard hated the idea that she'd taken Rowdy hostage, he'd guessed this would be how things went down if the homicide detective began snooping around the place. Turning him would ensure his silence, but it was too risky to do it here. No way did Howard want to be responsible for the guy as a newly turned shifter, even if he was really good at his job and they could use him in their line of work—once he got the shifting under control.

Rowdy tried to talk. Val peeled the tape off his mouth as gently as she could.

"I get it, okay. Hell, jaguar shifters too? All I could think of was that she was going to return and kill me." Rowdy sounded angry, but Howard thought some of his anger was to hide his fear.

Howard could smell it on him, and he wasn't surprised. If he hadn't known jaguar shifters existed and one had taken him hostage, Howard was sure *he* would have been afraid of the jaguar's big teeth.

"We can't let you take Benny in," Howard said. "That's what you have to realize. Our kind can't be incarcerated for long periods of time. Not unless we're born as shifters and have shifter roots going way back. We're just like the wolves in that regard, the only difference being that our shifting isn't tied to the phases of the moon. The wolves can have problems with being able to control their nature then. We have our human sides, sure, but we have the wild jaguar side too. Can you imagine if some guy tried to pick on a jaguar shifter? Do you think he'd take it? Most likely not. It would be a disaster for our kind. Though some jaguars prefer to be city cats and don't ever come to the jungle, most of us do. I swear, someday the city cats will be like big domesticated cats, unable to fend for themselves in the wild. But in jail? We'd all have that fight-for-our-lives reaction.

"You can imagine what it would be like if Benny went to prison and he took off his clothes and shifted. End of our anonymity." Howard paused. "I guess we should have introduced ourselves. I'm Howard Armstrong, and this is Valerie Chambers. I'm with the United Shifter Force. She's with the Enforcer branch, both part of a jaguar-shifter police force."

"A shifter police force." Rowdy cleared his throat. "I'm Rowdy Sanderson, but I guess you already are well aware of who I am. Though how, I don't know. I understand your point. This isn't necessary. Val could have told me what Benny was, and I would have understood the need for handling this differently."

She folded her arms. "I couldn't be sure. You *are* a human homicide detective."

"True, but I sympathize with the wolf shifters. Well, now with you too."

"As far as Benny goes, there's no going to prison, no going to our own jaguar prison either. For what he's done, he earned the death sentence," Howard explained. "I know you're the law and you think in terms of arresting murderers so they'll receive a fair trial. We don't do that. We all know the rules. Murder innocents, either the shifter kind or humans, and you're eliminated. It's as simple as that. We can't risk anyone discovering what we are. Many believe you're a danger to us. We normally would turn you or eliminate the threat in a case like yours."

"I'm innocent of killing anyone, except in self-defense," Rowdy said, looking exasperated.

"If we let you go, what are you going to do?" Val asked.

"I want to see this finished." Rowdy didn't force the issue, but Howard was certain if they told him to go home, he wouldn't.

"Why are you even here?" Howard asked. "You were her friend?"

"We dated on and off for two years. We were more than friends. But she didn't like the long hours I worked, or that I was shot three times on the job. After I left the hospital, she called it quits and moved back home to San Antonio. This isn't exactly your jurisdiction either."

"Any place is our jurisdiction when the perp is a shifter. We'll take Benny out as jaguars, if we can. The problem is he's got a girlfriend with him," Val said.

"He just murdered his wife, and he's got a girlfriend... Wait, was Lucy a shifter? I dated a shifter? A jaguar?" Rowdy looked a little pale.

"No. She wasn't. Not when you dated her. Benny married her and then turned her. The problem is that sometimes someone who is turned is so unmanageable that they have to be put down. We don't want that to happen, which is why we generally don't turn humans. There's no personality test we can give that will determine how someone will react if they're turned. Same with you. What if you were turned and you became a homicidal maniac?" Val asked.

"I wouldn't. Unlike with Lucy, it would be my choice. I wouldn't be turned against my will."

Both Val and Howard raised their brows.

"I mean, I wouldn't be in the dark about this like someone you might just turn who wouldn't have a clue as to your existence. Though I didn't realize there were other kinds of shifters out there. Listen, I helped an Arctic wolf couple prove an imposter was trying to take her inheritance. I was investigating the wolf pack in Montana when people started turning up murdered. Though they were wolves like, well, like them. I'm open-minded about…stuff like this. The wolves might change me, and I told them I'm okay with it. I'll have your superpowers then."

"Superpowers?" Val asked.

"Yeah, enhanced hearing, sense of smell, night vision. And the shifter always gets the girl. I'm sure I'd have a lot to learn and I'd have to deal with the issues, but I understand. I've read all kinds of were-books."

"Were-books?" Val asked, frowning.

"Werewolves, were-tigers, were-bears. Nothing about were-jaguars though."

Val rolled her eyes.

"There's also the problem with finding a mate if you're newly turned," Howard warned him. "Val and I were born jaguar shifters. We have a long history of shifters in our roots. No strictly human genes for centuries. A woman who might be interested in you otherwise might not want the trouble of dealing with a shifter who can't control his shifting."

"Also, what about your job? You couldn't go back to it," Val said.

"I have to admit I didn't think about possibly meeting someone. As to the job situation, I've considered I'd have to leave the force. You said you are with some kind of a police force?" Rowdy looked interested in that.

Howard would give him points for being determined when he wanted something.

"A jaguar police force." Val pulled out her Enforcer badge. It looked like an FBI badge, only with a different symbol to indicate she was an Enforcer.

"I have one too, but not on me." Howard patted the towel. "I work with the United Shifter Force, eliminating shifters—both wolves and jaguars—that hurt our kind or humans."

"And I am with the Enforcer branch that takes down murdering scum permanently," Val said.

"Generally, the wolves police their own, if they're in the pack's territory." Howard folded his arms again. "But a couple of wolves are with our USF."

Rowdy sat on the end of the bed as if this was all a little much to take in.

"In the meantime, what are we going to do with you?" Val asked. "You can't go over to Benny's place and spook him. We need to see if he runs as a jaguar in the morning and gives us the chance to take him down. We just need to get him away from his girlfriend. If you want, you can take care of her."

"Take care of her?" Rowdy frowned deeply.

Val let out her breath in exasperation. "Drive her to the airport after her boyfriend disappears."

"Oh. What do you mean, Benny would disappear?"

"He'll become crocodile fodder," Howard said.

"Oh."

Howard was sure Rowdy still wasn't getting the whole picture. "He can't go to trial."

Rowdy nodded.

"Where are you staying?" Val asked.

"I've got a cabin on the other side of the resort. Just let me know if you need my help, and I'll do what I can. I want to know this is finished before I return home. I cared deeply for Lucy. She was really vivacious and the life of the party. I can't believe anyone would kill her. But I have to admit seeing the two of you as jaguars, and knowing that Benny is one too, reminds me I might not have what it takes to handle a situation like this."

"All right," Howard said.

Val looked at him as if she wasn't sure it was a good idea to release Rowdy, but they couldn't keep him tied up in her spare bedroom for the entire time they were there.

"You can join us for meals if you'd like," Howard said. "I'm fixing a barbecue tomorrow for lunch or dinner, depending on what we're doing. But you can come over for breakfast in the morning. We'll let you know when."

"Sure thing. I'd like that."

Val left the room and returned with a pair of scissors. She cut off the ties, and Rowdy rubbed his wrists, then stood.

"I mean what I say. Just like I did with the wolf shifters I've helped. I'm on your side. I'm not one of you, but I'm only after the bad guys too." Rowdy seemed sincere.

Val gave him her, Howard's, and Jillian's cell numbers. "She's a wolf, one of Howard's USF partners, and staying at the cabin next door."

"So the two of you are together," Rowdy said, motioning to the two of them.

"It's complicated," Howard said, smiling.

"We're *not* together," Val quickly said. "He and Jillian are my backup, and he's staying with his partner."

"Marriage partner?" Rowdy raised his brows.

"USF partner," Howard said, imagining what Rowdy was thinking. "She has a wolf mate."

"Oh, okay, I wondered how that would work." Rowdy gave Val his cell number. "Thanks for trusting in me."

"Don't let us believe it was a mistake," Val said, her eyes narrowed.

Howard gave him just as dark a look to warn him it wasn't a good idea to cross them.

"It isn't a mistake. And…thanks for taking me into your confidence." Rowdy said good night again and stalked out of the cabin, looking damned relieved to still be alive.

As soon as Rowdy shut the front door, Val turned her attention to Howard, folding her arms and looking as if she was getting ready to defend herself or tear into him.

Thinking of only one way to show Val he was behind her all the way, he closed the gap between them, took her into his arms, and kissed her. Hard, and deep, and long.

Chapter 6

VAL LOOKED SHOCKED. HOWARD SUSPECTED SHE thought he would give her a lecture for taking Rowdy hostage, but he had kissed her instead.

"You're not angry with me for tying Rowdy up?" she asked, the two of them locked in an embrace.

Howard shook his head, smiling a little. "If I'd run across him in the forest like you had, I would have done the same thing."

"He was sneaking around in the dark, trying to reach Benny's place. I was afraid he'd try to arrest him and mess everything up. Not to mention I was afraid Benny in his jaguar form would come across Rowdy and kill him." Val impulsively ran her hand over Howard's shoulder. "I hadn't considered Rowdy could have an issue finding a mate if he's turned. That could be a real problem for him."

Howard was already feeling the heat between them. Though she was dressed, he was not, and her scent and touch were priming his arousal. Again. He'd never been around a woman who made him this hot and bothered in such a short time. "Not if he met the right woman and she felt the same for him. Besides, we're not turning him. We'll let someone else deal with it if it happens."

"Still, that gives me an idea. What if he worked for one of our branches as a human? And he got to know our kind better? Most likely he's had a lot of training in the field he works in. He could be a real asset for us. And if he was turned, he wouldn't have to worry about leaving his job. Everyone would understand."

"And if a shifter happened to really like him?" Howard asked. "She could turn him then." The idea had merit. Rowdy was bound to be turned by one of the shifters at some point. Hopefully, a shifter wouldn't terminate him for knowing about their kind before he became one of them. "I could run it by Martin and see what he says."

"My boss too. Rowdy might like to be with the Guardian branch though." Val sighed. "We need to get some sleep. Thanks for not being angry with me about this." She slid her hands down Howard's arms, which were still wrapped loosely about her waist.

He was trying to control how he was reacting to her, but he knew she could feel his arousal, and she didn't seem to be put off by it. What's more, she had to know her touching him—and her pheromones—were stirring him up.

Because of what had happened, he said, "Okay, listen. I understand how you felt after you lost your other partner. Jillian and I can continue to back you up like we've been doing, or we can be right there in the thick of it with you on this. I don't want you to feel you have to do this all on your own. It's totally up to you. Hell, I just want you to know that you don't have to go taking human homicide detectives hostage—"

She opened her mouth to speak.

He continued, "By yourself."

She smiled up at him. "I couldn't ask for your help quickly enough. He was already headed for Benny's cabin and totally clueless." And then she kissed Howard back. Parting her lips slightly, kissing him sweetly at first, but then she ramped up the sensation, tonguing him, sucking on his lower lip, and moving her hands to his towel-covered buttocks.

He was kissing her back, savoring her lips, her tongue, greedy for more. Her sweet body pressed against his, and he felt his other head stirring to full arousal. *Hell*. He had a job to do, and this wasn't part of the mission. It was past time for him to head back to the cabin and let Jillian know he and Val were fine. He pulled his mouth away from Val's, their hearts beating wildly, and looked down at her glazed green eyes. "I'm just glad everything worked out. I'd best be getting back to my cabin before Jillian texts Vaughn and tells him I've disappeared for good."

Val chuckled. "Good night."

"Sweet dreams. I know what I'll be dreaming about." He handed her the towel, and she gave him a hot-blooded once-over.

He shifted, and she opened the door for him. He paused on the steps, gave her a toothy grin, and raced off into the dark to reach his cabin.

First on the agenda was a cold shower. Again. But tonight, he was certain he'd have a hot dream featuring one beautiful jaguar siren.

***

Looking a little anxious, Jillian opened the door for Howard when he growled on the porch. Phone in hand, she asked, "How'd the run go?"

Howard headed to his bedroom and threw on a pair of boxer briefs and Bermuda shorts. Then he returned to the living room to tell her all the news. "Val is definitely a bit of a rogue."

"Which intrigues you."

He smiled, then frowned and took a seat on the couch across from the bamboo chair Jillian was now sitting on.

"So what did Val do now?"

"She had a run-in with Rowdy."

"Oh no."

"Yeah. He knows we're jaguar shifters and that you're my partner and a wolf shifter. And that we're all here to help take care of Benny, without Rowdy's interference."

Jillian was wide-eyed. "How'd he take all *that* news?"

"Surprised, of course. He agreed to go along with the plan. I don't know what he'd planned to do with Benny on his own anyway. Benny isn't in his jurisdiction, and Rowdy couldn't just arrest him. When I went over to Val's cabin, she had Rowdy tied up on the floor of her spare bedroom."

Jillian laughed. "I knew I liked her from the minute she gave us the slip at the hotel. Rowdy wasn't upset with her for doing that to him?"

"We both showed him our jaguar halves, and I think, if anything, that helped convince him we were serious about this. I believe he wants to be one of us. A wolf, more than likely. He seemed somewhat spooked to think the woman he'd dated had been a jaguar shifter. We set him straight about that."

"I hope that doesn't become one of our missions." Jillian yawned and rose from the chair.

"Turning people?"

"Deciding if someone should be turned and into what. See you in the morning."

"Night, Jillian. We'll have breakfast, and then Val

and I will go running early tomorrow morning to see if we can catch Benny in his jaguar form. You can keep watch for him in the meantime. Oh, and I invited Rowdy over for meals."

"You're determined to make him one of us."

Howard followed Jillian to the bedrooms. "I think it's inevitable."

"Sleep tight."

"You too." He entered his bedroom, thinking they'd made some headway with Val but had taken a step back in having to deal with Rowdy.

Howard sure could get into having sweet dreams about Val tonight—kissing, hugging, dancing, swimming, and more. But he could imagine having nightmares about Rowdy getting himself in trouble, and the woman Benny had brought with him getting into the middle of it.

───※───

Early the next morning, Val joined Howard and Jillian for breakfast, hoping they'd get somewhere with the case this morning. Rowdy came soon after. Val was still annoyed he was here and hoped he wouldn't cause problems for them.

"I checked out Benny's parking space and his car isn't there, but I heard his girlfriend banging around in the kitchen. Saw her too, so I know for sure it was her," Howard said, serving plates of waffles.

"What happened to us checking this out together?" Val was supposed to be doing this on her own, but the big, bad male jaguar seemed to be taking over completely.

"I texted you several times, but you didn't respond. I

was afraid you'd gone over there on your own." Howard set syrup on the table.

Not believing she'd missed the texts, Val pulled out her phone and checked. Ten texts from Howard, asking her if she was ready to go with him. "Well, damn it. I left my phone in the living room. I thought I'd gotten up early enough to catch you."

"No problem. I checked your cabin to make sure you were all right and heard you taking a shower, so I went on ahead."

"Okay, so then Val and I need to try to make contact with Benny's girlfriend," Jillian said.

Rowdy had to be brought up to speed on what they were talking about.

"And if Benny returns and finds them there?" Rowdy didn't seem to like the idea.

"We'll kill him, but hopefully not in front of his girl-friend," Val said.

Rowdy shook his head.

Val knew he was having a time coming to grips with what they were and how they dealt with their own. She got a call from her information tech at headquarters. "Yeah, whatcha got, Manuel? Putting this on speaker." She made the decision to let everyone hear what he'd found, even though Rowdy was a civilian and not part of their organization. He was already involved, and he might be able to help—on the sidelines.

"Benny hasn't been using his credit card. He might not need to, or he's gotten a new one. I'm trying to track that down. He transferred the money from his and his wife's joint bank account the day before he murdered her, but I can't locate where he moved the money."

Val buttered her waffle. "We froze the account as soon as we discovered she had been murdered. Too late, I guess. So it was premeditated murder."

"Yep. Even more of a reason to terminate him. I'll let you know if I learn whether he has a new card and bank account or anything else interesting that pops up."

"Thanks, Manuel. Talk later."

"Premeditated murder," Jillian said. "How did anyone know she'd died without alerting the regular police?"

"A jaguar informant told us some guy named Benny Canton had his wife chained up in the house," Val said. "Guardian agents were sent to check on her, smelled a dead body, broke in, and found her. Benny's scent was all over the place, no one else's. They were certain he had been the one to murder her. His saliva in the bite marks proved he'd bitten her, causing her death," Val said.

Jillian shook her head.

Rowdy was scowling. Val kept forgetting he had dated her.

As soon as everyone finished breakfast, Val and Jillian left the dirty dishes to the men and hurried to see the woman next door. They'd worked it all out in text messages, and Val figured they'd just wing whatever they hadn't been able to plan for. She was nervous about working with another female partner. She didn't know Jillian well at all, what her strengths and weaknesses were, how she dealt with issues, and how well she could play along.

They reached Benny's cabin and saw his girlfriend watching out the kitchen window. Val took a deep breath, and she and Jillian both waved at her and went to the front door and knocked.

When the woman answered, Val thought she looked pale, with dark circles around her eyes. "We saw you the other day, and we swore you were Camelia Whitson who went to school with us in San Antonio. You look just like her."

"No. I'm Izzie Summerfield. Which school did you go to?"

"Johnson High School," Val said.

"I went to Reagan High School."

"Well, our mistake," Jillian said.

"You sure look like her. Doesn't she, Jillian?"

"She sure does. I'm Jillian Greystoke, and this is my good friend for years and years, Valerie Chambers. We're staying at the two cabins in that direction that are nearest to yours." Jillian motioned in the direction of their cabins. "If you ever want to drop by and say hi, feel free to do so."

"Hey, we're going to walk to the pond right now. That's where we were headed, but we wanted to drop by and see if you were Camelia. Do you want to go with us?" Val asked. "My boyfriend didn't come with me. Work commitment." She rolled her eyes. "We've been planning this for a whole year. So I just came by myself."

"She came with us. If my boyfriend had done that to me, I would have dumped his butt," Jillian said and laughed.

"One more time and I will," Val promised.

"She's been saying that for two years. Don't believe her. So, did you want to come with us to the pond?" Jillian asked.

Izzie hesitated, looking as though she couldn't decide.

"If you don't have anything better to do," Val said.

Izzie finally relented. "Sure. Let me grab my key."

Yes! Val and Jillian smiled while Izzie moved into the cabin to get her key. They didn't say anything to each other, not wanting to be overheard. Then Izzie returned and locked the door on the way out.

"Have you ever been to Belize before?" Jillian asked.

Izzie shook her head. Val wondered if she was always this quiet or just around strangers. She hoped once they shared Izzie's name with the office, they could learn more about her. "It's a beautiful place. You can swim in the aqua waters and enjoy lying out on the white sand beaches."

"Snorkeling is my favorite," Jillian said. "And horse-back riding."

That surprised Val—about the horseback riding. Maybe Jillian just said that as a conversation starter. Though Val supposed if wolves wore hunter's spray, they wouldn't spook the horses.

Val sighed. "Canoeing, checking out the caves, zip-lining, nature hikes. Just all kinds of stuff. How long are you going to be here?"

They reached the pond and watched the fish swimming about.

Izzie let out her breath. "I wish I could do all those things. We're here for three weeks, but Benny…" She shrugged.

"Don't tell me he's not interested in doing all those fun things. I'd be in heaven if I was going to be here that long," Jillian said.

"Like with Val's boyfriend, Benny's work has taken priority. I didn't even know he had work commitments down here. He just made it sound like we were coming here on a fun vacation. He's always working different construction jobs, sometimes out of state, and he's too busy to take me with him. I mistakenly thought we were just here to have fun."

So she'd known him for a while. "That means you're stuck at the cabin? No way. We can take you around." Val suspected Izzie didn't want to mess up the situation with Benny, but she hoped they could get her to leave him and then they would be free to protect her and take him down. Maybe Rowdy could get friendly with her and take her away. If he thought he was rescuing a would-be victim, he might go along with it.

"We're only here for a week, but yeah, like Val said, if you want to do anything with us girls, just let us know. We're game."

"What about your boyfriend?" Izzie asked Jillian.

"Oh, he's a runner. As usual, he had to go for a run first thing. I go with him sometimes, but Val and I just wanted to take a walk around the pond and get settled in."

"I…really didn't believe Benny would be gone so much. I'd…Googled the location, and it looked like a real paradise." Izzie snorted. "Unless he finishes up whatever he's doing here soon, I can just imagine it being like this the whole time."

"Okay, well, if he's gone on business, just come over and we'll do something. Since you've never been here before, you choose. Or we can take you on some of our fun adventures." Val would love to get her out of there and as far away from Benny as they could.

"Howard loves to do his own thing too, a lot. That's why Val and I wanted to take this trip together. So we wouldn't feel stuck in the cabin for hours with nothing but four walls to stare at."

"I feel like that when Benny leaves in the car. I'm stuck here, and I don't know what to do with myself. I don't know the area, and I'm afraid to wander off by myself."

"Well, leave it to us, and we can be your tour guides. So, do you still live in San Antonio?" Val asked, leading the way around the pond.

"Yeah. I leave sometimes, but I keep returning home."

"To family?"

"Nah, just to the familiar surroundings."

Val said, "I hear ya. We both are elementary-school teachers in the Houston area now. We couldn't wait to get away from school, and now we're back in the school system. Go figure." Val had thought elementary-school teachers sounded tame and nonthreatening enough.

"Oh, I can't imagine teaching kids all day. I'm a secretary at a real estate office."

"Ever meet any rich billionaires looking for a mansion?" Jillian asked.

Izzie laughed, the first time she had lightened up since they'd met her.

"I met Benny when he came looking to buy some rental property."

"Not a billionaire, I take it," Jillian said, sounding disappointed.

Izzie smiled. "He makes really good money. But no, not a billionaire. I've met some really rich buyers, and lots who were mortgaged to the hilt, trying to purchase a place, who had the income but not enough collateral. You meet all kinds."

Hmm, okay, so Val was thinking Izzie had met him at

the club. "I bet. It would be a lot different than teaching all those little kids every day." Val pointed to the island in the center of the pond. "Look at the turtles on the island."

Izzie sighed. "And they're not even afraid of us. It's so different from San Antonio."

They saw a couple of howler monkeys in a tree on the other side of the pond.

"See the howler monkeys? Don't leave your doors or windows open unless they have screens, or one of them could get in and start eating your fruit. Two of them got into my cabin and not only ate some of my oranges but threw them at me!" Val said.

Izzie chuckled.

Jillian laughed. "You should have heard her and the monkeys screaming. Howard ran right over to save her."

Izzie glanced at Val. "Did he?"

"Yeah. He scared them right out the door. I would have done it once I got over my initial shock."

Izzie smiled, and they resumed their walk.

Val was glad they could make her feel a little better, considering what she'd gotten herself into by making friends with Benny.

"Okay," Izzie said, "I'll talk to Benny and see if he can give me his work schedule, and then I can ask if you're free to do something when he's gone."

Val was afraid that would mean a no if he was really controlling. But she still had high hopes they could remove Izzie easily from the situation. Since he did construction work in the States, she wondered what kind of business Benny had to do all the time while he was here. She would have asked, but she wanted to keep the interrogation to a minimum, afraid she'd clue Izzie in that they were either annoyingly nosy—and then she wouldn't want to have anything to do with them—or they weren't who they said they were.

They walked her back to her cabin and exchanged phone numbers.

"Let us know if you want to get together," Val said, and they left her off at her cabin.

"Thanks, I really had a nice walk with you both. I'm sure we can get together."

Val wasn't sure they could, if Izzie had to get Benny's permission.

They all said bye, and Jillian and Val continued on their way to Jillian and Howard's cabin. Inside, Howard and Rowdy were waiting for them.

"Okay, what do we have?" Howard asked, fixing coffee for everyone.

Val was already calling Izzie's name in to Manuel. "Hey, need you to find out everything you can on Izzie Summerfield of San Antonio. Okay, thanks." She ended the call.

Jillian was telling Howard and Rowdy all they had learned when Manuel called back with the info. Val said, "Manuel verified where Izzie was living—an apartment in Universal City—and her place of employment: a real estate office near there. No husband or children, parents live on the south side of San Antonio, no siblings. She graduated from Reagan High School, no higher education. She's never been married, never had kids, and she does volunteer work at a pet shelter after hours. So she can't be all bad."

"Do you think she'll call you to get together?" Howard sounded hopeful.

"I think she was afraid to upset Benny if she took off to have fun with us, even if he's off working all the time. I think she's unhappy being stuck at the cabin with nothing to do. So hopefully she'll get together with us. Maybe Rowdy could get friendly with her and 'steal' her away and that will make our job easier."

"You ladies did a great job. I'd say you might have gotten somewhere with her," Rowdy said.

"Did you doubt it?" Val asked.

Rowdy smiled. "Not even for a second. As to me 'stealing' her away, I could try, but I'm not sure I'd do a good job of it."

"Well, we could say you were another friend who dropped by and take you with us if she says she wants to go somewhere. I was thinking Jillian might offer to go somewhere with her because I couldn't, for some reason. PMS or something. And then Rowdy could run into you and Izzie and make friends," Val said.

"Okay, we could sure try that," Jillian agreed.

Rowdy nodded, and Val was glad he seemed willing to help them however he could.

"One other thing I thought was odd. She said he'd never taken her anywhere fun, and it sounded like she'd known him a while."

"While he was mated to Lucy?" Howard asked.

"Yes, it did sound like that," Jillian agreed.

"Huh, well, it's possible he was seeing her while he had his mate confined to the house," Howard said. "I wouldn't be surprised at anything we might learn concerning him."

They waited that afternoon, listening for Benny's car, but he didn't return. They continued to while away the time, not wanting to go out as jaguars until night fell. They took turns napping so they could stay up that night. When it was dark enough, Howard and Val ran as jaguars while Jillian and Rowdy watched Benny's cabin.

But all Val and Howard found were Benny's old scent trails. When they returned, they saw his car parked at the cabin and heard wild lovemaking going on in one of the bedrooms.

Val sighed, and then she and Howard ran back to his cabin. There, they shifted and dressed.

"I guess when they get back together, the sex makes all the waiting worthwhile," Val said, disappointed. She had hoped Izzie would give up on Benny, but Val didn't want her to fight with him either, in case that could make him angry enough to kill her.

"Yeah, here I thought you might have swayed her into thinking he wasn't worth being with," Howard said.

Jillian shook her head. "We won't give up."

"I'm going back to my cabin, and we can try again early tomorrow morning," Val said.

"Night, Val. Sleep well." Jillian yawned.

"I'll walk you back," Howard said to Val.

"I'll be fine. Get your rest. I want to be out there early."

"Gotcha. See you before first light," Howard said.

"I'll head out with her," Rowdy said. He left her at her cabin before he went off in the dark with a flashlight to find his way to his own. Val admired him for not being afraid of the dark or the rain forest when he couldn't see like they could.

———

Val was normally an early riser, but she'd gotten up especially early. She was determined to catch Benny

this time and couldn't believe she'd missed Howard's
text messages yesterday morning. This time, she had her
phone in the bathroom while she showered. She suspected Howard hadn't risen as early this morning and
hoped she wouldn't have to wait long for him to join
her. She would have just gone off on her own already.
Intending to run over to his and Jillian's cabin and wake
him, she opened her front door some, shifted, and leaped
to the bottom of the steps.

And ran straight into a large, male jaguar. Not Benny.
Not anyone she knew.

Shocked to see him, she gulped and didn't even
have time to react. But she knew from the predatory
gleam in his eyes that he wasn't there to be friends
with her.

The jaguar tore into her, biting her in the shoulder,
then struck her on the head with his deadly paw.

Early that morning, Howard texted Val to let her know
he was headed over to her place. She didn't text back,
but he was making sure he took her with him this time
no matter what. She was probably in the shower again.

He texted Rowdy after that: Val and I are taking an
early morning jog to stake out Benny's cabin. Jillian's
up and she said you could come over and visit with her
before we return and have breakfast.

Howard wasn't sure if Rowdy would even be awake
at this early hour. But he'd feel better if Jillian and
Rowdy could watch each other's backs in case they had
trouble while he and Val were out.

Rowdy texted: I'll be right over. Thanks.

Howard finished his coffee. "Rowdy will be over in a few minutes, Jillian."

"Be safe and keep Val safe."

"I sure intend to." He wondered what Jillian and Rowdy would talk about. Jaguars versus wolves? What life as one of them was like? The pros and cons of being a shifter versus being a human? Maybe murder investigations.

Howard stripped out of his clothes in the bedroom and shifted. When he left the bedroom, Jillian opened the front door for him, and he raced outside and into the trees to reach Val's cabin. All he could think of was connecting with Val and possibly eliminating Benny this morning.

When he reached her cabin, he didn't see any sign of her, but her door was wide open. Which gave him pause. He smelled a new male jaguar's scent and, damn it, blood! *Hell.*

Already his adrenaline was roaring through his veins. The male's scent wasn't Benny's. Howard heard rustling inside Val's bedroom. He ran inside the cabin, thinking it had to be her, but he smelled the man's scent all the way through the cabin. As soon as he reached the bedroom, he saw a naked, muscular man searching through Val's things. Heart thundering, Howard was ready to kill the bastard. The man turned to see Howard coming for him. The man's mouth was bloodied, and his steely blue eyes widened right before he shifted into a golden jaguar.

Howard slammed into the jaguar, conscious that he needed to keep him alive to learn where Val was. He didn't want to consider that she could be dead. The man wasn't injured. Which meant he had to have wounded Val, and she hadn't had the chance to strike back at him.

Filled with white-hot rage, Howard sank his teeth into the jaguar's flank. The cat was moving so much that Howard was having a time getting a firm hold to take him down. This asshole could have easily taken out an unprepared female jaguar, but he wouldn't stand a chance against Howard. Not as angry as he was. Even so, the cat's teeth grabbed hold of Howard's shoulder. Lucky damn strike for the cat, but he wouldn't get another.

Howard whipped around, growling, intent on getting hold of the cat's skull. They tussled, claws gouging, trying to get purchase to hold on to each other so they could bite at will. It would be better if Howard could just strike and not leave a bite that said a jaguar killed the man, but it was too late for that. The cat was wearing plenty of bite marks. The jaguar had hold of him, but Howard struck out with his paw, slamming it against the cat's head. The other jaguar released his hold on Howard, looking dazed for a second, then lunged for another showdown. Howard leaped straight into the air, calculating where the other cat would be, landed on top of him, dug his claws into the cat's flesh, and bit the cat in the skull, crushing it. There was no chance of questioning the bastard about Val.

Without wasting another second, Howard raced through the cabin. He didn't smell Val's blood inside, so the bastard must have injured her outside and taken her somewhere else. If she could have, she would have crawled to his and Jillian's cabin for help. And that had him sweating it out, praying she was still alive.

He leaped out of the cabin door, landing on the path

below the cabin, and raced around the area, feeling panicked and searching earnestly for Val. He was glad he'd asked Rowdy to stay with Jillian, in case Benny had anything to do with this. More of these men could be here, ready to take them out if they realized Val wasn't on her own. He suspected they believed she was a single Enforcer agent here by herself.

His heart thundering, Howard kept smelling blood but not Val's scent. She would have been wearing hunter's spray to run with him this morning. He was afraid the blood he was smelling *was* hers. She wouldn't have disappeared otherwise. And the man was wearing blood where he'd bitten someone before Howard killed him.

Howard wanted to call out to Val in his jaguar's roar, but he couldn't in case others were holding her hostage. They might kill her if they knew he was coming to aid her.

He had to believe she was alive. Injured, but alive.

When he reached the river, he saw a jaguar body. *Val's.*

His heart nearly gave out.

She wasn't moving at all. His mouth dry as sand, he ran toward her. She hadn't shifted into her human form, which meant she wasn't dead, but she could still be close to death. That's when he saw movement in the river and turned to look. Two black Morelet's crocodiles were swimming toward the shore, their long, ridged tails sweeping the brackish water back and forth. One of the crocodiles was nearly ten feet in length, the other around eight feet. Either could kill Val in the shape she was in. They were a danger to humans, not normally to jaguars, but with Val lying there unresponsive and bleeding, she would be easy prey.

Howard wouldn't have enough time to shift into human

form and carry her away from the river before the first crocodile reached her. He nuzzled her face to tell her he was there for her if she was conscious. She didn't respond, but he didn't have time to stay with her. He ran full force to meet up with the larger crocodile, which was closer.

Jaguars were stalk-and-ambush predators, unlike other big cats that chased down their prey. But crocodiles were also ambush predators and coordinated with one another to go after their prey. Which meant Howard had to ensure the other crocodile didn't attack him when he went to take out the bigger one.

It would have been much easier, and safer, for Howard to attack from the back of the crocodile, grab the beast with his claws, and bite into his head. That's how a jaguar would normally take one down. Howard couldn't sneak up on the crocodile, so he had to watch for the jaws of the beast. He leaped nearly twenty feet, hoping that maneuver would help him kill the first of the crocodiles. Howard landed on the croc's back, but he was turned the wrong way. He whipped around to kill the croc as he would have done if he'd been in the right position. Not that the crocodile was waiting for him to get into the correct killing form.

It whipped around, trying to bite at Howard, but Howard was too agile, too focused on protecting Val. His claws dug into the croc's sides while he struggled to hold on to the fighting reptile.

The croc thrashed to return to the water, the smaller one coming to his aid. The smaller one was quicker than the other, but Howard bit into the larger croc's head and crushed its skull. Then he whipped around to take care of the other menace.

The croc's jaws were wide open, but then it began backing up. Howard snarled and struck at it with his paws, claws extended, needing to force the croc to leave so he was safe to take care of Val. The croc suddenly twisted around, and sweeping its tail back and forth, it slipped into the river and swam away.

Relieved but worried about Val, Howard surveyed the murky water for any other crocs. Seeing none, he turned and ran to Val. He smelled her, nuzzled his face against hers, and licked her nose, trying to get her to stir. She was bleeding, but not badly. The other jaguar must have knocked her out with a swipe of his paw. Howard prayed she didn't have a severe head trauma.

He shifted. "Val, can you hear me? It's me. Howard. Thor. I'm your guardian, here to protect you."

Her eyes opened, and she even gave him a small smile, her whiskers testing the air, her nose taking in deep breaths of him, although she couldn't smell his scent because of the hunter's spray.

"The shifter who attacked you is dead. I'll carry you to my cabin. Rowdy and Jillian can look after you. I need to get rid of the dead guy."

She closed her eyes as if she was too tired to deal with any of this.

"Do you know who he was?"

She didn't respond, and that worried Howard all over again. He lifted her into his arms and walked back to the cabin as fast as he was able to carry her, trying not to jar her too much. He just hoped he wouldn't run into Benny or any other jaguars on the way. But he sure wondered if this guy and Benny were in league. Howard would have preferred to question the man who had injured Val first, but that hadn't been an option. The guy had to have known he was living on borrowed time, and Howard was certain he wouldn't have given information freely anyway. The priority had been to find Val, so Howard hadn't had time to play games with the jaguar. He just hoped Rowdy didn't give him trouble over killing the man.

As soon as he reached his and Jillian's cabin, Howard called out, "We need some help here." He couldn't get the door open on his own, and he didn't want to put Val down on the porch to open the door. He kept his voice low so it wouldn't carry. Though the proliferation of trees and vegetation muffled sounds, Jillian would be able to hear him because of her close proximity and enhanced wolf hearing.

The door opened and Jillian gasped. "I'll get my first aid kit. You smell like you tangled with a caiman or a crocodile. And you smell of another male jaguar."

"True on both counts." Howard carried Val into the cabin. "The shifter who injured Val is dead in her cabin."

Jillian shut the door and rushed to get the first aid kit.

Rowdy hurried to get water and some towels. "I take it you had to kill him."

"Yeah. Talking to him or taking him hostage weren't options." Howard laid Val on the floor in the living room, not wanting to get blood all over the sofa.

"He was a jaguar like you?" Rowdy asked.

"Yeah. Mean son of a bitch. Almost as mean as me."

Jillian carried the first aid kit, a pillow, and a blanket into the room. "Go get dressed. I'll get started on her."

Howard strode to his bedroom, pulled on a pair of Bermuda shorts, then returned to the living room.

Jillian had already tucked the pillow under Val's jaguar head.

Knowing it would be easier for them to see her wounds if she shifted, Howard took hold of her hand and caressed it. "Val, can you shift?"

She opened her eyes and growled softly. She nodded and groaned, but she didn't shift. Sometimes jaguars had a hard time shifting when they were badly injured. And sometimes they couldn't shift at all until they were much better.

Val furrowed her brow, closed her eyes, and appeared to be concentrating. The change was always so swift that when she finally managed, she turned into a blur of forms. When the shift finished, she was her beautiful human self. As if it was too much for her, she closed her eyes again.

Howard quickly covered her with the blanket Jillian had brought out and called softly to her, "Val."

Jillian shook her head. "It's better if she's out when I begin to sew her up."

Rowdy had been watching the whole scenario, which again reminded Howard of how the guy should be one of them after seeing all that he had. Rowdy crouched down to help clean Val's neck and face.

Howard would have done so, but Rowdy appeared to know what he was doing and seemed eager to earn a place with them. So far, the guy was doing all right by Howard.

Jillian stroked Val's hair and held on to her hand. "She was lucky he didn't kill her. He could have easily done so. Which makes me wonder if he wanted to question her about who she was and what she was doing here if he couldn't find anything about her at her cabin. On the other hand, he left her by the river where a couple of hungry crocodiles were coming to dinner."

Rowdy swore under his breath. "Then no one would realize a human had murdered her."

"Not when a jaguar chewed on her too." Again, Howard was reminded that Rowdy was thinking in human terms. It was so easy for shifters to think in both, but it would be a learning curve for Rowdy.

Jillian began to sew the bite marks on Val's neck while Howard spoke softly to Val. "You're one brave cat. I probably would have had a heart attack if that jaguar had blindsided me. He probably did when I came upon him in your cabin without him knowing it at first."

"It's not Benny's scent on her though. And you're wounded. You said the other cat is dead at Val's cabin?" Jillian asked, sounding as though she would have taken him down herself if he were still alive. But as a wolf, she couldn't kill a male jaguar. Probably not a female either. She could shoot him, but if the police found the body, they would believe a human killed a human.

"He's lying dead in Val's bedroom. Once I know Val's going to pull through, I'll take care of him."

"Who is he if he's not Benny?" Rowdy asked. "Hell, I thought Benny was on his own. Well, except for the girlfriend."

"Beats me. Benny's staying with the human woman, but she did say he was doing business down here. No telling who this guy was. I'll take pictures of him to see if Val or our headquarters can identify him. We have a database of jaguars who pursue criminal activities. Maybe Val knows who he is, and because she recognized him, he tried to take her out. For him to have had time to wound her, then haul her off and return to search through her things, she must have left her cabin much earlier, before I arrived."

"Was there any ID on him?" Rowdy asked, a typical question for a human homicide detective who wasn't thinking in terms of them being shifters.

"He was wearing a jaguar coat. No pockets for his ID. But he'd shifted to search through Val's things, probably trying to learn who she was."

"Unless he already knew who she was and was searching for some kind of evidence on who she was after. Which means he suspected she's here on business," Rowdy said. "Could you be mistaken about who killed Lucy? Maybe this other shifter did."

Howard ran his hand over Val's forehead. "No. Benny's saliva was in the bite marks."

"See, this business of being able to tell people by scents—even if they're shifters or not—is something I'd like to be able to do," Rowdy said.

"The perks of being a shifter come with a lot of trouble too," Howard reminded Rowdy.

Once Jillian had stitched Val's wounds, Val stirred again.

Jillian squeezed her free hand. "How are you feeling?"

"I've got a headache the size of Alaska, like the first time I had two Singapore slings without eating anything all day." Val paused to take a breath. "He bit me before I could react. I was just coming out of my cabin to get Howard, and this jaguar materialized out of the rain forest, bit me, and then knocked me out." She closed her eyes, then opened them. "I woke to find him dragging me through the forest. I smelled the river and heard it flowing by. I must have passed out after that until one of my guardians came to rescue me." Val offered Howard a small smile and squeezed his hand.

"That's my job," Howard said. "I'm going to carry you to my bed for now and then take care of the man who injured you. He's dead, if you didn't catch that part. Do you know who he was?"

"Not as a jaguar. I didn't recognize his scent."

"I'll take pictures of him in his human form and show them to you."

"Fingerprints too?" Rowdy asked. "I've got a kit. His fingerprints might be in our human database."

"Okay, good idea." Howard carried Val into his bedroom. After laying her in his bed, he covered her with a sheet and a light comforter.

"You're injured." Tenderly, Val touched his arm where his shoulder had bite marks. He also had a few wicked cuts across his side and back.

"Just a few scratches. With our fast healing, I'll be perfectly fine in no time at all. Jillian and Rowdy are staying with you. I'll be back shortly with pictures of the bastard."

"All right. Be careful. We thought Benny was the only one out here, but it looks like something more is going on."

"I'll watch out." Howard kissed Val on the cheek. "Get some rest." He turned to see Jillian watching him from the doorway. He knew that look. He wasn't leaving until she took care of *his* injuries. But he wanted to get rid of the dead guy right away.

Jillian folded her arms. "Rowdy's gone to get his fingerprint kit, and I'll stitch you up before you leave."

"No time."

"It's completely dark out yet. You'll have plenty of time." Jillian made Howard come with her. "You know, you are the worst of us when you're injured."

Val chuckled. Howard wished Jillian hadn't said that in front of her.

As soon as Jillian had sewn Howard up in the living room, Rowdy came back with the fingerprint kit.

"I'll go with you and get his fingerprints. And then return to watch over the women," Rowdy said.

"Do you have a gun?"

"Yeah, and Jillian said she has one too."

"She does. She can handle a big cat with one, probably not as a wolf though. It would still be better to take care of them as jaguars. I'll finish dressing, and we'll go over there," Howard said.

After Howard dressed, he and Rowdy headed through the trees to Val's cabin, climbed the steps, and entered the cabin. Rowdy locked the door behind them.

When they reached Val's bedroom, Rowdy saw the man's torn-up body and glanced at Howard as if he thought he had killed an unarmed, naked human.

"He was a jaguar when he tore into me and Val. Remember?"

"Yeah, sure."

"In death, we turn into our human form."

"Okay, gotcha. It just takes some getting used to. When I see a dead body, no weapon on him, well, it's easy to assume he's the victim. Especially the way he's torn up. But then again, so were you and Val." Then Rowdy frowned. "How are you going to take care of the body? Won't you need my help?"

Howard smiled. "As a jaguar, I can carry a lot of weight."

"Ah, yeah, right. I've done a lot of research about wolves, but I haven't learned anything about jaguars."

"We'll have to let you in on our secrets."

"Much appreciated." Rowdy took the dead guy's fingerprints and Howard's cell phone. "What if Benny or some other jaguar attacks you while you're trying to dispose of the body? Can you roar for help?"

"In my jaguar chuffing way, but yeah, Val and Jillian will hear me."

"Something else I'd love to be able to do."

Howard smiled.

Rowdy shook his head. "I can't believe I'm aiding and abetting in the disposal of a dead body."

"A would-be murderer. And if Benny hired him to take Val out, he's probably done this kind of thing before."

"I'm sure you're right."

"All right. Be back soon." Howard began removing his clothes.

"I'll get the door for you and clean everything up." Rowdy looked a little unsettled that Howard was going to carry off a dead body with his jaguar teeth.

If he was going to be a shifter, Rowdy would have to learn about their world and what they would do to keep it secret. Howard did appreciate that Rowdy was willing to help them out though.

Howard shifted and grabbed hold of the dead guy's arm. Even though jaguars had the strongest bite of all the big cats—beating out both lions and tigers—they could be gentle too, the female carrying a cub safely in her jaws. Howard didn't intend to injure the guy any more than he already had.

Rowdy watched Howard as he pulled the dead guy out of the cabin, then shut the door.

Howard dragged the man over the same route he had traveled before when the guy had hauled Val to the river. Would the crocodiles still be around after Howard had killed one? He saw two on the bank across the river. They were opportunistic hunters. If he left a meal for them, they'd eat it.

He dragged the dead man into the river and let the current pull the body away, then returned to shore. The crocodiles watched Howard, but their supper was getting away from them. They both left the riverbank and swam after the dead man. *Good. Less of him for anyone to find that way.*

Howard glanced in the direction of Benny's cabin. Rowdy was with Jillian, the two of them able to protect Val while she was recovering. Howard couldn't miss the opportunity to prowl around Benny's cabin. When he finally drew near, he saw Benny's car was still there.

As Howard moved even closer to the cabin, he listened for a sign of anyone but didn't hear anything. No lights were on inside either.

He climbed the stairs to the door, shifted, and tried the door. It was unlocked, so he opened the door and went inside. He heard snoring in one of the bedrooms and shifted, then walked on silent jaguar paws to the room, poking his head in. Only one body was in the bed—the woman. Howard quickly checked the rest of the rooms. Benny wasn't there. That meant he was probably running around through the rain forest. Had he known Val was here and after him? Had he hired the other jaguar to take her out?

If that was the case, the guy looked to be conspiring with other rogue jaguars. This wouldn't be just about murdering his wife any longer.

Chapter 7

WHILE VAL WAS STILL LYING IN HOWARD'S BED RECU-
perating, Rowdy showed her the photos Howard had
taken of the dead man, but she didn't know the man.
"Did you send them to headquarters?" she asked Jillian.

"Yeah. They're running them through their database."

Val glanced at the clock. "How long has Howard
been gone?"

"An hour," Rowdy said. "I'll get back to watching
things." He returned to the living room.

"Howard's been gone too long. He shouldn't be off
by himself." Val couldn't shake loose her concern that
Howard could get into real trouble on his own after what
had happened to her. She had a better chance of helping
him than a human or a wolf shifter would. But she had
such a severe headache that she didn't even know if she
could shift without passing out. Still, she couldn't let
him risk his life when he had no backup.

And she always felt better getting back on track with
the mission after she'd been wounded, to prove she
wouldn't be beaten.

"I agree, but I don't think you're in any shape to go
running after him." Jillian had just given Val medicine
for the headache, while Rowdy was armed and watching
out the windows. But he couldn't see half as well as they
could in the dark.

Val couldn't quit worrying about Howard. "I need

to go. I can help him fight other jaguars. I need to be there for him." She climbed out of bed, still naked, and shifted. A sharp pain shrieked through her skull. She quickly sat down on her rump to settle the dizziness.

"Are you sure you're going to be all right?" Jillian placed her hand on Val's head, her brow furrowed with concern.

Val nodded.

"You're not experiencing double vision, are you?"

Val shook her head. She stood and prowled toward the bedroom door. She wasn't certain wolf shifters made good teammates to deal with rogue jaguars. They just weren't as powerful.

Jillian followed her out of the bedroom and hurried to unlock the front door and open it for her.

"Whoa, she's not going out on her own, is she?" Rowdy asked Jillian, eyeing Val.

"Yeah, she's worried about Howard. So am I. He's taking too long. What if he had to deal with crocodiles again?" Jillian asked. "Or another jaguar?"

Val agreed and wasn't waiting for him to return. She ran out of the cabin and leaped to the ground. She followed the path Howard had taken to her cabin and then raced off through the rain forest along the path where Howard had dragged the dead man. She continued to run all the way to the river, but she didn't see any sign of the man's body or of Howard. She did see a crocodile sitting on the opposite riverbank. Unfortunately, Howard hadn't left a scent. Had he followed Benny somewhere? Alone? He probably was at Benny's cabin. She could bite Howard if he was, especially now that they suspected others might be involved.

When she raced off to get closer to Benny's cabin,

a jaguar shot out of his doorway, and her heart gave a start. *Howard*. She let out her breath in relief. He turned to see her, then just stared at her for a moment as if he couldn't believe she'd be out here after what had happened to her. Then he ran straight for her, and as soon as he reached her, he nuzzled her face and growled a little. Then he shifted. "Benny's not here. His wallet was on the bedside table. The woman is inside asleep," he whispered to Val. "He must be running in the rain forest."

She rubbed her body against Howard, which was a way of declaring he was her territory among cats, leaving her pheromones on him, just as he'd done with her. Then she shifted. "Let's find him and take him out."

Howard ran his hands down Val's arms in a caring caress. "Are you sure you're all right?"

"Yes. If we can find him, we need to do this."

"All right. But we stick close together."

"Right." Val shifted, and for the first time since she'd had her partner on a mission, she was glad to have someone—Howard—on her side.

Together, they ran in a different direction this time, both smelling for any fresher scents indicating where Benny had run. Val began to feel apprehensive when they got close to Rowdy's cabin. She smelled Benny's scent around Rowdy's place on the far side of the resort from their cabins and could tell he'd followed the detective there. His scent hadn't been here before. He must have known Rowdy was onto him.

They heard someone coming, and both Val and Howard slipped underneath the cabin resting on its stilts.

"Hey," Rowdy said, his voice hushed. "Howard? Val?"

They moved out from under the cabin and joined him.

"Your phone rang several times, and Jillian and I went to your cabin to check if it was your boss calling. Your mom called and said they were in trouble. She said if you could come and help, bring Howard and Jillian."

The three of them hurried to return to her cabin.

Val's heart was racing as she ran up her cabin steps, shifted, opened the door, and dashed inside.

Howard went in with her, though his clothes were at his cabin. She knew he came with her to watch over her.

"We'll get ready to leave," Rowdy said.

"But who's going to take Benny down?" Val asked from her bedroom as she hurried to dress. "We can't all leave here. He's still here somewhere."

"Did you see any sign of him?" Rowdy asked.

"No. But his car is still here. And Howard said his wallet was on the bedside table. The girlfriend was sleeping in their bedroom." Val finished dressing and tossed some spare clothes into her bag. She joined Howard and Rowdy in the living area, and they went outside with her. She locked up the cabin, then they hurried through the forest to Howard's cabin. "Two of us need to stay here. And two of us can go. Or I'll go and check on my parents. That would mean three of us against the bad guys, and three of you here."

Rowdy opened the door to Howard's cabin, and Howard ran inside.

"What are we doing? I've packed our bags in the event we're leaving," Jillian said.

Howard disappeared into his bedroom.

"I'm staying here," Rowdy said. "After I learned Lucy's husband had murdered her, I made a promise to myself that I'd take this bastard down."

Howard came out of his room, carrying his bag. "Jillian, we're supposed to stay together."

"Sometimes we get separated when we're doing a mission. Just like when I had to go after a shooter that I learned was a rogue jaguar shifter, and you and Vaughn went after the other jaguar. We each have our roles to play. I was going to go with you, but if Rowdy's staying, he'll need my help. If you and Val go to her parents' aid, Rowdy and I can keep track of things here. I can smell if Benny's around. Once you've aided Val's parents, you can return and help us, if we haven't taken care of matters already."

Howard opened his mouth to speak, but Jillian added, "Before you say anything about what Vaughn would say, I've already messaged him. He trusts us to do what's right. I think he's finally coming to grips with the fact that sometimes we have to go on separate missions, and he can't constantly worry about me when he has a job to do too."

"All right, but don't take any unnecessary risks," Howard said. "If you run into Benny and he's a jaguar, shoot him."

Jillian took a deep breath. "You and Val either. Rowdy and I might not have the claws and teeth the two of you do, but we're packing. If we manage to take him out, we'll move his body to the river and let the crocs handle the rest of him."

"You're sure the two of you are going to be okay?" Howard figured this was the best option for them, but he still worried about them.

"Yeah, we'll be fine," Jillian said, and Rowdy agreed.

"Let me know if anything comes up," Howard said.

"Same with you," Jillian said.

Howard offered to drive Val's rental car because of the way she was feeling, and she let him. Then they headed to where her parents were. "Are you sure you're all right?"

"Yeah. I'm worried about them. They should have retired last year. They nearly died after three male jaguar shifters about our age attacked them on a case. Sure, they have the training, but they're not as fast as they used to be. And yes, anyone could have been in as much danger if they'd been outnumbered like that. But early in their career, they wouldn't have gotten themselves into that bind in the first place," Val said, directing him to her parents' location.

"Are you sure? Anyone, no matter their age or training, can get themselves into trouble. Hell, even I did a few times."

"A few times?"

Howard smiled. "I was a hothead and thought I could do anything, that I was invincible. I have a dad who believes if you are going to be great at anything, you have to take chances, no matter how difficult or insane the task. I took his words to heart. And I've made some god-awful mistakes, nearly getting myself killed any number of times. Hell, that was before I was even twenty."

She chuckled. "But you lived."

"Yeah. It wasn't easy at times. I appreciated my dad's comment though. I might never have had the courage to do what I've done if it hadn't been for him."

"What did he do for a living?"

"He's a Guardian. So is my mother. When he told me I had to take chances, he thought I would join the Guardian force like them. It was too tame for me. I wanted to prove to my dad I could do just what he said I could do."

She laughed. "I bet you gave him early gray hairs."

"I did. He's told me that every year since I joined the Enforcers. He and Mom weren't sure about me transferring to the USF. He thought it could be as dangerous as the Enforcers' jobs. And it can be."

"Same with the Guardians, if they tangle with the wrong people." Val was texting on her phone.

"Which was what Dad was referring to when he said I had to take chances if I was going to be great at my job. He and Mom both have had some death-defying challenges while trying to protect shifters or jaguars from the rogues." He glanced at her. "Are you trying to reach them?"

"Yeah, first my mom, then Dad, but neither are texting back."

"Were they glad that you joined the same force as them? My parents wished I had joined the Guardians. They never thought I'd want to be an Enforcer."

"No, actually, they wanted me to be a Guardian. It was all right for them to be Enforcers, but they didn't want to worry about me. They met in the Enforcer branch, and they've always had each other to work with. They haven't liked that I've been working alone."

"Which is why they contacted my boss to see if I'd watch your back."

"Yeah. I can't believe they did that. Or that Martin Sullivan and my boss approved it. I have to admit you saved me back there. Thanks for that. Jillian said you had to fight off a crocodile to stop him from making me his supper."

"True. There were actually two of them, but I

convinced the other one to get lost so I didn't have to kill him too."

"Why in the world were you in Benny's cabin alone, with no backup? I was ready to bite you for it."

He smiled at her. He suspected she was serious. "I was angry he might have hired someone to take you out. But he wasn't there."

"What about the woman? What if she'd seen you?"

"The guy is dangerous to you, me, and most likely the new girlfriend. If he'd been there, I was going to… convince him to leave with me so we could have a talk. Privately."

"So that's part of your living-dangerously creed."

"The other man could have easily killed you. I wanted the truth out of Benny. Had he been involved in the attempt on your life? I'd say yes." Howard let out his breath. "When did you leave your cabin? You should have texted me you were coming."

"Around four. I couldn't sleep. I was anxious to be out there."

"So you hadn't gone anywhere close to his place?"

"No. I'd left my cabin, intending to wake you if you weren't up yet. Out of the dark, the jaguar attacked. Of course, at first, I thought it was Benny, but then I realized it wasn't his scent. It all happened so fast that I didn't even have a chance to warn you I was in trouble. I was angry with myself for letting him get the drop on me. Here I hadn't even wanted you or Jillian's protection. I was damn glad you had come with me and saved my life. I would have died if you hadn't."

"Hell. I was texting Rowdy to join Jillian to watch her back. I was angry I hadn't gotten to your place sooner. I would have taken the bastard out before he had a chance to injure you."

"You shouldn't have had to. This could very well mean our whole mission has escalated to something more serious." Then she changed the subject. "Enough about that. It's done. Your parents haven't retired either?"

"No. They love what they do. Their work as Guardians isn't usually as dangerous as what Enforcers do on a regular basis. I think their boss gives them more low-key assignments unless he needs them for something more challenging. I understand why your parents want to keep doing their job though. It gives them a sense of purpose. I also understand how you feel about it."

"I'm sure they worry about me as much as I do about them. My dad is so controlling that I couldn't work with him."

Howard smiled at her. "I wanted more excitement in my life. I couldn't imagine being a Guardian agent." He let his breath out. "I hope Benny doesn't injure either Jillian or Rowdy."

"I hope not." Val looked out the window.

"Can't you get ahold of either of your parents yet?"

"No. If Eric, the drug pusher, has hurt them… Well, even if he hasn't, if I get ahold of him, he's dead. My parents won't need to finish their mission."

"That was your parents' mission… Take him down, but just him, correct?"

"Yeah. But what if there are more jaguar shifters involved in this? My parents haven't had any luck in pinning him down."

"If he has any jaguar muscle helping him, we'll take them all down."

"If he's just got humans protecting him, we'll have to turn them over to the local police force."

"We will, if we don't have to fight them and take them out to protect ourselves or your folks." Howard wasn't about to mention what he feared had happened. Her parents were already dead. He was certain Val had already thought the same thing.

"Good. I hoped you would feel that way. Do you think you would ever want to work as an Enforcer again?"

"If I had the right incentive. The right partner."

"You would work with a partner again in the Enforcer branch, even after what had happened to you before you began to work solo?" she asked.

"Yeah. Working with agents of other branches, and now other kinds of shifters, has really helped me to see the advantage of sharing ideas and using one another's skills to accomplish the job with fewer casualties on our side. What about you? Would you ever be interested in joining another branch?"

"If I had the right incentive. The right partner."

He smiled. Sure, he could return to work as an Enforcer, but he really did like working with the mix of people he was with. They truly were a team.

They were quiet after that and had driven for a couple of hours when Val finally pointed to the street. "Okay, this is the area. The drug house is down the street to the right. It should be the third house. White siding. There's a vacant lot first. And another on the other side of it. It's a mix of homes, vacant lots, trees, shrubs, a few businesses. Looks like this area is zoned commercial."

"Do you know what vehicle your parents were driving?"

"Yeah. A gray Nissan Versa."

"I don't see one in the area." He drove by Eric's house, looking for a place to park that wouldn't make them stand out too much. "Laundromat, café, gas station, and grocery store are nearby."

"If we walk around at all, we're going to be noticed."

"Screw it. If your parents are in danger, I don't want to wait." Howard drove around the block until he was back on the street where the house was located. He pulled up next to the treed front yard. "Ready?"

"Knife, throwing stars, gun. Yeah, I'm ready."

"Okay, let's do this."

Howard and Val exited the car.

Three vehicles—a blue pickup and a couple of sedans—were sitting on the dirt road leading up to the side of the house. A couple of cars and trucks were parked along the street a few lots down.

"Could be more than we bargained for here," Val warned, motioning to the three vehicles parked at the house.

"Yeah. You still want to do this, don't you?"

"Yeah. If my parents are in trouble, we need to. Besides, we've already made our move, and if anyone's watching, they know it."

The two of them walked together, eyeing the windows to see if they noticed any movement. That was the advantage of their jaguar sight. They could detect the slightest movement that humans might be incapable of seeing.

"Window to our left, a woman peeked out," Val said.

"I noticed. They'll be ready for us."

They were close to the door when they heard a man say to someone, "Hell, you shot the agents. Now look at the damn mess you got us into."

Howard glanced at Val to see if she'd heard. He felt sick to his stomach, thinking that whoever the man was, he'd killed her parents. She looked pale as Howard knocked on the door, his free hand in his pocket where he had a switchblade. He'd rather take care of a jaguar shifter as a big cat, but for now, he didn't have any choice.

A woman answered the door but only opened it narrowly. She was a petite blond with blue eyes, her gaze darting from him to Val. And she *was* a jaguar. "Y-yes?" she asked, her voice stuttering a little with nervousness.

He hated that Eric and his partners had used a woman to cover for them. Unless she was involved in the drug deals. She looked sweet and innocent, but since she was here, she most likely knew all about the drug business. Unless she was here against her will.

"We're looking for Eric. Is he here?"

Her eyes widened again. "I don't know anyone by that name."

Howard pushed his way into the house. "He's a jaguar like you. Like us. Where is he?"

"Y-you're jaguars?" The woman looked shocked. Since they were still wearing hunter's spray, she hadn't detected their scents.

Val quickly shut the door, then secured the woman's arms behind her back. Even though she appeared mousy and unable to fight them, she could be just as dangerous as them if she shifted.

They heard movement in the kitchen. Val took the woman's arm, and she and Howard moved toward the kitchen.

"Who else is here?" Howard asked the woman, his voice hushed.

"Just a cat. He must have gotten into my plants again."

"Jaguar?"

"No, no, little cat."

He didn't believe the woman for a moment. "We heard men talking."

"Lie down on the floor," Val said to the woman. "Don't move." She showed her the gun she was carrying. "I'm an Enforcer. I won't hesitate to take you down if you interfere or try to run."

The woman's eyes rounded.

Yeah, tell someone you were an Enforcer, and that got the jaguar's attention. Howard had to admit mentioning being one of the Enforcers, who took a lethal approach in their missions, had a lot more of an effect on a perp than telling him he was a USF agent. Most shifters still hadn't heard of the newly formed branch, so he often used the Enforcer card when he wanted to impress upon the individual how serious his business was.

Howard and Val moved into the kitchen where a window was wide open, the breeze whipping the bright-pink curtains about. "Out back," Val said.

They peered through the window and saw two men running, both dressed in jeans, sneakers, and T-shirts, the one dark-haired, the other blond.

"I'll go after them. You get what you can out of the woman," Howard said.

"We're supposed to stay together."

"Right. But she might have the information we need. We don't want to lose her too if I miss catching up to either one of these guys. She might know what happened to your parents. If not, we can't afford to lose these men."

"All right." But Val didn't sound happy about it.

Howard ran through the house, racing out the front door and around to the back. There were no fences around most of the small houses; all had sizable lots with fruit trees and other vegetation that helped to separate the properties. He hoped he'd catch up to at least one of the men. They weren't wearing hunter's spray like he was, so he easily followed their trail through the properties. The problem was that they could have friends in the neighborhood who would offer them safe harbor. Maybe even provide backup for them.

He hadn't wanted to leave Val behind. He seriously hoped she could get something out of the woman about where her parents were. Though he did worry the guys he was chasing might call for support to protect the woman in the house or to take her out so she didn't talk. Which would put Val at more of a risk.

For now, he was running as fast as he could to catch up to the two men, hoping he'd have only two to handle at the same time.

Chapter 8

VAL HELPED THE WOMAN TO SIT UP IN THE LIVING room of the perp's drug house, worrying about Howard but praying the woman would know where Val's parents were and that they were still alive. Though the one man saying the other had shot agents didn't sound good.

"Okay, look, I know you're working with Eric or you wouldn't be here. He's sold that purple heroin shit to people who have died from it. He's a murderer, pure and simple. Our kind can't go to human jails long term. You probably know that means we have to terminate him. What does that mean for you? I'm taking Eric down. And anybody who works with him selling this shit. My parents are both Enforcers, and they were here to do that. They called me, and now they've disappeared off the radar. If you know something about it and can tell me where they are, I can just let you disappear, with strong advice to get out of this business before you're on the target list. You don't want to be there, believe me."

"I don't know where they are. I swear it." The woman's heart was racing, and she smelled of rampant fear.

"Okay, let's try this again. I'm going to ask you where they are, and you're going to tell me, because if you don't, I'm going to eliminate you right here and now and go help out my partner. There's no sense in me wasting my time here otherwise. My parents were watching this house. They were close by. So. Where. Are. They?"

"All right. All right. Eric said he saw them and thought they were bad news. He...he didn't say who he thought they were. I believed they wanted some of his business. Or...or maybe he was encroaching on their sales territory. I didn't know. I didn't ask. I figured they were all in the same business. All drug people. Not once did he say they were with the...the Enforcer branch. I...I would never have guessed it. I don't have anything to do with any of this."

Val felt nauseated. She often was when she found a murdered victim. This was so much more personal. She couldn't have lost her parents. "What did Eric do about it?"

The woman looked away. Val feared the worst. Eric and whoever else was working with him had murdered her parents. "Tell me. Who was the man that said the other had shot the agents?" Val's voice was hard with anger. She considered that she should have been soft and encouraging. But she was an Enforcer. Being sympathetic wasn't part of her mission. The woman could be just as deeply involved in this business as Eric. She could have watched him kill Val's parents. She could have helped.

"Ren said that to Eric. You promise you'll let me go? I'll...I'll leave. For good. I'll never see Eric again."

"As long as you had nothing to do with harming my parents." Val wasn't going to lie. If the woman had helped to kill them, she was a dead woman.

"I...I didn't. I didn't know what Eric did, but he said he was going to take care of them. And then I heard Ren say Eric had shot them right before you knocked on the door. But Eric and four other men had all been in on it."

"When did this happen?" Val ground her teeth to try

to keep her emotions in check. She desperately wanted to kill the men.

"An hour ago."

That gave Val hope her parents were still alive, but she figured Eric and his cohorts wouldn't have made that mistake. "Where are my parents?"

"Unless they moved the bodies, and I don't think they were going to until it got dark, they're at the house across the street."

A cold sweat covered Val's skin. "You lied about not knowing anything."

"Eric threatened to kill me. And he has a lot of men who would do the job for him. I didn't know he was into all this. Your parents rented the house across the street. An older man and woman? We didn't think anything of it until Eric grew suspicious for some reason. Not sure why. But he can be really paranoid sometimes. I didn't think they were anything but some Americans tourists. There's a beach near here and a rain-forest park nearby."

"You're coming with me."

The woman looked alarmed, the scent of her fear escalating, her eyes huge. "Wait, no. You said you were going to release me."

Her reaction concerned Val, making her believe the woman did have something to do with her parents' deaths. Maybe she was afraid Val would smell her involvement in the rental house. "After I find my parents."

"I told you. They're in the house over there. At least, I think so, if they killed them over there and didn't take them somewhere else."

"Come on then. Let's go see." Val's heart was beating out of control, and her palms were sweaty. She knew she'd find her parents dead, and she wanted to kill every last person who was involved in their murder and the sale of the heroin. She cut off the ties around the woman's wrists. "I can kill you easily with my bare hands. No need to use a gun or a knife, and I'm armed with both, so don't scream or call any attention to yourself in any way or you'll be dead. Understand?"

"Yeah…yeah."

"What's your name?"

"Emmie Bancroft."

"Your real name." Val escorted her out through the front door, watching for any sign of anyone observing them or coming to the house. She saw no one, just a black-and-white cat perched on a fence eyeing them.

"That is my real name. I haven't ever done nothing wrong. You won't find me in your databases or on your termination list. I just…I just started dating Eric because he was rich and fun. And when he said he had a house in Belize… Well, being a jaguar, it was all I could have ever hoped for. I…I didn't know the kind of trouble he was in."

Val gave her a look that said she didn't believe her as they walked down the long driveway.

"Well, I didn't. Not until we got here, and then I overheard some of his friends talking. I'm not involved in any of it. He never tells me nothing. I didn't have any money or a car to get out of here. I've been stuck, trying to pretend I'm clueless."

Val still didn't believe her. She wouldn't until she gave Emmie's information to headquarters and they ran it to see if Emmie Bancroft was who she said she was.

Val eyed the rental house but didn't see any movement. "Who are the other men working with Eric?"

"Ren, but I don't know his last name. Eric just calls him Ren. And Bixby. Eric keeps calling him Bro. I think he really is his brother, but he never came out and said so. Harington is the other man. I'm sure Eric is in contact with others, but I've never seen them, and I don't know their names. Eric sent Bixby on a job, but he hasn't returned. Eric was worried he might have met with foul play. Oh, and then there's Benny. He got into trouble in the States and ran down here, but Eric isn't happy with him. I don't know any of their last names though. Everyone is on a first-name basis only."

"Benny?"

They crossed the street and began to walk up the rental house's driveway.

"Yeah. I only met him last night. He looked nervous, his hands shoved in his pockets. Eric's really pissed at him. So he sent Bixby with him to take care of some problem."

"This Benny?" Val asked, showing Emmie her phone and the picture of Benny that the construction manager had on him.

"Uh, yeah, that's him."

Then she showed her the photo of the dead man. "Is this Bixby?"

Emmie's lips parted, her eyes wide. She looked up at Val. "He's…he's dead?"

"Yeah."

"That's Bixby. Eric is going to have a meltdown."

"Too bad. Bixby attempted to murder me."

"I'm…I'm so sorry."

They went to the front door of the gray house. It had a one-car garage, and Val wondered if she'd find her parents' rental car inside. She motioned to the front door. "Open it. In case someone's inside other than my parents, I want you to call out that you're Emmie, Eric's girlfriend, and you thought Eric was over here."

"He doesn't call me that."

"Whatever. Just don't tip anyone off that I'm with you." Though anyone could have been watching out the windows and seen what was going on. Val thought if someone had, he would have either come for her when Howard took off after the other men or called for more backup.

Emmie tried the door and found it was unlocked. She opened it and hollered out, "It's just me, Emmie. Eric sent me over."

No one answered.

Val was smelling the scents in the living room and realized Benny had been here too. So had some of the men who had been in the other house. Her parents' scents were also in here. She smelled their blood too, and she fought back the bile that threatened to make her vomit.

The back window in the living room had been shattered, making it appear the men had come in that way. Glass was scattered all over the floor.

"Move slowly." Val followed Emmie inside. She wanted to rush to where she smelled blood, but she had to make sure the house was clear and no one could attack her while she was here. Despite how desperately she wanted to see her parents, she bit back the inclination to rush headlong into the house to reach them.

"I think they're in there," Emmie whispered, her eyes filled with tears as she pointed to the hall to the right.

"I haven't been here before, but there's a trail of blood going all the way down the hall."

They checked the living room and the kitchen. No one. They moved down the hall to the bedrooms and bathroom. No one in there or in the first bedroom. Val kept Emmie in front of her as they moved to the second bedroom. Emmie was shaking, and Val didn't blame her. She would be too if she was in her predicament—Eric would want to kill her, and Val wanted to do the same, if she'd had anything to do with this.

Emmie came to the doorway, peered in, and gasped, genuinely shocked. Her skin turned ice white.

Immediately, Val grabbed her arm and rushed her into the bedroom—and saw her parents leaning against a wall, both of them bleeding from what looked like gunshot wounds to the chest. They were tied up, their mouths taped shut, but her mom's eyes suddenly fluttered open as if she knew Val had arrived.

Val forced Emmie to sit on the bed. "Stay." She hurried to reach her mom. "Ohmigod, Mom. You're... you're alive." But for how long? She couldn't think like that. All she could think about was getting them help and keeping them alive until then.

Then she heard her dad's faint heartbeat. "Help me," Val said to Emmie. "Get a pillowcase off the pillow. Help me stop the bleeding."

"Yes." Emmie quickly jerked the bedcover aside and hurried to get the pillowcase off one of the pillows, but she was so nervous, she couldn't get it free.

"Throw me the other pillow."

Emmie tossed it to Val and continued to work on the one she had.

Val jerked the pillowcase off, wadded it up, and held it against her mother's wound. Then she used the pillow against the pillowcase and wound. "Hold this tight, Mom."

Her mom tried, but she was so weak.

"Do the same for my dad, but hold the pillow against the wound for him," Val ordered Emmie. She cut her parents' ties and removed the tape from their mouths. Then she got on her phone and called Howard. She knew he could be in a fight, and she didn't want to distract him, but they had to get help for her parents immediately. She wanted him to know that her parents were in dire straits and that he didn't need to catch up to the other men right now, not without having her as backup.

When he didn't pick up the call, Val left a message. "My parents are badly wounded, gunshot wounds, loss of blood, weak. Stopping bleeding. Rental house across street."

Then Val called her boss. "Sir, need help. Agents down—my parents—GSW, loss of blood. Need help ASAP."

"Calling in reinforcements. Where are you?"

"Rental house where they were watching the perp." She knew he'd be telling someone in a message to get help to her pronto. She realized her boss probably had known where her parents were all along, damn it. Why hadn't she thought of that?

She held her hand against the pillow over her mother's wound. "There are four others involved that we know of: Eric, Ren, Bixby, and Harington. But Benny was working with them too."

"Anyone else?"

Val looked at Emmie. She was working hard to stop

Val's dad's bleeding, talking softly to him, telling him he'd be all right. That his daughter was here to take care of them.

"No one else. We didn't catch Benny, but we had to kill someone who tried to take me out this morning at our resort."

Emmie looked up at Val.

"The pictures Howard sent you of the dead man... Did anyone recognize him?" Val asked her boss.

"He was Bixby Erickson," Sylvan said.

Val said under her breath, "So he was Eric's brother. Well, he's out of the picture now."

Emmie swallowed hard.

Val had been serious when she said they took the bad guys down. *Permanently*.

"Our people have gotten ahold of a couple of Guardian agents who are down there. They're strictly on vacation, but they'll be at your location in approximately twenty minutes. Matt and his sister Katrina Sorenson. They're bringing medical packs. There's a municipal airport nearby. They'll transport your parents out of there and get them to a hospital right away. I know you'll want to go with them, but you have a mission to complete. And now it appears you have your parents' mission too, since Benny's connected to Eric and there's no one else available right now to take him down. Where's your backup?"

"Chasing down two of the men." Val didn't tell Sylvan that Jillian had stayed near Benny's cabin, nor that a human homicide detective was helping them.

"Did you tell Howard and Jillian what happened?" Sylvan asked.

"I tried but I didn't get a response back."

Her boss swore. "They're supposed to be watching your back."

Yeah, exactly what she was thinking. She couldn't think of the danger Howard might be in. Not when she needed to ensure her parents received help while their lives were hanging by a thread. All that had kept them from dying was their healing genetics. Even so, they'd lost a lot of blood, and though they would regenerate it faster than humans, they could still die before they regained enough to save themselves.

"I need to go," she told her boss.

"Stay on the line," Sylvan ordered. "I need to know if you end up in a battle for your life. If I had any other Enforcers or JAG agents down there, I'd send them. But no one else is as close to your location as the two Guardian agents."

"I'm glad that at least they are nearby." She put the phone on speaker so she could hold her mother's hand with her free hand. "Mom, you're going to be all right. Guardian agents are on their way. You have to keep fighting to prove these bastards didn't have what it took to take you out."

Her mother gave her a weak smile.

"Who did this to you? Do you know?" Even though Emmie had told Val who, she wanted to hear it from her mother, since Emmie hadn't witnessed it—or at least Val didn't think so.

"Eric shot both of us. He knew he didn't kill us outright. He wanted us to bleed out slowly."

"Bastard. Were the other men here too? I smell their scents. Any that you could identify?"

"Eric's brother, Bixby. Then he sent him to take care of you. By then, we weren't capable of calling you to warn you. We called when they first entered the house before they overwhelmed us. Harington was the other man. Brooding, sour-faced. You can't know how glad I am to see you."

"Howard killed Bixby."

"Good. I knew Howard would be good for you. We were worried about you, but then we were in pretty bad shape ourselves. Benny was here. We wondered what had happened that Benny was here and you didn't know about it."

"His girlfriend was still at his cabin. His car was gone, but then he returned. We thought he was running as a jaguar, so we went after him. Then Jillian got your call and we came straight here." Val let out her breath, hoping her parents really would retire after this. "Okay, Mom, you just need to rest." Val had to contact Howard again while she waited for help to arrive. She just *had* to reach him. "Boss, you've heard who all was involved here, right?"

"Yeah, every word. I'm having each of the men researched."

"Good. I've got to call Howard again to let him know about this situation."

"All right, then once you're done, call me back."

"Okay." Val ended the call with her boss and tried Howard's number, but it went to voicemail again. She left another message to let him know her parents were going to be cared for, in case he was able to check his phone later. "Guardian agents are coming for my parents. As soon as they leave, I'm coming after you."

Then she called Jillian and gave her an update on their situation.

"Ohmigod, Val. Do you want us to go there?" Jillian asked.

"No. It'll take you too long to get here. Stay there in case Benny or some of his men go there. I can't get ahold of Howard. I'm worried about him, but I have to stay here to protect my parents in case Eric or any of his cohorts return. We'll be back as soon as we can. Just watch out for anyone. I've learned Bixby was the man Howard had to take out this morning, and he's Eric's brother. Eric might very well go to your location to learn what happened to him and want to finish the job his brother was supposed to take care of if he thinks either of the two of you are with us."

"We're both keeping an eye out."

"They're all jaguars. None of them are human."

"Good, then we can eliminate them, no questions asked."

Val smiled. "Yeah, eliminate them to your heart's content. I've got to call my boss back. Let me know if you run into any trouble."

When they ended the conversation, she tried Howard once more. Again, the message went to voicemail. She prayed he was all right. If he was in a fight with them, or if he'd shifted, then she could understand why he couldn't answer his phone.

Then she called her boss back. She'd never known him to monitor anyone so closely on a mission, botched or otherwise. She hoped that didn't mean he felt she couldn't do the job. Or maybe he felt that in her current state of mind, she wouldn't be able to. She had to admit she was ready to kill every last one of the men, the adrenaline rushing through her blood. She hoped Emmie hadn't had anything to do with this.

Then Val smelled the air again. Emmie's scent hadn't been in the rental house. Not until now. But she still could have known just who Val's parents were working for, and she could have been just as involved in the drug business.

"Did you get in contact with your backup?" Sylvan asked.

"No. I'll track them down as soon as my parents are on their way. Wait. Someone's just pulled into the driveway." Val had to release the pressure on her mother's wound and pulled out her gun.

"It's Katrina and Matt. They just messaged me that they've pulled into the driveway."

Someone knocked at the open door. "Val?" a woman called out. "It's me, Katrina Sorenson, and my brother, Matt."

"We're in the back bedroom." Val had heard of them. They were a sister-and-brother team who had been working together for years like this. On an earlier mission to Belize, they'd flown down to take possession of shifter cubs left in the rain forest when the cubs' parents had been taken hostage as jaguars. A couple of JAG agents had taken care of the cubs until the Sorensons had arrived. She couldn't imagine how difficult that would have been for the JAG agents.

The Sorensons were both trained as physician assistants. They worked missions where there were wounded agents or other shifters in need of medical care or other guardian-type duties as assigned. Which was the case with the cubs.

"So glad you're here," Val called out. "Sylvan, they're here. I need to help them. I'll call back later."

The man and woman rushed back into the bedroom, carrying medical bags. They were dark-haired and dark-eyed, wearing brightly colored board shorts—his blue, hers neon pink—T-shirts, and water sandals. They smelled like jaguars, salty seawater, fresh air, and coconut lotion, so inconsistent with the overwhelming smell of blood and fear in the room. They looked like tourists on vacation, not jaguar shifters ready for this kind of medical emergency.

"My dad's been unconscious the whole time," Val warned them.

They began working on her dad first because he was worse off, and she admired how efficient they were, each working in perfect synchronization with the other as if they'd been doing this for years. Which they had. Val wondered if they had mates but thought it was noble of them to be so close and work and vacation as a team. Twins, probably.

"We need to do an emergency blood transfusion for your dad," Matt warned.

"I can give blood to Jasper," Val's mother said weakly.

"Absolutely not," Val said, frowning at her mother. She loved her mother for caring so much about her dad that she would risk her own life. Val was about to offer her own, but Emmie spoke first.

"I'm O negative. I can give blood to anyone. I can do it."

Val was surprised to hear her offer, but grateful too. Maybe Emmie really wasn't involved with any of this.

"Okay, let's do this," Matt said.

They hooked Emmie up to donate blood to Val's dad.

"I can do the same for my mother. I'm B positive. Mom's AB," Val said.

"Your boss said you have a job to do—track down these bastards. I'm B positive too. I'll give blood," Katrina said. "In the meantime, you need to protect us if these drug runners return."

Not that the Guardians couldn't fight too. They were just as armed and deadly, but Val understood they had other priorities for now. And they were right. She needed to help Howard, and if she gave blood, she would have a harder time. Not to mention that if someone came here looking to kill them, she wouldn't be at top form.

Matt hooked Katrina up to donate blood to Val's mother.

"Thank you, Emmie, Katrina, Matt. You're a godsend."

Both Katrina and her brother glanced at Emmie as if they wondered who she was. They probably assumed she wasn't an agent. Which meant she was most likely with the bad guys, if not one of them. Neither asked Val to enlighten them.

Once they had given blood to her mom and dad, Matt and Katrina brought in two stretchers.

"You have an ambulance down here while on vacation?" Val couldn't believe it.

"It's in a nearby storage facility for use by any of our people who are down here, have the medical training, and need it for emergencies. A lot of our kind like to come here for vacations, and sometimes for the kind of job you're doing. We just happened to be at a beach resort near here when your boss's people called. We're glad we were close by." Katrina and her brother finished loading Val's parents into the ambulance and secured them.

"Me too." Val kissed both her parents, squeezing their hands. "I'll see you both as soon as I can."

"Take care of yourself," her mom said, frowning.

Her dad was breathing steadily, his heartbeat normal now, but he was still unconscious.

Val said, "I will, Mom. I'll take them down. Every last one of them."

"*With* your backup."

"Yes, *with* my backup." Or at least one of her backups, if he'd managed to stay alive.

"We have to leave now," Katrina said. "Gladys and Jasper will pull through. We've got your number. We'll let you know as soon as they're in the hospital and keep you informed of their status."

"Thank you." Val waited as the ambulance pulled out of the drive. Then she returned to the house, planning to tell Emmie to leave now and never come back, if she hadn't taken off already. Val was surprised to see her watching out the living room window, then turned to speak with her.

"What do you want me to do?" Emmie asked, her eyes filled with tears. "I'm...so...so sorry."

"You've just given blood. You need to leave, get away from here and these people now. Don't pack, just go."

Emmie was wringing her hands. "You didn't tell them or your boss about me."

"You have a chance to start over. Do something good with your life before it's too late."

Emmie found some paper in a drawer in the kitchen and a pen. She wrote down something. "This is the address of two other houses they use for their business. I heard him telling Benny where they were. I don't know any more than that." Emmie gave her a quick hug. "Thank you for giving me a chance."

"Go, before anyone comes back and learns you've helped me."

"All right." Emmie ran out the door and crossed the street to the other house.

Val assumed she was going to get keys to one of the vehicles parked out front of the house. Or call a taxi. She closed the door to the rental house and hurried after Emmie. "Are you taking one of the cars?"

"The blue pickup."

"Okay, I'm slashing the tires on the other vehicles so they can't use them." Val pulled out her knife and cut the tires so that if any of the men returned, they wouldn't be able to come after her and Howard right away.

She still needed to remove her parents' things and the rental car from the house. If the rental car was in the garage. She knew her parents would have packed light, but she suspected Eric had taken their weapons before he attempted to murder them.

Emmie ran back outside, looking panicked. "Eric took the keys to the truck."

"No problem." Val hot-wired it for her. "Now go."

"Thank you!" Emmie got inside the truck, closed the door, backed out of the driveway, and tore off down the street.

Val ran off in the direction Howard and the men had gone, calling him on her phone to try to locate him, though she was following the other men's scents. Thankfully, they weren't wearing hunter's spray, or she could have lost Howard. On the other hand, what if he was no longer following them, and she was after them all on her own? The only way that would happen was if he'd been severely injured. Or was dead. She didn't want to consider that he might be.

At least she was glad her parents would probably pull through.

No matter what, Eric and his buddies were dead men. She kept running across vacant lots, behind buildings, and down alleyways. Off in the distance, she saw trees looming. At first, she thought the men were trying to reach another one of their drug houses, maybe where they might have reinforcements. She didn't have time to stop and check the locations Emmie had given her.

By the direction they were running, they appeared to be headed for the rain forest. If they weren't armed, maybe they thought they could take Howard on in the forest as jaguars. She hoped Howard wouldn't try to fight them on his own. She and Howard would try to catch up with the men again once they were a unified force. She suspected he was like a jaguar with catnip. He wasn't letting go of his prey until they were taken care of. Not to mention that he probably felt that if he lost them, he and Val could lose the information about where her parents were.

She didn't want to even think about why he couldn't call her back.

Chapter 9

HOWARD HATED LEAVING VAL BEHIND, BUT HE HAD smelled that Benny had been in the drug house, as well as the man Howard had taken out this morning. They were all connected and all had to go down. He didn't like leaving Val alone in the house with the other woman, not that he didn't think Val could handle her, but he worried others might be involved and come to find Val there.

If he could just take these two men down, then they'd deal with Benny. At all costs, he had to learn where Val's parents were. The two men were full-out running, and he desperately wanted to call Val to ensure she was safe. But he couldn't pause for a second, or he'd lose these guys. Not once had the distance shortened between them, but they hadn't widened the distance either. They had run him through vacant lots, leaped over wooden fences and concrete walls, never hesitating. He suspected they were headed for the rain forest about two miles ahead. Both men darted around the edge of a wooden fence and disappeared from his view.

Three thoughts ran through Howard's mind. They were waiting beyond the corner of the fence to ambush him. They were taking a detour to lose him while they were out of sight—but he could track them by scent, and they probably knew that. Or they were still trying to outdistance him until they could reach a place of relative

safety, someplace they might have reinforcements waiting for them. He believed they planned to reach the rain
forest, shift, and take him on. Two cats versus a human
who wasn't ready for their teeth and claws would spell
his doom.

His cell phone rang again, and he fished it out of his
pocket. *Val. Again.* He'd been too busy leaping over
obstacles to answer the phone.

Howard made the calculated risk assessment to keep
running, knowing if he slowed down at all, he'd lose
them for good. But he just had to answer Val's call when
he ran around the corner of the fence. The two men were
still running. What he hadn't counted on was an assailant hiding behind an upside-down boat to his left. The
man jumped out at him, stabbing at him with a knife.
Howard blocked the knife with the cell—thank God for
cell phones—but that knocked the phone from Howard's
hand. It flew across the lot, striking a concrete wall.

His assailant was a jaguar, smelling of weed and
eager to take Howard down. He was shorter than
Howard, sturdily built and grinning like a fool, his blue
eyes bright with eagerness.

"Where are the Enforcer agents who were watching
Eric's place?" Howard asked, not expecting the man to
tell him, not even expecting him to know.

"Dead, like you'll be."

Hell. Did Val know? Maybe that's why she'd been
calling him. Now he was worried she was trying to catch
up to him.

Howard didn't have his knife out, so he tried to angle
himself to break the guy's neck. Less messy that way.
Because of the citrus trees in abundance, the concrete

wall, and the wooden fence, no one could see them, but he didn't want to use a weapon. He was torn between doing this expeditiously so he could catch up to the other men and ensuring he didn't get himself knifed.

The guy was good at wielding a knife, striking quickly, but Howard's cat reflexes kept him from getting cut.

"I already put one of you down this morning. Guess it's my day to destroy your whole damn ring." Howard was certainly ready, his blood pumping hard with exertion and anger.

"Bixby?" the guy asked, his eyes widening. That little bit of hesitation gave Howard the time he needed.

He lunged forward and grabbed the guy by the arm that was wielding the knife and broke his arm with a quick snap. The man cried out. Howard went for a choke hold around his neck.

"Yeah, Bixby." Howard guessed that's who it was. He wondered just how important the man was to startle this guy so. "Two down." Howard snapped the man's neck, dropped him where he stood, and took off running, then remembered his phone and rushed to retrieve it from where it had fallen on the concrete next to the wall. The glass was broken, but the shield kept it in place. On the run again, he tried to call Val while chasing down the two men's scents. All he got was a black screen. "Well, hell." He pocketed his phone and sprinted even faster. "Damn it all to hell."

He considered turning around and going back to ensure Val was okay, but then he saw the men race into the rain forest. He couldn't let them go. But he knew they weren't going there to hide from him. They were going there to shift and kill him as soon as he entered the forest.

He accepted the challenge. He had to get rid of these men before they could hurt anyone else. They'd already killed Val's parents. As much as he was interested in her and doing a whole lot more about his feelings for her, she wouldn't forgive him if he didn't take the men down now.

Hating that it had taken her so long before she'd been able to chase after Howard and his prey, Val came around the corner of a fence and found a man sprawled on his back, knife by his side, his arm broken, his eyes wide open. It appeared his neck had been broken too. Unless Eric or the other man did this, she assumed Howard had killed him. Thankfully, there was no blood on the knife, but this guy's body was growing cold, so he'd been dead for a while. She took off running again, growing closer to the rain forest. There was no sign of Howard or either of the other men. She knew they were all in there, and Howard was going to have to fight two male jaguars. She just hoped she could get there in time to help him out, and that she could actually aid him.

She had barely reached the edge of the rain forest when she saw Howard's clothes lying in a pile near a group of bracken. She didn't see anyone else's clothes, and she suspected the other men had gone deeper into the rain forest to draw him in. But Howard had been smart to shift right away. Just as she was going to do. She stripped off her clothes in the dappled forest light and tucked her things with Howard's, finding his phone and quickly looking at it. Cracked glass, not working. *Damn it.* She hoped no one would find their clothes and steal them. She hid them better in the leaf litter.

Then she shifted and went on the prowl. The men would be using the jaguar maneuver of stalking and ambushing to deal with Howard, two on one. If Howard got himself killed, she would never forgive herself. She wished she could smell Howard so she could join him. Then again, the men couldn't smell him or her either, and that was a good thing.

That made Val feel a little better, since the others had the advantage of being two males against a male and a female. Not that she couldn't be just as aggressive as a male if her life and her partner's depended on it.

Partner. When had she begun to think of Howard in that way? She sure hoped he was all right.

She moved slowly into the shadowy rain forest, the howler monkeys warning she was in the area. *Damn it!* She hadn't thought of that. Then again, maybe they were warning about one of the other jaguars.

She moved cautiously, knowing Howard could be injured, or worse, and she could be facing two male jaguars. She continued to analyze the scents in the rain forest—the sweet fragrance of orchids and the testosterone-laced smell of the male jaguars.

The men had split forces, one going to the south, the other to the north. That worked for her. Fighting one instead of two was a much better deal. She just hoped that's all she'd have to fight.

She had walked for maybe a mile, climbing trees, looking for any signs of Howard, not wanting to be ambushed herself. And then she heard the sound of cats fighting off in the distance. It had to be Howard and one of the jaguars. She raced to join them, to help Howard kill the cat, hoping the other wouldn't circle around and attack too. She was certain if he heard them fighting, he would.

Val finally reached the two male cats, and she was thrilled to see Howard was alive, battling the other jaguar, and hadn't been injured badly yet. Still, as viciously as both of them were attacking, they had both drawn blood.

She waited for a chance to tackle the cat without taking Howard's attention from the fight. She was also watching for any sign of the second cat. If he pounced on her while she was unaware, she'd be dead. Then he and the other cat would finish Howard off.

The way the men were turned, and as much as they were concentrating on each other, they hadn't seen her in the shadows of the trees, courtesy of her rosettes. She remained perfectly still. Not even her tail was twitching.

She thought if she could catch the other jaguar's eye, Howard would take the advantage. But what if he thought the guy's partner in crime was coming?

She chuffed, letting Howard know she was here for him, and the other jaguar turned to see her. She leaped from where she was crouched, but Howard bit into the jaguar's skull. Male jaguars might fight with males in the wild to establish territory over females, but they normally didn't kill each other.

The shifter agents had to take their own kind down in a situation like this. They didn't have any other choice.

The jaguar collapsed on the ground and shifted into his human form.

Howard rubbed against Val, licking her face, and she

did the same with him, rubbing against him, licking him, so grateful he was alive. He wore fresh claw wounds and bite marks, but he was alive.

They didn't shift, not wanting to expose themselves as humans while they searched for the other jaguar. After running through the rain forest for another hour, they heard a group of tourists talking.

Val leaped into a strangler fig tree, and Howard joined her. Sitting on the sturdy branch, vines trailing along the massive trunk and down to the ground, they observed the five men and four women and their tour guide approach along a narrow path. The guide was pointing out some of the plants, lizards, frogs, and birds.

Several of the people were taking cell phone pictures. A man and a woman had telephoto lenses on their cameras, and Val worried they might spy the two jaguars if they began searching the trees.

She was sitting stiffly next to Howard. He was relaxed, watching the tour group. He turned and nuzzled her, as if to say she had nothing to worry about. The tour group wasn't here to shoot the jaguars, except with cameras, if they spied them.

"Ohmigod, right over there," a woman said, pointing her zoom lens in the direction of the cats.

The guy with the telephoto lens swung around and angled his camera in the direction she indicated.

"Jaguars. A pair. As big as they are, they're most likely a mating pair, a male and female," the guide said. "Not a mother and juvenile cub. We rarely see them as they usually hunt during dusk and dawn. Sometimes they're drinking water or fishing at a river, but it's very rare for us to catch sight of them." He sounded as excited about seeing them as everyone else was.

"The one…has blood on him. The bigger one," the one woman said, looking through her longer lens.

"He must have found some prey. They'll pull it up into a tree to protect it from other predators, but I only see the female up there with him," the guide said.

Val prayed the tour group didn't come across the dead, chewed-up guy. There hadn't been any sign of a trail through the rain forest where they'd run to catch up to him, so she hoped that meant the group wouldn't go in that direction. She knew Howard had wanted to catch the other jaguar, but they would also need to dispose of the dead guy before they left the rain forest.

Everyone in the tour group was trying to get shots of them, which didn't really matter. As long as they didn't see them shift or find their clothes and things, a jaguar photo op wouldn't hurt. But the delay could.

The group stayed there forever, watching them, taking pictures, the guide not ushering them along. Seeing the jaguars was too rare an experience. Even he was taking pictures, probably to show future clients what customers might see on the tour. She didn't think the group would ever leave unless she and Howard did first. She nudged him, and he nodded. Then she leaped down from the tree, and he joined her.

"Oh, oh, oh!"

"Ohmigod!"

"Watch out!"

"Don't run. Just stay put. They're leaving," the tour guide said. "They don't go after people."

These did.

"Did you see how they communicated with each other?" a man asked.

Another said, "You can see who wears the pants in the family."

Everyone laughed.

Val smiled as she and Howard raced off in the direction the other jaguar had gone. She figured they'd made the tourists' whole trip. That was a perk of being a jaguar in the rain forest if they ran across tourists. As long as they were *only* tourists.

They finally found the path the other jaguar had taken, which led to the dead man's clothes. They weren't a whole lot farther from their own. But there was no sign of the other guy's clothes, or of him. She suspected he had run off, letting his partner take the heat.

Val nudged Howard, and the two of them made their way back to where the dead man was. Howard took hold of one of his arms, and she took hold of the other. Then they dragged the naked, dead man to the river, swam into it, and let go of him. They watched his body float away. She didn't see any crocs, but that didn't mean they weren't lurking, hidden in the thick vegetation along the shoreline.

It began to rain, and she and Howard headed back to where their clothes were. They quickly shifted, but before she could begin to dress, he pulled her into his arms and kissed her hard on the mouth. "God, Val, I'm so sorry about your parents."

"They're alive. A Guardian brother-and-sister team took them to a hospital."

Looking shocked, Howard stared down at her. "Before I took him out, the guy I killed said they were dead."

"The bastards thought they'd killed them, but they hadn't. Thank God." Val hugged Howard tight. "Thanks for worrying about them."

"I was anxious about how you were faring if you had learned the truth—which now I know wasn't the truth."

He kissed her and then, conscious of the other jaguar still on the loose, they separated and began to get dressed.

"They needed blood. They'd both been shot, but the Guardians said they'll make it. I was so worried about you when you didn't answer your phone."

"I couldn't answer your calls right away while I was trying to navigate over walls and fences, and then the bastard broke my phone. I made him pay for breaking it, but I'll need to get another."

Val eyed Howard's new injuries as she pulled her shirt on. "We need to take care of your fresh wounds."

"I'll live." He tugged his shirt on.

"Don't act all tough on me." She sat down on the leafy forest floor to pull on her boots. "You know as well as I do how bad getting an infection in a jungle environment can be. What would Jillian do without you if you ended up coming down with a fever and couldn't do your job?"

Smiling, he crouched down and finished tying his own boots.

"Jillian was right about you not liking to have your wounds taken care of. I'm so glad you're okay. Chewed up and clawed a bit, but alive."

"I was glad to see you too, safe and sound." He helped her off the ground. "I hated that we couldn't get in touch with each other. But then I was running through the rain forest as a cat and couldn't have called you anyway."

"When I found you fighting with the one cat, I hoped my chuffing at you wouldn't unduly distract you."

They began moving through the rain forest again.

"It did, believe me, but it distracted the perp much more. All I could think of was that you were alive, but I needed to take the guy out as quickly as I could. He looked shocked as hell that you had come to my aid. I was damn glad for it."

"I'm glad you took him down." Val pulled her phone out of her pocket. "I'm calling my boss." As soon as she got ahold of him, she let him know what had happened. He was still trying to get more agents on the case. Then she called Jillian to update her and make sure she and Rowdy were all right. Jillian said they hadn't heard a peep from anyone. "We're on our way back there soon," Val told her.

"Good," Jillian said. "I'd rather we were together as a unified force, now that we know more rogues have banded together."

"Me too. Keep you posted." Val and Jillian signed off.

Val and Howard shared what they'd each been through as they walked back to the spot where the dead man's clothes were.

"Maybe we can find something on the guy's phone that will help us. In any event, you can use his phone until you can get another," Val said.

They searched the dead man's clothes for any ID. "This is Harington," she said, looking at his driver's license.

"Which means Eric was the one who got away."

"You killed Bixby this morning. He was Eric's

brother. I warned Jillian that Eric might be coming to learn what happened to him. And Benny's involved with this whole mess. Emmie, the woman in the house, gave me two more drug houses to check out."

"Did you already call that in? Martin or Sylvan needs to send another team. For now, we need to return to the resort to make sure Jillian and Rowdy remain safe."

"I thought we could handle it on our own. But you're right. We need to take care of this other matter with Benny first." Val got on her phone and told Sylvan about the "new" phone Howard had to use for the time being so he and Martin would have a number to call if they needed to reach him and would know who was trying to get ahold of them if he called them. Then she told Sylvan about the two other drug houses.

"I've already been working with Martin to see if we can get another team there right away. Our intel on this was bad. We'll let you know as soon as we have the names of the agents who'll be joining you."

"Thanks, sir."

"Just keep me informed on your end."

"Will do."

She and Howard avoided going near where he had killed the other man, in case the police were looking into the murder by now.

"We need to eat. We haven't had breakfast, and it's way past lunchtime," Val said.

Howard took hold of her hand. "All right. We'll head to one of the hole-in-the-wall fast-food cafés to grab some tacos or whatever you're feeling like somewhere along the way. We can get the food to go that way, no long waiting time in a restaurant."

"Sounds good, and I need to pack up my parents' things at the rental house. We also need to return their rental car to the airport when we can."

"We'll take care of those errands. Hopefully, we won't run into any trouble at their rental house."

She had considered that some of Eric's men might be there lying in wait. She sure hoped not.

Chapter 10

"By the way, I'm supposed to be your backup, not the other way around," Howard said, thankful Val hadn't run into the other jaguar on her own while she was trying to track down him and Eric's men.

"And Jillian is yours. Since she wasn't there for you, I had to be. Lucky me." Val smiled. "Besides, how would it sound if an Enforcer stayed behind, cowering in her boots?"

He chuckled. "Like that would ever happen. I was glad you showed up and helped me to deal with the other cat. I worried about you, and I had no way of telling you I was okay."

"Same with me. When you didn't answer, I was worried they'd taken you down."

"And you still came after me?" Not that Howard was surprised, but she could have put herself in a world of danger.

"Yeah. I don't know. I'm kind of getting used to having you around."

"Good. I feel the same way about you."

"I thought the two of them would have stuck together and ambushed you. If you and I had been able to, we would have."

"I agree. They ran for a long time, then finally split up. I was sure they would want to prepare an ambush, but if they tried to come around and search for my scent, they wouldn't have found it. They'd have to have a visual sighting, and I guess I seemed like an invisible predator stalking them both instead. Maybe I spooked them because of it. They split up, giving them a fifty-fifty chance for one of them to get out of there alive, and I followed the one trail. Still, I kept believing the other guy would come to help out his partner."

"No, he just tucked tail and ran."

"I wish we could have caught up to him, but we will. What will your parents do now?"

Val sighed. "Convalesce. Maybe work desk duty for a while. Maybe they'll consider retiring now. Though they'd been outnumbered, so it wasn't really their fault. Any of us could have ended up in their situation."

"Right."

The rain stopped when they finally reached her parents' rental house, and Val went in first, gun readied. She knew the layout of the place, which was why Howard was fine with her going first. She signaled the all clear for the living room and the kitchen, and he saw broken glass on the wooden floor in the living room. They headed down the hall to the other rooms.

He smelled the blood and saw a couple of trails all the way down the hall. He imagined the horror Val must have felt when she'd first seen the blood and hadn't known her parents were still alive.

The bathroom was clear. The next bedroom was clear. They went to the last room, another bedroom. This one was clearly where her parents had been tied up. Blood had pooled on the floor and was smeared on the wall. Discarded duct tape and cut plastic ties littered the floor. He felt terrible for Val and her parents, knowing how much it must have killed her to see them so badly injured. In that instant, he regretted not staying with her. His only thought had been taking out the bastards who had fled the house, certain he could get them to tell him where her parents were.

He couldn't have been gladder that they had survived.

Val grew pale when she looked at the blood.

He rubbed her back, and that brought Val back to the present. "I'll check the garage to see if the rental car's there while you're packing their things, and then I'll help you finish up."

"Yeah, all right." She began pulling her mother's clothes out of a bureau drawer.

He walked back down the hall and finally reached the door to the garage on the other side of the small house. He opened it, dagger in hand, but the garage was completely empty, smelling of the same men he'd been chasing, Benny, and the ones he'd killed. The garage window on the left side was broken, glass all over the concrete floor.

Howard returned to the bedroom and grabbed an empty field pack and began packing her dad's things in it. "Rental car's gone. We need to ask your parents if they left it somewhere else."

Val finished packing her mother's bag and pulled a first aid kit out of one of the bureau drawers. She got antiseptic and bandages out of the kit. "I'll text my mother." She pulled out her phone and began texting her mom.

Howard finished packing her dad's bag, and Val shook her head. "No response. She could be in surgery, heavily medicated, or asleep." She took hold of Howard's shirt. "I'll take care of your wounds before we leave."

He wasn't going to say it wasn't necessary at this point because he figured she'd just insist. He pulled off his wet shirt.

She ran her hand over the skin below some of the bite and claw marks, her fingers soft and warm against his skin. He wanted to kiss her again. "I'll be right back." She went into the bathroom and returned with a wet cloth. Then she got to work, wiping off the blood and debris. She added antiseptic to the wounds, then wiped her hands off on the towel. Then she carefully covered each of the wounds with a bandage.

"All right, hopefully nothing will become infected." She threw the rest of the supplies in the first aid kit and grabbed her mother's bag. "We can worry about their car later. We need to go."

"Thanks for doctoring me up." He felt the same urgency to rejoin Jillian and Rowdy, but while they were here, they needed to do whatever needed to be done. He wrung out his shirt in the bathroom, then pulled it back on.

They carried the bags out to Val's rental car.

Howard glanced at the house and vehicles across the street. The car tires were all flat. "Looks like they had some tire trouble recently. Some of your handiwork?"

"Yeah. In case they returned and planned to take off." Val studied the house, and he was sure she was thinking the same thing he was.

"What if the other man has returned to the house, thinking we won't catch him there?" she asked.

"I was thinking the same thing." They placed the bags in Val's rental car and locked it. "No sense in leaving business unfinished if the other guy returned there. What happened to the blue pickup and the woman?"

"I told her to run. I don't think she was involved, and she gave my dad blood."

They moved through the fruit trees to the front door. They didn't bother knocking, just shoved the door open, waiting safely on either side of the doorjamb. Then Val went in first, gun readied. Howard was right behind her, his knife out. They quickly checked the rest of the house, but no one was there.

"While we're here, why don't we look for anything important related to these guys and their business?" Howard wanted to get on the road, but if they could make a further break in the case, they had to make the effort.

Howard yanked the covers off the bed in the main bedroom and flipped the mattress over, frowning at the bulging fabric.

He cut through the fabric, and money spilled out.

Val stared at it for a moment, as surprised as he was, and then she said, "I'll see if I can find a bag." She opened the closet and pulled out one of the larger roller suitcases. Then they began filling it.

Once they finished in there, they found loose floorboards under a throw rug in the spare bedroom. When Howard removed the boards, they found forty-two paper-wrapped bricks of heroin, money-counting machines, debt lists, and digital scales. They'd hit the mother lode.

Howard called Martin. "Hey, this is Howard. We've got a new case we're working on, if Sylvan hasn't told you."

"Eric and his cohorts and their little drug empire."

"Yeah, well, we found money, drugs, and more. We

can send the money home with the Guardian agents who are flying out Val's parents. Drugs too? To destroy the drugs, we'd need an oven with about a 2200-degree temperature. I'd thought of sneaking into a mortuary and burning the drugs up in one of their ovens, but they only get to about 1700 degrees. I'd hate for the Guardians to be caught up in this if the local police check over the plane."

"Turn it over to the Guardians, money and drugs. They'll get it on the plane, no questions asked. I'll let them know to pick it up from you."

"Okay, sir." Howard nodded to Val as she motioned with another roller bag.

She began filling it up.

"Good job," Martin said.

"Thanks, sir. Out here."

After searching the two bedrooms, kitchen, living room, bathroom, and garage, they didn't find anything more useful. They checked the vehicles and found a couple of guns and three knives in one of the cars' trunks. "My parents'," Val said.

Howard had smelled their scent on the weapons, so he'd assumed they were her parents'. "Good. At least we've secured them and will return them when we can."

"You can use one of the guns while we're here."

"All right. Let's get out of here and grab something to eat on the way."

They returned to Val's rental car, shoving the suitcases in the trunk, and she got in to drive. But then she got a text from her mom. "Why don't you drive, and I'll answer this."

"Okay."

They switched places, and she said, "Mom says they parked the rental car in the garage. She heard the car's engine and the men talking in the garage. Then the car was driven off."

Howard drove off for their cabin resort. "How is she feeling?"

"Much better. Tomorrow, they'll be flying home in one of our jets that has medical transport equipment."

"Okay, good. How did Eric and the rest of his gang know who they were?"

"I didn't ask. They were in too bad of shape when I saw them. I'll ask now that Mom seems to be doing better." Val texted her mother back. She paused, then said, "Oh wow. Mom said they'd done the beach touristy stuff so it looked like they were really tourists. They did everything by the book, winged it when they were trying to look the part, but Eric recognized her." Again, Val didn't say anything as she texted back and waited for a return text.

"Okay, so she went to a grocery store to pick up some things for them to eat while Dad stayed at the rental house to keep an eye on Eric's place. Mom saw Eric but acted as though she didn't know him or that he lived across the street from the rental house. He didn't say anything and must have been pretending not to know her or that she was a new neighbor. She returned to the rental house, and Eric returned to his place. A short while later, others joined Eric at his house.

"It wasn't long before some of them made their way secretly around the back of the rental house and broke a window, and then the others barged in through the garage window."

"Had she tried to take him down before?" They

normally never assigned an undercover agent to go after someone they'd failed to eliminate before.

"No. That was the thing. She didn't know what he even looked like before she got the case. But Eric said he remembered her from when she'd gone after a friend of his. She hadn't seen Eric because he'd run. He'd seen her when she'd identified herself as an Enforcer agent to the perp before Eric had taken off."

"Okay, so that could have happened to any of us."

Val got a call and she answered it. "Thanks, Sylvan. I'll let Howard know." She ended the call. "Well, Jillian's mate is flying in tonight. Vaughn apparently thinks you aren't protecting her well enough."

Howard shook his head. "I'm not surprised. Jillian and Vaughn have been texting each other constantly since we got this mission. He's been worried about her the whole time she's been with me. Not because of me," Howard quickly said. "He just thinks no one can protect her like he can. SEAL wolf, you know. Not that she hasn't felt the same way about him."

"We wouldn't be that way."

"You mean if we were mated?" Howard was surprised Val would be thinking in those terms.

Val laughed. "As *partners*."

"They're partners and newly mated. And yeah, we would be the same way. You've already told me you were anxious about my well-being when I took off after the men, despite you being sick with worry about your parents."

She smiled.

"See?"

"Yeah, all right. I tried to get ahold of you several

times. But some of it was to tell you that my folks were barely alive so you didn't need to kill yourself trying to track down the perps on your own to learn where my parents were."

"I'm glad to know you worried about me."

"Of course I did. We're on the same team. Side." She was quiet for a moment, looking out the window.

He watched the road for any sign of a fast-food place along the way. They weren't like American franchises, which were few and far between in Belize. In fact, he'd traveled extensively all over the country and only found one. But the service and food were good in the Belizean eateries.

She turned to face him. "I have a…proposition to make. Strictly professional. You and Jillian can toss a coin to figure out which one will stay with me. Rowdy can stay with one of the teams. That way, everyone has backup until we put Benny and his cohorts down."

"A coin toss, eh?" Howard was certain she knew no one was going to do a coin toss to determine who stayed with her. Vaughn and his mate would stick together. The civilian was here of his own accord. Which left just Howard, and he was certain Val wanted him to stay with her, but she didn't want to openly suggest it.

"Yeah, so neither of you will feel left out or obligated," Val said.

"Professionally speaking, we'd just be doing our job." Not that he felt that way about Val in the least.

"Good. That's the way it needs to be."

Because she'd lost her partner before? He suspected that was the case. "Hey, that looks like a place where we could grab a bite to eat."

"Looks good to me. Lots of vehicles and foot traffic there."

They pulled into the parking area, and both went to the window to order. "How about garnaches as an appetizer?" Howard asked. "I've been addicted to them ever since I've come down to Belize."

"I've never tried them before."

"Fried corn tortillas topped with cheese, beans, shredded cabbage, and other goodies. I'm going to have tacos, and you?"

"The salbute. Corn tortillas with lettuce, avocado, pulled chicken, and tomato. It's the staple in Belize, and they sure are good."

Howard bought the food and a couple of bottled waters. Then they ate in the car. Howard finished his before Val did, so he drove to the resort while Val finished her salbute.

"Now I'm ready for more action. I needed to eat," she said.

"Me too. Here I thought we were going to share breakfast at my place."

"Depending on what's going on, maybe we can still have the ribs for dinner. I was looking forward to them. I haven't had grilled pork ribs in forever."

"Sounds good to me. How are you doing, Val? I mean about your parents."

"Better, knowing they're going to pull through okay."

"We'll make the ones responsible pay."

"We will. Thanks for getting some of them."

"I only regret I didn't get Eric. How about your injuries?"

"I'm feeling much better, thanks. What about yours?"

He smiled. "Same. We're a pair, aren't we?"

She chuckled.

It began raining again. Howard turned the windshield wipers to their fastest speed, but the rain was coming down so hard that it quickly obscured his view. Thunder crashed overhead. Streaks of white lightning flashed through the dark-gray clouds. The roads were wet and slippery, and it was hard making out the centerline in the road. Luckily, there wasn't much traffic. His rain jacket had been sitting in the vehicle the whole time. So much for using it in the rain.

"We sure made some tourist group happy," Val said.

Howard smiled. "Those make for some special times when we can do that. So you wear the pants in the family."

She laughed. "That was cute."

"I was like you, figuring they wouldn't leave until we did."

"Can you blame them?"

"No, not at all."

Val got a text and responded before saying, "Mom must be feeling a lot better. She wants to know what happened with regard to taking care of these bastards."

"Good. I'm glad to hear it. What about your dad?"

"He's starting to recover. Which means he's grouchy."

Howard smiled. He knew the feeling.

She reached over and patted his thigh. "Good to know you're just like him."

"Not just like him. I have no problem letting my partner take charge of a situation we're in. Whoever's got the best plan of action works for me."

"Hmm, I recall telling you that you had to stay on the other side of the resort so you didn't tip Benny off."

"Right. But that wasn't the best plan of action."

She smiled. "Uh-huh." Val texted someone and then told Howard she was letting Jillian know they would be there in another hour. And she told her mom Howard had taken down three of the men already.

Jillian called right after that, and Val put her phone on speaker.

"We have a problem. Izzie Summerfield, Benny's girlfriend, came to our cabin, and she's hysterical," Jillian said.

They heard a woman sobbing in the background.

"She says she thinks Benny gave her some kind of mind-altering drug because she was seeing things."

"He gave her that purple heroin?" Howard growled.

"Worse. Well, I mean, that could kill her, sure. But he turned into a jaguar in front of her."

"Tell me he didn't bite her." Howard was afraid that's what had happened, if Benny's past history was any indication. Couldn't the ass get a jaguar girlfriend? Then again, if he did have a jaguar girlfriend and he got her involved in his drug dealings, she'd be in the same trouble as him.

"He bit Izzie about half an hour ago. Then he shifted again, told her he was going to get groceries, and if she needed anything, just go see the neighbors. Afterward, he got in his car and drove off!" Jillian sounded just as exasperated as when Vaughn had tried to take her brother down. "She came over in a panic because she was having hallucinations and was feeling 'weirded out.' Those were her words."

"Don't tell us he did it on purpose so we'd be stuck dealing with her," Val said.

"I'm sure of it," Jillian said. "It ties some of us up with having to take care of her."

"Then he's not returning to the resort," Val said, which was just what Howard believed.

"I suspect that's the case. I've never handled a situation like this before. I wasn't sure how to deal with it. Rowdy's talking to her in the living room. He's good with people. He's calmed her down. At the same time, this gives him an inkling of how it feels to be newly turned. Though at least he knows about us, unlike the woman."

"Hell, so she's a jaguar shifter now. A Guardian family will have to take her in to teach her the ropes, and hopefully she'll adjust just fine," Howard said.

"Jillian, I'll call it in. Just help Rowdy keep the woman calm in the meantime. Hopefully, we'll get a Guardian agent out here right away. Maybe even the brother and sister who were taking care of my parents. We found money and drugs at Eric's house, and we need to transfer that to them as well. They can fly it all out on a private plane."

"Okay, praying that will be the case. Let us know what you learn."

"Will do." Val called the brother-and-sister team after that and reached Matt. "Hey, it's Val, and if you and Katrina are still in the area and can handle another mission, we have a new problem."

"Oh? Martin said we needed to take some stuff off your hands. Is it something else?"

"The guy we're after just turned his new girlfriend. He murdered his wife after he'd turned her. Now the new one is with the rest of our team, under our protection. We're still trying to destroy this drug ring, which includes the guy who did this. We're at the Tropical Rain Forest Resort, cabin three. It's about two hours from where you were. Can you handle it, or do I need to call my boss to have him ask your branch for another Guardian team?"

"We'll do it. Your parents are doing fine, and we're free to pick up the newly turned jaguar and take her with us. We'll go with her and your parents on the return flight to Houston. In the meantime, our boss will assign her a family to take her in."

"Thanks so much, Matt. We're still on our way back to the resort. It'll take us another hour to get there."

"Who's watching the woman for now?"

"Jillian, but she's a wolf shifter, and we have a human homicide detective there. Long story, but he knows about our kind. He's trying to reassure Izzie that everything will be all right. We'll see you in a couple of hours then."

"Uh, yeah. I'll let Katrina know we've got another assignment. We'll need to know who the woman's family is and will have to deal with that too."

"That's true."

Something Howard hadn't thought of. All he'd focused on was getting Izzie away from here and safely home without anyone else knowing what she was. He was relieved the Guardian agents would take care of her. They were trained more for that kind of work than the JAG, USF, or Enforcers were. He could hear it now though. The last time they'd had an issue like this come up, Martin had made them take training to deal with it. After this, Howard could see them having to learn how to cope better with newly turned shifters. He guessed it wouldn't hurt. He just hoped, since they were stuck taking care of this here, Martin wouldn't assign *them* the task of teaching others how to deal with it. That's usually what he did. Those with firsthand knowledge in the field became the instructors for the other agents.

Val called Jillian and told her the news. She was relieved Howard and Val would be there soon to help out until the Guardian agents arrived. She sounded harried, and Howard wished they were already there. Because of the rain and road conditions, he had to watch his speed, though his foot was pressing down a little more on the gas pedal than it should have been. Especially when he was carrying all this dope and money in the car.

After that, Val updated her boss, who was glad the Guardians would take care of Izzie but insistent that Val and Howard take Benny down before he bit anyone else. As *if* that hadn't been their intention in the first place.

When Val finished the call, she turned to Howard. "Okay, so we're going to have a full house, if Matt and his sister have to stay the night with us. And of course, so will the newly turned woman."

"I hate to say this, but because we're all jaguars and better equipped to handle her, all of us need to stay at your cabin. We can take turns watching her through the night until Matt and Katrina can take her with them in the morning. I feel for them though. They could have a challenge, just taking her anywhere."

"Maybe they can sedate her. Their vacation sure has been ruined."

"I'm sure they'll get plenty of comp time to make up for it."

Val smiled at Howard. "That takes care of the coin toss then."

Howard chuckled. She couldn't seriously have thought it would come to that.

He considered what Benny had done to the poor woman. If he wasn't already on Howard's terminal list, that would have done it. What if she was really close to her family, and now this happened? She probably couldn't see them for years, until she could get her shifting under control. It would be a nightmare for her for a long time. Here the woman thought she had been drugged.

So what was the next step? Tell her that almost all of them were shifters and not to worry? He imagined that would go over big.

"If he wasn't a dead man before, he would be now," Val said, thinking along the same lines as Howard. "From his action today, I'd say he was planning all along to do the same thing as before. Maybe he'd keep doing it until he found a woman who could handle being turned."

"He won't have that long to live. At least I hope he won't. At least in Emmie's case, she was already one of us."

"Right. Since Benny took off, assuming he's not going to return after saddling us with another crisis, Eric probably won't be showing up here looking for his brother either," Val said.

"Unless he wants to learn what happened to him. If Eric was close to him, he might. I hope he does. He'll have a whole bunch of shifters to deal with. We'll see if the Guardians have ever dealt with a case like this. It's not something I've ever had to take care of." Howard had thought they could take turns sleeping while someone watched Izzie.

Surprising both him and Val, Jillian called again. They were nearly to the resort, and he figured her call only meant they had more trouble. He just hoped Benny and his cohorts hadn't showed up.

Val put the call on speaker. "Yeah, Jillian? What's wrong now?"

"She tore off her clothes and shifted. I told Rowdy to run. To get out of the cabin. He ran for the door and opened it, and she nearly *bit* him! I interceded and she bit me instead, but she ran off."

"Ah, hell. Okay, at least she didn't turn Rowdy," Howard said. "We're nearly there. What about you? Are you going to be okay?" Howard worried Jillian might have been injured badly.

"I'm okay. She didn't bite hard. She…she's gone. I'm so sorry. When Rowdy opened the door to leave, she ran after him. He thought she was going to attack him, but then he realized she was trying to leave, and he attempted to shut the door so she wouldn't escape. That's when she tried to bite him. Then she ran off into the rain forest. Rowdy's cleaning my bite. She bit me in the arm, and I might need some stitches until the shifter genetics help me to heal."

"The Guardians are physician assistants. They can sew you up. Just stay there with Rowdy. We'll search for her as soon as we arrive," Howard said. "Benny is so dead."

"I agree. Rowdy's upset Izzie bit me. He wants to be a wolf, but no one has offered to turn him. He doesn't want to be a jaguar, so he was glad she hadn't bitten him," Jillian said.

"Well, hell, he's going to be what he's going to be. And that's being a jaguar or a wolf, depending on the trouble he gets himself into. If one of the branch chiefs agree, we'll take him into one of the jaguar branches—hopefully with the USF where we have both wolves and jaguars working together—and train him to be one of our agents. But it'll be a while before he can work in the field."

"All right. I'll tell him. He's pacing around here, furious with Benny for turning Izzie."

"He should be. Just don't let him run off after her. I wouldn't put it past him to think he has to chase her down and try to talk her into returning to the cabin. He doesn't know his way around, and he might run into Benny or any of the other jaguars."

"I agree."

"Okay, we're pulling up now." Howard parked, and he and Val hurried to leave the car so they could look for the woman. He just hoped Izzie didn't get herself into any further trouble in the meantime.

Chapter 11

VAL CALLED HER BOSS TO LET HIM KNOW THE NEW development and to get a feeling for whether they could employ Rowdy right away.

"What the hell do you mean you want to employ a human civilian just because he knows about wolf shifters?" Sylvan paused, then said, "Wait, he knows about us too? I want this under control now. If the woman and the homicide detective have to be eliminated, so be it. Sometimes it has to be done, or we end up having a domino effect. Hell."

"Yes, sir." Val knew if a newly turned shifter couldn't get themselves under control, they would have to be eliminated. But she wanted to get Izzie in hand and at least give her the opportunity to prove she could control her shifter half. Val also wanted to give Rowdy the chance to work with the jaguar policing force officially before he was turned or eliminated for knowing about them.

"What the hell was the human homicide detective doing there when the woman shifted?" Sylvan asked.

Val explained that she'd had to stop him from alerting Benny he was after him, reminding Sylvan he already knew about wolf shifters, but also now about them.

"So it's his own damn fault he was there investigating the situation when it wasn't in his jurisdiction."

"Can we give him a job?"

"What? Hell no."

"In the office? Until someone turns him and he gets his shifting under control?"

"He investigates murders. He doesn't commit them."

"Right, well, maybe Martin can hire him. Rowdy has extensive training. He would be a great asset," she said as she and Howard walked into the cabin to see Rowdy pacing across the living room floor.

"Maybe he could, but not at my branch. And try not to call me about anybody else getting turned on your assignment, will you?"

"I don't plan to. But if it happens, you'll be the first to know." Val ended the call.

"That went over well, I imagine," Howard said.

"Yeah. One too many humans turned for his liking, with another wanting to be turned."

Rowdy was so aggravated he'd nearly been bitten by a newly turned jaguar that Val didn't want to tell him her boss wasn't about to let him work for her branch.

"If I'd had a tranquilizer gun, I could have knocked Izzie out before any of this happened." Jillian ran her hands through her hair, looking distraught that everything had gone so wrong and she hadn't been able to stop any of it, but it wasn't her fault.

Val had already disappeared down the hall.

"No problem. We'll find her and bring her back." Though Howard didn't know how they'd be able to convince Izzie to return with them. He might have to resort to knocking her out with a swipe of his paw. But if he hit her too hard, he could kill her.

Val had stripped out of her clothes in his bedroom and loped out of there wearing her jaguar coat.

Howard eyed a scowling Rowdy. "You wanted to be one of us."

"Yeah. As a wolf. I didn't even know you guys existed." Rowdy was glowering at him, looking totally pissed off, as if it was Howard's fault for what had nearly happened.

"Hey, you play with shifters, you have to take the consequences. Besides, you'll have your enhanced senses if you are turned. In the meantime, while we're gone, don't get bitten or cause Jillian any trouble, or I'll return and kill you myself."

"I'm one of the good guys, remember?" Rowdy's brows were raised.

"If you're turned or shift and you bite or otherwise injure Jillian, you'll be considered a rogue and you'll be on my terminal list. Just a warning. You'd deal with me next. You don't want to have to, believe me."

"Hell, give me a little credit, won't you? I haven't been bitten. But if I had, as I understand it, I still have control over the beast. Right?" Rowdy looked a little worried that he'd need to be locked up for his own good and everybody else's.

"The shifter doesn't take control, but we never know when a perfectly good human who is turned will react in a negative way." Howard began stripping out of his clothes and said to Jillian, "Shoot him if Izzie returns, bites him, and he shifts and even growls at you."

Jillian smiled at Howard, and he suspected she'd reassure Rowdy after Howard left that she had no intention of doing anything of the sort. She was sweeter than he was.

When Howard gave her a growly look that said he

was serious, she nodded as if in agreement. Then he finished stripping off his clothes and shifted.

Val headed outside, and Howard raced after her. At least it had stopped raining.

They both immediately smelled the woman's scent and began searching for her. He hoped she hadn't run into any trouble while she was racing through the rain forest. She wouldn't know the ins and outs of being a jaguar yet. She could instinctively leap into trees, love to swim, be able to leap long distances, and roar like they did. But other abilities—fishing as a jaguar, hunting, fighting—would take some practice, skill, and training. She most likely wouldn't realize what scents belonged to what. Some, she would know. Like the fragrance of orchids or the smell of the rain, the woodsy scent. But animals? Distinguishing between shifters' scents? Even recognizing a jaguar's pattern to distinguish him from another jaguar? Those were things she would have to learn.

As a new shifter, she was being bombarded by sounds. He imagined it would be like turning the volume up on a hearing aid, and all the sounds would be confusing.

Her sense of sight would experience overload. Every little thing that moved—water drops dripping off a leaf, a leaf stirring, a mosquito buzzing overhead— would capture her attention. It could be frustrating and overwhelming.

Shifters born with the ability and growing up with their enhanced senses would learn about them gradually, taking baby steps at a time.

He hoped she didn't go for a swim and encounter a crocodile. Just as Rowdy kept thinking with his human brain, he suspected Izzie would for some time too, until she got used to being in her jaguar form. If she saw a crocodile, instead of tackling it, she'd probably swim for her life, attempting to get away from it. She probably wouldn't even know that crocs were on the jaguars' menu.

They'd been searching for Izzie for about an hour when the sun began to set. *Hell*. Not that they couldn't still see, smell, or hear her, but he could imagine how she'd feel when the dark descended. Any place a person wasn't familiar with could be even scarier at night.

Where the hell did she think she was going? As far away from them as she could go, most likely.

He suspected she wouldn't return to their resort for anything. And he wondered again how they were going to convince her to come with them when they found her without getting into a big fight.

Then he heard voices. Just great. Probably a tour group returning to the resort, or a group going out to see what they could of nocturnal creatures. He hoped the woman would stay clear of the humans and not think to seek their help. He had no idea what her frame of mind was, except for being panicked. She didn't seem to have any real destination in mind, and she was moving deeper into the rain forest.

He kept Val in sight because they were still wearing hunter's spray, and he didn't want to lose her in the rain forest where he couldn't track her down. He lost the woman's scent and then picked it up again. The group of humans—if they weren't shifters in human form—were getting closer. No one was screaming that they'd spotted a jaguar, no excited talk, so he suspected Izzie had moved out of their path already. But Val and he were headed straight for the people. He didn't want to veer off from the woman's trail and have to track it down later. He didn't want to sit in a tree for a time either, as they'd had to do earlier.

He thought Val was going to veer off the scent trail, but she continued on the same path, headed straight for the humans. He smiled at her tenacity.

But they had a mission.

Then he saw five men and two women on the narrow trail, all of them flashing flashlights at something on a tree. Val dashed off the path and around several trees, but she made the move before he could follow her lead, and one of the people saw him.

"A jaguar!"

Howard was gone in a flash, disappearing into the foliage, the dark shadows consuming him.

"Did anyone capture a shot of the jaguar?" a woman asked.

"No, she was too fast."

Howard wanted to correct the man who had called him a she. He soon caught up to Val, but she was circling the area, having lost the woman's scent. He smelled a river nearby, but they still would have smelled the woman's scent as she made her way to the river.

Val began to look up at the trees right in this area, and he did the same. That's when they both saw Izzie at the same time, sitting on a limb and watching them. She was more of a reddish-brown color than a golden and tan like he and Val. She was smaller than Val too.

Howard shifted, hoping he wasn't making a mistake. Or that the tour group would run into them here. Or that his nudity would offend the woman. Jaguars were used to shifting in front of other shifters, so nudity was something that didn't bother them.

"I'm Howard…and this is my partner, Val. We're with a shifter policing force." Not that Val was truly his partner, but he didn't need to get into the details right now. "We're after Benny because he turned his human wife, and when she had trouble dealing with shifting, he murdered her. We're going to take him down as soon as we can. In the meantime, we want you to come back with us." He paused. "A brother and sister who just saved Val's parents' lives—after they were shot by one of Benny's partners in the drug-dealing business— will take you to Houston. A family there will give you a home and teach you how to live as one of us."

The woman was just staring at him, taking in his nudity, and she didn't make a move from the branch. He thought about moving to his next plan of action— knock her out—but that would mean dragging her back to the resort. They'd come so far that he didn't think carrying her through the rain forest as a naked human was a viable option.

Val shifted and he figured she'd want to talk to the woman, so he shifted back to his jaguar self and lay down among the ferns to make it seem as though he was completely at ease. Which he wasn't. He didn't want to leave Jillian and Rowdy alone for longer than necessary in the event Eric or his men showed up. And he wanted to get Izzie back to the resort before they ran into any more night tour groups out here.

Val said, "You can't live out here, Izzie. You can't go back to the States, not without our help. And you can't return to your home. We need to learn more about you and your family. You can't leave here without going with Matt and Katrina Sorenson. They have a chartered private plane that will take my injured parents home, and they'll take you too. Not home, of course. You can't be around humans for the time being. You'll need to learn how to cope with all the changes. We can discuss all this civilly back at the cabin."

The woman's long tail twitched, her whiskers moving, sampling the air and scents and sounds, but she didn't make a move to get down. Howard really didn't blame her. This had to be a lot for her to take in all at once.

"You have to know you don't really have a choice. We'll do everything we can to make the transition the easiest for you." Then Val shifted, as if she was done talking. Now she was leaving it up to the woman to decide what she wanted to do. Val suddenly shifted again and added, "Oh, and don't ever bite a human. That can put you on a terminal list. I wouldn't recommend you bite another shifter either, not unless you want to see how fast one of us can take you down. We can't allow you to deal with this on your own. Either you come with us, or you don't. It's completely your choice. If you don't, we won't have any choice but to just eliminate you." Then Val shifted again.

He was surprised Val had become the "bad cop" in the situation. Then again, maybe she felt she needed to with the woman since she wasn't agreeing to the plan. They waited for a few minutes, but the way Val was eyeing the woman, he suspected she wasn't going to wait much longer.

She shifted and turned to Howard. "Okay, so I'll knock her out of the tree and you finish her off, or do you want to get in the tree and do the honors?"

He didn't think Val was serious.

"Forget it. I'll do both. Just pin her down after I knock her out of the tree, if I don't kill her right off." Val shifted and leaped into the tree.

Howard liked a woman of action. He readied himself to pounce if Izzie tried to leap from the tree and run any farther.

Izzie only hesitated a couple of seconds before she jumped to the ground and stayed put, eyeing Howard as if she was worried he might attack her. Val jumped down and shifted. "We're not running after you any more tonight. Stay with us, or we terminate you. I'll lead, and Howard will follow behind you. If you stray, your life is ended. Got it?" Then Val shifted again, then led the way, and just like she'd told her to do, Izzie followed her.

Howard was smiling at Val as he followed the woman. He hadn't been sure Izzie would go along with Val's command. The problem was that each person was different, with unique life experiences, values, judgments, and personality traits, so what might work with one wouldn't with another.

He was glad they were finally headed back to the resort. Val would make one damn good partner, and that got him thinking about returning to the Enforcer branch to partner up with her or convincing her to work with him in the USF. He wasn't sure if she'd like to work with a mixed shifter group, but he didn't know if he could go back to his old job either. He liked the diversification and the group he was partnered with now.

They heard the noisy tour group heading the same way they were. Val circled around the group, which meant they had to take a longer path when they didn't need anything slowing them down. He suspected that as long as it had taken them to find Izzie, the Sorenson team would be at the cabin by now.

Then they heard something running toward them in the woods. A wild pig, with dangerous tusks. And Val was standing still, looking ready to pounce on the beast.

Howard shifted and said, "Get up in the tree." He shifted back into his jaguar form.

Jillian leaped onto a branch first, and then Izzie joined her. Howard had been afraid the woman would run off, fearing for her life. He jumped into the tree with them and waited for the animal to pass. Then Howard and the others jumped down, and they began to run back to the resort.

It took them another half hour to finally reach the cabin, and he couldn't have been happier to get Izzie inside.

He wasn't surprised to see two more vehicles parked there. The Guardian twins must have arrived. Howard suspected the other vehicle belonged to Vaughn, and he figured Jillian's mate wouldn't be happy to learn about all that had gone on while she was here without her mate.

Howard chuffed at the door. Jillian answered it. "Good. You all made it back safely. Since it's not raining, Vaughn and Matt are going to barbecue ribs, if you want to help them, Howard."

He chuffed and headed to the bedroom to shift and dress. Val followed him into his bedroom, shifted, closed the door, and smiled at him. She grabbed her bra off the bed.

Howard shifted and pulled her into his arms before she could dress and gave her a warm embrace. If he was to remain completely professional, he wouldn't have done that. But he already knew he wanted more with her. And she seemed to feel the same way. At least she didn't pull away, leaning into his touch instead. Every time they got close, he smelled her pheromones and his own, saying they wanted each other.

"Hmm," she purred. "Ending a mission like this is really nice."

"Only with you."

"Not with any of your other partners, eh?"

He smiled. "Not even close."

"I never thought this mission could be such an adventure. At least we managed to bring Izzie here without having to kill anyone," she said.

"I hadn't expected you to be the bad cop in the situation." He kissed her cheek.

"It depends on the situation. I thought you were afraid to scare her into compliance, and when your talk didn't convince her to go with us, I figured it was my turn. Sweet and solicitous wasn't working."

He chuckled. "I don't think of myself in that way."

"Either you were trying to impress me, or you were worried about scaring her."

"If I was trying to impress you, did I succeed?"

"Always."

He chuckled. "I've never dealt with a situation like this. I wasn't sure how to handle it. You did great. I don't think I've ever seen an agent convince someone who didn't want to comply to go along with the program that fast. We could have been out there a lot longer if you hadn't stepped in and taken charge."

"I think she'd finally figured out she didn't have any

other choice, and she wasn't sure if I was serious about eliminating her. I hadn't wanted to intimidate her like that. She's dealing with enough right now, but it had to be done." Val let out her breath and ran her hands over Howard's chest. "I feel bad about Rowdy too."

"Why? By hanging around our kind, he's bound to get himself into trouble."

"He didn't know this was a shifter case when he started it. But it's not about that. It's about my boss not giving him a job."

Howard shouldn't have jumped to conclusions. "I'll check with Martin and see if he's more agreeable about hiring him. Or maybe the Guardian branch would take him in."

Val pressed a kiss against his mouth, and he began to kiss her, slowly at first, his body reacting to hers, soft and warm against his. Then she parted her lips for him, and he kissed her deeply. "Hmm, about the room arrangement… I'll share my bed with you, if you don't snore."

"You've got a deal." He kissed her again, damn glad she was letting him in, and though he planned to discuss this case further with Vaughn and the others, he couldn't help thinking about being alone with Val tonight.

Reluctantly, they separated and began to dress.

Once they left the bedroom, Howard told Val, "I'll help with the cooking. Just holler if Izzie gives you any trouble."

"I'm sure we can handle it." Val patted him on the chest and then went to join the ladies.

Howard glanced at them. "Rowdy, you coming?" Then they went out back to join Vaughn and Matt.

Chapter 12

Izzie was lying on the living room floor, still in her jaguar coat. Val wondered how long it would take before she could shift back. Matt and Howard had gone out to the car and removed the suitcases of drugs and money, and now the bags were sitting on the living room floor.

The list of debts was sitting on the coffee table. When Val picked it up and read over the list of names, Jillian said, "Vaughn took photographs of the two-page list. We'll send the original list with the money and drugs with the Guardian agents."

"Sounds good. I hope Vaughn wasn't too upset with the turn of events," Val said, not sure how a growly SEAL wolf would react. She imagined how Howard would be if she'd been his partner and that had happened to her. He'd be a growly jaguar.

Jillian brought in margaritas for everyone and sat down with a glass of her own. "Nah. Vaughn was just eager to see me. He only wanted to give Howard a hard time because he constantly does the same to him. Mainly because he's never seen a pair of wolf shifters working together. It was rather a rocky beginning for us, since Vaughn was trying to catch my brother for a suspected hit on a friend of both of theirs, but my brother hadn't done it. No way would Vaughn treat me as though I couldn't do a job on my own just because he or Howard wasn't here to watch my back.

YOU HAD ME AT JAGUAR

"I have to admit I wasn't expecting Benny's girlfriend"—Izzie growled, and Jillian rephrased the comment—"for Izzie to suddenly shift. Or for her to try to bite Rowdy. I should have realized it could come to that, but everyone was acting…civilly up to that point. I've never had to deal with anything like this before."

Val agreed. "I don't blame you. Though I probably would have turned into a jaguar and fought her. About the sleeping arrangements… The jaguars will be at my cabin next door. You and Vaughn will be staying here. Right?" Val asked Jillian, in case they had other plans.

"Yeah. If you don't need us for guard detail for Izzie. Or we can go over when we're needed. Otherwise, we'll keep a lookout for any signs Benny or his cohorts are returning to the area. We're thinking Rowdy should stay with us. Safety in numbers."

"Sounds good to me," Val said.

"Vaughn and I are going over to Benny's cabin to search for anything you might have missed when you were over there earlier. And we'll pack up Izzie's things. She'll need them when she leaves here tomorrow." Jillian set her margarita glass on the table.

Katrina sipped from her margarita. She was quiet, just taking everything in.

Howard returned to the living room with his phone in hand. "Good news for our United Shifter Force team and for Rowdy. Martin said he'd take him on."

Rowdy came in with a margarita in hand. "I don't know what I'm really getting myself into, but I've always taken risks."

"Food's nearly done." Howard rejoined the other guys.

"Well, that's good news," Val said to Rowdy. She was

glad Martin had given him a job. It might take him a while before he actually was able to work in the field, but at least he was going to be part of their police force. "You'll need to give your work notice, and we can help with that." She corrected herself. "The USF agents can, I mean."

Izzie suddenly shifted, screamed, and grabbed a pillow off the couch to cover herself.

Jillian got Izzie's clothes from where she had tossed them in the living room. "You can change in one of the bedrooms, but one of us needs to be with you at all times."

"So I'm a prisoner. I hook up with a murdering drug dealer, he bites me, I turn into a...a jaguar shifter, and now I'm treated like I'm a criminal who has to be watched every second."

"No, but you're dangerous to our kind if you run off again and shift in front of humans. Believe me, if you are seen shifting and they catch you, you'd be locked up and studied. Alternately, a hunter could kill you, and then you'd be a dead human. Or someone might stick you in a zoo enclosure. Then what would you do?" Jillian walked Izzie back to her room. "With us, you stand a chance of having a normal life again. Different, but you won't be an oddity to be examined and tested by humankind. Not to mention what would happen to the rest of us." They disappeared into the bedroom.

"What are you going to do about your job?" Rowdy asked Val.

"What do you mean? I'll finish the mission, but I'll have a whole lot more help than I bargained for. Of course, the mission has expanded from what I was initially tasked to complete. If taking out the drug dealers had been part of the deal, more of us would have been sent to handle it in the first place."

Rowdy gave her a small smile. "I mean about you and Howard. The two of you are interested in each other. So will you be joining the USF, or will he be switching back to working for the Enforcers?"

Howard came into the cabin carrying a platter of the ribs. "Hot off the grill."

"Sure are," Val said, not meaning the ribs at all. To Rowdy, she said, "Wolves mate for life. Cats don't always. Not that we don't hope to find that special one and stay with him or her permanently, but it's not always a sure deal. With the wolves, they have to be sure."

"Then there's hope for me yet."

"Hope for you? You're not talking about me, are you?" Val asked, wondering if she'd given him the wrong impression.

"He wouldn't dare be talking about you," Howard said, smirking, but there was a hint of darkness to his tone, and she was certain he was already becoming a little territorial.

Which was all right with her. She felt the same way about him. When Izzie had been eyeing him in much too fascinated a way while he was naked in the rain forest, Val had felt the urge to knock her out of the tree. Val had already claimed the cat for her own. Even if they hadn't made anything official. Yet.

Everyone headed to the kitchen table.

"We need to know about your family," Matt said to Izzie.

"You'll need to let them know you're fine but that you have a job in a new place, and you're staying with a family near your workplace," Katrina said.

"I don't have any family that I have anything to do with," Izzie said. "My dad died a few years back. Drunken driving. My mom has a new boyfriend I can't stomach. I don't have any siblings. My dad had a sister and brother, but neither of them had anything to do with the family. No surviving grandparents." She shrugged. "I have a lot of online friends but no one who will know that I've changed. Do I get a choice as to who I stay with?"

"Not at first. If the family and you don't get along, we can find another family, but it can take a while. You'll have to adjust to them, just as much as they will have to adjust to you," Matt said.

Val knew if they had real trouble with someone who was newly turned, they could incarcerate them in the facility they had for rogue jaguars that hadn't done anything bad enough to be on the Enforcers' list. She was sure the family wouldn't mention that to Izzie unless they had a lot of trouble with her.

"Do you want to know about me in case I get turned?" Rowdy asked, dishing up some more ribs. "These are great, by the way." He leaned back in his chair. "I have an ex-wife, no kids, lots of friends at work, a brother who has family out in California, but I never see him, and my mother remarried after my dad died, and he doesn't like me. I keep asking him if he's got skeletons in the closet, but he's not amused. Which makes me think he does."

Everyone laughed. Val liked Rowdy.

"You can't have any boyfriends or girlfriends who aren't shifters," Val warned, just in case they hadn't considered that. "We can't risk having you turn someone else."

"Like that's a big consideration right now." Izzie let out her breath and said to Rowdy, "Listen, about trying to bite you, Rowdy, I'm sorry. I…I just wasn't thinking straight. And, Jillian, I'm so sorry I bit you. All I could think of was running away from all this. I didn't know Rowdy was human. Or that I could turn him like Benny turned me. I don't know if I would have done anything differently if I'd known. I was just desperate to leave this nightmare behind.

"But truly, I'm sorry. And I don't intend to do anything like that again. I'm just feeling really overwhelmed. I appreciate that all of you are here to help me. As for Benny? I wish I could help you take the bastard down, but I'd probably just get in your way. So I wish you the best of luck in finding him quickly and killing him before he hurts anyone else."

"Thanks," Rowdy said. "But no need to apologize to me. I understood why you did what you did."

"Izzie, I know you're afraid of your future. All of us have our own fears to deal with. In this line of work, fear can't get the best of you, and I wonder what everyone fears the most. Val?" Howard asked.

"Losing control of a situation. Any situation." Val liked to be on top of things all the time. It didn't always happen, and she hated when things were out of her control. Like when she'd learned her parents were in trouble. "What about you?" she asked Howard.

"Losing control on a case," Howard said. "Here you think you've got it locked down, the perp in hand, and then voilà, he slips through your fingers and you're back at the beginning again."

"Same with me," Rowdy said. "If I can't find the

perp, there's a good chance he, or she, will kill again. We can't trust that the person won't have another 'episode' and do it again."

"For me, it's everything—the shifting, where I'm going, the unknown. It's all really scary," Izzie said.

Jillian leaned back in her chair. "I'd have to say losing my mate or any of my family members."

"Like when Vaughn thought your brother was an attempted murderer and went after him," Howard said.

"Yeah, like that. Which is why I shot Vaughn. Good thing he had a forgiving nature."

Vaughn smiled. "I just had to get even. For me, I'd say it's losing my mate or pack mates."

"Hunters," Matt said, "when I'm out running, worrying someone might want to take me home as a trophy."

Jillian agreed. "I totally avoid being anywhere near farms when I'm a wolf for the same reason."

"And bear traps. That's something I fear," Katrina said.

"Oh yeah, those too. They're bad for even hikers or their dogs. No regulation, nothing," Val said.

"Yeah, one of the wolves in Silver Town broke his leg because of one of those traps," Jillian said.

Rowdy was taking it all in. So was Izzie.

"Not saving the life of someone we're trying to save," Katrina said.

"That goes for me too," Matt said. "I've had nightmares about the ones we've lost. Worst thing ever."

"Thanks for saving my parents," Val said again. She couldn't tell them enough how grateful she was.

Katrina reached out and squeezed Val's hand. "Your dad was ready to get out of his hospital bed and wipe out the men you're going after." She smiled.

"He would too, given half the chance." Val loved her parents.

After they finished eating dinner and cleaned up, Matt escorted Rowdy to his cabin so he could pack and move in with Vaughn and Jillian. Val was glad they were sticking together, just in case they had any further trouble. The jaguars all said good night to the wolves, but then Val asked Vaughn and Jillian, "Wait. Are you going to pack Izzie's things tonight so they can leave early in the morning?"

"That's the plan," Jillian said.

"Howard and I will go with you," Val said, even though she hadn't discussed it with Howard yet. She figured he'd want to search the place too.

"Yeah, safety in numbers, and more eyes might find something Val and I missed the last time." Howard asked Katrina, "Will you and Izzie be all right without Matt or us being over there right away?"

"Yeah," Katrina said. "We just need to figure out the sleeping arrangements."

"The farthest bedroom in the cabin is mine. Howard will be staying with me," Val said, trying to sound perfectly professional about it, not like she was claiming him for her own.

Howard tried to remain impassive when she made the announcement, as if he'd known all along she would make the declaration, but his mouth curved upward just slightly.

"The spare bedroom is yours."

"I'll share the bed with Katrina," Izzie said. "If I

leave the bed or shift in the middle of the night, you'll wake all right, won't you?"

"Yes, light sleeper. Matt won't mind sleeping on the couch," Katrina said.

"Okay, we'll join you in a little bit," Howard said.

Katrina and Izzie said good night to everyone and headed over to Val's cabin.

Jillian locked up the cabin, and then the four of them walked through the trees to reach Benny's cabin. "Do you think Izzie will behave tonight if she shifts? Or even if she doesn't?" Jillian asked.

"I believe so," Howard said. "She sounded like she really spoke from the heart at dinner. I don't think she was making any of it up."

"I agree. I believe it was just a knee-jerk reaction before. She shifted and wanted to run away from it, from us, from what her life had become," Val said.

"I believe so too. But I think she'll have some rough times ahead of her, and she could very well lash out at the people who are trying to help her see this through." Vaughn wrapped his arm over Jillian's shoulder.

Val was smelling rain forest scents, trying to pick up any scents that would indicate Benny or Eric had come through here more recently. She didn't smell any sign of anyone. Though she'd wanted to give the place a last check, she'd been more concerned Vaughn and Jillian were without more backup in case some of the rogue jaguars showed up.

When they reached the cabin, it was unlocked. Probably Izzie had left it that way when she ran over to Howard and Jillian's cabin in her panicked state. The lights were on in the kitchen and living area.

Everyone had their guns out now, and Vaughn proceeded into the cabin while Howard brought up the rear. Val headed off to the back bedrooms, Jillian right behind her.

Val was listening, watching, smelling for any indication anyone was in here. She didn't sense anyone. "All clear," she called out as she and Jillian checked each of the bedrooms, turning on the lights and checking the closets and under the beds.

"Bathroom's clear," Howard said.

"We're in the bedroom they used," Jillian said.

"We'll work on the rest of the cabin," Howard said, and they heard him opening cabinet doors in the kitchen.

Val found a black suitcase that smelled mostly of Izzie, and Jillian began pulling the woman's clothes out of the closet. Val emptied the drawers of Izzie's neatly folded clothes and set them on the bed. She and Jillian went through them, looking for anything that would be helpful to their investigation.

Jillian found Izzie's purse and emptied it out on the bed. "Her passport, driver's license, and a credit card. And her cell phone. I'll pack her things away if you want to check her phone. You might find something important on it. Maybe a clue of where Benny could be."

"We have a lead on two drug houses we can check out tomorrow too. Though after what we found in Eric's house, I'm not sure we'd find much more at the other places. I'd say we should do it at night, but we need to get some sleep, and I'd rather the Sorensons take Izzie to the plane to transport them out of here first."

"What about Rowdy? He's still a civilian. He

shouldn't be here on this mission. Not until he is really one of us, credentials-wise," Jillian said.

Val was reading through text messages but hadn't found anything important yet. "I suspect he'll be stubborn about leaving this to us to handle. He's angry Benny killed his ex-girlfriend. He wants to see Benny taken down. I think once that happens—"

"He'll want to see the rest of the rogue shifters terminated." Jillian folded the clothes from the closet and tucked them into the bag.

"You're probably right. I'd still rather he be with us than trying to do this on his own, which I'm sure he'd try to do."

Jillian finished packing the bag and searched through the wastepaper basket. "No condoms. I didn't see any birth control pills in her stuff either."

Val looked up from the phone. "Unprotected sex? Maybe?"

"Unless she gets shots for it."

"Or she has birth control pills in the bathroom. I can't imagine she'd carry them on her person." Val went back to searching through text messages.

Jillian looked through the rest of the drawers. "It's something we need to ask her about. I don't know what would happen if a human were pregnant and then was turned. Would the baby also be turned? Or would it be human? With wolves, it rarely happens, but there are known instances. I don't know about jaguars."

"Same with jaguars mixing it up with humans. It's rare to have a child from the union. I sure hope she's not pregnant."

"None of Benny's clothes are here. I'll check the bathroom." Jillian rolled the bag into the hall, and Val followed her. Leaving the bag outside, Jillian walked into the bathroom. "Finding anything on her phone?"

Val waited in the hall while she checked messages. "Just older texts. She's known Benny for a while. Just like she'd told us. The love affair between them wasn't brand new."

Jillian was searching the wastepaper basket. "No condoms. We can smell they had sex on the sheets, so it's not like they weren't doing it." She emptied the contents of the drawers. "Makeup, toothbrush, hairbrush, deodorant. No birth control pills. Or any other kind of medicine." Jillian glanced at Val. "Was she seeing him when he was married to Lucy? She wouldn't have been able to smell the other woman's scent on him at the time."

"Yeah, she was. We need to learn if she had known about Lucy. Not that it would make a big difference now, but it would say something about her character."

"What if she had something to do with Lucy's death? Maybe she didn't have anything to do with actually killing her, or you would have noticed her scent in their home when you went to investigate it. But what if Izzie was instrumental in inciting him to get rid of her?"

Val frowned. "Okay, now that would have dire consequences for her. I hope she wasn't involved."

"She might be the reason he wanted to get rid of his wife so he could be with her instead. Not that Izzie actually had anything to do with it. Which makes me wonder if she knew his wife had been murdered. Had he told her he'd left his wife and wanted to be with her instead?"

"Okay, all great points. We'll have to question her about it." Val frowned at one of the messages. "She says she wishes she could get pregnant and thinks she actually might be pregnant."

"Great. But she doesn't know for sure? No mention of a pregnancy test?"

"No mention, so I'm not sure why she thinks she might be. Maybe she's late."

They joined the men in the living room and finished searching all the sofa and seat cushions.

"Did you find anything?" Jillian asked.

"Nothing," Howard said, "except that he cleaned out most everything. None of his clothes are in the bedroom, I take it."

"No," Jillian said. "And nothing of his in the bathroom either. No razor, toothbrush, or deodorant. It was all her stuff. And no used condoms."

Howard and Vaughn smiled at her.

"That's been Jillian's main focus," Val said. "Though she has a good point. What if Izzie had been pregnant before he turned her? In her texts, she did tell someone she wished she could get pregnant. And that she might be."

"Ah, hell, I hope not. It would just cause more concern," Vaughn said. "Both for the family taking her in and for Izzie herself."

"Unless she is pregnant and she loves the child, and this changes her outlook on what she's become," Val said. "She'll want to nurture and raise her shifter child as a shifter mom."

"Or it could have the opposite effect," Howard said. "Not to be a wet blanket, but if she's having trouble coping, it could put her over the edge if she learns she's having a baby by a murdering jaguar who will soon meet his demise, and now she has to cope with a baby with shifter genes and also with her own shifter changes."

"If the baby is a shifter. It's rare that a human and

shifter are able to create a baby, but there have been some instances that I know of, and in those cases, the child wasn't a shifter," Vaughn said. "But the offspring had an affinity for wolves. Uh, because the shifting parent was a wolf. I'm not sure how it would be for jaguars."

"I don't know of any case where a jaguar has impregnated a human," Howard said.

Val shrugged. "I know of a couple of cases."

Jillian sighed. "That is saying that Izzie is pregnant. We had another discovery. Tell them what you found on the phone."

Val explained how Izzie had been having an affair with Benny while he'd been married.

Both Vaughn's and Howard's brows rose.

"That's not good," Howard said.

Val agreed. "It may be that she knew nothing about Lucy. We just need to learn the truth."

"If we're done here, I'll grab her bag and we can return to our cabins." Howard stalked down the hall to secure Izzie's bag, and they turned out the lights, then headed out of the cabin. "I guess we don't need to check her out of her cabin, if Benny was the one who made arrangements for renting it. He'll be responsible for it."

"What about us?" Val asked.

"For now, I'd say we'll make this home base. Even though Eric's crew knows where we are, we can still take them out if they try to come for us," Howard said.

"We'll let you and Val question the lady." Jillian grasped Vaughn's hand and hauled him toward the steps to the cabin. "You can tell us all about it in the morning after they've left."

Val wished she and Howard could have some privacy

too. It wasn't that they couldn't have some kitty-cat loving, but with everyone's sensitive hearing, they'd all be well aware of it. Then again, they'd probably assume that if she was declaring Howard was staying with her in her bed, they weren't planning to just sleep.

As soon as they entered her cabin, they were met by Matt armed with a gun.

"Sorry, I should have announced we were coming in. It's just us," Val said. "Is Izzie asleep?"

"She's taking a shower."

"I'll leave her bag by the bathroom door." Howard rolled it down the hall.

"Is Katrina with her?" Val asked, wishing she could trust Izzie. After seeing her text messages, she was having second thoughts.

"Yeah, sitting in the bathroom. She was going to sit outside by the window, but it was safer if we all stuck together, at least until you returned. You look as though you have something you want to talk to Izzie about."

"Yeah, some important issues." Val showed him the text messages indicating Izzie had known Benny for some time. "And she might be pregnant."

Matt's eyes widened.

Yeah, none of them could really see that as a good thing.

Chapter 13

"I JUST BROUGHT YOUR BAG OVER," HOWARD SAID FROM outside the bathroom. He heard the shower shut off. "It's by the door if you need anything from it." He thought he heard someone crying in the bathroom.

The door opened, and Katrina got the bag from him. "Thanks, we'll be right out."

"Is everything all right?"

"No. We'll talk to everyone in a moment." Katrina shut the door.

He hoped she didn't have to say Izzie was pregnant. That she was just weepy about the other changes in her life. He returned to the living room to sit with Val and Matt.

"She's crying," Howard said. "They'll be out in a moment."

They sat in awkward silence, waiting for Katrina and Izzie to join them.

"She may have to go to the facility if she had anything to do with Lucy's death and she's pregnant," Matt said quietly.

Howard wondered how the Guardians would handle it. If Izzie had had a hand in Lucy's death, would they terminate her? She had been a human at the time, and she would have been brought up on charges in the human court system. Not now that she was a shifter though. He tried not to think about it until they learned what they needed to know from her.

The bathroom door opened, and the two women joined them.

"Izzie has some news. She's pregnant, first trimester. She was worried that the baby would have been harmed by the change."

"Benny's baby?" Val asked.

Izzie nodded, her eyes red from crying. "I…I didn't want to say anything. I was afraid to even think about it. That was one of the reasons I had run. I thought I was protecting the baby."

"You knew Benny had a wife," Val said, her voice dark.

"Not at first. He slipped up once and said something about his wife liking a red wine I liked. He quickly said they were no longer married. They didn't have any kids, and he said they hadn't been together for a couple of years. He was busy with his work, trips out here to do with his job, and I believed him."

Howard wondered how much of what Izzie was telling them was the truth as far as what she knew about Benny's wife.

"I had no way of knowing he had murdered his wife. Or that he'd turned her into a jaguar. I didn't know he was one! Everything he said was lies. He said he was working for a company that had a lot of ties with Central and South America. I had no reason to believe anything he said wasn't true. Oh, and he wanted to know if I liked cats. I do. I love them. I had one when I was growing up. He said his former wife hated cats, so he wanted to make sure I loved them. I asked him what kind of cats he had, and he said he didn't have any currently. But he wanted to get one after we got married. I guess he lied about that too. He just wanted to know if I would hate being one."

"Did he know you were trying to get pregnant?" Val asked.

Izzie shook her head. "He didn't ask. Like he didn't care. I'm twenty-nine. I just wanted to have a baby with him. I thought we were going to get married. He said we would next spring. I had no reason to believe he'd lied about any of it."

"Rarely can a jaguar shifter impregnate a human," Matt said. "I don't know about other shifters. Often, they don't worry about protecting against pregnancy. We can't get STDs or give them. It's rare for a human to get pregnant by a jaguar shifter, but it does happen sometimes. I know of three cases. In those, the baby couldn't shift. But they were drawn to big cats. In two of the cases, the shifters were women, and they turned their babies so that they would be shifters too. In the other case, the shifter was a male and he ceased having anything to do with the human, not wanting to turn her and her baby. But this is different. Since Izzie was already pregnant when she was bitten, it could very well be like a case of a pregnant woman taking a drug and it affecting the baby," Matt said.

"Then the baby would be a shifter too?" Izzie asked, fighting tears.

Katrina patted her hand. "Yes, which is a good thing. The baby will only shift when you do. When you're a jaguar, even while your baby hasn't been born yet, she or he will shift into a jaguar fetus. The same thing will happen after the baby is born—when you shift, the baby will shift. You can even give birth to a baby as a human, or to a jaguar as a big cat, depending on if you have any control over your shifting. The baby won't be shifting on its own until he or she is old enough to control his actions. At least you won't have the issue of deciding whether to turn the baby or not. We'll have to discuss with the family about the issue of you having a baby. It shouldn't be a problem."

"What about having the baby?"

"We take care of our own. And just so you know, if anyone were to check your blood when you're a jaguar, you would only appear to be a genuine jaguar. When you are human, the same thing—strictly human DNA. We heal faster too. Which means you'll have an easier time giving birth and getting back on your feet."

Izzie looked relieved.

"You'll have to see a doctor when we return. He will get you started on prenatal vitamins and talk to you about what to expect. If the rest of you don't have any other questions, I think it's time for us to get some sleep. We'll have a long day ahead of us tomorrow," Katrina said.

After that, everyone headed for their bedrooms, while Matt made a bed for himself on the pullout couch. Before they all retired for the night, he said, "Izzie, if I shift, it's not because of you, but because I do sometimes in the middle of night."

"Good to know. If I have to get up in the middle of the night to go to the bathroom, and I see you as a jaguar, don't be surprised if I scream. I haven't gotten used to seeing jaguars outside of zoo enclosures yet."

"I understand."

Once Howard shut the door to Val's bedroom, he quietly asked, "Do you think she's telling the truth about not knowing that Benny was still married?" He began stripping off his clothes, boots first, then socks, and setting them beside the chair in the bedroom.

"As far as I could tell from her cell phone, she never once said in a text that she wanted him to leave his wife, and he never mentioned Lucy to her either. Either they were being careful not to leave an evidence trail, or it's like she said. He lied to her about his wife. That happened to my mother when she was dating some guy before she met my dad. I think that's why she really joined the Enforcer force."

"She wanted to go after rogue jaguars like her boyfriend?" Howard got a kick out of her mother.

Val smiled and set her shirt on the dresser. "She fell for my dad right away because he kept telling her she couldn't manage the job as a female Enforcer. That she wouldn't have the killing instinct and she would react too slowly and end up getting herself killed." Val sat on the bed and began removing her boots.

He raised his brows, surprised to hear it. "I would think his concern would have turned her off." He unzipped his pants, and she watched him. He wondered just where they were going with their relationship tonight. He hoped they would take it to the next step.

"He had the biggest crush on her. Everyone kept telling him she'd suckered him right in. Every time she was assigned a partner, Dad was all gloomy. Finally, their boss, who retired a few years ago, couldn't handle it any longer. He said for them to mate or else, and then they could be partnered up. My mom asked, 'What if I don't want to be partnered up with him?' Their boss told them if they didn't work together, he was kicking them both off the force."

Smiling, Howard shook his head and pulled off his pants, then stripped off his shirt.

"She was just giving my dad a hard time because he'd always given her one." Val pulled off her pants, then reached into a drawer and set a long, black T-shirt on top of the dresser.

"You said he always takes charge of the situation." Howard always slept naked, but he figured he'd better take it slow if Val wasn't ready for that. It was one thing to hug her naked in the woods and another thing to sleep naked together in bed. Unless she was ready for more.

"Yeah, and it works well for them. Not for me though. Not that I can't follow a partner's lead, but if I have a plan and it seems to be the best option, I'm ready to take action."

He smiled. He couldn't help it. He was hoping she meant she was ready to take action with him. In bed.

She reached back and unfastened her bra, then put it on the dresser top and pulled the T-shirt over her head and arms.

He read the message in white on the black T-shirt that stretched nicely across her perky breasts: *I didn't say I was smarter than you. I'm a redhead. It's implied.*

He smiled.

Since she wasn't sleeping naked, he pulled back the covers and didn't ditch his boxer briefs.

She smiled at him. "You don't sleep nude?"

"Yeah, I do, but since you're dressing for bed…"

She laughed and reached up under her shirt and slipped off her panties.

He smiled. "You don't sleep naked?"

"Sure. When it's hot."

"It's going to be hot." He moved around the bed, took hold of the bottom edge of her shirt and pulled it up until he drew her shirt over her head and tossed it on top of his clothes.

She gave him a wicked smile that said *Prove it to me*. And he aimed to do just that.

He removed his boxer briefs, then pulled her into his arms and began to kiss her.

She pulled her mouth away from his and caught his bottom lip with her teeth in a gentle manner. That little action shot need and pleasure straight to his groin. He groaned and tightened his hold on her, pressing her against his arousal, breathing in her pheromones and the sweet, heady fragrance of her.

She kissed him while his hands caressed her back, moving lower, cupping her buttocks, making her blood hot with craving. The kiss intensified, her tongue sweeping over his—intense, hot, and wild.

She was wild, a force to be reckoned with, determined and focused. She was tender too, and soft where it counted: her skin, her body, her touch. Then she was fierce again, driven by the same need as him. To have, to conquer, to explore a deeper relationship. It was more than sex. It was a deeper bonding between two big cats. A melding of wills and wants. A mix of respect and education. Learning what she liked. Learning what he preferred. A lesson in love.

Their heartbeats quickened, their breathing more ragged, their pheromones on fire.

He kissed her lavishly, and she broke free for a moment to look up at him, her green eyes glittering in the light of the room, darkened, aroused, a total turn-on for him.

Her hands had been sliding down his skin in loving caresses, but now they clung to him as if she couldn't stand upright without him being her anchor in the sea of sensations swamping them. He slid his hand down between them, caressing a breast, fondling a nipple, then moving lower. He moved his hand over the smooth curve of her hip, sweeping it around to the center of her, dipping a finger between her drenched curls, knowing she was ready for him.

"Yes," she whispered, the breathless quality of her voice tantalizing him, arousing him.

He savored every second, every sigh, the pressing of her body against his in a natural kitty-cat rub, her ragged breathing, the warm, wet touch of her tongue licking at his collarbone, the movement of her pelvis as he began to stroke her clit.

She was desire personified and he wanted to make her his. And not just during this mission, but forever. He wasn't sure she was ready for that. Not yet. But he was damned determined that they were right for each other in all things.

He stroked her harder, his free arm keeping her locked against him as he felt her trembling, her knees weakening, and her hands tightening on him. He kept up the pressure, stroking back and forth, then dipping a finger inside her. Plunging his finger deeper, he stroked inside her, but when he pulled out, she cried out. For a fraction of a second, he missed the cue and thought she had objected to him removing his finger from deep inside her. Instantly, she was pulling him onto the bed, spreading her legs, and letting him know she was ready for him.

He moved between her legs like a big cat on the prowl,

yet he hesitated to enter her. They were not mated. Even after having sex, they would not be considered mated unless they said so. Which meant unprotected sex could result in babies they weren't ready for.

"Covered," she said, grabbing at his hips and pulling herself toward him.

He was ready, past ready, to join her all the way.

Howard was a sexy jaguar god, Val decided. She'd never known a big cat to be this hot for her and so attuned to her needs and wants before he sated his own. His face was taut with desire as he licked a breast and then the other, sending a spark of need through her. Caught up in the heat and passion of the moment, she kissed him again, her tongue tangling with his with raw desire. She felt more alive than she had in years.

She wasn't going to plead with him to finish this, as much as she wanted to. It wasn't in her nature to beg for anything. She might have to make an exception in his case if he continued to tease her nipples like that. No. She wouldn't beseech him to get on with it, but she could command him. That was more her style.

While she was opening her mouth to tell him to finish it or else, he pressed his cock into her, slowly, and then slid nearly all the way out in the same methodical way. And repeated the motion. And again. Building the momentum, deeper, harder. His expression was rife with determination as he tilted her world on end. She couldn't believe he could bring her to climax again so soon after the last time he'd spun her for a loop. Now, she was spinning out of control again. *He* did it to her.

Him keeping up the pace and slowing down, then speeding up his thrust, deepening and nearly pulling his cock out was doing a number on her. In a deliciously wonderful way.

Howard was going full throttle, as if he knew they both needed the faster pace, her breath ragged, their hearts beating hard. He dipped his head down to kiss her, licking her lips, and plunging his tongue between them. That did it! Val shattered into millions of fragments of untold bliss.

He followed with a *holy hell* right afterward.

"Good, huh?"

He smiled down at her with a wicked expression that told her this wasn't going to happen just once. She gave him the same look, telling him she was ready for more.

"Hot enough, right?" he asked, motioning to her T-shirt, as if she'd want to dress again, when she was repositioning herself to snuggle against his hot, naked body.

"You know it." She wasn't going to tell him how he compared to other men she'd been with. The one guy who'd come close was only around a seven now. And she knew that was because there was much more between Howard and her than just the sex. A real bond, maybe because of the job they both did. Maybe because of their personalities. They just seemed to fit together, unlike any other man she'd ever gotten close to. "That better not be all of it."

He chuckled. "Just tell me when."

When ended up being about an hour later.

But in the middle of the night while snuggling against

the big cat, Val woke to hear growling. Instantly, she left the bed and shifted, glad she hadn't worn anything to bed. Not to mention that she felt totally invigorated after she and Howard had made love. She was glad he didn't treat this business between them as all about just sex. She knew it wasn't for him either, not the way they were so attuned to each other. Not the way he wanted to snuggle with her the rest of the night like a man who really wanted her in his life for now and always.

For now, though, she had to investigate who was growling in the hallway. She was used to leaving her bedroom door open, but with them making love last night, Howard had closed it. She had to shift again to open the door and came face-to-face with a prowling jaguar. *Izzie*.

Val's heart tripped. She hadn't expected her to be right at the door, not to mention that she appeared extremely agitated, as if she was ready to bite anyone close by. And that meant Val. She tried for the lighthearted approach first, to win her over, unable to communicate with Izzie as a jaguar in a way that she thought Izzie could understand. "Hey, Izzie, do you need some company?"

Izzie shook her head, turned around, and padded down the hall into the living room. Val assumed Matt was awake and watching her, but neither he nor Katrina had asked Val or Howard to pull guard duty. If Matt could sleep while a newly turned, agitated jaguar paced through the living room, Val would have to watch her. She shifted and walked down the hall to join her.

Izzie was standing at the door.

Matt was sitting on the couch in his human form, watching the two of them. Val heard movement down

the hall and turned to look. Howard was wearing his
jaguar coat, and she smiled. She hadn't meant to wake
him, but she was glad he wasn't a heavy sleeper either.

Izzie pawed at the door.

Ohmigod, had she gotten up to go to the bathroom,
shifted, and hadn't had time to pee? That was the problem with being pregnant.

Val shifted right behind her. "Do you have to go to
the bathroom?"

Izzie nodded.

"Okay, Howard and I will go with you. Not to make
sure you don't run. We know you won't do that, but just
to protect you if Benny or any of his henchmen show up."

Izzie nodded again, her tail and whiskers twitching.
Val opened the door for her and quickly shifted. She
didn't think Izzie had any notion of tearing off, but she
wasn't risking it.

She thought that only she and Howard would go with
her, but Matt did too. And before they knew it, Katrina
was joining them. Val hoped Izzie didn't believe they
were all treating her like a prisoner but rather were in a
protective mode. Like a family. Even though jaguars in
the wild didn't act like a wolf pack, the shifters often did
because they had to help each other out when it came to
problems with humans or rogue shifters.

They heard movement in the forest. Val and Katrina
stuck close to Izzie while she relieved herself, while
Howard and Matt checked out the sounds. Howard
roared at whoever it was. Then everyone headed back
to Val's cabin.

As soon as they were inside, Izzie returned to the
bedroom with Katrina. Matt curled up on the pullout

couch as a jaguar, and Howard and Val retired again to their bedroom.

"What were you roaring at?" Val asked after she and Howard had shifted.

"Wild pig. He took off running. That was a morning run I hadn't thought we'd have to go on." Howard climbed into bed.

Val joined him. "Did you hear her pacing in the hall? I think she wanted Matt to let her out, but he didn't know what she wanted."

"Good thing you did. I wouldn't have figured it out either, probably."

"Katrina must have been asleep. I think Izzie was hoping one of us would figure it out." Val snuggled against Howard, the ceiling fan whirling around, keeping them comfortably cool. "I could really learn to love you, you know?"

"Good, then I'm doing something right." He pulled her tighter into his arms and kissed the top of her head.

"Lots of somethings right." She could really get used to this on an everyday basis.

It didn't seem like any time had passed when they heard Katrina and Matt moving around between the other bedroom and bathroom. Howard was happily wrapped around Val, thinking she was a dream of a she-cat.

Val caressed Howard's chest. "I guess it's time to get up, have breakfast, and say goodbye to them. It's going to be awfully quiet around here when they're gone."

"Hell, not if I have anything to say about it." He smiled down at her, and she laughed.

"Promises you'd better keep."

"I sure will, unless we're busy dealing with the bad guys." Howard took a shower after Val did, but once the others left for the trip back to Houston, he had every intention of sharing showers with her.

After he dressed, he left the bedroom to join the others in the living room. Jillian had texted him that breakfast was ready.

"Jillian and Vaughn prepared breakfast for everyone, so we should head over there," Howard said. Val looked like one sleepy, well-satisfied cat as she gravitated toward him as if they were a couple already, and they followed the Sorensons and Izzie out of the cabin. "Good night, right?" he asked Val.

She chuckled. "I'm going to need a cat nap later."

"I'll join you for one." He wrapped his arm around her shoulders.

"That is if we're not in a new mess as soon as we get back to the other mission."

"That's the problem with a budding romance during a mission."

"I don't see it as much of a deterrent. Fighting bad guys with a partner just deepens the relationship." She smiled up at him.

He smiled back. He imagined all the things they could do together—running, swimming, and climbing as jaguars, dinners in, and dinners out. Enjoying the sunset when it wasn't raining. Even taking a group tour to be tourists for a change.

They knocked on Jillian's cabin door and announced themselves.

Jillian unlocked the door. "Good morning, everyone."

"Morning, Jillian. Vaughn." Howard and Val let everyone enter the cabin before they did.

Howard asked, "Did the three of you get enough sleep?"

"Yeah," Matt said. "Except for the one time we all went outside, Izzie slept the rest of the night. At least we can all sleep on the plane and don't have to worry about anyone shifting."

"What if I have to go to the bathroom and I shift on the plane?" Izzie asked, sounding worried.

"Go whenever you have the urge before you shift," Katrina said. "And we can have a litter box for you otherwise. No problems. We'll do everything we can to make you feel comfortable."

"Litter box." Izzie sounded disheartened.

"Yeah, but you might not have to use it. If you do, don't worry about it," Katrina said. "Just embrace your wild cat side, and it'll get better."

At least no one had to worry about Izzie taking off on them if she shifted, and they didn't have to protect her from Benny or any of his pals. She would be perfectly safe.

Howard thought she seemed glum. He didn't blame her. She had to deal with all these changes, not to mention that she was going to have a baby. That could add to the emotional stress for anyone, but being a shifter and taking care of a shifting baby too? Even more stress!

"Where's Rowdy?" Val asked.

"He ran over to check out of his cabin since he's not going to be using it any longer," Vaughn said.

Howard called Rowdy's number, but there was no answer. "No answer. I'll go check it out." Howard headed for the door.

Vaughn and Val went with him. They saw Rowdy hurrying to join them from the direction of the lodge. "Sorry. I just wanted to take care of that since Vaughn and Jillian insist I stay with them."

"Okay, we were just worried about you, given the events of yesterday," Vaughn said.

Rowdy looked pleased that he was already one of the team—so to speak.

A half hour later, after escorting the team to the private airstrip and helping to load the drug money, drugs, and equipment onto the plane, the Sorensons wished them luck in eliminating all the rogue jaguars. The team, in turn, wished the Sorensons well on their trip home. So far, Izzie was still in her human form and looked to be in pretty good spirits. The team members watched as the plane took off, making sure there weren't any problems before they headed for the next part of their mission.

They were dressed and ready for a fight, determined to finish off the rest of the rogue jaguars. "Are we ready to go?" Val asked.

"Yeah. Two cars, right?" Howard asked.

"Two cars," Vaughn agreed.

Time to take out some more bad guys.

Chapter 14

ROWDY RODE WITH VAUGHN AND JILLIAN IN HIS rental car while Howard and Val led the way. They knew Belize, while the other three had never been there before.

"Either Rowdy's afraid of me, or he figures we're courting and he's giving us some space," Howard said, hoping it was the latter reason.

"He's not afraid of you."

"Then he assumes we're courting." Howard was so ready to spend time alone with Val, realizing how much of a workaholic he normally was and how much Val had changed his feelings about that. He wanted to make time for her. For them. Uninterrupted time. Fun time.

"My dad would have to approve."

Howard glanced at her, not sure if she was joking or not. "Are you serious? I wouldn't think you'd let him decide something like that for you."

She let out a heavy sigh. "Let's just say I have all the luck when it comes to dating the wrong guys."

"But you ought to know I'm right for you." He was certain they were meant to be together. If she had any doubts, he wanted to get rid of them right away.

"Yeah, see, as soon as I begin thinking that way, I find myself in trouble."

"Such as?" Howard asked, concerned. Here he thought everything was going fine between them.

"If I bare my soul to you about past relationships, are you going to do the same with me?"

He hesitated to answer.

She laughed.

"It's not that I have anything to hide, but you'd probably find my dating life rather boring." He'd dated a lot, but usually not more than a single date with each woman. He'd always thought that being such a workaholic was what worked against him. He'd be out on a date, get bored, and start thinking about his next case.

"Okay, well, I'll be the judge of that," Val said. "I don't date bad boys. Ever."

"That's good to know. I don't date bad girls either."

She laughed, sounding tickled by his response. "One of the guys I dated was way too much like my dad—overbearing and in charge of everything. Dates, what we did with our spare time. Just everything."

"Sounds like a cat I dated. Then there was the one who had set routines for everything in her life. She wouldn't change them for anything. I like some routine in my life, but if something comes up that I want to do, the routine goes out the window."

"I do like a cup of coffee first thing before I start my day, but you know with the kind of work we're in, every day can be so different."

"Yep. Which is the way I like it. No regular nine-to-five job." Which could be a real problem with a relationship. His mate never knowing when he'd return home. Missed meals. Missed weeks. Like him being here for now.

"Same with me with loving a varied schedule like this. Okay, so then there was this one guy I went out with who didn't like me to beat him at anything. I thought maybe he just didn't like to lose, no matter who he played with. Nope. He didn't like it that *I* beat him."

"Because you're a woman."

"Exactly."

"I'm surprised he'd play *any* games with you."

"He kept trying to beat me. Table tennis was the worst. I know how to put a perfect spin on the ball so it flies across the net at a different angle every time, and he could never return it. Dad and I used to play all the time. I could never beat him, but it never stopped me from trying. The first time I won against the ex-boyfriend, he thought it was a fluke. After three more games, he practically slammed his paddle on the table in anger."

"Poor sport."

"What about you?"

"At table tennis? I always win." Howard smiled at her.

She smiled back. "I mean when you lose. What kind of a sport are you?"

"Good. I never lose."

Val laughed. "Next time we have a chance, I'm beating you."

Howard chuckled. That was part of why he really liked her. She had the drive and determination to do whatever she set her mind on doing. Just like he did. "What chance do you think I'll have at convincing your dad that I'm good for you?" He'd like her father to approve of him, so he would do anything to help that along.

"You've already blown it."

Howard paused, a little surprised. How the hell had he already screwed that up? "Oh?"

"Yeah. You were supposed to be protecting me on

the mission, but instead, you were trying to chase down Eric and the other man in the rain forest."

Howard wouldn't have done anything differently. He'd had to discover the location of her parents in case he and Val could still save their lives. "Yeah, I chased after Eric and the other guy. To learn what had become of your parents. We didn't know that the woman we had taken into custody knew they were across the street."

"Yeah, you know, afterward, I realized I should have called my boss to learn where they might be. Then again, if Eric had killed them, he could have already moved them somewhere else. As to my dad, he still would have preferred for you to stay with me to protect me. *That* was your duty."

"How do you feel about it?" That's all that really mattered to Howard. He'd thought she would have been glad he had tried to learn what had happened to her parents.

"You needed to go after the bad guys. That was a given. Dad might not see it that way, but I sure do."

Howard took a relieved breath. He hadn't realized how important it was to him for Val to see him in a good light.

"Okay, we're nearly there. The first drug house is on the left, four houses down."

"White stucco house, four vehicles out front," he said.

Sounding concerned, Val asked, "Do you recognize any of them as being the ones out in front of Eric's place?"

Howard had a sickening feeling. "That blue pickup inside the carport. Isn't that the truck Emmie drove off in to get out of here?"

"Yeah, same license plate too."

Howard reached over the console and squeezed Val's hand. "You couldn't have done anything for her but tell her to leave."

"Right. But what if she went back to him? Either because he forced her to or he convinced her to return to him?"

Howard couldn't understand why some people did the things they did. "Or she wanted to return to him on her own. If she had any sense, she would have gotten far away from him, but people fall for criminals all the time, so we can't discard that possibility." He was past ready to complete this mission. "Ready for some action?"

"Yeah. The others are right behind us. Let's do this."

As soon as Howard and Val were out of the car, Vaughn and Jillian hopped out and headed their way.

His blood pumping hard, Howard knocked at the door while everyone else took up positions that would afford them protection from the windows if anyone started shooting.

No one answered the door, but there was a lot of movement inside.

Howard smelled Benny's and Eric's scents. He also detected scents for the men he'd terminated and four more male jaguars. Damn it. And he smelled Emmie's scent. Was this a rescue mission now? Or was she just as guilty as the rest of them?

Val mouthed, *Emmie*.

Howard nodded, though her scent didn't mean she was here. She might have escaped the men and they had found Eric's truck. Or she might not have gotten away and was no longer alive. He and Val would treat it as though she was alive and being held hostage. Just in case.

Val indicated she was going around back. Vaughn went around the north side of the house with Rowdy while Jillian followed Val. Howard waited where he was until everyone was in place.

Gun out, he tried the doorknob. The door opened, making him wary of an ambush. He shoved the door aside but jumped back to keep out of anyone's line of sight. He suspected whoever was inside wouldn't shoot. Not when neighbors might call the cops. At least once the police verified Howard and his team were here looking to take care of the bad guys, they would be fine, though they'd have to explain why Rowdy was with them. Thankfully, the jaguar branches provided a big donation to the Belizean government annually, and they believed the jaguar policing force was a special, secretive unit of the FBI. The jaguar agents had helped them round up human criminals involved in the trafficking or killing of the big cats or any other human criminal activity they ran across while in Belize. In this case, the shifters still couldn't take these men into custody.

Suddenly, there was a skirmish at the back of the house, and Howard moved inside quickly. A worn couch sat in the middle of the living room, three chairs on either side of it, with dingy curtains hanging from the windows. He moved toward the kitchen and saw dirty dishes stacked in the sink and beer cans littering the kitchen counters and coffee table in the living room. The place smelled of beer, dust, spoiling food, and jaguars. He couldn't see how shifters could live in such squalor and not be bothered by the odor.

He headed for the bedrooms, the doors closed to both of them, and came to the first one. He twisted the knob and pushed the door open, moving behind the wall in case someone took a potshot at him. Then he got a glimpse of the bed and saw Emmie tied to it. She was wild-eyed and gagged, her head twisting toward the closet, warning him someone was hiding in there. Howard moved quickly into the bedroom, careful not to make any noise, though he was sure whoever was hiding in there would hear him moving toward the door.

Then he heard someone coming down the hall. Afraid he was going to have a fight on two fronts, he slammed his boot into the closet door, splintering it. A jaguar leaped out at him.

That Howard hadn't expected, thinking the guy would be armed with a gun instead. Before he could get a shot off, the jaguar pounced on him and knocked him to the floor. Having lost his gun, Howard grabbed the jaguar's neck. He was trying to hold on to the jaguar so he couldn't bite him with his deadly jaws. Furious with himself for not being better prepared, Howard struggled to keep the jaguar from killing him, but he couldn't hold him off for long. Already, his biceps were straining with the effort.

Rowdy suddenly ran into the room and fired a couple of shots at the jaguar. *Hell, Rowdy!*

Howard knew the jaguar would devour Rowdy alive as soon as he released Howard, so Rowdy could forget about getting bitten and turned. The jaguar twisted around to pounce on Rowdy, who bolted out the door and slammed it shut in the jaguar's face. Trying to get to Rowdy, the jaguar ran into the door with a thud.

Freed from the jaguar, Howard stripped out of his clothes the fastest he'd ever done, intent on saving Rowdy's life and his own. Howard gave Rowdy credit for coming to his rescue and shooting the jaguar while giving Howard the time needed to strip and shift. He just hoped no one would alert the police. What a fiasco that would be. He could see the headlines now: *Jaguars and Wolves Fighting at Drug House in Belize!*

Howard shifted and tore into the jaguar with snarls and growls of his own—deadly, dangerous, determined to kill the jaguar quickly, his teeth sinking into the jaguar's shoulder instead of his throat like he'd intended. The jaguar was wearing two nonfatal bullet holes, the areas bloodied. He lunged to tackle the new threat. The very real danger.

Howard couldn't kill the jaguar easily, not as big as he was. Or aggressive.

He dug his fishhook claws into the sides of the cat to hold on as he tried to bite him in the head. The jaguar did likewise, his claws digging into Howard's flesh, his teeth clashing with Howard's.

Howard's teeth collided so hard with the other jaguar's that he heard a crack as he broke off one of the cat's teeth.

Rowdy opened the bedroom door and was about to shoot the jaguar again. As the big cat turned to look at him, Howard slammed his paw against the jaguar's head. The jaguar collapsed on the floor and expired on the spot. The rogue quickly resumed his human form, showing he wasn't Benny or Eric.

Leaving the room, Howard prowled through the house as a jaguar, determined to learn if the others needed his help. He was grateful Rowdy had come to his aid but worried about him too, both that he might alert the police by firing his weapon and by the real risk of him being torn to shreds.

Rowdy hurried to free Emmie, but they still had to eliminate the rest of the bastards and make sure the place was safe for her. Howard shifted at the second bedroom door, threw it open, and shifted again, much preferring his jaguar form if he was going to run into another shifter wearing his jaguar coat. He couldn't believe the other guy had blindsided him like that.

Howard heard a wolf howl. He didn't see anyone in this bedroom and raced out to join the others. A high fence and thick vegetation kept any neighbors from seeing what was going on, thankfully. Jillian was lying on her side, panting, and Howard saw red. He leaped from the back patio to where a jaguar was fighting Val. It appeared Vaughn and Jillian had tried tackling the other jaguar, but the wolves were no match for the big cats. Howard tore into the jaguar Vaughn was fighting, wishing to hell he could help out Val. She was much better equipped to fight the big male cat than Vaughn was, but the male jaguar she was battling would wear her down. Vaughn immediately went to her aid while Howard fought the other male jaguar. Emmie, as a jaguar, and Rowdy came running out to help them.

With Emmie and Howard both ganging up on the bigger jaguar, Howard was able to get in some hefty bites. The guy thought he could pick on wolves, much easier prey, but now he really had to fight for his life. As soon as Howard killed him, he leaped toward the jaguar Val and Vaughn were fighting. Emmie quickly joined them.

Rowdy carried Jillian into the house. With Val, Vaughn, Emmie, and Howard all helping, they quickly killed the remaining jaguar. Howard prayed Jillian wasn't too badly injured.

Vaughn and Howard shifted and carried the man they'd just killed into the house. They would do the same with the other while Val ran to the side yard. Howard didn't like seeing her disappear from their view by herself. Then Emmie joined her, and he was glad she was helping to watch Val's back.

Howard assumed Val was shifting and getting dressed. Sure enough, when he and Rowdy headed back outside to collect the other dead man's body, Val was dressed and carrying their weapons, cell phones, and Jillian's clothes into the house with Emmie at her side. Val set the clothes and other items on the floor and left again, Emmie running beside her as her jaguar protector. He suspected Val was going for Vaughn's clothes on the other side of the house.

Once he and Rowdy had dumped the second body with the others in the spare bedroom, Howard went to help Vaughn with Jillian.

"I'll get the first aid kits," Val said to the group and hurried out the front door to their vehicle.

Rowdy went with her while Emmie returned to the bedroom to shift and dress.

Vaughn was cradling Jillian on his lap so she wouldn't have to lie on the filthy floor. He knew they needed to bandage her wounds and find out what other injuries she had before they moved her.

Val returned with the first aid kit and began to clean and bandage Jillian's wounds while Howard hurried to dress.

"The jaguar struck with his paw and knocked Jillian out. I was afraid he'd murdered her," Vaughn said. "I could have killed him, I was so angry, despite the fighting inequities between our species."

Howard hadn't seen Vaughn fight that fiercely before, but he understood why. Vaughn had to kill the rogue jaguar before he reached Jillian and finished her off.

"If you hadn't worn him out, Emmie and I would have had a rougher time of it. When I heard you howl, I knew you were in trouble." That had surprised the hell out of Howard, and he knew Vaughn would never have done so if he hadn't been losing the battle.

"I was afraid someone had killed you in the house when Rowdy left me to go to your aid," Vaughn said.

"Hell, I assumed the jaguar had attacked you when you were still human, from all the snarling I heard. I was certain it wasn't you doing any of the growling," Rowdy said. "I hadn't wanted to leave the others in a bind, but I figured if we didn't have your help out back, we weren't going to win against those two jaguars either."

"I was glad to see you, but I believed you were going to get yourself killed. I was surprised the jaguar didn't break down the door, he hit it so hard," Howard said.

"I won't lie. I was certain I was facing imminent death." Rowdy shook his head. "I know you didn't want any gunfire, but I reckoned you'd be dead if I didn't do something."

"Yeah, but that means we really need to get out of here," Val said.

Jillian groaned and looked up at everyone, her eyes half-lidded. "We won, didn't we?"

They all chuckled. "Hell yeah, honey," Vaughn said, kissing her cheek.

Once Val was finished bandaging Jillian's wounds, she and Vaughn helped Jillian to dress. Then Val turned to Vaughn. "You're next."

He had been torn up pretty badly too, but he was either too macho or too worried about Jillian to notice. Val took care of his wounds and then he dressed.

"I swear...the next time, I'm just shooting them. No more trying to take them on in my fur coat," Jillian said.

"I agree with you there," Vaughn said. "We need something to even the odds against a rogue jaguar."

———

Val wondered just how viable a united shifter force was when the wolves couldn't fight the jaguars. But she knew they all needed a force like this to deal with mixed groups of shifters or lone wolves that were creating issues. Packs took care of their own, but they didn't have a policing force that would do that kind of work.

She realized that before they got into any more fights, they needed more supplies.

"We've got a first aid kit in our car," Jillian said, still not making a move to get up.

Val hoped the wolf hadn't suffered any internal injuries. "I'll get it."

Emmie came out of the bathroom, tears trailing down her cheeks, and Val was glad to see she was alive. Bruised, beaten, but alive.

"I didn't get away," Emmie said, sobbing. "I'm so sorry they did this to you."

"I'm afraid it comes with the kind of work we have to do. We'll have to get you out of here. I wish the Sorensons could have taken you with them," Val said.

Emmie wiped away her tears. "I thought I could do it on my own. Thanks for believing in me and not turning me over to your people."

"I'll put in a good word for you, if it comes to that."
Val hurried outside to get the other first aid kit. Howard
quickly followed her.

"How are you doing?" Howard asked.

"I think I'm going to be sore tonight, just like everyone else. The shifters wanted to take us on as shifters,
maybe guessing the wolves couldn't hurt them, nor
could a female jaguar. If we'd had silencers, we could
have shot them all. I was afraid to start shooting everyone and have to face a police inquisition. It's one thing
for us to turn these guys over to the police, quite another
to start a shooting war."

"I'm surprised they didn't just run off."

"They couldn't. The fence was electrified. I was disappointed Benny and Eric weren't here," Val said.

"The other drug house then?"

Val and Howard walked back into the house.
"Maybe."

She took care of some of his wounds, and he ban-
daged up hers.

"After what happened to Jillian, we need to regroup
and head back to the resort," Howard said.

"I agree," Vaughn said.

Jillian nodded.

Howard turned to Rowdy. "Thanks, man, for saving
my ass."

He smiled, but Howard noticed he looked a bit
flushed.

"I guess you're one of us, even if you don't have
the credentials. Or the shifter powers," Howard said.
"Are...you okay, Rowdy?"

"Yeah, sure."

Everyone studied him. Val placed her hand on his forehead. "You're burning up."

"I didn't get a whole lot of sleep last night."

"What about them?" Emmie asked, motioning to the dead men in the bedroom where she'd been tied up.

"Either the police will find their rotting corpses and investigate how wolves and jaguars had killed them, or the other rogue jaguars will bury the bodies. No one's going to be able to figure it out," Howard said, glancing back at Rowdy's flushed face. "Good thing this was a team effort. Totally confuses the issue. Let's get out of here before anyone comes to investigate the shots fired."

Val had to agree with Howard there. She also thought the world of Howard for saying what he did. She knew he really liked working with Vaughn and Jillian and wondered if he'd lose them as partners if the USF believed the wolves couldn't do the job they were there for.

"Did you overhear anything that could help us take these men down?" Val asked Emmie.

"They were careful not to talk about their plans in front of me. Well, most of them, anyway. The new guys you killed? I hadn't seen them before, so I hadn't known about them."

"I'm surprised Eric didn't kill you for running off, thinking you could be a traitor," Val said.

"I think Eric planned to use me as bait to draw you out. Which was the reason I had run. I did overhear him bragging to the other men that two jaguars couldn't take them down, and they'd deal with them soon enough. He said the rest of the shifters would be easy kills. Despite his bravado, he called in reinforcements."

"So he didn't say anything else that could help us?"

"He did get into a fight with Benny. Said if it hadn't been for him turning and killing his wife, they wouldn't have had to deal with all this. Benny reminded him your parents were in Belize already, and that had nothing to do with him."

"Sounds like they're having some issues among themselves. Good," Howard said as they quickly moved to the cars, Vaughn carrying Jillian.

"How did you know to come here? Did you already go to the other drug house?" Emmie asked.

"We chose this one first. We're glad we did so we could rescue you. If we'd hit the wrong house, they might have warned Eric, and he might have realized you gave us the intel on their drug houses." Val pulled out her phone.

Normally, she would have called their situation in to her boss right away. She would have maintained a purely objective stance concerning what had gone down. She couldn't this time. For the first time since she'd had a partner, she felt the shifters working to bring the bad guys to justice had to come before the mission, and she was afraid her boss would change the game plan.

"Are you all right to drive?" Howard asked Vaughn.

She thought Vaughn would take offense, as if Howard was implying the wolf wasn't as strong as the jaguars.

"Hell yeah. Are you?" Vaughn arched a brow at him.

Howard gave him a cocky smile, and Val realized that was part of the way they joked with each other, reducing some of the tension after a high-conflict situation. At the same time, she suspected Howard really wanted to ensure Vaughn was all right to drive.

"I can drive, if anyone needs me to," Emmie said. "I wasn't injured like the rest of you."

"Not in the fight, but you look like they beat you," Val said, furious with the bastards.

"Yeah, Eric didn't like that I had run off. I told him I'd escaped you, and I was trying to leave so you wouldn't catch up to me."

"I'm so sorry, Emmie."

"We're good as far as the driving goes, Emmie," Howard said. "Thanks for the offer. Rowdy, are you okay riding with Vaughn and Jillian again?"

"Yeah. Jillian can stretch out in the back this time. I'll watch over her since Vaughn won't give up the wheel. I think he believes I can't drive as well as he can."

Howard chuckled. "Emmie, why don't you come with us then."

"Let me grab my bag. They threw it in a closet." She rushed to get it and rejoined them.

Val just hoped they wouldn't have any further trouble before they could get Emmie safely away.

Chapter 15

EVERYONE LOADED BACK INTO THE VEHICLES AND headed to the resort. The other drug house was an hour away, and Val wished they could go there now. But some of their team members needed to recuperate sufficiently. Well, all of them, truthfully. She didn't come away from the fight unscathed either.

She wanted to talk to Howard about the situation with the wolves, but not in front of Emmie. She wondered what they were going to do with her. She was worried about Rowdy too. Val finally said, "Okay, about Emmie, I've considered different options. I think the only thing we can do to keep her safe is to put her on a flight and send her to Houston for her protection until all of this gang is dispatched for good."

"I agree," Howard said.

"We can take her to the airport and see her on her way without any trouble this time. I'll call and ask my boss if he can have a Guardian agent on hand to meet her at the airport. It would probably take too long for the branch to send an agent or two here. We got lucky with the Sorensons vacationing here."

"I would be fine with that," Emmie said.

"What if Eric, Benny, or anyone else they're working with ends up flying out at the same time she does, thinking things are getting too hot for them down here?" Howard asked.

"That's a risk, but we can't leave her at the resort alone, and if we take her with us when we try to track down these men, she could get in harm's way. I don't think there's any way around it. If the Guardian branch chief sent a private plane for her, it probably would take some time." Which again made Val wish she had sent Emmie back with her parents. She'd had the notion Emmie could just disappear and start over and not have to deal with the JAG police questioning her.

"What if someone goes with her?" Howard asked.

"Like Jillian?" Val was thinking she might need more time to recuperate so it would be good for her to go home. On the other hand, she might not be able to protect Emmie that well if she had to.

"I doubt she or Vaughn would leave us to do this alone."

"You're thinking Rowdy might go with her? I don't know. He seems to stubbornly resist the idea of leaving here until he sees us take Lucy's killer down."

"He's still a civilian and doesn't have one of our badges. Maybe we can convince him that if we get into a mess with these people and the police get involved, he wouldn't be protected like we are because of our status with the JAG policing force, though the local police believe we're a special unit with the FBI."

"Rowdy saved your life," Emmie reminded Howard, as if she thought they could use his help again.

"It's worth a try. See if you can get Emmie a flight out and make arrangements for the Guardian branch to take care of her. I'll ask Rowdy if he'll serve in a bodyguard capacity for Emmie, since he is a homicide detective. The USF can even pay him for the job."

"Good idea." Val made reservations for Emmie for the first available flight out the next day at noon, then called her boss about getting a Guardian agent to meet her at the airport.

"No one else has been turned, correct?" Sylvan asked.

"No, sir." Val only told her boss they had taken down three more of the gang, not anything about everyone's injuries or how the human homicide detective had saved Howard's life. When she ended the call, she heard Howard talking to Rowdy on speakerphone since he was driving.

"We've got a damsel in distress whose body needs guarding. Yeah, it's not your job, but we could really use your experience to help out here. And to protect her on the way home. After what happened the last time she tried to get away from these guys, we don't want to take any chances. You know we're staying here until we get this done. You have our word on it."

"What if I can't get a flight out when she leaves?" Rowdy asked.

Yes! He was going for it! Val quickly spoke up. "There were still five seats left on the plane. I reserved a seat for her that has an empty one next to her. If you're agreeable, I'll add your reservation for the other seat, at our expense."

"Why didn't you mention that the first time?"

"And we can pay you a stipend for doing the job," Howard added.

Val quickly made the reservation for the other seat, in case Rowdy said yes for sure. "Okay, and the other thing is we need to learn if Rowdy is running a fever because he contracted malaria. It can be a real problem for visitors to the area who haven't taken an antimalarial drug."

"Aww, hell," Howard said. "We all take the medicine because we frequent the areas that are prone to malaria. Everyone in the agency is required to take it. Rowdy?"

"No, you're right. I didn't have time to start any medicine. But some of our officers where I work had the flu. If anything, I think that's what I might have," Rowdy said.

No one said anything for a moment. Flu was contagious. Malaria could be shared through the blood, but otherwise, you couldn't catch it.

Val looked up the incubation times for malaria. "Says here it takes seven to thirty days to incubate before symptoms appear."

"Okay, then it's probably a case of the flu," Rowdy said.

"What about you, Emmie?" Howard asked.

"I took the medicine. Eric had malaria once and nearly died from it because he ignored it for so long, despite our healing genetics. So he insisted I take the medicine," Emmie said.

Val suspected Rowdy often stuck to his guns on something he really wanted to do, so this was a big concession for him. She almost felt sorry for him, but she thought this was the best for everyone concerned. "I've got you a seat on the next flight out tomorrow at noon."

Rowdy chuckled.

"Just in case you said yes."

"You'd better take Benny down," Rowdy said.

"You've got our word on it," Howard assured him.

Val knew they weren't leaving until they did.

When they ended the call, Howard said to Val, "Thanks for not telling your boss about what actually happened out there. He would have told my boss, and Martin might have made some reassignments. He most likely would have shipped Jillian home. Maybe Vaughn too. And taken us to task for having a couple of civilians in the line of fire."

"We need to rethink how wolves can fight against jaguars if this is going to continue to be a team effort."

Howard glanced at Val as if wondering if she meant she was considering joining the USF. She had to admit she thought this group was adventurous, worked well together, and still took down the really bad guys. She liked them a lot as individuals too, and she was already feeling the kinship. Before working with them, she hadn't been sure what they did.

"I mean, for this mission. And for your future missions. Handling a wolf would be easy for one of us. The wolves need to have something more they can use against jaguars," she explained.

"We've discussed tranquilizer guns, Tasers, and silencers. The problem with tasing or tranquilizing is that would only be used if we were taking the perp in to be incarcerated," Howard said.

"Right. You couldn't knock them out and then kill them." As evil as some of the perps could be, the agents couldn't resort to the bad guys' tactics.

"Do you ever have cases where the bad guy gives himself up?" Emmie asked.

"In the USF's case, yes. We take care of those on a case-by-case basis. But if the perp is trying to kill us or others, we take them down. Period," Howard said. "This is a special case where we're helping out an Enforcer whose job was to take down a murderer. But our cases vary.

Sometimes we have to terminate the perp. Sometimes we don't. In those cases, we have used tranquilizer guns when needed. We try not to use bullets when eliminating a shifter, unless we have no other choice."

"Eric said you killed that one drug runner by breaking his neck. The guy had been bragging about getting women hooked on the heroin at some bar and thought it was pretty funny. I'm glad you took him out," Emmie said. "He kept telling me he was going to get me started on it, and Eric told him he'd better not. A couple of times, Eric was ready to kill him. He threatened to cut him and to shoot him another time. But the guy was too useful to him. Still, Eric protected me from him." Emmie took a deep breath. "What is your job exactly?" she asked Val.

"As an Enforcer, we normally only get the cases where a jaguar is scheduled for termination. They don't have any incentive to give themselves up. They always come out fighting."

"Sounds to me like the wolves need to subdue the rogue jaguars in hand-to-hand combat before the rogues can shift," Emmie said.

"Vaughn does, when he can. Jillian has shot a couple of shifters when they were shooting back. That was in the States and in a red wolf pack's territory. And that was in a case of dealing with rogue jaguars. With wolves, they hold their own. We also work closely together to fight the bad guys." Howard looked over at Val. "We sure could use another jaguar on the team though."

Val smiled at him. She was still trying to work out what she might do. She could be impetuous at times, but she wanted to make the right decision.

"I'd go for it if I were you," Emmie said. "I think Howard can use some extra help on his side. At least from where I was observing the fight."

Val chuckled. Howard would never live that down.

"You could have warned me the guy hiding in the closet was wearing his jaguar coat," Howard said, though he didn't sound serious.

"How? I was tied up and gagged. All I could do was motion with my head toward the closet to let you know he was hiding in there. It was just a good thing two of them weren't in there. I was glad Rowdy gave you enough time to strip and shift. He wasn't even working for your organization, and he risked his life to come to your rescue."

Val was surprised Emmie cared about any of this. "What do you do back home?"

"I was a secretary at an insurance company in San Antonio. I met Eric at the Clawed and Dangerous Kitty Cat Club and began dating him. He promised me a fun trip to Belize after we'd been dating for a couple of months. I had no idea how dangerous he could be. Or the kind of people he ran with and the business he was in. As bad as these guys are, they haven't been trying to sell the drug to the shifters. At least from conversations I'd overheard. One of his men mentioned it, and Eric and the others said no. Not that selling to humans is any better."

"Eric knew we'd be down on them as soon as we learned about him selling the heroin. As it is, he thought we wouldn't know he was involved. We were lucky an informant came forth and told us about him. That's why my parents were sent to handle it. But the informant said it was just Eric, no other jaguars involved. They were to take him down and then report the other dealers to the local police," Val said.

Emmie's eyes widened a little. "An informant? I hope he managed to stay alive. I was wondering, since I'm going to have to stay with you for the night, what is the situation exactly?"

"Rowdy is staying with the wolves. We have a separate cabin next door," Val said.

Emmie ran her hands through her hair. "I'll stay with them, if it's all right with you."

"We'd have more room for you." Val wondered if Emmie had a crush on the homicide detective who had risked his life to save Howard.

"I'm a jaguar. Female, sure, but if jaguars attack in the middle of the night, at least I can help the wolves until the two of you get there."

Val knew then she had made the right choice in not turning Emmie over to be investigated by their people. Emmie had done nothing but tried to help them all along.

"Sounds like a good plan," Howard said.

"I suggest tomorrow we consolidate what's left of the team and stay in one cabin," Val said to Howard.

"I concur."

They finally reached the resort, and as a group, they investigated each of the cabins. They also checked Benny's cabin again—to ensure the sneaky bastard hadn't returned, or that some of his partners in crime weren't planning a night strike from there. Not that they still couldn't arrive sometime in the middle of the night.

All the places were clear, and Jillian was looking much less pale.

"Do you have a headache still?" Val asked her.

"Yeah. Per Vaughn's orders, I'm going to bed soon. Are you sure you don't want Rowdy at your place so he can help you listen for any trouble tonight?"

"I'm staying with you to protect you as a jaguar," Emmie said. "Rowdy should stay with Howard."

Val laughed.

Rowdy agreed.

Howard shook his head, but he was being good-natured about all the ribbing. She loved that about him.

"Does everyone want a little dinner before we retire for the night?" Howard asked.

"Yeah. How are you feeling? Are you up to helping me cook up a batch of chili?" Vaughn asked.

"Sure am."

"I'll keep an eye on Jillian," Val said.

"Do you need me to help with anything?" Rowdy asked.

"You can help us," Howard said.

Rowdy joined them in the kitchen, and the three men began comparing notes on how they fished, the shifters talking about how they did it while wearing their jaguar and wolf coats. "I swing my tail in the water. Great fishing lure," Howard said.

The guys all laughed.

"I like to ice fish," Rowdy said.

"Leaping and grabbing is a great wolf fishing technique," Vaughn said.

Val wasn't surprised that the guys would be talking about fishing—even about when they were in their wilder animal forms.

"What will I do when we get to Houston?" Emmie asked.

"Guardians will take you in and provide you a safe place to stay and work. Until we feel it's safe for you to return home," Val said. "They'll provide for you until then."

"What if I don't want to leave Houston after this business is done?"

"I'm sure if the job they set you up in works out, you can stay. You could get your own place by then."

"Okay. I guess I can't let anyone know where I've gone for the time being."

"No, not until we're sure we're finished with these guys." Val was still concerned about Jillian, and she turned to her. "Are you certain you're all right? We don't need to take you in to see a doctor and run some tests, do we?"

"No, thanks, I'm fine. I was just seeing double for a while. I slept in the car on the way here and feel much better. Though I would have slept even better if Rowdy hadn't kept waking me to see if I was still okay."

Val smiled. "With head injuries, you're not supposed to sleep."

"Yeah, but fighting with a jaguar wore me out. I know the policy is to take them down in ways other than just shooting them, but I sure would rather do that."

"I don't blame you. After the way I feel tonight, I would have preferred doing that too," Val said.

When the meal was cooked, they all sat down to eat chili and have margaritas, the beginning of a good night to end the day. Following dinner, they said their good nights.

Rowdy, Howard, and Val walked through the woods to Val's cabin. They were quiet, listening for any sounds that might indicate trouble. They didn't hear anything but the usual sounds of the rain forest settling down for the night.

Once they were inside the cabin, Rowdy eyed them speculatively. "Does anyone mind me taking a shower first?"

"Go ahead," Howard said, leading Val into her bedroom.

"Night, all." Rowdy closed the door to the bathroom behind him.

"I'm serious about needing another jaguar shifter in our ranks," Howard said to Val when he shut the door to the bedroom.

"Any will do, right?"

"Okay, let me word that differently. I need a *partner*." Howard rubbed her arms with his big, capable hands.

"Because everyone else has one, and you're feeling left out?" Val didn't think that was the only reason, but she was sure he wanted someone to keep him company when they had a minute to relax during a mission.

He smiled darkly at her and moved her to the bed, the backs of her legs hitting the mattress. All at once, she felt the power of the big cat—him claiming her for the night, territorial, possessive. And needy. Oh, so needy. "Not because I feel left out." He looked at her with a predatory gleam, his hands caressing her shoulders.

She ran her hands up his chest. She loved knowing he needed her and how much he desired her.

His hands kneaded the tension from her shoulders. He sure knew how to get her motor purring. He pressed his body close to hers, his arousal already stirring against her. She sure knew how to rev up his motor too. She slid her hands around his waist and pulled him closer, wanting to feel his rampant need for her.

He nuzzled her neck, licked her skin, and before she was ready for it, he tackled her to the bed. Holding her arms stretched out, he pinned her body to the mattress. "I've been wanting to do this since the last time we made love." He kissed her forehead, her nose, her cheeks, her mouth. Then he lifted his head. "I need you. A mate. A partner. For work *and* for pleasure."

She smiled up at him. "Just keep thinking those thoughts. In the meantime, I want more of this." She pulled him down for a searing kiss that told him she was thinking along those lines too. Every time they began to kiss, their pheromones did a happy dance, mixing and colliding, telling them in no uncertain terms just how intrigued they were with each other.

Val loved making love to him. He entranced her with his kisses, his ardor, the way he didn't hold back but continued to ply her with kisses. He started working on her clothes, pulling her shirt over her head, unfastening her bra, and tossing both aside. She yanked at his shirt, and he quickly dispensed with it.

It was so much quicker to just make love after they'd shifted from cats to humans. No clothes to bar them from getting down to the finish line.

He began to massage her breasts. Her panties were wet, and she wanted them off and him stroking her there. And she wanted to feel his cock pressed against her, skin to skin, no fabric between them.

She worked her hands between them and tried to unfasten his belt. She couldn't manage, so she rubbed his cock through his cargo pants instead. His arousal jumped and he groaned.

Her action had him refocusing on their clothes, and he quickly removed his boots, his socks, and then his pants. She just lay there, her hands behind her back, watching him, smiling.

He smiled back. Then he began to remove her clothes—one boot, massaging a sock-covered foot. The second boot hit the floor, and he massaged her other foot. He was a keeper.

Then he peeled off her socks and massaged her feet again, his warm hands working the tension out of them, and she hadn't even realized her feet were so tense! He ran his hands up her pant legs, his thumbs sliding up her inner thighs in a sexy caress. When he reached her button and zipper, he slipped the button through the hole and pulled her zipper down, then pulled her pants off.

He rubbed his hand against her mound, his fingers pressing the silky panties between her folds, and she groaned aloud. God, how could he touch her like that and nearly make her come? Just the anticipation of what he would do next, the hot, hungry look in his eyes, the way he undressed her and touched her brought her to near climax faster than any man had ever done.

He continued to stroke her through her panties, then slipped them aside and inserted two fingers into her. She cried out, unable to help herself. He slowly pulled off his boxer briefs as if he were a male stripper, his cock springing free at full mast. Then he slid her panties off and tossed them to join his boxer briefs on the floor.

She licked her lips, right before he loomed over her,

then pushed his cock between her feminine folds and began to thrust.

———~w~———

Howard was serious about making Val his mate. Everything they did together made that clearer to him. It wasn't just the incredible sex, but that was part of it.

He lifted her legs over his shoulders and thrust deeper, keeping the momentum going, then slowing when he felt the end coming, trying to prolong the connection.

He slid a hand over her breast, squeezing and rubbing the taut nipple. She looked ravished and beautiful, her green eyes holding him hostage, her red hair splayed across the pillow, her hands caressing his arms. He meant to extend this, his body taut with need, but he was so nearly there. He pulled her legs off his shoulders and she seemed ready to protest, but he wanted to kiss her again before he came, to lick her nipples and to suckle, and so he did. That stopped her from feeling dissatisfied. And then he separated from her while he thrust, his hand stroking her clit again, hoping to coax another orgasm out of her.

It didn't take long before she was thrusting her pelvis at him, and he couldn't hold out any longer. He rubbed her and thrust until he came, feeling the heady satisfaction that she was his. Maybe she hadn't said as much and wasn't ready to commit all the way, but in his heart, he hoped she was. He sank down on top of her, feeling her climax gripping his cock in delicious waves. She'd come, silently this time, and she wrapped her arms around him, holding him in place. He felt at home here with her, locked in a loving embrace.

He rolled over to cradle her in his arms again. To sleep, to dream of her, to keep the feelings alive.

Besides eliminating the bad guys, the only other obstacle he was facing was how to convince Val he truly was the only one for her before they ended this mission and she decided she'd better return to work as an Enforcer—without a partner.

Chapter 16

THE NEXT MORNING, THEY ALL HAD BREAKFAST together. Emmie was coating butter on a piece of toast as if in slow motion. She appeared to be considering something, and Howard was confident he wasn't going to like it.

Emmie set her knife down on the plate. "Are you certain you can't use my help? I mean, I *am* a jaguar."

"Absolutely not. We appreciate all your help so far, but we can't chance having you hurt in the face of another battle." Howard forked up some more of his cheesy omelet. He could just imagine the trouble they'd be in with their bosses if anything bad happened to Emmie. She wasn't trained for the kind of work they did. Not to mention that he didn't want it on his conscience if one of those guys killed her. What if he was trying to protect her and left his partners in a lurch? "You're a civilian and we're meant to protect you, not put you in the line of fire."

Everyone agreed with Howard on that.

He did appreciate the offer though. He wondered why she had made it. Wanting revenge? Trying to prove to the agents she was on the good guys' side? Guilty conscience because she really had been involved in this nefarious business, and she wanted to make amends?

"You did enough by giving Val's dad a blood transfusion and sticking around to help her out until the

Guardians came to aid her," Howard said, appreciating her efforts. "And with everything you did when we were at the drug house." His cell rang, and he pulled out his phone. The call was from another of his team members in the USF. Everett Anderson.

"Demetria and I are on our way to join you. We heard you are interested in partnering with an Enforcer." Everett sounded amused.

"Who told you that?" Howard was certain Val hadn't.

"Jillian. She said it's a sure thing. She already told Martin to request her from her branch to work with us. No way can we afford to lose you from the team if you were to decide to return to the Enforcer branch to partner up with Val. You're stuck with us, and we're stuck with you."

Howard smiled, enjoying the back-and-forth hassling they gave each other. "It's not a sure thing. Val hasn't said she wants to join us, even though we have a lot more fun than the agents in the Enforcer branch. But I haven't given up changing her mind yet either."

Smiling, Val shook her head.

"Did you take care of your mission already? I was surprised Vaughn came out to join us. Well, not entirely surprised." Howard hoped they had terminated the guy.

"Yeah. It turned out to be a lot easier than we thought. The hardest part was locating Redding, but once we did, we eliminated him, and he had no backup. The opposite situation has occurred with you, so we need to regroup. We were just making sure everything was taken care of out here before we joined you."

"You have no other mission at hand?" Howard was glad they'd get reinforcements from their own team.

"Hell no, not when you're up to your ass in jaguars.

We told Martin if he had any other assignments pending to put them on hold. He said he planned to send us right out to your location anyway. How are you all faring?"

"Jillian suffered a concussion. She seems to be doing much better today. All of us had some stitches to close bite and claw wounds." Howard normally wouldn't have mentioned that, but he wanted to be honest with the Andersons so they'd know the difficulty he and his team had had. Especially when they were going to be up against those same people themselves. "We'll be glad to see you. When are you getting in?"

"We'll be at the airport this evening at five. Can you pick us up?"

"Yeah, unless we're in a fight or a chase, we'll be there."

"Okay, if we can't get ahold of you when we arrive, we'll get a rental car and drive out to your resort. Jillian said she and Vaughn want to vacation out there when this is all done."

"If we don't have another mission right after this, I don't see why not. Maybe we all can."

"Val too?"

"Yeah, Val too, if she agrees. That would be the only way I'd want to stay."

She raised her brows and smiled at him.

Was that a yes? Howard sure hoped so. "About the rental vehicle: just get a taxi. We've got to return a car to the airport today, and we still have an extra rental car. We're escorting Rowdy and Emmie to the airport now." Howard didn't bother to explain who Emmie was, figuring Jillian or Vaughn had probably told them some, if not all, of the story. "We'll see you tonight."

"See you tonight. Don't terminate all the bad guys before we get there."

Howard chuckled. If they could, they would. And he knew Everett and Demetria wouldn't mind if they did. Then they could all enjoy a vacation. He just wished they knew how many they still had to deal with. He was truly glad they'd have some additional jaguar power to tip the scales in their favor. He didn't want to see anyone else get injured in the fight to finish taking the rest of these men out.

After they ended the call, they decided to use Vaughn's rental car so the vehicle wouldn't be recognized, since they'd driven Val's and Jillian's when they had gone to the other drug house. Now, they drove two of the rental vehicles to the airport: Rowdy's and Vaughn's. After dropping off the other rental car and parking Vaughn's car, they all walked inside the airport with Rowdy and Emmie. As additional protection, they stayed with them until they were checked in. They wished them both luck. Emmie and Rowdy went through security, and once they were out of sight, the Greystokes and Val and Howard returned to Vaughn's car.

Then they were on their way to the next drug house.

"I'm glad Demetria and Everett are joining us," Vaughn said. "We could use some more cats on this adventure."

"Me too," Jillian said. "And I'm glad the civilians are all safely away."

Howard knew the wolves didn't feel they couldn't be useful on the mission. That was what was great about their team. They knew their strengths and weaknesses—even if the guys didn't like to admit they had any weaknesses—and they complemented each other.

"I don't imagine these guys are going to be at the second drug house," Val said. "If Eric believes Emmie told us about the other drug house, he'll know she told us about this one too."

"I even had the thought that we could return to the first drug house to see if they showed up there to clean up the bodies," Jillian said. "But that could be a different sort of trouble."

"I agree with you there," Howard said. "No telling what we could run into."

"The dead bodies and maybe the police," Jillian said. "Before you joined us for the meal, I was watching the news. They only talked about the one dead body found in the alley where you had to break the guy's neck. No mention of the guy you had to kill in the rain forest. Or the one you had to feed to the crocs nearer our resort."

"Good. Hopefully no one will find them," Howard said. "There was no mention of the drug house and the three bodies we left there?"

"All quiet on that front. I did think about going to that house Eric owned, but the police might know there was some connection between the broken-necked guy and Eric's place," Jillian said. "They don't have an ID on the dead guy yet either. And no mention of all the blood spilled in the rental house where Val's parents were staying."

"At least we've probably put a crimp in Eric's drug dealings. He's too busy keeping one step ahead of us."

"Serves them right for Benny turning Izzie and every-thing else they've done." Val's phone began ringing, and she pulled it out. "Speaking of that…" She answered her cell and put it on speaker. "We're all here listening. How are you doing, Izzie?"

"I just had to call you and tell you I'm settling in and had my first OB check at a jaguar clinic. I actually shifted at the clinic, which terrified me. Can you imagine me being in the waiting room, yanking off my clothes as fast as I could? They took me into the exam room calmly, no one reacting like I was a crazed woman, like this happened all the time, when I'm sure it doesn't. The doctor and nursing staff were so patient with me. They showed me the ultrasound of the jaguar cub while I was lying on the exam table as a jaguar. Before they were through, I shifted again, and they showed me what the baby looked like in human form. It was a miracle. They said they couldn't be one hundred percent sure at twelve weeks, but by the angle of the dangle, the baby looks to be a boy."

Val swiped at her face, and Howard looked over to see her brushing away tears. "I'm so glad for you, Izzie. See? What did I say? Everything would work out for you." She gave Howard a dark look as if saying he'd better not comment on her tears.

He worried about Val though. Was she just sentimental about the woman's baby being fine? Or was it something that went deeper?

"I'm thrilled. And I wanted to thank you all for saving my life. I realize you could easily have terminated me for the way I had behaved."

"We knew you were going through a tough time and only wanted to do what we could to help you cope with it," Val said, sounding a little choked up.

"They have me in counseling to deal with all of it: what I went through with Benny, having a baby, and having a jaguar cub, and of course the changes in my senses. Sometimes, they're useful. But I haven't been sleeping well. Too many sounds and smells to deal with when I need to sleep. And everything distracts me."

"It'll get better. It might take some time, but you'll learn to live with your enhanced senses."

"That's what they keep telling me. Just like the shifting. Part of my counseling program was to let you know how I'm feeling and to thank you for all that you did. But I keep worrying Benny will come after me. My counselor said I should call you to get an update on him and maybe that would help settle my concern."

Since they hadn't gotten anywhere with the bastard, Howard was certain their news wouldn't be good news.

"We're still working on getting ahold of him," Val admitted. "We've taken down more of his henchmen, but he still has eluded us."

"I'm glad you've gotten rid of some of the others. Will you remember to tell me when you've taken care of him?"

"Absolutely, Izzie. As soon as we can."

"Thanks. I think that's another reason why I can't sleep very well. And well, because I keep shifting into a cat in the middle of the night. It always wakes me. I'll let you go, but I just wanted to say thank you."

"You're so welcome, Izzie, and congratulations again on your baby. We're thrilled for you."

When they finished the call, Howard said, "We're coming up on the location."

"That same blue pickup is sitting out front," Val warned.

"No other vehicles," Vaughn said. "Which could mean they've set a trap for us and are hiding the other vehicles so we'll think only Eric is here."

Howard drove past the house. "What does everyone

want to do?" They worked as a team. He wasn't about to decide this for everyone.

"Someone moved a curtain at the window," Val said.

"Okay, so someone is in the house. Not necessarily Eric or Benny," Howard said. "I'm thinking we should wait for reinforcements." He was only thinking of the Greystokes and Val's welfare. Normally, he would be eager to finish the mission, no matter what the stakes. After the last clash with the rogue jaguars and the injuries his fellow team members had sustained, he was thinking they needed to be more cautious. Everyone was still suffering from bite and claw wounds. Vaughn had been especially worried about Jillian this morning, though she appeared to be feeling all right.

"I vote for waiting. It won't be much longer until the Andersons join us," Vaughn said. "I thought we could do this, but I agree that it looks like a trap. If it is, they'll be prepared for us, and we won't know what we're going up against."

"I want to get this over with and get on with vacation plans," Jillian said, snuggling against Vaughn in the back seat. "But if any of us get killed over this when we could have waited and had much better odds, I would never forgive myself."

"I agree," Howard said. Waiting would benefit them all.

Emmie called Howard on her cell, and he put it on speaker. "Yeah, Emmie?"

"Rowdy and I haven't boarded our flight yet, but Eric texted me. He said I was the only woman he'd ever trusted, and I'd pay for abusing his trust."

"We'll get him, Emmie. As soon as we can," Howard

said, feeling all growly. The bastard didn't deserve to have anyone special in his life, not while he was conducting the kind of business that he was.

"I…I didn't want to tell you this, because I really think Eric said it so I'd overhear him and relay the message to you. Rowdy told me to let you know what's going on though. Just in case the information was for real and you could use it to take him and Benny down. He said Benny was going to be at the beach near the resort making some heroin sales in about three hours. My gut instinct tells me it's a setup," Emmie said.

"Okay, we'll discuss it. Thanks for giving us the information. Have a safe flight, and just know we'll get them," Howard said.

"Thanks. Let me know what happens," Emmie said.

"Will do."

They ended the call, and Howard asked, "So what do we do?"

"It's lunchtime," Val said. "Why don't we grab some lunch at a local place? We could pick up some swimsuits and go swimming at the beach and see what happens. We could explore the area first, make sure they're not there. If no one shows up, we return to the cabins and wait for the Andersons to get in, have dinner, then take care of this business. If we see Benny, we move to shore to take him out. Or a couple of us could be sitting somewhere in the trees—hidden, possibly—while two of us are swimming, so it looks like we're just taking a break."

"Val, you have got to join our team. Seriously," Jillian said. "The job isn't about taking the bad guys down 24/7, but about knowing how to be a team and play when we can relax and be ready for the next conflict—or look like we're playing—and prepared to take the bad guys down."

Howard smiled at Val as he drove them to a fast-food restaurant. "I keep saying the same—that she needs to join our team."

Vaughn shook his head. "Are you sure you want to hook up with Howard? You know that's his whole intention."

"Maybe he's not ready for it," Val said, glancing at Howard as if waiting to see if he was.

"Oh hell, I'm ready. Past ready," Howard said. Jillian was right. It wasn't just about the mission but all the time spent around the mission. It was about the little things too: sharing a funny moment, letting down their guard, talking about their futures, sharing secrets, being there for each other—before, after, and during the mission.

Vaughn had gotten Jillian a coloring book when she'd been injured on their first mission together, and they'd all ended up coloring pages from it. Little gestures like that made them a cohesive team, a family of shifters who were protective and loyal and could still have fun. Admittedly, he had been a little envious when the mated shifters retired to their rooms for the night. They had each other to complete the night and share intimate moments with during the day. Not that he'd met any woman up to that point in his life who would complete that need. He hadn't thought he'd ever find a jaguar who would make him feel that way. Val was that woman for him.

"Hmm, Val, you're not saying anything," Howard said.

Val opened her mouth to speak, but then she got a call. "Hold that thought." She answered her phone and raised a brow at Howard. "Yes, sir. What? A transfer?"

"Yes!" Howard said, loud enough so her boss, as he figured that's who it was, could hear.

She chuckled. "No, it wasn't my idea. Not right away… Of course, I love being an Enforcer. No, my mom and dad won't mind. They'll be happy for me…" She let out her breath. "How about I try it out? Just for a time, and you keep my old job in case it doesn't work out." She smiled at Howard. "Okay, that's a deal… We're still hunting them down, but you probably know we'll have more jaguars here in a few hours to help us out." She paused. "Yes, sir." She smiled. "Okay, thanks. I'll keep you…yes, better informed." She chuckled and ended the call.

"You said yes! You're transferring? To join us? Me?" Howard couldn't help how excited he was.

Val and Jillian laughed.

Vaughn chuckled. "Hey, old man, I didn't know a woman could bowl you over like that."

"She's the only one who has taken me down to the mat in training exercises. I definitely need a mate like that."

"I have to admit he's the first guy I did that to that didn't want to get even. Wait, don't tell me that's a proposal."

"Uh, well, if it works?" Howard smiled again at her.

"It didn't."

He sighed. "Okay, next time, I'll do better."

She smiled at him, and he was glad she still seemed… somewhat agreeable concerning the idea, if he did it right. Which was his next mission, until they had to take care of the bad guys again.

"I've enjoyed working with all of you. It's definitely not the same as doing this on my own as an Enforcer. There's never any enjoyable downtime during a mission." Val sighed. "I didn't expect Martin to tell my boss I was transferring per the team members' request though. I haven't even met the Andersons yet. What if they're opposed to me being part of the team?"

"Sorry," Jillian said, "if I jumped the gun a bit. But we need you to join us!"

Val smiled at Jillian over the seat.

"We discussed it last night with the Andersons," Vaughn said. "Demetria said make it happen. Everett was in full agreement."

Val laughed. "Thanks. I don't think I've ever met a group of people who wanted to work with me that badly."

"Me more than anyone," Howard said.

Everyone laughed.

"We need to go to a beach shop," Jillian said. "I need to pick up a swimsuit. I didn't think my mate would be here with me, or that we might have a minute to enjoy aqua waters and white sand beaches."

"I've got board shorts with me," Vaughn said. "I always take them with me on trips to hot places in the summer."

Howard was reminded of the time they went swimming in the hotel pool and couldn't wait to be with Val again in the water.

Val looked up stores for swimsuits on her phone. "I'm with Jillian. I need something to swim in." She gave him directions.

"Since it's daytime, we'll have to have two of us armed with guns and badges, hidden in the foliage, waiting to ambush our prey. If Benny does show up to sell drugs, we can arrest him and take him somewhere else to eliminate him," Vaughn said. "We won't be able to shift and take care of this. He probably won't want to scream bloody murder and get the police involved. Jillian and I can remain in the bushes, armed and ready, while the two of you swim. Then we can switch off if no one shows up for a while."

"I imagine this is a setup, but they can't take us out very well either in broad daylight," Jillian said.

Then they drove to a beach shop and picked up souvenir beach towels to use and take home with them. Howard had to get one with a jaguar prowling through the jungle. He was a jaguar all the way. Being a SEAL wolf, Vaughn immediately grabbed the only seal towel he could find— two harbor seals on the rocks sunning and swimming. Jillian smiled at him. Before Val could pick out her own towel, Howard found just the one for her. Two black howler monkeys, just like the ones that had seized her oranges, in memory of her first day at her cabin in Belize.

"Just missing the oranges and jaguar to make it complete," Val said.

Vaughn waited to hear an explanation. Jillian smiled at him. "Val had visitors in her kitchen, nibbling on her oranges, when we first showed up at the resort. Howard chased them off."

"As a jaguar?" Vaughn was grinning. "Hell, man, I knew you were the best man for this job."

"Hey, lady in distress? You know it."

Jillian picked out a mermaid towel that said *Sorry, I Can't. I Have Important Mermaid Stuff to Do*.

"You sure do," Vaughn said to Jillian, giving her a hug.

She laughed. Val smiled. They were a cute couple.

They picked up waterproof pouches for their phones, drivers' licenses, credit cards, passports, and badges.

They didn't want to leave them in the car. They also selected fins, snorkels, flip-flops, and sun block. They were ready to have some real fun and do away with the bad guys.

"We'll have to bring Demetria and Everett to the shop if we get a chance to take them to the beach while they're here." Jillian was eyeing swimsuits, and Vaughn was pulling out several he wanted to see her try on. Red. Hot pink. Shimmering blue.

Howard was watching them, and then he began to do the same for Val, just as she and Jillian had picked out rain jackets for him to try on. Only the swimsuits were a lot hotter.

"What about this one?" Howard showed Val bikinis in emerald green, cobalt blue, and tomato red.

"How about this?" She pulled out a long-sleeved black swim T-shirt.

He eyed it and then her bust. "Yeah, that would fit nicely."

She smiled at him. "You would prefer a bikini."

"I prefer whatever you feel comfortable in. If you need protection from the sun, you wear that. I can wrap my arms around you in the ocean just as closely and with as much enjoyment no matter what you wear. Besides, I won't have to growl at as many guys who would be ogling you in a bikini."

She chuckled and took the selections into the dressing room.

He waited while Vaughn actually went into the dressing room with Jillian. That's what Howard wanted to do with Val. He wanted that closeness that came with a mating.

Jillian came out with three she'd decided to buy. "I couldn't decide so Vaughn insisted I get all of them. Where's Val?"

"Still in the dressing room."

"I'll see if she needs any help deciding." Jillian went into the dressing-room hall. "How are you doing?"

"Do you want to help me decide?" Val asked.

"Yeah, sure." A few minutes later, Jillian said, "Oh yeah, that one is perfect. And that one will work."

A few minutes later, Val carried out two bikinis—the emerald-green one and the cobalt blue—and the swim T-shirt. Howard eyed the suits, approving of both of them, and couldn't wait to see her wearing them.

"Redhead." She held up the T-shirt to Howard. "I turn into a crispy critter when it's sunny out and I'm in the surf or an outdoor swimming pool."

"That would ruin a good outing," Howard said, having been there before. He tanned well, but he could also burn.

"Believe me, after having been burned to a crisp once, yes! It does. And for a couple of days afterward. No sleeping, burning up, just miserable."

"Even though I don't burn as easily, it's happened to me a couple of times, so I know your pain. I hadn't applied sunscreen often enough." He reached his hand out to her to take the clothing.

She hesitated to give them to him.

"My treat. I'm trying to prove I'm the right one for you. I'm still trying to come up with a good way to make a proposal you can't refuse." He would do whatever it took.

Val chuckled and handed him her clothes and appeared to like the way he was going about this.

Howard paid for the items, then took her hand and led her out of the store, following the others.

Then they returned to the cabins so the guys could get their board shorts. They changed into swim gear and wore their clothes over it. After that, Vaughn drove them to the beach nearest to the resort.

They checked the whole area, laughing, smiling, kissing as couples, pretending to be Americans enjoying their vacation. They were also breathing in the scents of the sea, sand, and vegetation. Of fresh air, fish, and flowers, searching for jaguar scents. They were looking for the perfect location for Jillian and Vaughn to hide and observe the beach to watch for Benny or anyone else who might be selling drugs there today. Sea grape and coconut palms provided the perfect cover.

"Just don't stand beneath a coconut palm," Val warned. "A falling coconut can do serious damage."

Howard was glad she'd mentioned it because he kept forgetting the wolves had never been here before.

"We're all set," Jillian said. "Go play for a while, and then we'll switch off."

"Will do," Howard said.

He and Val grabbed their towels, snorkels, and fins from the rental car and headed across the white sand beach. When they were close enough to the water, they spread out their towels next to each other. Hopefully, the towels wouldn't go missing while they were playing in the water, but they could always chase down the suspects if they didn't just take the towels and get in a vehicle and drive off. Val and Howard left their flip-flops, flippers, snorkels, and sunglasses on their towels. Howard was only too happy to apply lotion on Val, even though she was wearing a long T-shirt. She did the same for him, her hands rubbing the lotion all over his bare skin, making him hot and interested.

She smiled at him and kissed his lips. "Sorry, I didn't mean to stir things up."

"Can't be helped when you're rubbing your warm hands all over my body."

Then they walked across the hot sand to the water. The waves were gentle, the water clear aqua, darker the deeper it got.

"I hope this works," Val said. "I hate leaving the Greystokes to do all the sitting and watching while we're playing though."

They raced out into the waves. It was invigorating to get in some playtime in between the rough times. Howard noticed Val's wounds were healing, the same as his, but they were still visible.

"We'll relieve them in a bit. As team players, we all love to take the bad guys down. They're as eager to wait there and watch for the bad guys, hoping to make another break in the case, as we will be when we switch places."

They splashed into the water, running deeper until they could swim and put on their fins and goggles. Howard and Val made sure they could watch Jillian and Vaughn's location, lined up directly with their towels, in case anyone tried to harm their teammates. He was paying attention to the ocean currents too—to make sure he and Val didn't drift down the beach—and watching the shore. With her head in the water, Val was keeping close to him, observing the fish swimming beneath them. Some came up to nibble on their legs. She pointed to them, looking thrilled to be here. With him.

At least he thought so. Both jaguars and wolves loved the water. Jaguars especially, so they were in their element out here.

She suddenly came up for air. He looked down at her, afraid something was the matter, though he didn't see what it could be—unless she had another idea about the mission.

Chapter 17

VAL COULDN'T HAVE BEEN MORE DELIGHTED TO TRY
out this new working relationship with several partners
and to have a mate while she did it. Still, she was serious
about returning to her job as an Enforcer if she didn't
feel she fit in with the team. The rest of them had already
worked together on several missions. Would she truly be
able to contribute?

If she returned to the Enforcer branch, would Howard
come with her? She didn't know, but she had decided
that more than anything, she wanted him in her life. She
wasn't going to wait for him to propose to her in a special way. This was special enough—snorkeling together
in the pristine waters of the jaguars' playground, Belize,
while watching for the perps.

When she returned to the surface so suddenly, she
was afraid Howard would believe something was
wrong. He might not like her proposing to him instead
of the other way around, but she suspected he would be
thrilled. At least she hoped he would be.

As soon as she reached the surface, the waves carrying them up and down gently, she grabbed hold of him
and let him be her flotation device while she readied
herself to ask the question. She'd never imagined she'd
be doing this with a jaguar someday. Certainly never
with one who was as brawny, interesting, funny, and

clever as he was. Or here, in the Caribbean, the warm waters lapping at their naked skin.

He kept her back to the beach while he switched his gaze from her to the beach, watching the situation there.

"If having me with the USF doesn't work out, for whatever reason, then I'll return to the Enforcer branch. I don't expect you to do that. You make a great USF agent, and I can see how much your team members love working with you, so I wouldn't want to take that away from you," she said.

It looked like it was killing him not to respond, but he nodded, waiting for her to finish what she had to say before he did, and she appreciated him for it. In fact, that was what she loved so much about him. He was really attuned to her feelings, just as she was to his, and that made all the difference in the world to her.

"So when I ask you if you want to be my mate—" she said.

"Hell yeah, under any condition," he quickly said.

She laughed. "Don't try to act like you're Mr. Nice Guy and go along with everything I say. I know you better than that."

He chuckled. "Okay, let me put it this way: if we're working as USF and as mates, we'll have each other's backs, as usual. Only...it will be a little different."

"We'll be mated."

"Right. Because you love me."

"And you love me."

"*So* much. Now, if you work this mission and you really don't feel like you can work with a team, that's completely up to you. I respect your wishes. You have to feel right about your partners and about the job we're doing. Otherwise, you won't be able to do your best, and you and your teammates could suffer."

"What about you?" She wrapped her legs around his hips while he kicked to keep the two of them afloat, her hands caressing his shoulders.

He settled his hands on her hips. "We'll see. If you don't want a partner as an Enforcer, I'll stay with the USF. Though it will kill me, I have to admit. I'll be like Vaughn is with Jillian, making a total nuisance of myself, texting or calling you constantly to see if you miss me. Or what you're doing next. Or how things are going. Or when we're going to be together again."

She smiled. She loved when he was being honest with her.

Howard kissed her wet cheek. "That's completely your choice. If you want me as a partner, I'll make sure someone takes my place in the USF, and then I'll join you." He glanced again at the shore.

"I wouldn't want you to have to leave them when I can see how well you work with them, but I would want you as my partner wherever I work."

"A mate takes priority. I've worked both jobs, so I know something about them. I prefer being a USF agent because of the partners I have now, and with you on the team, it would be even better. If I'm an Enforcer with you as my partner? I'll be just as happy. You're the one who makes me complete. Not just the job. You. Yet, if you decide at some point you don't want to work as my partner, I'll let you have your space. As long as we can make up for it when we're together again."

"Okay, then that decides it. I want you to be my mate. Will you be?"

He shouted out with glee.

She laughed, glad he wasn't shy about letting others know how he felt. "I think all of Belize knows it now."

They looked around to see Jillian and Vaughn's location, and she wondered if they'd heard them.

"Hey, since we're going to be mates, I wanted to ask you about being so distressed in the car when Izzie told us she was going to have a baby boy. I worried about you."

"I don't know." She kissed his chest. "I just felt bad all of a sudden about having bullied her to come with us—threatening to eliminate her if she didn't. We didn't know she was pregnant at the time. It just hit me when she announced she was having a baby boy."

"Okay. I'm glad that's all it was. One of us had to convince her for her own good. Everything you said to her was true, and you *weren't* going to eliminate her. If nothing else, I would have knocked her out and carried her through the rain forest back to our resort. You were the one who convinced her to return with us without either of us having to resort to violence. I was proud of you, and she was grateful to you." He hugged Val tight. "No worries. Next time, I can be the bad guy."

She smiled up at him. "Thanks, Howard. I think with a guy, you would have more of an impact. With a woman, it worked out well with me taking on that role."

"See? We're already a great team."

"Agreed. Why don't you snorkel for a bit, and I'll watch the situation on the beach and make sure we don't drift," she said.

"I like the way you keep bumping me below the water. Go ahead and keep swimming, and when you're done, we'll switch off with the Greystokes." Howard hesitated to release her, his hands still wrapped around her back, but then he leaned down and kissed her mouth, lowering his hands to cup her buttocks to press her against his arousal. She rubbed up against him, and he bit back a groan. "You're killing me."

She smiled. "We'll have to do something about that when we return to our place. All right. I'll snorkel. I haven't been down here in eons."

"I can't wait."

They swam around for a good half hour, and then Val finally said she was ready to switch off with her teammates. She couldn't believe she was actually calling them that, or that she and Howard had agreed to be mated jaguars. She couldn't have been happier, except if they'd finish this business with Eric, Benny, and the rest of Eric's henchmen.

They wrapped their towels around them, wearing their flip-flops, with goggles and fins in hand, and walked through the sand to the parking lot. They were talking about what to fix for lunch—Belizean tamales wrapped in plantain leaves filled with seasoned chicken appealed to everyone. But they needed to throw on their clothes over their swimsuits and drop off their gear at the car before they took Vaughn and Jillian's place.

That's when they saw three men talking together in the parking lot, wearing jeans and T-shirts and sneakers, not looking like part of the beach crowd. None of the men were Benny or Eric. But one of the men was passing a bag of something to another who was handing him cash.

They might not be dealing drugs, but it sure looked like they were. Even if they had nothing to do with the jaguars, Howard and Val needed to do something about the men. The three men suddenly looked over at them as Val hugged Howard and looked up at him, smiling as if she had no idea what the men were doing. He glanced down at her and kissed her forehead.

"There was supposed to be twice as much here," one man growled, his voice low, but the jaguars could hear him.

"My supplier's stuff was stolen. This is the best I could do."

Supplier? As in Eric?

Howard and Val heard movement behind them and saw Jillian and Vaughn hurrying to catch up to them.

Dropping their beach gear, Howard and Val ran to intercept the men. Jillian and Vaughn pulled out their guns and hollered, "Undercover agents! Get down on the ground! Now!"

Of course, all three men ran, but it didn't take long for Val to reach one of them and trip him, making him sprawl onto the pavement. Howard and Vaughn took down the others, while Jillian kept her gun trained on the men. They were all human, and once the men were tied up, Jillian called the police.

Then Jillian and Val searched the men for IDs. Vaughn took pictures to forward to Emmie to see if she knew them. She would be getting off her flight in a couple of hours, so they wouldn't know until then.

One of the men had a driver's license on him, and Vaughn smiled at the name. "One of the guys on the list of debts." He turned to the drug dealer and eyed the other guy's passport. "Where's the other man who was supposed to show up?"

"BC? He set me up?" the drug dealer growled.

"Yeah, him," Vaughn said.

BC? As in Benny Canton? That meant Benny had sent someone else in his place.

---~~~---

Twenty minutes later, the police arrived, arrested the men, and took everyone's statements. Since the jaguars and wolves all had Martin as their boss, the officers verified with him that the agents were here on vacation.

When one officer got off the phone, he eyed them with suspicion. "You work together and come down here on your time off to play together?" Gonzales sounded like he doubted that.

"Sure," Val said. "And Howard and I love it here so much that we just got engaged." She hugged Howard tighter and smiled up at him. "So it's kind of a pre-honeymoon trip."

"Congratulations," the officer said. "Try to enjoy your vacation."

"Thanks," Vaughn said. "We will."

When the police officers left, Val asked Jillian and Vaughn, "Okay, so do you want to get in some swimming and we'll keep an eye on things now?"

"We were thinking we would, but since we probably took care of any action going down here, we could just return to the cabins and have some lunch," Jillian said. "We can swim later."

"Are you sure?" Howard asked.

"Yeah, I'm starving," Vaughn said.

They packed their gear in the car, but when they arrived at Vaughn and Jillian's cabin, they had a new problem. One of Jillian's rental car's windows had been smashed, and the door was wide open.

"Hell," Vaughn said as they all hurried to exit the car and check out the cabin.

He reached the cabin first, the door wide open, and they heard someone still inside. Vaughn handed Val his gun and began stripping out of his clothes. Howard was removing his clothes too, but Val didn't think Vaughn should be seen as a wolf out here.

Howard and Vaughn shifted and Vaughn raced into the cabin, while Howard ran around to the back door.

Val started to jerk off her long T-shirt and her bikini.

"You're shifting?" Jillian asked, sounding surprised.

"Yeah, in case the guy makes it past Vaughn. We need to stop shifters without using bullets, if we can." Val shifted, headed inside the cabin, and planted herself in the entryway, readying herself for action. She stared at the mess the perps had made of their place—couch and chairs turned upside down, throw rugs tossed about, decorator pillows in a pile on the floor. She could just imagine what they'd done in the other rooms.

Then someone cried outside at the back of the cabin. Val wanted to tear around and see what was going on or help Howard. Doing something was better than doing nothing.

Howard gave a frustrated jaguar roar. Vaughn barked at him, and Val assumed Vaughn had gone out the back door or a window after the culprit. Even though she wanted to join them, she stayed put in case they had more trouble on this side.

Then Vaughn loped into the cabin and shifted. "The man got away. He must have heard our voices and taken off before we could reach him."

Jillian frowned. "Aren't we going to chase after him?"

"Could be an ambush. I was waiting to see if Howard wanted to go, but he indicated no," Vaughn said.

Jillian and Vaughn went outside, and he dressed.

Howard came into the cabin, rubbed against Val, then headed outside. She joined him so she could shift and dress alongside him. "No going after him?" She pulled on her bikini bottoms.

Howard pulled on his board shorts. "Nope. It wasn't Benny or Eric either. The guy took off as a jaguar, and by the looks of things, a jaguar tore some of the things up in the cabin, so they didn't just ransack it as humans. Did you smell Eric's and Benny's scents in the cabin?"

"Yeah," Val and Vaughn said.

"Well, going to the beach was a setup. Benny sent someone else to do his dirty work, and that gave the others time to ransack the car and cabin. Most likely to search for the drugs, money, and other stuff we took from the drug house. I didn't want to leave the two of you here alone in case they'd try to take you out while we were off chasing the one guy." He helped her fasten her bikini top.

Vaughn said, "Let's check out the other place—I suspect it will look like this one—and then we'll fix lunch."

When they entered the other cabin, they found everything tossed about like at the other place.

"Benny and Eric were here too," Howard said.

"Letting us know they're onto us, and they aren't taking this lying down," Jillian said.

"They have to know that if they killed us, a ton more agents would descend on the area," Vaughn said.

"Yeah. But Eric will want his stuff back, and he'll want revenge. And then he'll disappear. He had a nice little drug operation going here too." Howard headed for the bedrooms to check them out.

Vaughn went with him. Val noticed how well they worked together, acting in sync, no one having to tell the others what they were doing, just doing it.

"Did they steal anything?" Val asked Vaughn.

"Doesn't look like it. They were just looking for their stash."

"They won't find it here." Val was glad they had sent it with the Guardian agents, who had turned it over to their chief when they arrived home.

"I opt for a quick shower," Howard said.

"Jillian and I can wash off in the outdoor shower since we didn't get in the ocean. We just need to rinse off our sandy feet and legs."

"Okay, sounds good," Val said. She and Howard were sandy, salty, and needed to wash up and change. "Does everyone feel safe enough with two to a cabin for now? Or should we post guards?"

"I'd say post guards. You can buddy up in the shower to make it quicker," Vaughn said.

Jillian and Val laughed. "You think it would be quicker that way?" Val asked.

Smiling, Howard took Val's hand and led her to the bathroom while Jillian and Vaughn rinsed off outside and watched over the place.

Howard turned on the shower, and Val hurried to pull off her shirt and bathing suit in the bathroom. She carried them into the glassed-in shower stall and rinsed them out before setting them on a faux marble shelf. He yanked his board shorts off and followed her into the shower, rinsing his suit out like she'd done and setting it on top of the shelf too. If it had been just him, he would have tossed his board shorts on the floor and washed them later. And gotten down to the most important business first.

Since they had agreed to a mating, what better way to enjoy their first mated lovemaking than in the shower? Howard was eager to enjoy every minute of it with Val. They first rinsed off some of the salt water covering their skin. Then he poured peach body soap on his hands and she did the same with hers. They began to wash each other, warm hands stroking over heated flesh. Her skin was satiny and smooth even without the soap, but with it, his hands just slid down every inch of her body with silky caresses. She was doing the same to him, and every lingering touch was sending his pheromones into a tailspin. His cock was already stretching out to her, straining with need.

"I'm crazy in love with you," he breathed out, his voice rough with desire, his heart and hers thudding in overdrive.

"I'm crazy about you too, you big ol' cat," she purred against his mouth.

He kissed her mouth with passion and craving. Her lips and his were still salty from the sea, hers soft and malleable beneath his. Their tongues tasted and teased each other's as he pressed his cock against her belly, showing her just how much she aroused him.

He moved his hands down her back, lower, until he reached her buttocks, cupped them, and pulled her tight against him.

She moaned against his mouth and ran her hands

down his sides, kissing his shoulder, licking his wet skin. His hands shifted to her breasts, and he massaged them before moving his hand lower between her legs and beginning to kiss her. Her hands shifted to his cock, and she began to stroke him as he was stroking her. She was a slice of heaven on earth and all his.

He was already wringing her out, her hands stilling on his arousal. Then she transferred her hands to his hips and clung to him as if she was ready to collapse on the tile floor.

She kissed his mouth with exuberance, and he thought she was struggling to be as quiet as she could be, but she needn't have been. The others would understand.

He stroked her clit faster and harder, knowing she was close to reaching the pinnacle, and she came apart under his touch, crying out, dissolving. He quickly lifted her against the tile and sank his cock deep inside her as she wrapped her legs around him and he began to thrust.

Howard was so good at this. He had already pushed Val to the limits, his finger stroking her clit, his other hand caressing a breast, their tongues mingling before they pressed their lips together again and kissed. Her fingers dug into his hips to keep some semblance of control, but when it came to him, she was lost in his ministrations. She'd felt the climax rising and then slamming into her. She'd tried to stifle the cry that had bubbled up but only partly managed it. Howard quickly kissed her, lifting her so that he could embed his cock deep inside her. Then he thrust.

Ohmigod, he was an amazing lover, and she treasured

every new experience with him. She loved being mated to him and kissed his jaw as he settled her against the wall and continued to thrust into her. She reveled in the powerful feel of his hot cock sliding inside her, loved the way his hands gripped her buttocks to support her, the way his muscles strained with the effort, the way his face was tense with concentration and pleasure.

She could tell from the strain on his face that he was about to come, and she kissed his chin, right before he growled low with relief and his hot seed bathed her deep inside. "You...are...amazing," she gasped out, then licked his chest.

He groaned, then hugged her tight and kissed the top of her head. He finally set her down on the tile floor, pulling out at the same time. "You are too, honey. Just beautiful."

They took their time washing each other again, exploring, getting to know each other.

Once they were done, Howard turned off the water and smiled down at her, and she chuckled. "So much for a quick shower to clean off."

He laughed. "Hell, the wolves would have expected no less from us."

They hung up their bathing suits and her shirt to dry, grabbed towels, wrapped themselves up in them, and hurried out of the bathroom to go to the bedroom and dress.

As soon as they were wearing jeans, boots, and T-shirts, they left the bedroom. Val and Howard checked all their stuff and didn't find anything missing. "Nothing missing that I can see," Val said to Jillian and Vaughn when they joined them outside.

"Let's have lunch and plan our next move," Vaughn said, and everyone agreed.

Chapter 18

AT JILLIAN'S CABIN, VAUGHN SAID, "OKAY, SO WE talked of all staying in one cabin before Everett and Demetria said they were arriving. We won't have an extra bedroom, but the couch in each of the cabins makes into a bed."

"We can draw straws and decide who takes the couch," Val said as they entered the cabin.

Howard would have been sleeping there if he hadn't just found a mate. And since Val didn't even know Everett and Demetria, Howard preferred that he and Val had a bedroom.

Everyone straightened up the place, and then they congregated in the kitchen to make lunch.

"We'll take the couch." Jillian pulled out the ingredients for the meal.

Howard really thought jaguars should sleep in the living room, in case anyone had the notion of breaking in. They would be foolhardy if they did. Everyone would be sleeping naked and ready to shift at a moment's notice.

"Unless Everett or Demetria don't want to go along with it, I vote they stay in the living room. Better protection for everyone," Howard said.

"That's what happens when you come last to the party." Jillian smiled and began cooking sliced chicken in a pan, adding chicken broth and seasonings to a corn dough, then steaming tamales in plantain leaves.

Howard was certain the Andersons wouldn't mind in the least. They'd been mated the longest, though it hadn't been all that long. Last year, actually. He pulled out bottles of water for them while they worked on lunch. Val set the table.

The aroma of the seasoned chicken made Howard's stomach rumble. Val ran her hand over his stomach and smiled up at him. He was hungry for her too.

"So which cabin should we stay at?" Val asked as they sat down at the table to eat.

"I'd say we should stay here, since it's closer to Benny's cabin. Just in case," Jillian said.

Vaughn mixed up margaritas for everyone.

Everyone agreed. The one room had already been Howard's, so Val could move right in with him. And Jillian and Vaughn had been staying in the other room.

"I wonder if they ransacked Rowdy's cabin. They would have smelled his scent around our places and the drug house where we had the fight, so they'll know he was with us. And maybe believe he's still with us." Howard picked up his tamale.

"Unless someone else has already moved into the cabin," Val said.

"True." Howard bit into his tamale. "Damn good."

"They are. I love making a different version back home, so I wanted to try this one out here. Now when we return, it will feel like we've brought some of Belize with us," Jillian said.

"We need to learn to make them." Val smiled at Howard. "As to the bad guys, they probably believe Rowdy's here to help us fight them and that he wouldn't run off like that. We could check Rowdy's cabin after lunch. Somebody else might be staying there and get a real shock."

Jillian sipped some of her margarita. "I had another thought. Eric and the others would have smelled Emmie's and Izzie's scents at our cabins. They might have been trying to learn if the women were still here too."

"Oh, I hadn't thought of that," Val admitted.

Vaughn pulled out his cell. "I need to bring the Andersons up to speed." He called them and put it on speaker. "Hey, guys." He told them all that had happened.

Everett swore. "You guys haven't taken them down yet? I was hoping we could land and just have a vacation."

"Yeah, I know you want to take part in this," Howard said. "Besides, we already took some time off to enjoy the beach."

"Don't tell Demetria that. She packed bathing suits, beach towels, and suntan lotion. I keep telling her we're on a mission first," Everett said.

Everyone smiled. Jillian said, "Soon, we hope."

"We have two cabins, but we're putting the two of you on the couch in one and we'll take the bedrooms. Last one to show up, you know…" Howard said.

Everett laughed. "Sounds like a good plan to me. We just hope we don't disturb your sleep too much if the couch is kind of squeaky. Wait, you're staying with Val?"

"Yeah, we're mated."

Jillian raised her margarita to the newly mated couple.

Howard knew the wolves were pleased to see them mate and bring Val onto the team.

"Well, hot damn!" Everett said. "We're getting ready to board our flight. We've got some celebrating to do when we meet up with you."

Demetria said, "Congratulations, you two. Can't wait to see you."

"Same here," Howard said, and then they signed off so the Andersons could board their plane. "Okay, so the sleeping arrangements are all set."

Once they finished their lunch, Val poured everyone a glass of lemonade, and they all took seats in the living room. "Okay, so what's their next move? And our next move?"

"I don't think Eric will leave until he takes us out and gets his stuff back," Jillian said. "He probably assumes we couldn't have taken his money and drugs anywhere, not counting on the Guardians leaving on a private plane."

"I agree." Vaughn took a swig of his glass of lemonade.

"We keep hitting him hard. I suspect he's going to want to return here and take us out but learn first where his stash is. We brought both Emmie and Izzie here for safekeeping, more of their 'property,' I'm sure Eric and Benny feel. The cabins are our safe houses. By ransacking them and breaking into our cars, they're telling us to be afraid of them. That we're not safe, here or anywhere else. Belize is their territory." Howard drank some of the lemonade. "Great stuff."

"Thanks." Val smiled at him. "Been giving this a lot of thought, have we?"

"Yeah. I put myself in their shoes. What's going through their heads? Of course, they have a criminal mentality, but still, it's a combination of tactical plans and revenge. We stole their women; we took out Eric's brother and more of their men. We invaded *their* 'safe houses' too. It's time for retaliation. I doubt we have to go looking for them. I imagine they'll be coming here to fight the war. The rain forest retreat is the perfect place to fight us without being seen, and a handy place to dispose of the bodies, if they're so inclined."

"I agree with Howard," Vaughn said. "So we dig in, get prepared, and take them down."

"All right. As a former private investigator and army military intelligence officer, I'm not used to this kind of operation. I'm more used to chasing the culprit and turning him over to the authorities. In the USF, I'm chasing the perp down, not waiting for him to show up," Jillian said. "What if we set up the other cabin as a decoy? Maybe this one too. We could turn the TV on in one of the cabins, music on in the other, lights, but keep the shades closed. Can we simulate movement in the room? Talking? Walking around? Shadows randomly moving? As former PIs, Vaughn and I both have recorders. We could set up some conversation they can hear. So they know it's not just the TV. Maybe plans of attack that we're contemplating."

"Sounds like a good idea to me. I think we should have the jaguars in the trees, watching for any movement. We need to warn the Andersons about what we think might happen, or they could be ambushed when they arrive in the parking lot," Val said.

"I agree," Vaughn said. "They're on their flight now, but they'll call as soon as they get in. If the jaguars are in the trees, where do you want us to be?"

That's what Howard loved about this team of agents. The wolves knew they were at a strong disadvantage and understood the jaguars would know better how to handle other jaguars. In wolf territory, Vaughn and Jillian took the lead.

"Okay, we can do a couple of different things that I can think of. Join us in the trees as humans, not as wolves. We know you can't climb them as wolves. But you can be armed and stay there until we've dealt with Eric and the other men. Or you can stay in one of the cabins together and wait for them there if they try to come for you. We'll come at their backs," Howard said.

"We'd be bait then," Vaughn said, nodding with approval.

"Or you could stay at Benny's place," Val said. "But then they might try to gather their forces there."

"They'll come at us as jaguars, don't you think?" Jillian asked.

Howard rubbed his chin in thought. "Unless we can hit them before they shift. They have to drive in from somewhere. If they tried to run for miles to reach here, they'd be worn out before the fight began. I suspect they'll drive as close to the resort as they can without tipping any of us off, and then they'll shift and move through the rain forest to our location."

"Then we should try to intercept them first. Jillian and me," Vaughn said.

Howard knew the wolves were itching for a fight. They didn't want to hide in a house or trees, waiting for the jaguars to finish the mission. He just hoped it all worked out as they were planning it to.

"There's only one road in," Jillian said. "It splits off to the various cabins, but there's really no place to drive a vehicle and park it without someone seeing it."

"Except at one of the cabins," Val said. "They could park it out some way from one of the cabins so the occupants wouldn't be aware of it unless they're moving around at night, and most people wouldn't be."

"Unless they dropped off their army of jaguars and the driver left the area. Then the shifters would be running through here in their jaguar form." Vaughn let out his breath. "Without a crystal ball, we won't know which is the best option. Will they move in before dark, or when the sun begins to set, or after?"

"If it were me, I'd get here early, before the sun begins to set, and try to learn where everyone is first, if I could get close enough. But I might get caught by people still taking rain forest tours or just walking to the pond or on other trails. Or I might be seen by the people I'm trying to ambush if they're already lying in wait for me."

"So the cover of dark would be better," Jillian said.

"We can still see well at dusk and when it's a little darker. They'd be able to see figures moving around that are highlighted by the cabins' lights."

"What if we all are in one location having a celebratory party, then split up to go to the separate cabins, pretend to be drunk, turn off all the lights like we went to bed, and lie in wait?" Jillian asked.

"That's an idea," Howard said.

"Okay, as jaguars, we stalk and ambush," Val said. "It's in our blood. And wolves track, pursue, and encircle their prey. I think we should do both."

Howard didn't get what Val meant.

"Jillian and Vaughn track, pursue, and encircle any rogue they can find. We watch their backs. Once

they've found one, we ambush him and take him out."
Val smiled.

"When?" Howard asked.

"Now. We look for any signs of them now, in case
they're in the area. If not, then we'll move to plan B and
wait for them, hiding in the trees. Jillian and Vaughn can
choose their best plan at that point: join us, wait it out
in one of the cabins, or watch from the forest and give
early warning."

"And the Andersons?" Vaughn asked.

Howard poured himself another glass of lemonade.
"We'll text them that we think Eric and his men are
going to attempt to ambush us. We're going to try to
take them out before Everett and Demetria get here, but
if we don't, they need to know they may be walking into
a killing zone."

"Okay, will do." Vaughn got on his phone and began to
send the text. "They'll be here after the sun sets. And if we
don't find anyone out there, we regroup and return here?"

"I believe we should stay out there until this is done.
I'd rather not be a sitting duck in the cabins," Howard
said.

"I agree," Val said.

"Let's do this then," Vaughn said.

"If anyone gets into real trouble, return to this cabin,
howl, roar, let us know to regroup," Val said.

"I'm ready." Jillian turned on the TV and a few
lights. "I'll leave my tape recorder playing PI cases I've
recorded." Then she headed to the bedroom to remove
her clothes.

Vaughn joined her.

Val hugged Howard. "I hope this works."

"We can't know what they're up to exactly. We're doing the best we can under the circumstances. Come on. Let's remove our clothes and shift."

They returned to their bedroom and took off their clothes.

"Be careful. Don't do anything rash," Val said.

Howard snorted. "I was going to say the same thing to you."

They kissed and hugged, not wanting to let go. Then they shifted and headed for the front door.

Jillian and Vaughn were waiting for them in their wolf coats. Vaughn shifted and opened the door. Once everyone was out, he shut it again, then shifted.

They went to Val's cabin, where she shifted and turned on some lights and the TV. Then she turned back into her jaguar and joined the rest of them outside.

Vaughn and Jillian began trying to track any of the men's scents they could find in the rain forest—jaguar scents, whether they were Eric's, Benny's, or someone else's. Val and Howard moved through the shadows of the trees like mythical creatures hidden from view, watching the wolves' backs but listening and smelling and watching for any sign of danger too.

For over five hours, they searched for signs of anyone prowling the rain forest, believing they might be wrong about this. Then the wolves found their first jaguar target, and everyone froze in place.

Chapter 19

Whoever the jaguar was, he hesitated to fight the wolves. His heart was pounding, and Howard figured he was probably shocked to see the wolves in the rain forest, if he hadn't been forewarned they were working with the jaguar policing force. Or even if the jaguar had known about them, he'd been unprepared to see them out here, roaming through the woods.

For a moment, Howard wondered if the big cat was all jaguar and not a shifter. But then the jaguar jumped to take down Vaughn, the bigger of the two wolves. Howard leaped out of the shadows of the trees and swiped at the jaguar's head, killing him with one blow. The jaguar dropped to the forest floor, dead, and shifted into a naked man, but no one they recognized. Val remained hidden in the shadows as backup in case someone else attacked. Howard quickly grabbed hold of the dead man's arm and dragged him to the river. One down, but how many more did they have to deal with?

The wolves followed him, serving as his backup now, and Val stayed out of sight, but Howard knew she would be watching for trouble. He wondered if this guy had been a scout, looking to see what the situation was with them. Or maybe there were others here too, and they were prowling separately through the rain forest toward the cabins and getting into position before they struck.

So far so good as Howard dragged the man to the

river, no sign of humans wandering about as the sun began to set. No sign of anyone else, though jaguars could be so elusive that even Howard might miss seeing them. He suspected the jaguars didn't have hunter's spray down here, not believing they'd have trouble with the Enforcers or other jaguar agents. They were wrong.

He pulled the man into the water and released him, then swam back to shore. The wolves waited a moment, observing him and the dead man floating away. Both Vaughn and Jillian turned and resumed the search for prey.

When Howard had first started to work with them in their shifter coats, he wasn't sure they could all communicate well enough to coordinate tactics on the fly. But they were good at their jobs and everyone worked together to bring out the best outcome they could, given the situations they encountered.

A strangled cat cry was muffled before it could travel far in the noisy rain forest. It came from the direction where Val had been. Heart racing, Howard ran toward it. His teammates followed. When they reached Val, she was panting hard, blood staining the fur around her mouth, and a dead, naked man lay at her front paws. Damn glad she was fine, Howard nuzzled her face with affection, and she returned the love.

The guy wasn't Benny or Eric either, but he was a shifter, and like the other dead man, Eric's scent was on him. A handshake or a slap on the back would have been enough to leave his scent on the men.

Val took hold of the man's arm and was about to drag him to the river—her kill, her situation to deal with—but Howard shook his head at her. He was stronger and

could move the man faster. He needed her to stay and
protect the wolves.

As before, they followed him to watch his back. Val
remained hidden among the trees, a silent predator waiting to terminate the next shifter that showed himself.

Howard wondered if Eric had sent two men to scout
out the situation or if the whole gang was out here. At
least the number of men working for him was dwindling.

The sun was beginning to descend, the clouds growing
darker, the shadows of the forest deepening when they
heard the sound of a car driving toward their cabins. The
timing was about right for the Andersons' arrival. On the
other hand, maybe the car belonged to Eric or his men.

Howard met up with Vaughn and Jillian. Their ears
were perked, twisting, listening, their tails straight
out behind them. Then they raced toward the cabins.
Howard glanced around for Val, but she remained
hidden from view. He took off after his other teammates to protect them.

When he reached sight of Val's cabin, he saw the
driver and passenger doors on the car were open, no sign
of anyone. Vaughn and Jillian split up to smell the scents
on the car. They both woofed softly at Howard, telling him
it was Everett and Demetria's vehicle. They hadn't gotten
a taxi, maybe worried the taxi driver would see a jaguar
ambush. Howard and the wolves followed their scents
because their teammates had moved into the rain forest.

A few minutes had passed when cat snarls from
three different directions pierced the darkening forest.
Howard ran in the direction that was closest to where
he'd last seen Val. Vaughn and Jillian raced toward the
other cat cries. Howard was almost to Val's location

when a jaguar jumped out of a tree, slamming into him
and taking him down.

———⁓⁓⁓———

Val had killed the jaguar who had made the mistake of
prowling beneath the tree she'd been sitting in while
watching her teammates checking out the car. She knew
Howard and the others hadn't needed her there too. She
suspected Eric, Benny, or their henchmen would make
a move to check out the car, and she had been ready
for them.

She didn't think they could have many more people
left.

Then she saw Howard coming for her and no wolves
in sight. She was worried about them when a jaguar she
hadn't seen hidden in a tree pounced on Howard as he
approached her.

Her heart in her throat, Val leaped over the man
she'd killed, desperate to save her mate. Howard was
lying on the ground, stunned. The attacking jaguar had
been primed to kill her mate but turned his wrath on
her instead. She snarled and struck with lightning-fast
paws, claws extended, biting and thrashing like a wild
cat. She wasn't exactly using a jaguar's killing form, she
was so angry and wound up. This was her prey—Benny
Canton. He was a dead man. And she was relentless. She
thought she surprised the big male cat, who couldn't win
against her constant battering and biting him.

She prayed Howard would come out of his stupor,
but in the meantime, she was killing this bastard before
he could hurt anyone else.

Benny was bloodied and so was she, the iron scent and

taste of it compelling her to finish him. He'd clawed and bitten her, but she attacked him with such ferocity that she could see he was wearing down, his paws batting at her less effectively, his bites more glancing than penetrating.

Someone was coming, but she didn't take her focus off the threat in front of her. Benny turned to look though. Afraid another male, a stronger opponent, was ready to attack him from behind?

Benny was a fool to take his eyes off her. She took advantage of his distraction and bit down on his skull, killing him instantly. He fell to the forest floor and shifted into his human form, dead. That's when she saw who was coming. Her heart nearly stopped. The jaguar wasn't one of her own teammates, as she'd hoped, and the wind sending his scent proved the jaguar was Eric.

And damn him, he ran straight for Howard, who was still looking dazed and trying to get to his feet. She knew Eric wanted to get rid of the bigger male threat first, easily, before Howard *could* be a threat.

As if *she* didn't count!

She tore into the jaguar, feeling as though she was on catnip steroids, feeling no pain, white-hot rage filling her veins. No one attacked her mate without paying the consequences.

But Eric was just as relentless as she'd been with Benny, trying to hit her with his paws, trying to knock her out or kill her outright. She was having to dodge more than attack him, trying to keep out of his killer's reach. He hadn't been fighting, no blood staining his coat, so he was fresh. She was panting, her heart beating wildly, tension filling every pore, her muscles taut.

She leaped into a tree, and he followed her. She

jumped to another branch, and he leaped to the same one. She meant to move away from where Howard was so Eric would follow her and give Howard time to recover.

Val prayed Howard wasn't permanently injured and would regain his wits soon. If she didn't manage to kill this SOB, both she and Howard would be at risk. She backed away from Eric on the thick limb. He moved toward her, his eyes gleaming with threats. Before she ran out of room, she leaped for the ground. It was a mistake, and she knew it was from the moment she'd started the descent. As soon as she landed on the ground, he'd pounce on her like Benny had pounced on Howard.

She hit the ground and immediately leaped away from the spot where she'd landed to avoid being pummeled, but Howard was no longer barely standing in his stunned state where he'd been. And Eric hadn't followed her to attack her. She whipped around to see Howard in the tree crouched low on the branch near Eric's, his gaze focused on him. Eric had turned to face his new foe. Her beautiful mate.

Val jumped back onto the branch behind Eric. He ignored her, conscious of the bigger threat in front of him. Worried Howard wasn't ready to tackle the male cat in his condition, she would take Eric on. She'd do anything to save her mate. Like Eric, Howard didn't glance in her direction, his focus solely on the male cat.

Eric's tail was twitching slightly, and she made the decision to attack him, hoping Howard was able to follow through and take Eric out if she wasn't able to. She was afraid if Eric pounced on Howard, her mate might not have recovered enough to fight him back and win. She leaped on Eric's back, digging her fishhook claws into his flanks. He tried to turn and strike at her, but the branch wasn't wide enough. She tenaciously clung to him and realized she had the advantage. At least for the moment. She couldn't take him out with a killing bite from her position, and he suddenly jumped from the branch toward the ground with her still holding tight to him. She knew he'd kill her as soon as they were on the ground.

Seeing double, a jackhammer pounding in his head, Howard could barely see or think straight. All he knew was that his mate was desperately trying to protect him from Eric and take him down, and Howard had to snap out of his disoriented state now. If he jumped at Eric on the other branch and missed, the bastard would kill Val. Howard was trying his damnedest to see more clearly and make the jump as two Vals clung to two of Eric, biting him as best she could when Eric leaped from the tree toward the ground, taking Val with him.

As soon as he saw the jaguars on the ground, Howard jumped from the branch, landing on Eric's head and breaking his neck. At least that's what he thought happened when he heard the crack of the spine and suddenly two dead, naked Erics were lying beneath him.

Howard turned to make sure both Vals were okay. She nuzzled him, rubbing him as if she was feeling no pain, tears running down her jaguar cheeks. As much as she was bleeding, he knew she was feeling pain. He licked her face and nuzzled her back, wanting to assure her that he was okay. They had to be prepared for the next onslaught, but he was damn glad they were here as a team. He was worrying how the others were faring when he heard Vaughn howl.

Jillian howled back, letting her mate know she was alive and well.

If Howard had been up to speed, he would have raced off to join the others, but he could picture himself running into trees, so he just waited with Val to see what she wanted to do. She stayed put, listening, watching, waiting. He sat down, hoping some of the dizziness would subside. It didn't, and he felt as though he'd had way too much to drink during a celebration with friends.

Then movement to the west caught their attention. Another male jaguar, not one of their own. Val waited for him to approach. Howard was damn glad. Let the bastard come to them. The jaguar had no blood on him, and he was in top form. It appeared he'd come late to the party and missed out on any of the fighting. He was sizing them up, a male and female jaguar.

The jaguar looked down at Eric's body. Did he assume he could take the two of them on? Or think better of it since they'd terminated Eric?

The jaguar didn't run off, so he must have figured they couldn't manage him. That something was wrong with Howard for not coming after him. He didn't have long to wait. Everett and Demetria were leading the pack, the wolves right behind them, as they came to join them. Everett and Demetria tore into the lone jaguar, and once he was dead, Jillian hurried to join Howard and Val. She was bloodied too, like all of them were.

Jillian shifted. "Vaughn and I are serving as guards in case there are any more of them out there. We're disposing of the bodies now."

Howard planned to shift and talk to her, but as soon

as he tried, his head splintered in two and his world turned to midnight.

———∿∿∿———

"As wolves, I thought *we* fought hard," Jillian said as they all sat in Val's cabin having margaritas, though Howard was only drinking water after Val had brought him home from the hospital.

"Yeah, the jaguars are brutal," Vaughn said.

Everybody was wearing bandages and looking like they'd been in a battle for their lives, which they had been. Val was curled up next to her mate, who was no longer seeing double, which she was glad for, but she still worried about him.

"I say Val and Howard get top honors for taking out Eric and Benny." Everett saluted them.

Everyone agreed. Though if the others hadn't been there to take out Eric's other henchmen, they wouldn't be sitting here to talk about it.

"Damn glad the two of you showed up," Howard said. "It was bad enough I was seeing two of Eric. Two of Val was fine."

Val smiled up at him and kissed his cheek.

Everyone chuckled.

"Okay, so what happened with the rest of Eric's men?" Val asked. She and Howard didn't know how many more they'd taken down. She had taken Howard straight to the hospital while the others had disposed of the bodies.

"There were four others, all jaguar shifters, and I smelled weed on one of them," Everett said. "We worked well together, the wolves acting as bait and confusing the issue, and Demetria and me taking the jaguars out before they could fight us too much. Not that Jillian and Vaughn didn't get in a whole lot of bites too."

Jillian and Vaughn smiled.

Val knew the cats they fought had given them a real workout, as evidenced by all the bites and claw injuries they had. She was glad they had prevailed and hadn't needed her and Howard's assistance in taking the others down. She loved how they teamed up to work together.

"When you were in the exam room with Howard, having him checked out, Jillian called your parents to tell them we'd taken down all the bad guys, Val. Vaughn called Emmie, I called Rowdy, and Demetria called Izzie with the good news. Everyone is grateful," Everett said. "I called both Sylvan and Martin to let them know the good news. And the best news? Martin's giving us two weeks to play in the surf down here. Of course, he said if we learn there are any loose ends running around down here—part of Eric's drug network—we're to take them out if they're jaguars or turn them over to the police if they're humans. That's part of the reason he's giving us the extra time off, all expenses paid. But two weeks, folks! Martin never gives us that long of a break. We have Howard to thank for that."

Val patted Howard's leg. "I wasn't sure if you could help me out there at the end."

"I was afraid to jump at Eric and miss the branch."

Everyone laughed. The notion a jaguar couldn't jump from one branch to another was unthinkable, though Howard had had good reason. She'd wondered why he hadn't made his move.

"You know, the boss is going to want you to train agents on how to do that," Everett said.

"Do what?" Howard frowned.

"Take down a cat in a tree when you are seeing two of them. That takes some special maneuvering." Everett smiled at him.

Val loved how the team members supported and teased each other in a way that made the fighting take a back seat to the whole mission.

"I had a wild cat taking the brunt of it," Howard said, draping his arm carefully over Val's shoulders. "She was amazing."

"I was only keeping him occupied until you could take him down. Without you? I would never have won that battle." Val still couldn't shake loose the image of poor Howard standing on the ground looking dazed, or in the tree looking mean and growly, but not taking any action.

"Which is why we do things as a team." Demetria poured everyone fresh margaritas from a pitcher.

"Two weeks of fun in the sun," Jillian said.

"Just remember, before we leave, we have to drop by a grocery store and pick up some wangla for our boss," Everett said.

Val raised her brows.

"Yeah, I know. When I heard about it, I didn't believe it, but he tells all his agents if they end up in Belize, they have to bring him back the brittle sesame seed candy," Demetria said.

Instead of one package, they each got him several, their mission done, and all of them had a great time in their jaguar paradise over the next two weeks. But now it was time to return home to Houston and set up new housekeeping for Val and Howard and plan a wedding.

Epilogue

VAL AND HOWARD ORDERED MARGARITAS AT THE Clawed and Dangerous Kitty Cat Club in Houston, where they were waiting on the rest of their USF team to show up for happy hour, when they saw Emmie dancing with a guy. The boss hadn't yet given them another assignment because of the tough situation in Belize, despite the vacation having helped them all to heal and be ready for their next mission. They'd taken five more of Eric's human dealers into custody and turned them over to the police and had permanently taken out one more of Eric's jaguar henchman who'd thought he might still recover the money and drugs the agents had confiscated. With that many agents on the mission, the perp didn't last long.

They were still chilling out upon their return to the States.

"Whoa, I sure hope she's being more careful about who she's seeing these days," Val said about Emmie.

Emmie turned and saw them and waved, then leaned over and talked to the guy she was with. He glanced back at them and gave them a thumbs-up.

"Hell, he's a Guardian. Good deal for her if things work out between them," Howard said.

"Yeah, I'm glad she's with one of the good guys this time." Then Val spied Izzie at a table across the dance floor from theirs. "Ohmigod, what's Izzie doing here?

What if she shifts?" Then she frowned. "She'd better not be drinking while she's pregnant."

"It appears she's not with anyone. What happened to her Guardian family?" Howard asked, getting ready to leave the table to investigate the situation.

"Wait! Look there! Look who's coming out of the back where the restrooms are," Val said, excited.

"Well, I'll be damned. What's Rowdy doing here?" Howard sounded as surprised as she felt.

"He sees us, and he's bringing Izzie with him to join us." She just couldn't believe he was here. Or that Izzie appeared to be with him.

Izzie was all smiles when she and Rowdy joined them at their table. "We didn't know you were here," Rowdy said.

"We just arrived. We're meeting up with Jillian and Vaughn and the rest of the team members that you haven't met: Demetria and Everett. When did you get in?" Val wondered if he'd ever gone home to Montana.

"Last night," Rowdy said. "I gave notice at work and put my house up for sale. I started training with the USF this morning, and I'm celebrating at the club where so many of our agents hang out." Rowdy proudly showed off his agent-in-training badge.

Val and Howard smiled.

Howard's cell jingled, and he pulled it out and frowned. "Hey, Martin… Yeah, we're all at the club… What do you mean you've got a job lined up for us already?" He glanced in the direction of the front door. "Yes, sir, they're all headed for our table."

Val turned to see the other USF team members coming to join them.

"Yeah, just a minute." Howard held up the phone, indicating he had an important call. "Since the whole gang's here, I'll give them the news. What's the new mission?"

—◦◦◦—

Val was ready to take on a new mission with them. And everyone else was too. She couldn't imagine working with the Enforcer branch on her own any longer. She squeezed Howard's hand. She loved him. Her parents had retired from the Enforcer branch, thankfully, deciding from now on, the younger cubs could help out their kind. Though she knew they were volunteering to do anything they could to assist the jaguar police force.

Howard would have liked another week alone with Val, just the two of them having fun, but he was ready to work the new case with her by his side. And when they had a break? He was making use of every second of it, loving his beautiful and clever mate. When they were in Belize, they'd found a place that had table tennis and she still hadn't beaten him, but he loved that she kept trying. And she was the best of losers, tackling him in the bed at their cabin afterward to make love.

"Ready to pack it up?" Howard asked the gathered team members.

"After one more dance," Val said.

All the team members took to the floor—the couples dancing together, while Rowdy was dancing with Izzie. He appeared to be having fun, even though he still couldn't go with the team on a mission. But as soon as he was fully trained? He would be part of the team too.

"Love you," Val said to Howard, dancing nice and slow and close.

"Love you and all your roguish tendencies back."

Val smiled up at him. "You mean for giving you the slip at the hotel in San Antonio? Just a test to see if you could handle being my backup."

"I passed with flying colors." He placed his hands on her back and pressed her closer.

"I like how much you protect my front...too."

He chuckled and kissed her thoroughly. One dance led to two, and then three, when they finally had to leave and pack for the trip out of there. "More of this later."

"Yeah, but we're not leaving without a quickie," she said as they left the club.

"And that's why we were meant to be together. We think so much alike."

"It helps set the proper frame of mind for the next assignment."

He smiled. "You give me superpowers."

She laughed, and they waved at the others, who they'd be joining soon enough for another USF adventure.

*Keep reading for a sneak peek at the next
book in Terry Spear's SEAL Wolf series*

SEAL WOLF
SURRENDER

Coming soon from Sourcebooks Casablanca

Chapter 1

HER PARENTS' GARDEN NURSERY HAD BEEN OPEN FOR A brief time that morning when Natalie Silverton, who was loading flowers into the back of a customer's pickup, realized it was time to leave for the airport. "Thanks, Mrs. Nesbitt," she said, barely waiting for the woman's response.

She ran back to the shop where her mom was cashiering. "I've got to leave." Having helped all she could before she departed, Natalie grabbed her purse from a locked drawer under the counter. Her dad had left to deliver trees to a customer's home, and Natalie had been handling everything else except the register. She hated to leave her mother alone in the nursery.

"Go, give our Angie a hug for us," her mom said, giving Natalie a quick squeeze. "Have a good time, and don't hurry back. Your schedule is clear for five days. See some sights while you're there. Have some fun."

Her mom knew Natalie wouldn't see any "sights" on her own. She suspected her mom was hoping she'd go out with some of the wolves of the Greystoke pack while she was away.

"Love you, Mom." As their master gardener, Natalie gave classes and tours of their nursery all the time. But she had to catch a flight from Amarillo, Texas, to Denver, Colorado, to celebrate the marriage of her best friend, who was like a sister to her. Half a decade earlier, Natalie's parents had learned Angie lived in the Amarillo area and didn't have a family of her own. They had promptly taken her in as part of their family.

Natalie rushed back through the garden to reach the gate that led to her carriage house behind the Silverton Garden Center. She should have parked her car in front of the garden shop, but she had intended to leave a little bit ago.

Her bags were already in the car, so she changed out of her jeans and Silverton Garden T-shirt, yanked on a dress and heels, and tore out of the house. She jumped into her car and drove off, tamping down the urge to speed. She would make it, but without a lot of time to spare. She would much rather arrive at the airport early and relax before she took the flight. Better yet, if she hadn't given a gardening workshop last evening, she would have just driven to Denver. It was only about a six-and-a-half-hour drive.

A half hour later, she parked and rushed into the airport, pulling her bags behind her. Inside, she paused, looking for the right airline counter to check her bag, then saw it and hurried toward it. Without warning, a little girl ran in front of Natalie to catch up with a woman who appeared to be her mother, forcing Natalie to stop suddenly. The abrupt stop caused a man to stumble over her bag and fall, sprawling out on the floor. She was so used to apologizing to customers that she let go of her bags and hurried to help him up. He looked to be in his early thirties, so it wasn't as if he needed the help, but she immediately made the gesture. Getting closer to him, she smelled he was a wolf, and that took her aback. She didn't know of any living in the area other than her parents and Angie.

"I'm so sorry." She offered her hand to him.

Blond-haired and mustached, he narrowed his blue eyes at her and cursed. "Hell, woman. Don't you ever look where you're going?" He took a deep breath of her scent, his eyes widening a little when he realized she was a wolf too. He ignored her offer of help, rose to his feet—towering over her at six-foot-plus—and brushed off his jeans.

He had the situation a little backward since *he* was the one who wasn't watching where he was going and had run into her bag. Was he just passing through, visiting the area, or did he live in Amarillo?

The wolf jerked his bag past her and headed for the same check-in counter she had to use. Great. She smelled liquor on him. Whiskey. She sure didn't want to have to put up with a drunken wolf. Though he could be on a different flight with the same airline.

For a moment, she thought about whether to get in line behind the surly wolf or wait until someone else came up to give her some distance. She decided not to wait and moved in behind him, keeping some space between them.

He was already arguing with the agent at the counter, wanting to carry his bag on the plane, but the woman said he couldn't. "It exceeds the maximum size for a carry-on. You'll have to put it in the cargo hold."

It was the same size and style as Natalie's bag, and she knew she'd have to check hers. She would have shipped Angie and Aaron's wedding gift to them if she'd had the time. Then she wouldn't have had to check a bag.

"They let me carry it on the last flight I took it on. I had no problem at all."

"That may be, if you flew on one of the bigger planes. This one just doesn't have room." The agent wasn't backing down from the growly wolf. Good for her.

"Hell, lady." He slammed his bag on the scale. "Someone should have said so beforehand."

"I'm sorry, sir. It's just that the bag won't fit under the seats or in the overhead bin." She gave him the claim tag for his bag.

He jerked the claim tag from the agent's hand and stalked off. Natalie felt embarrassed for being a wolf, considering this man was one too. His rude behavior would have given the wolf kind a bad name, if humans had known wolf shifters existed.

Natalie checked her bag and hurried to security, where she ended up behind the wolf again. How lucky could she be?

"I always have precheck stamped on my ticket. That ticket agent didn't like that I was annoyed about not being able to carry my bag on the plane. I want to report her."

"Sorry, sir," the man said, "but it's really random."

"I still have to go through all of this crap?" the growly wolf said.

"That's the rule, sir. Please remove your shoes and step through the screener."

The wolf grabbed a bin, jerked his sneakers off, then slammed them into the bin and shoved it onto the conveyer belt. Natalie wondered if he was always this disagreeable or if the liquor was the reason. She felt sorry for anyone who had to cross paths with him today.

She removed her heels and put them and her purse in a bin. After she put her carry-on on the conveyer belt, the security officer motioned her through. She grabbed her stuff and hurried to put on her shoes. Then she began looking for her gate. Of course, it had to be on the other side of the terminal.

At least she had a straight flight and no transfers. She saw the wolf ahead of her. There were a lot of gates in this direction, so he could be headed to any of them. She was counting on that, but then he took a detour to a bar. She shook her head. He'd already had too much to drink. He didn't need to make any more of an ass of himself than he already had.

When she reached her gate, the attendants were already calling for boarding. She was in group two, and with relief, she boarded the plane. If by chance the wolf was on her flight, maybe he'd miss it. She smiled. That would serve him right.

Natalie took her seat, and it wasn't long before she saw the wolf coming down the aisle. As soon as he reached his row, across the aisle from hers where she had an individual seat, he began to complain about being seated next to a mom and her toddler. Passengers were backed up behind him as he balked about sitting in his assigned seat.

The hostess hurried to see what the difficulty was, and the wolf said, "The kid's diaper needs to be changed. It probably hasn't been changed since yesterday. I can't sit and smell that piss the whole flight."

"She was changed right before the flight!" the irate mom said, her voice elevated.

Refusing to sit down, the wolf stood in the aisle, glowering at the hostess. "I demand a new seat. Anywhere. The kid smells like pee."

"The flight is full. Please have a seat," the hostess

said, her cheeks coloring though she was trying to pacify him in a cool, collected manner.

Natalie was about to offer her seat to him, just so they could get on their way. He was already delaying them, and if they didn't leave now, they would miss their place in line on the runway. Not that she wanted to sit by the mom and her toddler if the girl had a soiled diaper, because like him, Natalie had an enhanced sense of smell. But as annoying as he was, she didn't want to accommodate him. That would only encourage such bad behavior.

"I won't sit next to the damn woman and her filthy kid."

Natalie saw one of the crew members coming, and from the set of his jaw, she didn't think he'd allow any guff from the wolf. At least she hoped he wouldn't. "You're going to have to leave the plane," the man told the wolf.

The next thing she knew, Mr. Drunk Wolf was being escorted off the plane. He was cursing up a storm, but at least he wasn't fighting. Their kind could be trouble if they ended up in jail, especially if they couldn't control the urge to shift during the full moon.

Conversations filled the air while the flight was delayed about fifteen minutes. Natalie hoped no one would miss a connection because of him.

She texted her friend: Crew had to escort a drunken wolf off the plane. Arriving about fifteen to twenty minutes late.

You're kidding. A wolf? In Amarillo? No problem. We'll save you a seat. Love ya, Angie

Now *Natalie* was ready for a drink!

———∿∿∿———

Brock Greystoke was having a beer with his twin brother, Vaughn, at the rehearsal lunch for their cousin Aaron, when Angie announced, "My best friend, Natalie, is delayed, so I want everyone to give her a special warm welcome when she finally arrives." Angie was a vivacious gray wolf and had fallen in love with Aaron and the Greystoke pack right away. Brock was glad for both his cousin and the pack.

Brock knew Angie was really hoping that one of the bachelor males of Devlyn and Bella Greystoke's pack would mate Natalie, and she would move there so Angie could continue to be close to her best friend.

"You *especially* intend to give her a warm welcome, right, Brock?" Vaughn asked.

"Don't even mention it. After the mess I went through with Lettie, I'm staying clear of she-wolves for the time being."

"Hell, it's been two years."

"Yeah, which isn't long enough. And I'm certainly not going to lay claim to a she-wolf who will only be here for a couple of days. Besides, she's not with a pack, and her parents have a nursery where she serves as their master gardener. She won't want to move here and join a pack." Not that Brock hadn't liked Natalie's appearance. Dark-haired and blue-eyed, Natalie was striking. Angie had made sure all the bachelor males had seen a picture of her friend, saying she wanted everyone to recognize her when she arrived. So why had she sent *only* the bachelors Natalie's picture?

"Been thinking about this a lot, I see." Vaughn smiled, as though he knew Brock better.

Brock couldn't get over Lettie because of the crazy situation she'd gotten him into. As a PI, Brock had tried to locate and eliminate a *lupus garou* bank robber who had killed a woman and her child at a local bank. Learning Lettie was the robber's sister—who had only gotten to know Brock because he was after her brother—had really irked Brock. Hurt too. He couldn't believe she'd only had plans to convince him to let her brother disappear. Well, her brother did disappear, but he needed Brock's assistance in disappearing permanently. They couldn't allow a wolf to get away with murder and chance him getting caught and going to prison.

Brock sat back in his chair, not the least bit interested in Angie's friend. From what Angie had said about her, she sounded like fun, but she wasn't local. "Natalie's not looking to relocate or find a mate among our bachelors. She's staying at a hotel far away from all of us. She doesn't want anyone to pick her up at the airport. Her actions prove she doesn't want to get involved with the pack. She's only here to attend her best friend's wedding," he said.

"Right, and that's what Angie wants to change. She wants her friend to meet someone and ultimately join us. Hey, if I hadn't met and mated Jillian, I might have been interested." Vaughn waved at his mate, who was headed back from the restroom.

"You weren't looking to settle down either. I still can't believe Jillian shot you for going after her brother, and you mated her."

"Our two situations were eerily similar, with you going after Lettie's brother, though quite a bit different." Vaughn slapped Brock on the back. "Life is really

good, Brock. You just have to find the right woman.
You know Jillian wasn't with a pack either. She was off
working on her own."

"The two of you work all over. It's not like she's
dealing with wolf politics all the time," Brock pointed
out. "Besides, you work together, and her parents moved
here so you'd all be close. I wouldn't expect Natalie's
parents to pull up roots to join our pack. And I'm not
talking about me, but about any of the bachelors who are
eager to meet her. If Devlyn hadn't read them the riot act
and told them they had to let her do this her way, half of
them would have been there vying for the chance to pick
her up at the airport."

"Maybe she would have been amused. What do we
know?" Vaughn chuckled.

Jillian joined them and gave Brock a hug. "You really
should join the United Shifter Force. After that wild trip
to Belize with the jaguars, we wondered if you wouldn't
like to partner up with us. We could use your help. And
I'm sure you'd love it."

"No, it's not for me. I love being a PI. But see? The
two of you are perfect for each other," Brock said.

"Has your brother been trying to convince you to
make a play for Natalie?" Jillian took a seat and sipped
from her glass of wine.

"He has, and I won't be trying to win her over."

"That's what I told him too. She's only going to be here
today, for the wedding tomorrow, and then she's leaving
the day after. There's no time to get to know her." Jillian
smiled at Brock. "Besides, she's probably not your type."

Brock raised a brow. He knew Jillian was not-so-
subtly challenging him to get to know Natalie better.

"Why would you think I have a specific type of woman in mind?"

Jillian just smiled. Brock wondered what his brother had been telling her about him and his dating ventures. And why she thought Ms. Natalie Silverton wouldn't suit.

Natalie finally made it to Denver International Airport. She rushed to get her bag and pick up a rental car, hoping she'd only be about a half hour late, no later.

She still couldn't believe Angie had met her mate at the Denver airport when she was flying there to go skiing. She had ended up skiing with him at Breckenridge for the whole two weeks when he hadn't planned to be there at all. Three months later, Angie was tying the knot and moving to his gray wolf pack's territory near Granby, Colorado. Aaron Greystoke was the pack leader's cousin, but he also owned a horse ranch. Angie Pullman loved horses, and Natalie wondered if *that* wasn't the deciding factor in her friend falling in love with the wolf.

Natalie immediately texted her friend: I'm in Denver, just got a car.

Angie texted her back: There are a ton of guys in the pack who were willing to pick you up.

Yeah, but you know me. I like to have my own car.

Natalie didn't like to have to rely on anyone but herself. Besides, she wasn't here to date any wolves, and she knew that's what Angie was up to. She enjoyed being an

independent wolf, just like Angie. Though it appeared
her friend had changed her mind about that. Natalie
would miss all the fun she'd had with her back home.

Thanks for coming. I can't wait to see you.

Me too, Angie. See you soon.

Wolves mated for life, and they lived so long—
aging so much slower than humans once they reached
puberty—that it was important to find the wolf they
couldn't live without. Natalie just hoped Angie wasn't
making a mistake with her whirlwind romance.

Using her GPS, Natalie drove from the airport toward
Granby, but somewhere along the way, she took a wrong
turn, then another. After fifteen minutes of rerouting
directions on her GPS, she called Angie. "Hey, my GPS
is going crazy. Can you guide me there?"

"I'm sending a SEAL to the rescue. I'm in the middle
of toasts. Here, talk to Brock."

"No, that's okay, I'll just—"

"Tell me where you are," a sexy, deep-baritone
male voice said. "I'll meet you there, and you can
follow me here."

Ugh, if it didn't mean so much to both of them for
Natalie to be there, she would have just skipped it.
She wondered if the SEAL was as sexy-looking as he
sounded though.

She blew out her breath in an annoyed way. "I'm
at—" She looked around. "I don't know where. I parked
at a garden nursery called the Denver Garden Center."

"There are four of them."

Of course there were.

His voice calm, as if he was used to helping women in distress, Brock asked, "What are the intersecting roads?"

Oh, just great. "Wait just a minute." She couldn't see any intersecting roads! She looked at her GPS. "Um, I think I'm off North Boulevard."

"Okay, that's the nearest one to the restaurant. I'll be there in fifteen minutes."

"You can just give me directions." Otherwise, she would be thirty minutes late instead of fifteen.

"It's your call, Natalie. I'm one of Aaron's cousins, Brock Greystoke, by the way."

"Nice to meet you, Brock. Yeah, it will save us both time, so just give me the directions." And *hopefully*, she could make it there without having to be escorted the rest of the way. She could hear all the noisy lunch guests having fun without her. She preferred working with plants more than partying with people. And she had a total love-hate relationship with the GPS. She loved it when it worked. She hated it when it got her lost.

"All right, I'll stay on the line and get you here that way," Brock said.

She could listen to his calm, soothing, masculine voice all day. She imagined hers sounded frazzled and annoyed. "Okay."

"Turn right onto North Boulevard. Stay in the right-hand lane. You'll turn on the first exit to the right."

"Okay, leaving the nursery. I'm on North Boulevard, coming up to the first exit on the right."

"Good," Brock said, and she was glad he didn't sound as if he thought she was an idiot.

"Okay, exited North Boulevard."

"Go down to the third signal and turn left on Elm Street."

"Oak Street. Ash Street. Elm Street."

Brock chuckled. Okay, she knew she sounded silly, but she really, really hated getting lost in a strange city, *especially* when she was already late! She was really nervous about meeting all these strange wolves. Despite working in her parents' garden shop and being used to meeting customers—human customers—or presenting educational programs to humans, she wasn't used to meeting a lot of wolves.

"Keep going. You're nearly there. Stay in the right lane, and at the third signal you'll turn right. Dallas's Steak House is three buildings down on your right."

"Thank you. I so appreciate it. I'm nearly there." She should have just thanked him and signed off, but he wasn't ending the call either, and she felt more at ease knowing if she missed the steak house somehow, Brock would redirect her and make sure she got there all right. "Okay, I see the steak house, and I'm pulling into the parking lot."

"You're driving a blue Toyota?"

"Uh, yeah." She turned to look at the deck leading to the front door of the restaurant, where a large fountain was flowing into a basin.

Wearing blue jeans, a dress shirt, cowboy boots, and a Stetson, Brock was standing next to the fountain, appearing bigger than life, but he looked as though he was into roping steers rather than scuba diving as a SEAL wolf. Dark hair, dark eyes, and a sensuous mouth, curved up in a slight smile, greeted her. His gaze was intense, all-consuming. She parked her car and joined him.

"You must be Natalie, Angie's best friend. Brock Greystoke, Aaron's cousin." Brock offered his hand to her and she shook it, but then worried hers was a little clammy from sweating out the drive there. She should have wiped her hand off on her skirt before she shook his hand.

"All Angie's talked about was one of us running to the airport and picking you up so you wouldn't get lost. You know, instead of staying at the hotel, you could stay with any of the families in the town of Greystoke out in Wolf Valley. That way, you won't have to make the long drive there in the morning for the wedding. I know how it is when you want to have your own getaway vehicle though. Oh, and welcome to Colorado. Angie said you've never been here before."

"Thanks, and no, I haven't." How could she tell the darkly handsome wolf she preferred staying at her own hotel because she didn't want to put anyone out? They'd insist she wasn't, but she just needed...her own space. She wondered how much Angie had told her new pack members about her.

She sighed, and Brock opened the door to the restaurant for her. The noisy conversation inside was nearly deafening, partly because of their enhanced wolf hearing. That's why she preferred her garden nursery to this.

The aroma of hickory-cooked steaks did appeal though.

"Are you ready for a good-sized steak after all the flying and rushing to get here?" Brock asked.

"Yes. I hate being so late."

"Don't worry about it. We just started at noon, and it's only a quarter of one. Everyone is enjoying cocktails and appetizers first."

Natalie figured no one would realize she hadn't been there earlier since no one even knew her and Angie would have been too busy enjoying herself. But Natalie hated arriving late to anything, as if she were the star of the occasion and needed a big entrance. Yet, she was vitally aware of the man walking beside her, his arm brushing hers as they moved closer together so that customers could get by them. When a waiter nearly ran into her, Brock adroitly slipped in behind her, pulling her out of the waiter's way.

Heat spread through her whole body, and Natalie tried to think of anything other than the way his body was pressed against hers in the sudden crush of customers as a large party was leaving the restaurant. "Angie told me you and your brother, Vaughn, are Navy SEALs. Are you just here on a visit?" she asked Brock.

"No, we're both out of the navy now, retired. You know how it is. We didn't look like we were aging, so as soon as we could, we retired. Both of us had been private investigators. Vaughn hooked up with a jaguar policing force that's called the United Shifter Force, and he has a mate now. They live out here, but their headquarters is in the Houston area. They travel there whenever they need to for a mission. I'm doing the PI business on my own now."

"You look like you wrangle steers too."

He smiled at her.

She felt her face flush with heat. Maybe that was the wrong thing to say to him. She saw men wearing western wear in Amarillo too, so she was used to seeing it.

"I help out on Aaron's ranch when I can. I just like getting out and riding a bit. Do you ride?"

"Uh, no, actually. A bicycle, yes. A horse, no. Angie's the big horse nut. I guess that's some of why she and Aaron hit it off."

"Yeah, it is. And the skiing. Do you ski?"

"No. We don't have any mountains around Amarillo. I guess the closest is New Mexico. To think Angie switched her plans to go to Colorado instead of New Mexico and met Aaron because of it! I guess it was meant to be." Natalie was much more of a warm-weather person, though they did get snow in Amarillo. She really couldn't imagine falling down a mountain on two skinny skis for fun. She figured once Brock learned she didn't ride horses and she didn't ski, he wouldn't find her very interesting. Which was fine with her. She wasn't looking to hook up with a wolf, even as sexy as he appeared to be.

"Well, sometime when you come back to visit, you can ski with Angie and Aaron."

She noted Brock didn't offer. He probably didn't want to have to deal with a total newbie skier.

They wound their way through the large building until they arrived at a banquet room where the private rehearsal lunch was being held. There were about thirty people in the room, and everyone looked in their direction as they entered.

Angie quickly left her chair and gave Natalie a hug. All of a sudden, the pack members surrounded Natalie, giving her handshakes to welcome her. As stiff as she was around them, they must have realized she needed her space—so no one but Angie and Aaron gave her a hug in greeting.

"I'm so glad you made it. I told you that you should

have let someone pick you up at the airport. And you can't stay at the hotel in Denver. You're too far away from the fun." Angie glanced down at Natalie's hands and *tsk*ed. "You have green fingers. Not just a green thumb."

"I was working in the garden when we first opened, helping a customer with an order, when I realized it was time to catch the flight. Spring and early summer are such busy times for plant sales at the nursery."

"No problem at all. We're going straight to the ranch after the lunch. The ranch house has eight bedrooms, and since most everyone lives here in the area, most of the rooms are empty. You know we'll be having margaritas, and you don't want to be driving all the way back into Denver. What if you got lost?"

Natalie could never win an argument with her friend. Besides, if she was going to drink, she agreed about not driving back into Denver. "I'll have to cancel my hotel reservation for tonight, but after the wedding, I can stay the night in Denver to catch my flight the next day."

"Why don't you just stay at the ranch house, and then you can have breakfast with some of the pack members before you leave? For now, you can just follow Aaron and me to the ranch after the meal." Angie sat Natalie next to her chair, while Aaron was sitting on the other side of Angie.

"All right. But only because I *know* you. We'll be partying all afternoon. I still can't believe you're getting married."

"You can come and visit us any time you want." Angie smiled. "Now, let me tell you about all the bachelors in the pack."

Natalie chuckled. "You know I'm not interested.

Period. I love Amarillo and the garden center. What would my parents do without me? I can't plan on them wanting to relocate again either. So no. I'm just here to help you have fun."

"Well, I'll tell you one person who really, really isn't interested in finding a mate. That's Brock. Which is why I asked him to help you out with the directions."

"Oh?"

"Yeah. He broke up with a girlfriend a while back, and he hasn't been interested in one since. She's not with the pack. He met her under some rather unusual circumstances. Suffice it to say, he's not looking for a special someone right now. I figured if I sent any of the other bachelor males to help you, their tongues would have been hanging to the floor and their tails wagging behind them, way too eager to win you over."

Natalie laughed. "Thanks." Now she was curious about the experience that had made a man like Brock swear off women.

Chapter 2

AFTER LUNCH, A CARAVAN OF CARS HEADED FOR AARON'S ranch house to continue the party, but not before Angie arranged it so Brock would drive Natalie's rental car for her so she wouldn't get lost.

Brock had been up to the task; it wasn't any imposition. He'd ridden to Denver with some of his other cousins, and even if they lost the caravan, he knew the way and wouldn't have to give Natalie directions.

Natalie settled back against the seat. "It wasn't really necessary," she said, as they followed Vaughn and Jillian's car to the town of Greystoke, while the wedding couple was in the pickup ahead of them. "I couldn't have gotten lost, not with all the cars to follow."

Brock chuckled. "No problem. I rode with my brother and his mate, so I didn't have my Humvee here. I would have worried about you, if we'd somehow lost you."

They lost sight of the first two cars in the caravan at a signal.

"I don't think my GPS works in Denver," Natalie said.

He laughed. "Mine's gone haywire a time or two. So what does a master gardener do?" He envisioned her with bright-orange garden gloves, dirt smudges on her cheeks, her dark hair pulled back in a ponytail, and a trowel in hand as she dug around in the garden.

"I teach about gardening, plants, and wildlife to a lot of groups. What does a SEAL wolf do?"

"Rescues, retrievals, and removals."

"They all sound the same."

He smiled. "They're not. Rescues of people and equipment from hostile situations. Retrieving data and other important items. Removing bad guys from the scene."

"Sounds dangerous."

"It could be. Sometimes it was just tedious. It depends on how hostile the situation is."

"Are you guys going to be at Aaron's ranch too?"

"Yeah, we're using the guesthouse to party. You ladies will be in the main ranch house."

"He's got a lot of room for visitors."

"Yeah, he's one of the most welcoming wolves of our pack. He wanted a place for visiting wolves to stay who weren't with our pack."

"Does he have them stay often?"

"They come through and check out our pack, and most move on. But sometimes we have visitors who end up staying."

"It's a beautiful area. I love the mountains as a backdrop."

"It is beautiful. I don't think I could live anywhere that's flat." He'd traveled all over, but he still loved the view of mountains.

"It would be fun to run through them as a wolf."

"If we had time, we could go there together."

She smiled at him. "'Time' is the keyword."

"Yeah." He knew she wasn't interested in staying any longer than she had to. "If you need anything, don't hesitate to ask anyone while you're here."

"Thanks, and thanks for offering to drive."

"No problem."

They finally reached the ranch, where Natalie joined the other ladies and entered the ranch house, while the guys gathered in the guesthouse out back.

"You are so slick," Vaughn said to Brock as they walked inside the guesthouse. "I never thought of doing that."

"What's that?" Brock grabbed a beer out of an ice chest and joined the guys as they were telling war stories.

"Suggesting you aren't interested in a woman, but you're always there for her."

Brock smiled and tapped his frosty beer bottle against his brother's.

Their cousin Shawn joined them. "Yeah, he's slick all right. He moved in to protect the lady in SEAL-wolf mode right away."

"Hell, you're an Army Ranger. I would have thought you'd figure out how to snag her attention," Vaughn said to Shawn.

"I would have, but Angie wasn't buying it. She bought Brock's story—no more she-wolves for him."

"Natalie is so not interested in being here long-term," Brock said. "She will probably visit Aaron and Angie in the future, but you know how that goes. Everyone's busy with their own lives, so that could be rarely." Brock got a call on his cell and saw it was Angie on the caller ID. "Hey, Angie, what's up?"

"Hey, Brock, I swear I won't ask another thing of you this afternoon while you party with the boys, but we need a man to light our fire."

He laughed.

"We're all dressed up and don't want to get sooty or anything," Angie further explained.

"I'm on my way."

"Thanks, Brock. I knew you were the man for the job."

Vaughn and Shawn were waiting to hear what Angie wanted now.

"I need to light the ladies' fire."

The guys laughed.

"Do you need help?" Shawn asked.

"No. A SEAL can handle this." Brock headed out of the guesthouse and walked to the ranch house where the women were playing loud music and sounded like they were having fun. He smiled.

Bella and her sister, Serena, the two redheads of the gathering of ladies, were kicking off their sparkly sandals, then setting up a huge assortment of nail polishes to choose from for the nail-painting party. The pretty brunette, Brock's sister-in-law, Jillian, was preparing footbaths for the ladies. And Natalie helped Angie prepare finger baths. Natalie had never done this with anyone other than her mom and Angie, so this was fun. She removed her sandals and saw Bella and Serena making margaritas in a blender, just like they'd fixed when her mom and Angie needed a ladies' night!

"This is in memory of all the times we did this with your mom," Angie said.

"This is great, Angie. I love it." Natalie glanced at the stairs leading to the bedrooms. "You could have a ton of kids in this place."

Angie had always wanted to have more than one. Being an only child—unusual for *lupus garous*—and then losing her parents early on, she had always wanted to have more of a family.

"That's what Aaron keeps promising me." Angie laughed and so did everyone else.

Bella and Serena served everyone margaritas while the other ladies soaked their feet in the footbaths. After drinking their margaritas, the women soaked their fingers in little containers of soapy water. Natalie was glad when Angie scrubbed Natalie's fingers to remove the green stain from handling plants that morning.

After that, Angie made a call in the kitchen while the ladies began painting toenails. By the time they were in the middle of painting fingernails, Brock arrived at the house, surprising Natalie.

"I was told you ladies needed me to light your fire?" Brock asked, and all the ladies whooped and hollered, all except Natalie.

She only smiled at the sexy wolf. She imagined he could make for a sizzling encounter. Though she immediately wondered why he would have been asked when the ladies could have done it themselves.

Natalie knew Angie was up to something. She just hadn't thought her friend would try to match her with a wolf who wasn't interested in any she-wolf.

"Thanks, Brock, yes," Angie said. He started the fire for them, and Angie said to the ladies, "So, I met Natalie when I was vacationing in Cozumel. I had a boyfriend who got food poisoning at the salad bar. Such a drag. It was one of those trips that went downhill fast. Until I saw Natalie with her parents at the same resort. You know how it is when you meet others like us. We got to talking, and Natalie and I decided to go scuba diving.

The boyfriend went home early, and I eventually ended up in Amarillo to visit with her and her parents again. They realized I didn't have any family, and I just stayed. We've been best friends ever since."

Natalie noticed Brock was slow to make the fire. Natalie was certain Angie had told their story in front of Brock so he'd know Natalie was a scuba diver too.

"Hey, did you get your bags out of the car yet?" Angie asked Natalie.

"No, I was going to get them after we had our girls' party."

"Brock, can you get them? You can carry them to the first guest room up the stairs on the right," Angie told him.

"No, that's all right. I can do it." Natalie didn't want him thinking he was their errand boy.

"I'll get them." He held his hand out for Natalie's key, and she fished it out of her purse, then handed it to him.

"Thanks, Brock."

"No problem. Be right back." He left the house, and if it had been just her and Angie, Natalie would have said something to her friend about her matchmaking attempts. But she didn't want to do that in front of the other ladies, and it *was* Angie's wedding party.

Brock came into the house with the bags, and Angie said, "If you don't mind, you can haul them up to Natalie's room."

"No trouble at all. I'll join the guys as soon as I drop these in her room."

Unless Angie had other odd jobs for him to do, Natalie was thinking. Brock winked at Angie as if he knew her game.

"Oh, wait. I'll get my wedding gift for you out of the big bag. Let me grab that first. And thanks, Brock, for doing this for me."

"My pleasure."

Natalie unzipped the bag. She stared at the rolls of wrapping paper filling the bag instead of her clothes and the wedding gift. Underneath were a few men's clothes and a shaving kit—smelling like the drunken wolf who had collided with her bag at the airport.

Natalie's heartbeat quickened, and she felt her stomach turn.

Appearing shocked, the ladies all looked at the rolls of wedding and birthday paper.

"Ohmigod, I got someone else's bag!"

Acknowledgments

Thanks so much to Donna Fournier, who is there for me from beginning to end, cheering my word count on, eager to read the book, make suggestions, and reread it all over again. And on short notice! Even with Easter looming. Thanks to Deb Werksman for always believing in my books and acquiring them so readers have more and more to read! Thanks to all the various people at Sourcebooks who make this happen—from publicists to cover artists and everyone in between.

About the Author

Bestselling and award-winning author Terry Spear has written more than sixty paranormal romance novels and eight medieval Highland historical romances. Her first werewolf romance, *Heart of the Wolf*, was named a 2008 *Publishers Weekly* Best Book of the Year, and her subsequent titles have garnered high praise and hit the *USA Today* bestseller list. A retired officer of the U.S. Army Reserves, Terry lives in Spring, Texas, where she is working on her next werewolf romance, continuing with her Highland medieval romances, and having fun with her young adult novels. When she's not writing, she's photographing everything that catches her eye, making teddy bears, and playing with her Havanese puppies and her grandbaby. For more information, please visit terryspear.com, or follow her on Twitter @TerrySpear. She is also on Facebook at facebook.com/terry.spear.

Also by Terry Spear

THE LAST WOLF

First in an extraordinary new series
from Maria Vale: The Legend of All Wolves

Silver Nilsdottir is at the bottom of her Pack's social order,
with little chance for a decent mate. Until the day a wounded
stranger stumbles into their territory, and Silver decides to
risk everything on Tiberius Leveraux. But Tiberius isn't all
that he seems, and in the fragile balance of Pack and Wild,
he may tip the destiny of all wolves…

*"Wonderfully unique and imaginative.
I was enthralled!"*

**—Jeaniene Frost,
New York Times bestselling author**

For more Maria Vale, visit:
sourcebooks.com

X-OPS EXPOSED

More thrilling action and sizzling romance
from *New York Times* bestselling author Paige Tyler

Lion hybrid and former Army Ranger Tanner Howland
has retreated into the forests of Washington State to be
alone. He's too dangerous to be around people—including
his love, Dr. Zarina Sokolov. Little does he know, she's
following him, determined to save Tanner with the anti-
serum she hopes will turn him human again. But a vicious
ring pitting hybrids against each other for sport lies in wait.

*"Does it get any better than this?
Tyler...is an absolute master!"*

—Fresh Fiction

For more Paige Tyler, visit:
sourcebooks.com